'An assured and visceral page-turner, as convincing as it is bold . . . it also offers arresting insights into the craft of fiction itself, and raises provocative questions between life and art.'
Stephanie Cross, *Lady*

'As engrossing and tense as one of Highsmith's own.'
Good Housekeeping

'Funny, horrific and moving in turn this is a riveting read and an intriguing glimpse into the murky depths of an extraordinary writer. Jill Dawson captures Highsmith's eccentricities brilliantly'
Mel Mitchell, *Nudge*

'The sharply drawn characters and clever plotting are hard to resist'
Sydney Morning Herald

'This brilliantly melded fact and fiction digs deep into the psyche of the darkly gifted Patricia Highsmith.'
Sainsbury's Magazine

'The story is edgy and becomes darker as it unfolds, which when you first think of a story based out of a cottage in Suffolk is the last thing you'd expect, but trust me, having read *The Tell-Tale Heart* only last year I can promise you that Jill's writing is as good as it gets.'
Robert Bradley, *Huffington Post*

JILL DAWSON

THE CRIME WRITER

SCEPTRE

First published in Great Britain in 2016 by Sceptre
An imprint of Hodder & Stoughton
An Hachette UK company

First published in paperback in 2017

1

A CIP catalogue record for this title is available from the British Library

ISBN 978 1 444 73113 2

Typeset in Sabon MT by Hewer Text UK Ltd, Edinburgh
Printed and bound by Clays Ltd, St Ives plc

Hodder & Stoughton policy is to use papers that are natural, renewable
and recyclable products and made from wood grown in sustainable
forests. The logging and manufacturing processes are expected to
conform to the environmental regulations of the country of origin.

Hodder & Stoughton Ltd
Carmelite House
50 Victoria Embankment
London EC4Y 0DZ

www.hodder.co.uk

For Kathryn Heyman, with love

Something pursued her. Dreams – phantoms – woke her in the small hours, driving her from her bed to walk the darkness of the strange English village. She'd thrown a coat over striped pyjamas – what was the likelihood of meeting another person at this late hour on a Thursday night? – and pushed bare feet into the cold men's brogues she kept by the door for the purpose of these night-time prowls. There was no light in Bridge House, the house behind hers, Bridge Cottage, which meant that the old hag, Mrs Ingham, was not awake at any rate. High, bristling hedges hid her, lining the long road that she now stepped onto, there being no sidewalk here – or, pavement, as the British would call it. This road sliced through the village in a 'nice bit of straight', encouraging a fellow to drive on through. Down towards the Victoria bar or up toward the cemetery? A quick glance assured her there was a hunter's moon and a clean sheet of stars. She chose the cemetery.

A car approached: a soft sound like a waterfall. She quickened her steps in their tap-tapping shiny shoes, and pulled closer to the hedges, tugging her coat collar up to hide her face: was someone following her? The car released her from its beam and slid past, and her thoughts returned to Sam and the Problem. The situation was this: Sam was married. Sam had been married since the age of twenty: for fifteen years. Sam had a child, a girl called Araminta – Minty. Sam would never leave. Love was a kind of madness, not very logical.

The smell of woodsmoke and onions told her that someone was awake, even at this hour, perhaps enjoying a cosy fireside meal. Her stomach contracted. That reminded her: she must chop some wood – perhaps she should offer to chop a pile for

Mrs Ingham too. Fall was almost here, the season turning. And Sam was coming to visit for the first time this weekend.

As she reached the cemetery another car appeared, illuminating the gravestones, each with their shock of mossy hair: malevolent trolls. She tensed: two cars in one late evening in a place like this was unusual, she was sure. An inner voice started up immediately: Don't be silly, he couldn't possibly find you here, no one knows this place . . . She had barely been at Bridge Cottage a week, half of her boxes were still packed, but she was already sure that for most of the obedient people of Earl Soham, chosen for its anonymity and its proximity to London and to Sam, not much happened after the local bars closed. And in this second car – a white car, she'd noticed, in the moonlight – it wasn't a man but a young woman. Even so, it had been a woman she'd thought she recognised. Red hair? No, not really possible to see the hair colour, she'd concede that much; she was being dumb. But the shape of the head then, the familiar silhouette made by that particular hairstyle. Something of a Jackie Kennedy swing to it, that image seen over and over on TV screens at the end of last year. Bouffant on top; flicks at the end.

The car rolled out of sight and she realised she was breathing hard, although the walk was short and not uphill. She felt in her coat pockets for the gold Dunhill lighter and the cigarettes she'd brought with her from Paris. The fat white moon looked about ready to pop. There was easily enough light to see the bench, so she sat down and breathed out noisily. *It's all in your head, it's all in your head*. Then, as she flicked the lighter on, she was startled by a noise, a noise as if someone was standing close behind her angrily sucking in their cheeks. She sprang up and crashed down again, her hand trembling as she slipped the lighter back in her pocket and put the cigarette to her lips. Just a branch, rubbing against another. This place had some impressive, old, *old* trees, well established, like everything here. A rope swinging, squeaking in the breeze. She longed for a bottle of Scotch to go with the cigarettes – why had she not thought to bring that out too?

Tomorrow – Friday – would be the visit from the lousy journalist, at 10 a.m., which didn't help her mood any. She ought to telephone from the booth outside the cottage and call the whole thing off. Jesus – how could she be anonymous, safe, if people wrote about her and named Bridge Cottage? The earlier conversation, making the arrangement for the interview, had been awkward and no doubt offered a foretaste of how it would be. 'Matter of fact, I was rather hoping to keep my stay here private, as I'm having a hard time getting to finish a couple of books,' she had begun, only to be cut off with 'But it's *sooooo* exciting to have a famous crime writer in Earl Soham . . .'

She'd had to explain, for possibly the hundredth time in her career, that she didn't write *crime* novels; she wasn't a crime writer. The damn fool girl had protested by naming some of the best-known novels, as if Pat didn't know her own work, to which she'd patiently explained: 'Would you call Dostoevsky a crime writer for writing *Crime and Punishment*? Edgar Allan Poe? Theodore Dreiser? I don't happen to care for the label "crime writer". There is not much detection in my novels. There's rarely any police involvement at all . . .'

She finished her cigarette and stubbed it out under her shoe. She thought she heard sounds of car tyres popping on gravel near the village hall beside the church. And then she gave in to a powerful compulsion to bend forward and scuff out signs of her smoking with her hand, picking up the cigarette butt and stuffing it into the pocket of her coat, then looking left and right up the street, as if she was in a bad movie, covering up the evidence. She felt as if she watched herself doing this, carefully. She'd had that feeling from childhood. Narrating herself, was how she thought of it. *Pat did this, Pat did that*: a running commentary that she couldn't tune out.

As her hand dug into the pocket, she discovered a tiny snail she'd snuck in there yesterday, meaning to return it to its home. She held it close to her face, to examine it in the moonlight. A less-experienced observer might believe the baby snail to have vacated the shell but she knew it was in there, hiding. She had

3

torn off a piece of lettuce and felt the crumpled pieces of it now, inside her pocket, along with the little snail, bouncing in there as she walked, like a lucky pebble.

Her mood lifted as she pictured herself showing the snail – with its beautiful stippled brown and cream shell, its tiny body cautiously extending, its horns flailing inquisitively – to Sam. She picked up speed, striding back towards Bridge Cottage in her brogues, finding her way without a flashlight because the moon drenched everything in milky light – the telephone booth, the allotments, the gas pumps on the little forecourt next to her cottage. Rain threatened, and she didn't want to get the shiny brogues muddy. The smell of woodsmoke had evaporated. This time no cars passed her. Not one single house in that dull, pleasant place had a light on. She'd forgotten to lock the front door, she realised, as she grabbed the handle, brushing aside a dried-up rose that trailed near her face; another tense moment. What if someone had managed to sneak inside while she was out?

The door gave its customary jerk as she opened it and stepped inside: the living room in darkness, a faded Turkish mat, sludge colours, which had once been red and blue. She sniffed, relaxing her shoulders. No one was here. No one had been following her. Maybe she was half cracked. Ready for the booby hatch. The cottage smelt just as it had when she'd left it: damp, English and ridiculous. Sure, it was exactly as she'd said to herself. Earl Soham wasn't much of a place. Once again, she'd ended up in the middle of nowhere. It was a lonely neighbourhood. She was hidden, invisible; she wasn't being watched. It was perfect.

In the morning, she fixed herself the breakfast she always had, the one that made her feel terribly British: hardboiled eggs doused in salt. She knew the English actually ate them soft with a spoon in a little cup but she drew the line at that. She drank from the bottle most of the creamy milk she'd found at the front door, which the milkman had left with a note saying that if she wanted more she was to leave him her request along with the empty bottle. The mail arrived – she had not written to Mother since Paris, she remembered – and this bunch was only a letter about a new bank account, a letter from Peggy in London, and one she wasn't yet ready to read from her agent. She went out back to check the garden before the journalist arrived, taking the walk she did in every new property she rented in whatever country; the one where she imagined the prowler. ('Having a prowler or *being* a prowler?' Sam had teased her.)

The garden was large, wet with dew and unkempt. At the front, trees protected it from the road, and there was also a ghastly, oversized hedge that Pat rather admired for its unruliness. She wouldn't trim it, she thought. The front lawn was pretty bad. The back lawn was in better shape, and a murky green ribbon of water ran along the bottom. The colours in the garden, in the entire village, were the limited palette of an English autumn. A russet apple. Brown, rusty red, green: the water pulsed with these colours. Upstairs she had her easel set up already and her watercolours and she knew the lozenges of colour that would soon be wet and mucky; knew the exact shade the water would turn in the jam jar, and knew whose portrait was the only one she wanted to paint – Sam's.

Well, now that she was standing in the back garden – shaking off a damp leaf that had stuck to the toe of one shoe – she wondered whether this little strip of soupy water would more properly be described as a stream or a brook. She imagined the prowler hatless, young, damp hair, tufty like the patchy lawn, face down in the cold water, where she had pushed him, after finding him crouching in the garden casing Bridge Cottage. A bloodied stone lay beside his head where she'd clouted him and pressed his face into the sluggish stream. Brook. A man can drown in a couple of inches of bath water, every schoolchild knows that. Then she remembered that she had no tea; the English journalist could probably use a cup of tea.

It wasn't that she minded a brisk walk to the village store – putting her coat on over her pyjamas for the second time in twenty-four hours – but that crank Mr Fremlin (Mr Gremlin in her mind) would so want to *yak*, as if it wasn't bad enough that she had to gird herself for the intense conversation she was undoubtedly about to have at 10 a.m. with Miss Virginia Smythson-Balby. As a precaution against this, she stuffed some wads of cotton-wool into one cheek, preparing to pantomime and point to her swollen face, implying that she couldn't talk to the grocer on account of toothache. Matter of fact, now she came to remember it, this was dimly true. She did have some residual aching in one tooth; probably why the idea had suggested itself to her. Perhaps the Earl Soham store stocked tincture of myrrh or clove oil.

It didn't. It sold Fry's Chocolate Cream and Gold Cup Jaffa Juice and Limmits cookies and a brand new newspaper, the *Sun*, which she bought too when the old Gremlin pressed it on her, though privately she thought it looked about as goddamn awful as one might expect. 'Election soon,' he'd said. 'Wilson's the man for me. We do it differently to you Yanks. Quieter, you know.'

She almost replied, 'I'm hardly a Yank. I've lived in Europe most of my life,' but the cotton-wool in her cheek prevented it. Infuriating. Of course everyone knew who she was. Hadn't he even greeted her, as she'd entered, by name? She glanced down at the headline, read its bouncy 'Good morning! Yes, it's time for a new newspaper . . .' swallowed the protest and shook her head, as if in pain. At any rate, one oughtn't to need to explain that one didn't think of oneself as American, not really; more of a wandering European. She also picked up a packet of Limmits, orange flavour, as the idea of cookies 'medically tested and approved', cookies you could 'eat to help you slim' amused her. Perhaps the Smythson-Balby girl would be fat and she could offer her one. Once outside the little store she glanced up and down the street but there was only a man trundling an empty wheelbarrow and whistling; he tipped his cloth cap to her as if they were at a tea-dance. Her stuffed-cheek ruse did the trick and, with one hand cradling the aching jaw, she managed not to speak at all, only to point and wave.

On the walk home she thought of the portrait she'd begun, from memory, of Sam. Fall colours – muted, soft – apricots and greens – building up to the blonde, the bedazzling blonde of Sam's hair. It was naturalistic in style and she knew – suspected – Sam would despise that. Realism was something unfashionable these days. But no matter – soon she would be able to work on it again, with the live model.

Just as she reached her own front door, there was Ronnie, leaning on his bike. She registered with mild annoyance the fresh white sports shirt, rolled-up sleeves, the bleached hairs on his forearms; the sense of glowing health and cheer that always emanated from Ronnie. Yesterday he had arrived at the same time, insisting he showed her the great elm at Nayland, which had escaped the plague. Today she was armed against such enthusiasms. She removed the soaked wad of cotton-wool from inside her cheek. 'I don't care to sightsee today. I've barely unpacked. She'll be here any minute.'

'I know. I've been snooping around and it seems it's not just a piece for the *Ipswich Star* or whatever codswallop she told you. She's a biographer.'

Ronnie leaned his bike against the dead roses and crisped camellias still lingering at the back door of Bridge Cottage – several shrivelled leaves crumbled to the ground – and followed her into the kitchen. He glanced around the smoky, dark little room: red-tiled floor, low ceiling beams, some old flower-sprig curtains; a faintly fishy smell as if an aquarium bubbled there. On the table there were mugs still wrapped in their newspaper, a shoebox of packed cutlery. He found the kettle inside a cooking pot in one of the packing cases and filled it with water from a spluttering faucet. Taking matches from his back pocket, he lit the stove, began busying himself with unwrapping things for her with the proprietary ease of long familiarity, opening the packages from Mr Fremlin's and spooning tea into the tea-pot.

'I brought you more bits of painted boat and driftwood,' Ronnie said. 'I've popped it in the shed. My dear, there are some

7

excellent pieces of Southwold pier in that little lot. They'll make a splendid salty blue blaze.'

'I don't care to have you here when she arrives,' she told him. 'It will look funny. It will find its way into the article. "Miss Highsmith's gentleman friend, renowned local poet . . ."'

'I'll slip out the back. She'll think I was the grocer's boy, delivering.'

The kettle screamed at them and Ronnie poured water over the tea-leaves.

'I'd better put something else on,' she muttered, and went upstairs to change from the coat and pyjamas into Levi's and a pressed white shirt.

'Quit trying to help me,' she said, buckling her braided lizard-skin belt, when she reappeared.

'So secretive! Don't worry, I'm leaving. I'm sure our journalist – did you know she was the Right *Honourable* Virginia Smythson-Balby? – will assume that a single gentleman like me, living alone and writing all that nature poetry, must be a fairy, wouldn't you say?'

'Fix me a Scotch before you go,' she said, handing him the bottle.

'And how did you find this charming place?' asked Virginia Smythson-Balby, legs awkwardly crossed, mug of tea perching on the uppermost knee in its pantyhose. The living room was cold; Pat had not fixed the fire. It was dark too, and unfurnished apart from the sofa, a red leather chair that Pat sat on, the boxes, the Turkish rug, and a lamp at such a strange angle that it looked like someone with their head thrown back, laughing. Smythson-Balby – was she really titled or had Ronnie been teasing? – had arrived in such a breathless, over-excited state that Pat had feared the girl was about to have an asthma attack. She had been shaking, as she came in through the kitchen door, and looked horribly as if she had wanted to hug her. Fans! *Ghastly*. She had worn bright yellow patent knee-high boots, and when Pat suggested she took them

8

off, they were unzipped and abandoned, like peeled banana skins. As the girl stood up, she seemed at last to compose herself.

Good legs, Pat noted. Calves not too muscled, but well-formed. Lacrosse player, she reckoned, or whatever it was that English schoolgirls took seriously, these days. Smythson-Balby had given up on the pen and notebook for the moment. They lay menacingly beside her on the sofa.

'Friend of mine,' Pat replied carefully. 'Ronnie. He knows this village. English quietude. Cottage was rather a good price at three thousand five hundred pounds.' (Was that crass, she immediately thought. Would a girl of her type think it bad manners to talk about money?) She added quickly: 'Ronnie said it would be, you know, good for working. I have two books to write: one a novel, one a sort of "how to" book. Matter of fact, three books as I always keep a *cahier*, a notebook, too . . .'

And none of them going well, she might have added. The back door from the kitchen slammed shut and both women jumped.

'Delivery boy,' Pat said, swallowing the Scotch in her tea mug and trying to avoid fidgeting, in case the leather chair she was sitting in made a lewd noise.

Smythson-Balby sipped her tea and suddenly grimaced, obviously finding the sludge of leaves at the bottom (Ronnie had not been able to find a tea-strainer among her boxes, though Pat did possess one). As she leaned forward her silky blouse fell open a little and she clutched distractedly at the neckline.

'So, this will be your – tenth crime novel, is that correct? And you had been living in . . . New York and then travelling in Venice and Paris, Europe for many years, is that right, but wanted to set this one in England?'

'*Suspense* novel. One of the books I'm writing here is called *Plotting and Writing Suspense Fiction*. Not crime. Not detective fiction. As I mentioned on the telephone, I don't happen to like the term "crime fiction". Dostoevsky wrote suspense stories – that is, stories where there is felt to be a threat of imminent violence or danger. I don't feel ashamed of the category.'

Smythson-Balby smiled, but she did not apologise.

'Is the one you're writing now your tenth novel, then, or the eleventh? I like to get these things right,' the young woman said.

'Tenth,' Pat replied, but warily. What was behind the question? Was the girl smarter than she looked?

'It seems safe to say – I hope you won't be offended – that you're better known in Europe, rather than your native America. Any thoughts on why your books might sell better in Europe, Miss Highsmith?'

'None whatsoever.'

Next she'll be asking me where I get my ideas from.

Smythson-Balby had her notebook open and was now reading from it.

'A lady called Margaret Marshall called your work "unpleasant, unnatural and unsavoury". She says that your criminals often get away with the crimes they commit and there is rather too much – too much *relish* on your part in describing their thoughts of murder, the deviant things your protagonists want to do. She even suggested in her last review that perhaps you *admire* your famous anti-hero rather too much . . . and the policemen in your novels, the forces of law and order, are always depicted as weak and toothless. Evil, she says, prevails in the novels of Patricia Highsmith. What would you say to this, Miss Highsmith?'

'I'm sure Miss Marshall is a fan of Miss Christie and Ngaio Marsh. Let her go ahead and read their novels.'

Smythson-Balby looked at her keenly, as if expecting more.

'I don't happen to – I don't care to read the implausible fantasies of simpering ladies where everyone in the parlour is equally capable of committing a deadly murder, whether an eighty-year-old duchess or a sweet-natured stable boy.'

'"Implausible fantasies of simpering ladies" . . .' Smythson-Balby murmured as she wrote, using the squiggles of shorthand. To disguise what was really being written?

'Not a fan, I take it? Of the Golden Age writers, I mean?' she asked.

'I've sworn off them.' Pat hoped this might deflect her, but no, Smythson-Balby was waiting for a full reply.

Pat took a slug of whisky. 'They're nothing great. The only thing Agatha Christie did that interests me is go missing for a few days. Fake her own death. She obviously *planned* to punish Archie – her husband – since he was the one who would get turned in for it and he'd been playing around. But then she decides to duck out and get herself discovered in Harrogate. That's the closest she's come to conjuring up a *real* crime in her life.'

There was a pause while Smythson-Balby wrote this down.

'Matter of fact, I don't happen to give two hoots for Miss Christie.' Pat took another swig of the Scotch, longing to be able to shut up.

She was aware of a quickened heartbeat and a strange feeling, as if someone was trying to peel away her skin, edging a little palette knife between her and the outside world. This always happened in interviews. Despite what the interviewer thought – she was invariably described afterwards as taciturn or difficult – she was unable to be anything other than bracingly truthful: to say whatever came into her head. She could feel the words as they surfaced and the simultaneous instruction: Jesus, don't say that! But the necessary filter was not there and say it she would, as if in defiance of herself. A curious, tragic honesty and one she was sure no one appreciated. And, at any rate, the devil with Smythson-Balby! Imagine repeating that Margaret Marshall quote to her and expecting no reaction.

'Do you happen to know how many murders actually occur in English villages?' Pat found herself saying. 'Wait – I had figures somewhere for 'sixty-three, let me look . . .' She fiddled through her scribbled notes, under the craning gooseneck lamp.

'Approximately three hundred. I've counted them, using newspaper reports . . .' She sat back down and nodded towards another of her opened boxes beside the sofa, where the newspapers were stashed; the notes in her hand she had recovered from the top of the box. 'Not that many, is it? And how many of the murderers were beautiful middle-class ladies, or old ladies using poison, or educated gentlemen killing for complex and puzzlingly well planned "motives"? Hey, guess what – not one!'

She could feel herself growing a little swimmy with the whisky but she couldn't cut it out. 'Violence is not an act, it's a *feeling*. Some people give in to it – others never feel it. Most of the murders committed here in England last year were as they are every year, everywhere – sordid, spontaneous, ugly. Often not planned at all. Hoodlums. Young bums. Punks, child molesters, creeps. And who do they kill? You think we're all equally likely to be the victim of a murder? Think again. Murder comes from places of intense hatred and anger, not "cold-blooded calculation". Cold-blooded! The favourite phrase of crime writers, who *know nothing*.'

Smythson-Balby continued with her brisk smile.

'Most victims are known to their killers. Most are wives, girl-friends, children or buddies. Not everyone is capable of murder, not at all. That's a phoney idea. Capable of thinking of it, *wanting* to, of course. But doing it? That's something else. The ultimate crime, a boundary very few people cross, and yet if you read Christie or Ngaio Marsh and the rest, you'd believe *all* were capable of it with impunity. That's the lie being pulled. And I object to it.'

'You speak as if murder were an accomplishment,' Smythson-Balby said, with a bright stare.

Pat took a breath. 'A murderer is cursed with aloneness. Forever. Once he's committed this – ultimate anti-social act, he's condemned to a lifetime spent in terror of being found out. But perhaps he longs to tell all, to boast, because his crime took some kind of courage or daring – certainly a lack of care for convention. Not everyone is capable of murder because most people are not brave and are afraid of breaking society's rules. What goes on in the mind of a man who has killed somebody? Matter of fact, I am interested in *that*.'

She cursed herself again. Why couldn't she hold her tongue? The Scotch was probably not helping but she craved a top-up just now and the mug was empty. She stood up to fetch her cigarettes from the kitchen table. Pausing before offering the packet to her, Pat noticed as she came back into the room how the girl gave off a powerful perfume, musky and nervous, and the smell of newly washed hair. Her hair was long, silky and the colour of horse-chestnuts, snatched up into a ponytail high on her head, leaving her neck exposed, the backs of her ear-lobes presenting little tips of gold pierced earrings. Her blouse was rusty-red silk and must have shrunk, or been bought too small: there were spaces gaping between buttons that seemed to make the girl self-conscious. An extravagant bosom that aimed at her, like two juggernauts. The young woman accepted a cigarette from the packet, and Pat hesitated before going to light it for her. Instead she gave her the gold lighter, too, and sat back down in the leather armchair.

After a quick pull on the cigarette the girl handed back the lighter and said, in a slightly smoky, warmer voice: 'You said *man* just then. I've noticed the women don't commit murders in your novels. Are women incapable of murder?'

'They're capable. Ha! But they have fewer opportunities. And they have – well, most of them do – the nuisance of their sensitivity to others. This ability to feel sorry for whoever would be on the receiving end. Empathy. Sensitivity. Imagination. Whatever. They can't stay in their own feelings long enough to go through with it . . .'

The young woman smoked thoughtfully, then wondered what to do with her ash. Pat leaped forward, sweeping some snails out of a saucer to offer it to her. She pocketed the snails. She knew Smythson-Balby had seen her do that, but tactfully pretended to be scribbling.

'Miss Marshall says you don't like women much. Your women characters might not commit the murders but they all come to a grisly end. I believe she called you a . . . misogynist.'

'Ha! Miss Marshall is a women's libber, then? A bra-less wonder. The men in my novels rarely fare better.'

Smythson-Balby smiled then. A full mouth and a little gap at the front between the teeth. She finished her cigarette and screwed the end into the saucer.

13

'May I ask you about your working habits? How about describing for me an average day?'

The day was bleeding away, and all these hours talking about writing when she could be doing it. Pat drew on her cigarette, then sighed in a showy way and said nothing.

'And what is it that you're writing while you're here?'

'It's bad luck to talk about the novel one is writing. Like opening the oven on a soufflé. Pouf. It's gone.'

'Just a hint?' The frisky ponytail swung optimistically.

'It's about a woman who believes she's being followed. A prowler of some sort. A voyeur. Perhaps a rejected lover. Someone from her past. She might be a little paranoid about it. Perhaps she's imagining it . . . she can't be sure. She receives letters from him, not threatening but meaningless, troubling. She's afraid . . .'

This wasn't the novel she was working on. It was a lie. She trailed off, finished her cigarette, drained a tiny dreg of Scotch in her mug. At last the young visitor seemed to get her point, and suddenly sat up, alert, glancing at her watch.

'Well, that's terrifically helpful, thank you,' Smythson-Balby said, snapping the cap on her fountain pen. 'I've enough to be going on with.' She stood up.

Ronnie's comment suddenly came back to her. Was the damned girl a biographer, really, writing a longer piece for some other publication, not the short article for the local paper they'd agreed? There was a sizzle in the room. Smythson-Balby's pupils were dilated and her cheeks a little flushed as she tugged at the rust-coloured blouse, re-tucking it into the waistband of her skirt. Either she was nervous, or excited, or it was something else; Pat couldn't tell. She remembered the feeling yesterday, and it wasn't the first time, either, of being watched. And although the girl was in front of her, and fooling around, pretending to be putting fountain-pen and notebook into a small, schoolgirl kind of satchel, Pat had exactly the same feeling again now.

Christine Keeler, Pat thought suddenly. That's who she looks like, or would do, if she were a darker brunette, naked, with booted legs astride a chair.

'You don't have a television set?' the younger woman asked, nodding towards the empty wall beside Pat's leather chair – faded rosebud wallpaper, yellow on blue, lightly stained by smoke. Pat had gone to fetch Smythson-Balby's short fur coat from the chair in the kitchen.

'I plan to rent one. In Ipswich.'

The ponytail swung free of the fur collar of the coat: an expensive-looking black jacket that was rather conservative, a little too old for her, compared to the yellow boots and silky blouse. 'Oh, perhaps I could offer you a lift? I have my car here and I noticed there wasn't one parked outside . . .'

It was just an excuse, Pat knew, for Smythson-Balby to question her further, to get more unguarded comments out of her while they pretended to be idly chatting, both staring straight ahead at a dead squirrel on the road or the wobbling ass of a village mailman passing on his bicycle. The scrutiny wasn't yet over: she should refuse. But it had started to have possible compensations – she could use a ride, and Ronnie could never offer her one since he'd refused to learn to drive – and as she watched Smythson-Balby fasten her furry jacket around that pointed English bosom, she wondered at what point, if any, the younger woman might begin to suspect what the compensations were.

'Yes, a ride, thank you . . .' she conceded, and Smythson-Balby finished sweetly with 'And we can continue chatting in the car.'

Pat checked the snails before she left. A couple had escaped along the window ledge; she would need to find lids for the containers. She felt like a heel as she had to keep putting them back, but they were getting the message. There were two more, bigger, snails on a saucer upstairs in her bedroom; bought in a market in France and smuggled in in her suitcase. The snails liked to eat – come out – only when unobserved. The fact that

15

they seemed to know when they weren't being watched amused her. There was a new snail in the bedroom too, and she didn't know how it had got there. She hadn't been nettled, only amused. A paranoid person would say someone had put it there: it was a big one, with bits of dried grass stuck to its shell and its horns out exploringly, sitting on her pillowcase. She picked it up and watched its grey underbelly flute and flower, just like an anemone, as it tried to orient itself. Bubbles of silver formed at its mouth. Then she felt sorry for it, and put it back, careful to place it in the right direction along its own jewelled trail. How simple that it had told her exactly where it was going. Sam would hate to find it there. A smile then at the thought of it: Sam's head would rest on the pillow in only a few days' time.

The car was a white Anglia. Not for Smythson-Balby the three-box-shaped Ford that everyone else drove, no, this was quite the stylish number: small rear fins, chrome bumper with over-riders, chrome side-trim and hooded headlights. Touch of the 1958 Lincoln Continental about it. The cop cars round here were Ford Anglias with contrasting panels of blue or black and white; she'd heard them called 'Pandas' by locals. Next to the cottage was the only gas pump and village garage for miles and the car was parked on the forecourt.

The car last night had been white, too. She asked the young woman if she'd been in the village the night before, perhaps looking for Bridge Cottage. Smythson-Balby seemed unsurprised by this question – she was putting on large black-plastic-framed sunglasses to drive, the light being bright, though the October day was cold. She said she hadn't; Pat couldn't see her eyes.

The inside of the car smelt of cigarette smoke and orange peel, the strange padded-plastic fascia covers on the dashboard, and the perfume Smythson-Balby wore, which must have been very liberally applied. The bright yellow toes in her shiny boots pressed on the pedals as if it was the sexiest thing in the world to be doing, driving this foolish little car.

They didn't pass a mailman, only Ronnie, cycling towards the cottage. Pat hunkered down in her seat, hoping he hadn't seen her. His silly grin seemed to suggest he had but was playing along. His sandy fair hair flapped away from his forehead, like the crest of a waxwing. The Suffolk countryside was full of waxwings, Ronnie had said, showing her a rather fine sketch he'd done, using coloured pencils to show the black mask around the eye, the pretty rusty-red of its plumage, the yellow-tipped tail. Looked like a girl she once knew, who frequented the L bar in Greenwich Village dressed in those colours. She was disappointed that she hadn't seen a gaudy bird or a girl like that in the tasteful Suffolk countryside. Until now.

After a few miles Pat regretted accepting the ride. She'd promised to ring Sam at six o'clock from the telephone booth outside the cottage; what if she wasn't back in time? She didn't actually know how far Ipswich was from Earl Soham; perhaps it would take longer than she'd assumed. Virginia Smythson-Balby was, at any rate, a rookie driver for all her confidence. She was cocky, jerky with the gear changes, giddily swerving a couple of times on the spidery lanes and tight bends. The journalist was trying to keep up a conversation – 'And Mr Hitchcock made a film of one of your earliest novels. What did you make of that?' – but kept breaking off, saying, 'Sorry, oh!' as another driver appeared around a sweep in the road and she had to cut sharply left to pass. It wasn't a squashed squirrel but the huge grey rump of a badger that they saw bloody and upturned at the side of the road, and as they flew past it, Pat had an unpleasant mental image of herself meeting a similar fate under Smythson-Balby's wheel. She began to shake and fidget in her seat, the Scotch sloshing around her stomach, and at last the younger woman noticed and slowed down.

They had passed Ronnie's village – Debach (it wasn't on the way but Smythson-Balby had no sense of direction and had to turn around in a tight lane) – and Pat had managed not to give herself away over it. She counted this as a small victory: if she could keep her friendship with Ronnie to herself, perhaps she could learn continence on other matters of importance, too. Her thoughts kept returning to Sam. She'd noticed that during the day when she was writing she could keep these things at bay, but as the afternoon wore on and the hour when she would speak to Sam again, hear Sam's voice, drew closer, the thoughts loomed up more vividly. Last night there had been a dream, a horrible dream, in which she had drowned a naked Sam in the pond. But as Sam stepped out, arms dripping water and green weeds, just as Pat thought, I've killed her, she saw that it wasn't Sam at all, but Pat herself who stood there.

Smythson-Balby was chattering away about the character of Earl Soham, a place she held in contempt. 'You ask them, "What do you make of Vietnam?" They've been listening to the radio, reading the paper, but they only say: "Oh, it's a place far away." Vietnam's not in East Anglia. That's as far as their imagination will travel . . .' The countryside, she gathered, held few charms for Smythson-Balby. It was clear from hints that she'd travelled a great deal and hoped to do plenty more. At any rate, it was easier to imagine the girl in those yellow patent boots in a night-club in London, or perhaps Eve's bar in Munich (a place Pat knew well), eyes sandbagged in mascara and giggling over a martini with a man on her arm. Or even – here she let herself go a little further – on a spotlit stage with a mike in hand, in a floor-sweeping halter-neck dress, singing 'An Englishman Needs Time'. Had she seen her in such a role somewhere? Different hair, perhaps, rigged up differently – younger? A show-girl: that fitted. That was where the Christine Keeler thought had floated from. This girl pretended to be a bouncy fresh thing, with no ulterior motives. Pat knew the type. 'I was just having a good time,' she would protest. Could it really be her fault if people kept getting the wrong idea?

Ipswich was a town gearing up for something. Small groups of girls and boys formed lines outside the Savoy ballroom on St

Nicholas Street, and they were also at the railway station. The boys were smoking and polishing the toes of their shoes with their handkerchiefs, the girls laughing and shrieking in white gloves and courts and fur coats. Smythson-Balby was not impressed. 'Joe Loss. Harry Gold and His Pieces of Eight. Not my thing,' she sneered, as Pat's eyes followed the young women with their bouffant curls. No, Pat thought. She could picture Smythson-Balby doing a much more extravagant sort of dancing than the ballroom kind.

'We used to call girls like that round-heels. I guess you don't know that word any more,' Pat murmured.

Smythson-Balby remained silent.

Of course, she should turn the tables, hammer Smythson-Balby with a few questions of her own. 'Who are you, really? A friend of mine claims you have other . . . biographical, book-length intentions, not just an article . . . Matter of fact, would you mind declaring yourself now because I'd like to know what it is I'm confessing to?' but something prevented her. She believed it impolite to ask personal questions, despite having to endure them so often herself. She wouldn't dream of voicing them. She found herself wondering over the name 'Smythson'. Hadn't she heard it somewhere, mooted as one of the mysterious backers of the Great Train Robbery last summer? The trial was still going on, and the English newspapers' obsession with the hopelessly bungled crime was undimmed. She puzzled, too, about the state Smythson-Balby had been in when she'd first arrived. What had provoked it? Such a prickle around her, such an overwrought, giddy little drama?

Strange, sickening, really, how other people never thought it rude to ask *her* those kinds of things and make cracks at her, then had the nerve to complain afterwards about her unwilling-ness to answer. And they would offer her spiteful quotes and comments on her work and watch to see if she got rattled. And, yes, she was still smarting about the Margaret Marshall quote and who wouldn't be? Her characters *deviant*, her work

19

unnatural. Sure, yes, she'd always understood the insinuation. Damn them – did they think she was a fool?

At last Smythson-Balby lurched to a squealing halt in a parking lot and pulled up the brake with a flourish. She explained – slightly breathlessly – where Ipswich High Street was and where she'd find the store that arranged television-set rentals. They rolled up the windows of the car, which had been opened an inch so that they could smoke, and stepped out. The fur collar on Smythson-Balby's coat was tugged up around her chin; her bright dark eyes seemed to be smiling and she'd pushed the sunglasses onto her head, but her mouth was covered. The young journalist danced from foot to foot, clapping cold hands together. For the first time her brisk summer-camp-leader persona deserted her and she glanced at her watch a little shyly, saying: 'I could meet you back here in an hour. Unless you would like me to . . .'

'No, that's swell, thank you. See you back here at five?'

Pat strode away from the car with an absurd fear that Smythson-Balby might follow her. Perhaps she would never now shake her off. It wasn't the first time she had had that thought about a younger woman. 'You have a new fan,' Ronnie would say, if he was there. Ronnie was always vigilant. He liked to remind her of how attractive she was, take the glass from her hand, refresh it for her, tell her gently as he gave it back: 'This will ruin your looks.' Ronnie. She could have been chopping wood in the garden of Bridge Cottage just now, in fierce fall sunshine, Ronnie with his sleeves rolled up, sharpening the axe.

At ten minutes to six she was installed at Bridge Cottage, a fire chuntering in the grate, a whole pile of chopped logs stacked by the back door and a Scotch in hand. The television set was fixed up and being delivered next week. So she wouldn't be able to watch it with Sam, but no matter, there would be other occasions, other weekends. This thought, the real reason behind her moving to Suffolk, gave her a jolt of pleasure so strong that she paused, in the kitchen, and noticed it, and wrapped her arms around herself.

She had marked the Scotch bottle, scoring it with pencil at the point she felt she should drink to today, but the visit earlier meant it was almost empty. On the kitchen table two fat steaks lolled. She'd bought them from a butcher in Ipswich (taking care to conceal them from Smythson-Balby: she didn't want questions about weekend visitors). There was also a fresh lettuce and three tomatoes in a brown bag and some strongly vinegary salad dressing she'd made up in a pickle jar. There was a new warm loaf of bread. The kitchen curtains were tugged closed, but they were a little short of meeting in the middle: there was always a gap with a slit of dark sky in it. The telephone booth across the road loomed in her mind with supernaturally vivid presence. She had not heard Sam's voice since Paris, since she'd arrived in England, as they'd both thought it risky.

Moments later she stood in the booth, inhaling the faint smell of cat urine and cigarette smoke, her heart pattering as if she had been running.

'So, what time will you arrive tonight?' Pat asked. Hearing Sam, she immediately pictured her exactly as she was painting her. She had decided to change from fall colours to a background of intense cobalt blue and red. Sam, the figure of Sam, stretching through those colours like a white orchid (she would put an orchid in the painting, too, she decided) or a swan. Naked, her neck outstretched, winding a strand of her white-blonde hair in one finger. To Pat, Sam had the look of a Modigliani painting, though she couldn't remember ever seeing a blonde one. Almond eyes, heart-shaped face. Elegant neck, a little longer than is common. And, curiously, this portrait Pat was making of her – unfinished though it was – was easier to conjure up just now than the real Sam.

Sam's voice was somehow wobbly on the line. A crackle and then a loud, hacking cough.

'I don't feel so chipper,' Sam said, when she recovered. 'And there's another problem, darling. Minty's home for the weekend. She has a fever and the school sent her home. I can hardly leave her here with Gerald.'

Pat groaned and didn't trouble to disguise it. 'Gerald is perfectly capable of looking after his eight-year-old daughter by himself for one night, isn't he?'

'Yes, but it will look odd. Fair enough, I might go for a week-end by the sea with some old girlfriends from work, but not when my daughter is poorly. It would look . . . strange.'

'But I've been waiting and waiting!' Pat exploded. 'I've been here days already. Does that mean I have to wait a whole other week?'

'Well, if Minty's better tomorrow I might manage Sunday afternoon. Afternoon tea at Aldeburgh and a walk by the sea, and then drive back? Don't be angry, darling.'

Pat *was* angry. The Smythson-Balby girl had nettled her, the day's routine was spoiled and she hadn't written a single word of her novel. Worse, she felt an appalling dread that Sam's resolve was fading. If she mentioned this, Sam would prickle and sulk and nothing would be achieved, so she couldn't think, just at that moment, what to say at all.

'I – rented a television set,' she mumbled, her hand cupping the receiver. That was her last coin being eaten up. Mrs Ingham passed the phone booth, head wrapped in a red scarf like the Queen, walking her terrier in the soft, drizzling rain. Mrs Ingham spied her and waved cheerily.

'I bought two very nice rump steaks,' Pat said. The line went dead before she could say: I love you. Would she have said it? She wasn't sure. She stared at the little black shelf, the fat telephone directory, the sign saying Earl Soham, Woodbridge 6852. What was the point of anything? Sam wasn't the demonstrative type and in Pat's experience such lovers needed careful handling if they weren't to feel too overwhelmed, too 'smothered' (as her girl-friend, Ginnie, another cool type, had once witheringly put it).

22

She tried to slam the phone booth door behind her but it was on some kind of powerful hinge and closed in its own sweet time, so she stomped back to the house, reaching for the new bottle of Scotch before she'd even taken her coat off. The fire – so lively only a short while ago – was now completely out, the logs powdering to soft grey ash that a poke wouldn't ignite. She gave it a kick and a cloud of pale dust billowed. The room was pretty chilly; Pat's habit of keeping the curtains closed against nosy neighbours also prevented any sunlight warming it during the day, so she took herself upstairs with the drink to the bedroom, facing out over the back garden – looking onto Mrs Ingham's house, in fact. The room was north-facing too and wasn't any warmer. There was the portrait Allela had done of her, glowering, scowling, facing the bed.

She was about to fling herself under the covers when she noticed the two snails on their saucer on the window ledge. They were moving, swaying. Pat bent close and studied them. Now they were *kissing*. There could be no other word for it.

The Scotch bottle in her hand, she poured a generous shot into the tooth-mug she found herself holding. The entranced creatures in the saucer fascinated her. Look at that, she longed to say to Sam, who was a keen gardener and bird watcher. (She pictured Sam as she thought it, kneeling in front of a flowerbed, her slim spine curved over, wearing something blazing in peacock-blue and red, sunlight surrounding her in a frill of golden light.) She needed to get a book from the library about snails. That was her last thought before she tumbled into a bottomless pit of sleep, slipping under the top counterpane, still dressed in her jeans and shirt.

Thumping at the back door woke her. She glanced at her travel clock beside the bed at the green numbers: 3 a.m. Crazed, frantic banging, from a fist, Pat thought, small and desperate, like a child's. And then a voice, a woman's voice, calling. Pat felt for her pyjamas under her pillow. She didn't want whoever it was to think her ready to go out, or just arrived home, at this hour. If it was Sam, she had some crazy jealous thoughts sometimes. She took a second to step into the pyjamas before hurrying downstairs – banging her head on the low ceiling – and rushing to the kitchen door.

'Oh, Miss Highsmith, I'm so sorry to disturb you this late but – there's – oh . . .'

Her neighbour, Mrs Ingham, was standing in the back garden bathed in the light she had just flicked on in the kitchen, which dazzled them both. The older woman was chalky-faced, wearing slippers and a navy-coloured bathrobe over something incongruous and lacy, her elderly chest horribly on display. Pat motioned her into the kitchen – the slippers were wet and muddy – and Mrs Ingham breathed audibly, struggling to regain some composure.

Pat stood at a loss, then thought to offer a glass of water. Mrs Ingham glugged the water and dabbed at her eyes with a cotton handkerchief from the pocket of her bathrobe.

'Would you go to the phone box outside and call the police for me? I hear someone in the garden! I don't have a telephone in the house and I daren't go around to the front but you could from your front door without being seen . . . in case he's still there,' Mrs Ingham whispered, cringing towards the wall as if whoever it was might join them.

Pat looked round the kitchen and took a step back from her.

An intruder. A burglar – or an obsessive, a fan? Stanley – Brother Death – had he found her?

'Are you sure? Did you see anyone?'

'I heard – oh, terrifying sounds in the garden. You know, a plant pot being knocked over and scrabbling sounds by the chicken coop. I imagine he was trying the windows but I didn't actually see him . . . There used to be a torch that I kept by the window for, you know, such occasions, but I seem to have mislaid it. Oh, I'm so sorry again to trouble you.'

24

'Not at all.' The two women were both standing in the kitchen; Pat's bare feet were cold on the tiles. She tried to usher them both through the open doorway into the living room, where she'd flung her coat and brogues on the sofa. She grabbed her own large flashlight from upstairs, and from a drawer next to the bed she pulled out her switchblade, used for grooming plants, and slid it into the coat pocket. She put her shoes on.

Downstairs, Mrs Ingham was standing by the window in the living room, not quite brave enough to lift the curtain and peer at the darkness. She made a little gesture, anticipated by Pat, to clasp Pat by the arm, like a maiden in despair, but it was skilfully deflected with an almost imperceptible jerk away.

'I'm so sorry to trouble you like this,' she whispered again. Pat suspected the old snooper was enjoying herself. Probably a long time since something had happened in her life in the wee small hours. 'I'll wait here and re-lock the front door once you've run out to the phone box,' Mrs Ingham said breathlessly, then – 'Wait! I think I heard him again.'

Both women stiffened, listening intently. The tinny sound of something – perhaps the watering can – being kicked over in the back garden made them turn around and head back through the doorway towards the kitchen. It was irritating and ridiculous, the way Mrs Ingham followed her, as if she was one of those plastic toys, attached at the waist. The kitchen light was still on and the gap between the curtains made it possible they could be seen, so Pat hung back a little and Mrs Ingham quickly followed suit. Better to surprise him, not the other way around, once the door was flung open. They were behind the door now, breathing heavily, Pat with her hand on the wooden handle. There was an unmistakable scream, a horrible squeal as Pat shoved the door open.

The kitchen light pooled over a knocked-over plant pot, black soil heaping on the path. Pat let out her breath slowly, staring at the path that led to the lawn to Bridge House, Mrs Ingham's place. Did she see a shape? A dark figure anywhere? She wasn't sure. Her heart scampered a little, but not too fast. She saw some black smears on the path from the plant pot and went to put it upright. Then something else: a grey lump with ears. Mrs Ingham, still inside the kitchen, crumbling at the doorway, squeaked a little cry as Pat tiptoed towards it and nudged it with the toe of her shoe.

It was the severed head of a rabbit. Black eyes. Neck straggling with black blood that smudged over the path.

Mrs Ingham's pet rabbit: Bunnikins.

'No need for you to see this,' Pat said, stooping closer to look, then straightening up. She went back into the kitchen, passing Mrs Ingham, but managed with the tone of her voice – horribly *paternal*, even Pat was aware of it – to prevent her neighbour going outside. She fetched newspapers from the basket next to the fire, copies of the *Ipswich Star*, to wrap the little head in.

'I'm afraid our intruder was probably a coyote or some such. Do you get them in England?' Pat dimly remembered that they didn't. 'Or a fox.'

'Yes, foxes. Oh – did it get in the hutch? The wire was rather weakened. Did it hurt Bunnikins?'

Pat's instinct for an honest reply got the better of her as usual.

'I'm sorry but it did. Must have bitten through the wire at the top of the hutch. I reckon you'll need to check the chickens too.'

Mrs Ingham nodded, grimaced and, with Pat beside her, padded outside in her slippers to check. Strangely, the chickens, although beady-eyed and dazzled awake by the flashlight now spraying at them, appeared unharmed; they immediately began scratching at their feet, as if grateful for the sudden light to eat by. The limp body of Bunnikins was discovered, wet and flopping, across the grass.

Once back inside Pat offered her neighbour a shot of brandy to calm her nerves.

'Well. You must think me quite the fool,' Mrs Ingham said, sipping from an expensive bowl glass that Pat had unpacked when she had been expecting Sam. Pat assured her she didn't.

'I've lived on my own for so long. Not used to Bridge Cottage being occupied. Lucky that you were here. It's a big wild garden, isn't it? Have you been to the bottom, where the stream is? Always found it creepy myself but when my husband was alive it wasn't such a problem. And if there were strange noises – new sounds, you know – Alf would check on them. Poor Bunnikins. I don't care for him myself. I keep him for when my grandson, Paul, visits. He'll be heartbroken.'

Mrs Ingham's eyes glittered.

'I'll fix us another drink,' Pat said. Mrs Ingham seemed to be recovering rather well from the night's excitement, Pat noticed. This told her two things: the old snooper was not as dumb as she seemed and she was nosy as hell. The brandy made her voluble. A bit more drivelling – *Oh, you're a writer aren't you, how lovely . . . and American, I believe, but you don't talk like one, do you? Did you know there's a mobile greengrocer and a mobile butcher too, Wednesday afternoons?* How soon would it be acceptable for Pat to yawn and hint that she really must get back to bed?

It was a good half-hour. Yawning and hints didn't do it. Pat practically had to shove her through the kitchen door.

Locking it behind her, she rewrapped the newspaper more firmly around the rabbit's bloodied head so that she couldn't see again its open glassy black eyes. It reminded her of an English fish-and-chip packet; it was still disgustingly warm. She would put it out in the garbage tomorrow; somehow she didn't want to venture outside at the moment. The sense that something – not a fox, but a person – was watching her now through that slit in the curtains made her want to go back into the living room, find her cigarettes and smoke two, one after the other. Her new concern was how on earth she would spend a weekend, an evening or afternoon in the cottage with Sam and the goddamned snooper just over the lawn like that. At least there'd been the mention of a grandson. Perhaps Mrs Ingham went away sometimes to visit him. Pat made a note to introduce the question into the conversation at some later date to try to discover when. She changed her mind suddenly about the rabbit and quickly unlocking and wrenching open the back door, lobbed the newspaper package into the metal garbage can at the side of the house (the lid propped beside it was knocked rolling to the ground). The rabbit made a satisfying thud, and the lid clanged rudely. Strange noises, new sounds. Mrs Ingham had better get used to it.

She drifted to sleep thinking of Sam. The portrait she was working on in her little art room next door loomed up, life-sized and luminous, as if it was finished at last. But instead of her picture of Sam, there was a Modigliani painting that she'd seen many times in Paris. It annoyed her, the way this image superimposed itself on her consciousness, as if she wasn't able to create anything new at all, only to inhabit the form of another, ghostly, artist. Every time she closed her eyes, she had a troubling sensation of something small and worm-like swarming over her nose. She remembered the snails suddenly and opened her eyes, reaching for the little square button to press on the base of the bedside lamp. Of course the snails were still on the window ledge. In the lamplight they seemed to be paused, waiting for something. Or – she peered harder – utterly still. They had abandoned their earlier behaviour with no sign of anything amorous or aggressive at all. To all intents and purposes they might be dead. She felt an urge to get out of bed and go check them with one finger, pick them up and poke inside the shell to be sure they had not met the same sad fate as Bunnikins. She lay still and fought the urge. She had a bottle of Scotch beside the bed and she needed a large tooth-mug full before sleep at last descended on her. She thought of sleep like an anchor, a plumb-weight, pulling her down.

'It's an easy route – the A1120. You pass a mill as you approach the village, then cut right. You'll know the cottage when you see a little bridge – there's a stream runs through the garden. Oh, and you can't miss the colour – salmon pink! Well, I guess plenty of the houses round here are that colour.' Pat tried to slow down.

She was gabbling, her warm breath steaming up the telephone booth, and she feared again that Sam might accuse her of being 'intense'.

'I'll be there as soon as I can, darling, as soon as Gerald leaves for golf. Do write something first and don't worry about me. I have a map. You know you're awfully cranky if you haven't managed to write.'

What a stroke of luck! Minty had rallied and gone to spend the weekend with her cousins, as arranged, and now it was Saturday, and Sam said she was feeling a little better, and could come after all. The pips went and Pat hurried back to her cottage; the door was on the latch.

Her typewriter was still snug in its coffee-coloured cover, stickered with the peeling labels of the many countries visited, tucked under the bed. She had told Sam proudly that the new cottage had three small rooms upstairs and sang to herself as she unwrapped the typewriter: '"I'm gonna hug you in the morning, hug you in the evening too . . ."'

The disturbing thing about moving house, not to mention the boxes and cases that were meant to follow one but usually went missing, were the days lost while deciding where to set up her workroom. The options were the cramped kitchen table downstairs (risking being interrupted when Mrs Ingham or Ronnie came by and opened the back door on her, like shining a flashlight on a specimen in a Petrie dish . . . No, that would never work). Or a makeshift desk in her low-ceilinged bedroom with the flaking overhead beams and the portrait of herself in the red jacket looking like grim death that Allela had painted, and that she had brought with her to every house she lived in and then regretted, longing to turn its face to the wall . . . No. That left the living room and the problem of the front door and the mailbox. The mailman and his little stooge (she thought it was his son, somehow), the newspaper boy. He was particularly unexpected, with his rude and forceful thrusting of the goddamn *Ipswich Star*. Last week she was so shocked she'd opened the door after him and shouted: 'What's the idea?' But he was already on his bike and away as far as the row of almshouses near the bar.

Such interruptions sounded trivial to others (to Sam, for instance), who seemed to believe one should recover momentum at once, continue typing as if nothing were amiss. But being in the throes of a novel when it was going well was like being submerged under water. Being disturbed was like coming up for air too quickly. It gave one the bends. And it was not easy to go back under again.

And here, yes, just as she'd dreaded, here already was more knocking at the kitchen door and more disturbance. 'Yoo-hoo!' came a voice. A female voice, but not Sam's. A young voice.

'Sorry – the back door was open!' She had stepped into the kitchen, uninvited. Pat was astonished.

Smythson-Balby. Looking awful fresh. Washed hair. Sunny yellow shift dress, straining over the bust, short; worn over tan pantyhose and topped with a fringed suede jacket. The same banana boots. Huge owl sunglasses pushed up into her hair.

'I'm so sorry. But you don't have a telephone,' the younger woman said. 'And I wanted to ask if I could drop the article off tomorrow – my deadline is Tuesday – and whether you wouldn't mind awfully checking it over. You know. For facts. Errors. Titles of your books, that kind of thing. Might that be OK?'

'Tomorrow? Sunday? No. I – I'll be out.'

'Monday, then?'

Pat heard the engine now. Realised that Smythson-Balby was not alone. Both women wandered into the front room where Pat distractedly opened the living-room curtains to see through the window that another young woman was at the front of the house, smoking in the driving seat of a red sports car, its roof opened, like a peeled tin.

'That your friend?' Pat asked.

'Yes, Izzie. She gave me a lift.'

'Where do you happen to live?'

'Beg your pardon?'

'Do you live here in Suffolk?' Pat's difficulty with asking direct questions made her sound brusque, she knew, but too late to check that now.

'No. I live in London. In Notting Hill, in fact. But I'm staying at Aldeburgh. With Izzie . . .'

Damn her. Aldeburgh. Half an hour away. Damn girl could keep materialising like this at any moment. She would have to start locking the doors when she was home. Use the excuse of Mrs Ingham's 'intruder' if anyone queried it. Or perhaps her being from Texas would be explanation enough.

The girl was waiting for an answer.

'Bit chilly for the roof down, isn't it?'

'I'm sorry?'

Pat nodded towards the window, towards Smythson-Balby's pretty friend in her headscarf.

'Oh, Izzie doesn't mind. She loves driving with the wind in her face!'

Pat watched Smythson-Balby carefully for the way she said 'Izzie' but there was nothing to be read there.

'Yes. That's fine,' she replied. 'Monday. If the door is locked, knock loudly. I might be writing.'

'Of course. I wouldn't want to disturb you. Toodle pip!'

And then she was gone. Pat heard the driver say something like 'Hey, Ginny,' and the little car roared into a youthful burst and took off up the road. Pat was left adrift in a fog of oppressively sweet perfume. Once more she had the impression that the girl reminded her of someone she knew and couldn't identify. Now she wondered whether she'd met Smythson-Balby before, in another life. In another country. Neither thought was comfortable.

And then at last she's here, and filling the little cottage with the scent of honey and almonds. It's a baked tart in a little blue dish that she made herself and brought for after lunch; it hangs around her when I kiss her, her cheeks and hands smelling of vanilla and marzipan. She has on the peacock-patterned shirt-dress in a gauzy material that we bought together in Paris, the one I always picture her in. Her hair is artfully piled up, perfectly smooth, Grace Kelly-style, and when she stands in the garden to admire the stream and the deep English green of it all in her wellingtons, holding the little glass of Italian vermouth and soda I've made for her, the material becomes transparent in sunlight and I can see her legs through it. Over that she's slung a thick fisherman's-style sweater in dark brown wool, man-sized, probably one belonging to Gerald. It emphasises her slenderness, her elegance, and though it looks casual, thrown on, it isn't. Nothing about Sam is unstudied; no effect unsought. A woman of elongated lines – I sometimes feel she has been pulled and stretched, so tall, so slim, like a kind of pliable clay, but this could never be true, because nothing about Sam is pliable. Isn't that why I love her? The one woman I've ever met who in her quiet, solid, cool way matches my strength of personality with hers, matches me steel for steel.

I'm showing her a handful of delicate hazelnut-sized snails, explaining how many I've already amassed. She laughs at me, but her eyes are vivid, glittering: two vivid blue fish. Around her neck is the gold locket I gave her. When she frees her hair from its exquisitely well-arranged grips the last pale coil of it will reach down to her marzipan-scented waist. She will allow me to kiss her there: maybe, maybe.

Sam couldn't make it. More waiting, lunchtime passed, 2 p.m., another pained conversation in the telephone booth, more excuses (as far as Pat was concerned), something whispered about Gerald not having left yet, changed plans again, and then in anger, and suddenly sober as a trout, Pat clomped home and threw a splat of steak onto the lit fire in the front room, watching it melt into a fat black lump, stinking the place out with its acrid greasy smoke.

Pat was mad enough to hit someone. She smoked three Gauloises, one after another, letting out a loud shriek when she realised the packet was empty. She paced the room. She considered going back to the telephone, risking Gerald answering, and making some kind of demand. An ultimatum. A declaration. Gerald had a temper, he was volatile; Sam, she knew, was sometimes afraid of him. There had been that time. The very first occasion of meeting Sam: a small dinner party for some publishing people in London at the home of one of them, a dozen or so people present and Pat there too, eating quietly, hoping no one would speak to her, stealing glances at the beauty at the end of the table, the wife of a banker, someone connected to the publishing world only by some association she hadn't understood. Then Gerald had suddenly – there had suddenly been some commotion, Pat wasn't sure what, but others at the table had fallen silent and become embarrassed, aware of shouting, and there was Gerald, his silly skinny self, leaping up and bellowing something, and a glass of wine had been knocked over, and she hadn't really seen or heard properly what had happened, but with her antennae flickering she'd felt her pulse quicken anyway, her ribcage tighten, and she'd understood. Violence always has a smell, a temperature, to those familiar with it.

And Sam, tense, charming, trying to look as if nothing had happened, had stared gracefully down the dinner table at the guests, with her look of absolute poise and grace, murmuring to her husband, 'Darling, do sit down,' but she hadn't dared to touch him, Pat noticed. Sam – trying to stare at no one in particular – had accidentally caught Pat's gaze and somehow, between them, something fizzed.

Strange that Gerald did not know about his wife's tastes. The man was not naïve. There had long been rumours; even Pat had heard them before meeting the exquisitely lovely source of so much gossip. He preferred to remain in ignorance, like Queen Victoria. If such things were not named they could not exist. *When We Dead Awaken*, Pat thought bitterly – the title of the

Ibsen play she'd seen with Sam in London once, a phrase she loved and that had lodged fast. '"When we dead awaken . . . we see that we have never lived . . .".' Pat had whispered it urgently into Sam's ear that night, outside the theatre in Soho, kissed her hard in the glare of a streetlamp, repeating the phrase again and again, saying: 'If you never leave Gerald, you will never *live* . . .'

Sam had pulled away from her, smoothed down her coat, retied her silk scarf under her chin, said coolly: 'Please, Patsy, don't . . .'

And Queen Victoria, the thought of her now jogged something. There were two bars in the village: the Falcon and the Victoria. There would be cigarettes there (why hadn't she thought to buy some in Ipswich?) and 'a change of scene', as Mother used to call it, when she was in the doghouse with Stanley. 'Honey. You need a change of scene. Freshen yourself up and let's take a drive.'

She freshened herself up now. It was – she checked the watch by her bed – still lunchtime opening hours. She changed her shirt – her drawer was full of folded white shirts, and nothing gave her more pleasure than seeing them there, neat as sheaves of paper. She picked one out and splashed water on her face. Even swiped a smudge of pink lipstick around her mouth, patted powder on her chin and nose, a concession. (There was only so much being talked about that she could stand.) A visitor, a foreigner, a still-handsome woman in her forties (this wasn't vanity: all her girl-friends had said so), with no husband or children; a famous writer. The 'pub', the English village hub, with its dangerous darts players, would be the greatest test so far. Buying cookies for slimmers at her local store would pale in comparison.

She locked the door behind her and shoved her hands into the pockets of her Levi's. The hedges at the front of the cottage bristled and a leaf flipped over and over on the road, as if trying to escape. She marched in the direction of the bar, head down, over the little bridge, which the stream in her garden passed under; in her coat pocket bounced one of the snails. This time it was empty, an empty shell the birds had plucked, and she slipped her little finger into the comforting space, wearing it like a ring.

And yet what greeted her, as she scraped the creaking wooden door over the red tiled floor (she entered through the back door that led from the car park, figuring this for a less brazen way in), was surprisingly dark and consoling. Smoke, the smell of smoked fish, if she wasn't mistaken, and two fireplaces blazing in a rather cosy, masculine space. They were all men, of course. Most were elderly and sat alone, cradling their pint glasses. They did nothing more than nod at her or suck on their pipes. The appraising eyes – female eyes – she'd expected were not there. The men would have assessed her at once as attractive but not young, and not game, and with that appraisal over, her invisibility would be assured. The faded tar-coloured curtains were closed. The nicotine-stained walls and the wallpaper the exact shade of smokers' teeth, all testimony to a bar of dark secrets and noiseless musings by men used to their lonely days in the field, who did not see why they should forfeit silence.

'Would you push the door shut? We've just got the fire going,' the toothy redhead behind the bar asked smilingly, and Pat obliged by returning to the door and closing it with a firm shove. She ordered a whisky with ice – the ice was a luxury as she had no way of making it at the cottage – and, that received, arranged herself at one of the rickety wooden tables, nearest the fire. The table, she discovered, when she tried to tuck her feet underneath, was a Singer sewing-machine table, complete with little drawers that she longed to peek in and a metal frame trailing cobwebs. Everything about this bar surprised and pleased her – the curious portrait of Queen Victoria above the fireplace, with her wistful gaze, and below that the cartoon with its considerably less respectful take on 'the longest reign in history'; the weird trophy above the fireplace that had three horns (what goddamn animal had three horns, for Christ's sake?) and its great swags of straggling black hair; a laughably tiny and wobbly wooden bookshelf with no rhyme or reason to its presence (it was lined with dusty bottles); floor tiles pocked black by a lifetime's cigarette butts, ground under farmers' boots. She would not have been surprised if a pig had sauntered up to the bar and asked for a drink.

No one would speak to her here; the English pub was not what she'd imagined at all. She could think about the Problem over her whisky, stare into the fire, watch her face burnish in the reflection from the copper kettle beside it, and not one lousy lunk would care to chat to her. She rubbed her thumb against the ridged shell of the little snail in her pocket before removing her coat and hanging it from the back of her chair. She had brought a book along in the other pocket; a paperback she'd picked up in Ipswich, in the second-hand store next to the television rental place. It was a book on Gastropoda. She felt confident no one would start up a conversation about *that*.

She had scrutinised each snail, but there was no further strangeness, except for that one tiny snail with the particularly beautiful, glazed shell – whorls of pearlescent amber alternating with hazelnut brown – it was her favourite and it wasn't moving. She was thinking about that now – was that poor snail about to die? – and about Sam, and opening the cellophane on a fresh packet of cigarettes, Embassy (beggars couldn't be choosers) bought from a machine next to the ladies' room, when the door opened and a blast of daffodil yellow heralded the arrival of Virginia Smythson-Balby.

Damn girl! I thought she was staying in – where did she say? Aldeburgh? What was she doing in *this* village then, every minute of every goddamn day?

'Oh, hello! I hoped I might find you here. I brought the article, you know. I finished it sooner than I thought.'

Wasn't it only a matter of hours ago when she'd promised to bring it round Monday? She must have had it with her all along.

Smythson-Balby stood at the bar, smiling down at her. She bought herself a shandy with obvious inexperience, having to ask the price twice, dropping money as she fumbled with her pocket book, then turning, rather awkwardly, to offer to buy Pat a drink. Another whisky was secured and then the girl sat next to her, gushing:

'Just, you know, as I say. Whenever you can. Thank you so much for agreeing. The book titles, the spellings, that kind of thing. I'd hate to get anything wrong.'

Pat did not remembering agreeing, but said nothing. She glugged back her drink too quickly; the ice knocked against her teeth. The girl had pushed some typewritten pages towards her.

'I've actually never been in here,' Smythson-Balby confided, leaning forward in a gust of that overwhelming scent. 'Or in fact . . . probably *any* pub, on my own. Don't you feel as if everyone is staring at you?'

They were now. The old men looked as if someone had run a shot of electricity through them. Their hair practically stood on end, Pat noticed. They were trying *not* to stare at the mini-skirt, the legs, the deep crease between Smythson-Balby's attention-seeking breasts when she leaned forward to pick up a pound note she'd dropped on the floor. Her hair today was glossier and redder in colour than ever, and piled on top of her head like the Eiffel Tower – could that actually be all her own hair or was it some kind of elaborate hairpiece? It looked like plastic; Pat was tempted to put her hand out and touch it.

'Actually, there is something I'd like to ask you,' the young woman said.

Here it comes: she's writing a novel, Pat thought at once. She wants to ask me to read it. It had happened many times before; a hazard of the profession. Pushing her fringe out of her eyes, she tapped the ash from her cigarette into an ashtray that said *Guinness is Good for You,* wondering how she would manage to say no.

'Might you be interested in buying my car?' Smythson-Balby continued. 'I've bought the red one from Izzie – she was taking me for a spin in it just now and, well, of course, it's not very often in

England one can drive with the roof down but *still*. It's such a joy. And that means I have to get rid of the Anglia and . . . I thought of you. You're pretty stuck out here without a car. A new one would be nearly five hundred but, of course, I'd let you have it for a good price.'

Pat pulled on her cigarette and considered. Sure, she could use a car. She'd thought of that when Sam said she couldn't come to visit. She'd wanted at once to drive to London and snatch her away, elope with her. She'd driven cars with stick-shift gears in France and Germany, she was a confident driver, and the Ford Anglia was quite an appealing little model. But what was this young woman really asking? Did it insinuate her into Pat's life in some way, oblige her? If she said yes, would the girl find fresh excuses to visit her at Bridge Cottage every five minutes, to make herself indispensable to her?

'How much?' Pat asked.

'Two hundred pounds? You can have a little drive in it if you like. It's outside.'

'What's the perfume you're wearing?' Pat asked.

'Coty. L'Aimant. Do you like it?'

Pat stood up, placing the book on Gastropoda in her jacket pocket and her arms in the sleeves. Smythson-Balby's typed pages lay on the Singer table with a faint ringed stain where Pat had rested her whisky glass; she picked them up. The younger woman beamed and nodded towards the front door. As they left, the old men lifted their heads and noses, like pigs beside a trough as the bucket approaches.

'I won a *Vogue* contest,' Smythson-Balby was saying. 'Mother is really thrilled about it. A writing competition. Fifty pounds. Mrs Kennedy won the American one, you know, years ago, so it's rather something . . .'

'That dreadful Cutty Sark whisky,' Pat mumbled, not listening. 'I can't get the taste out of my mouth.' The advertising slogan was: *A man's drink that women enjoy*. That summed it up. Dumb women of no discernment, who were afraid to drink whisky, of course. It was the only kind the Victoria served.

The bar had closed late, something the locals called a 'lock-in'. It was dusk now. The car hurtled rather pleasingly down softly darkening lanes, its full beam catching and freezing a muntjac deer as it sprinted across the road, and then a tiny stoat, dashing for its life. The wattle and daub houses of Earl Soham, with their thatched roofs and some with pantiles that glowed orange in the car's headlamps ('Roman tiles' particular to this part of Suffolk, Ronnie had lovingly explained), were replaced by empty fields, spidery lanes and black ditches. Tail-lights from a jet at the Bentwater airfield sailed over them, like fish in an inky black tank.

Pat was enjoying being behind the wheel. The dumb girl's chatter and the smell of the L'Aimant nonsense was barely penetrating her consciousness; she was thinking only of Sam. Sam and Gerald, with his big hands and his square head, the strange, deceptive softness that flowed from him; the way that his pupils blackened his irises sometimes, black saturating the blue, like ink flooding water, when he was angry. Was Sam in danger? Had Gerald found out something – had something monstrous happened? Sam had sounded overwrought on the telephone earlier. Not herself, now that Pat came to think of it. Constrained. Pat had not believed she was ill. Or that Minty was ill. It was something else, and now that she was in the car, careering past a suddenly illuminated vicarage with its handsome cedar of Lebanon, she realised, with a chill shock, what it was. Sam had sounded frightened.

'Izzie's a grand girl.' Smythson-Balby was still prattling.

Pat interrupted: 'One hundred and fifty pounds. The clutch is shot to hell.'

Smythson-Balby's face was unreadable. 'Well, Daddy said it was in awfully good condition.'

'One hundred and sixty. It's pretty banged-up. I didn't ask you to bring it. I can live without a car.'

'Done!'

Pat swung the car to a wild turn in the middle of the lane and began driving home. Would she dare to call Sam? She needed to talk to her – she had to know she was safe.

'Thanks for the offer of the car, and the article. I'll see you tomorrow. Could you bring the car early? There's a journey I should take. I'll have the cash for you. Matter of fact, I have it now,' Pat said.

'I could pop in and get it?' There was a note in Smythson-Balby's voice that Pat thought she recognised.

'Sure, but how will you get home?' Pat was distracted. The obvious answer did not seem apparent to her.

'You might drive me?' the girl said sweetly.

Pat cut the engine outside Bridge Cottage. She had a glimpse of Smythson-Balby's startled expression in the interior light. She was thinking only: With a car, I could retrieve Sam. I could drive to London and rescue her from that old dope. Inside the cottage, she was almost running. She switched lights on, rummaged roughly in an old tin money box near her bed. She liked to keep cash the way she liked to keep folded shirts, and snails. She knew she had the cash. But the girl could go jump in the lake if she wanted a ride. Pat had a better idea.

'Why don't you call your little friend Izzie from the telephone booth? She can come for you in the red sporty number and we can have some highballs here while we wait.'

Again, Smythson-Balby looked startled. Pat stared at her, feeling as if she was watching the little mind working, the girl trying to figure out some logical reason to refuse. At last, admitting defeat, she asked for coins, then went outside to telephone Izzie. She didn't look behind her. Pat didn't see her expression, but she was sure the girl was angry.

*   *   *

Pat stood in the same phone booth, in a gusting wind, several hours later. She had finally got rid of Izzie and Smythson-Balby and the white Anglia was waiting like an angelic little saviour on the forecourt near the cottage. Izzie had been hammering at her, some nonsense about paperwork and road tax, but Pat was certain one journey without such things would not be a risk and was planning to go fetch Sam just as soon as they left. She had found her resolve, and now she was shivering and coatless, feeding coins into the phone and waiting. Gerald's voice came across the line, croaky with sleep, wary: 'Hello?' She immediately cut the call dead.

Goddamn him. She loathed him. She felt desolate as she remembered again the strained conversation with Sam and the curious thrumming tension, the weight in Sam's voice as she'd said she wasn't coming. Pat's tussle to repress her own disappointment had meant she hadn't been willing to listen properly. But now she went over it in her mind and the inconsistencies, the facts, seemed to be there. The Minty being sick story had been dropped. There was now no mention of Minty. There was a mention of Gerald, though, and a little nervous laugh when Sam had said that Gerald was in a 'filthy temper'. Did he suspect something? Had Sam told him, in a reckless gesture of self-defeat (this one she could hardly credit, because Sam was the silky-smoothest woman she had ever met; the one most able to keep a secret to the point of death)? What then? Had he struck her?

Pushing open the unlocked front door of Bridge Cottage, Pat tossed her coat onto the sofa and put the kettle on the gas hob to make herself some Nescafé. She paced the room a few times, then snatched up the five pages of typed script that Smythson-Balby had left. Reading quickened her heartbeat. She immediately spotted a split infinitive. She was secretly rather impressed with the phrase 'the low, flat, compellingly psychotic murmur' that Smythson-Balby had used to describe Patricia Highsmith's voice in her fictions. But the article did nothing to quell her dislike of circling vultures.

She flung the pages down and did not bother to rearrange them when they fanned into a sprawl over the table. A groggily ashamed feeling flooded over her, the one she always felt on seeing her name in print.

Sleep would never come now. The cover came off the Olympia and she abandoned the Nescafé, pouring herself a whisky instead, using a red plastic tooth-mug because there were no washed glasses. She picked up the notebook marked 'Notes on an Ever-present Subject' but she wasn't in the mood for that one; equally threatening was her soon-to-be published novel and the pile of Joan's notes on the manuscript. She rolled a fresh page into the machine and began tapping out some lines. After a time she was calmed by the sound of the typewriter's thoughtful peck-ing, as familiar as her own heartbeat.

Darling, I want you to creep up me like ivy, tattoo me like ink in my blood, I love you, I long for you, I want you, I love you now, then and forever . . .

She ripped this page out, put a fresh sheet in the typewriter. She should be working on her novel, but she was out of the mood to continue. How to get out of a fix? Plain hard work. She carried on typing, sipping the whisky intermittently.

It is hard for a free fish to understand what is happening to a hooked one.

Maybe that was the trouble: too many things under way. Her diaries, her book on how to write suspense fiction, her new novel hammering at her; her attempt at a first-person account of her times with Sam. She had an idea of writing all of them at once. But then there was the shady dread she felt every time she glanced at the manuscript of the soon-to-be-published novel she was supposed to be checking.

In the end, she had set up her desk slightly away from the window in the living room, facing the flower-pocked wall (she craned the goose-neck lamp over her and kept the curtains closed), and that suited her just fine. The cottage was so cramped that this was best if she wanted to avoid having her back to either the front or the kitchen door. And she did want to avoid that. A creepy feeling of someone being behind her would tickle up her spine if she allowed it; someone ready to tap her on the shoulder. This way, if she kept the door between front room and kitchen open, she could keep one ear out for Mrs Ingham or anyone approaching via the back door. This irritating sense of vigil never left her. She knew that someone was always in danger of bursting in, of interrupting, of wrenching her away from what she wanted to do most in the world. Lose herself in work, dissolve into work and disappear.

She smoked and typed. A quiet bump-bump accompanied her: the window had become unlatched and was knocking in the wind but she didn't care to get up and close it. Her head ached around the scalp, as it did most days. And Sam, a vision of Sam in all her blue and white elongation, all her extended loveliness, hovered over her, as sinuous as blue smoke.

Now she had the car she would drive to Sam's place in London. She'd make an excuse. Gerald would let her in. Gerald knew nothing, she'd been wrong about that. Gerald would never hurt Sam – the man hadn't enough courage to do anything that would draw attention to himself. And that disturbing melting softness, limpness, that hung around him. The way he dropped your hand the second you offered it, without shaking. The smile, out of the side of the mouth, designed to deflect. Perhaps Sam was simply ill in bed, had been taken ill, had sounded frightened because she was worried about upsetting Pat. That now seemed plausible, though it hadn't an hour ago.

She could hear an owl hooting softly in the back garden and the reply – a sharp, silly little yap from Mrs Ingham's house – as Reggie perked up. That dog was very selective in his barking, she noticed. Shame he hadn't seen off the fox that had killed poor Bunnikins, instead of yapping at an innocent owl. The wrong things always got it in the neck. And, with that thought, she finally quit typing random sentences, and felt able to turn to her novel again.

Her own neck was cold and ached from the hunching, from the tension. Hours flew by and she typed on, more awake now than she'd been all day. She stretched. She balanced the cigarette she was smoking on the saucer beside her, occasionally poking at the hot ash. It was a pleasure to feel the burn it gave her. It helped her keep awake.

When she'd typed enough pages of her novel to feel satisfied (six usually did it), she turned to proofing the manuscript that had arrived in Friday's mail, a task she hated, one that filled her with anxiety. The fear of making an idiotic error if she didn't do it well enough. The horrible feeling that the book was done now, and it was too late to claw it back. The horror of another round of interviews, talks, the whole damn embarrassing circus. And the title! No one had liked her suggestion. 'I'm afraid "Janus" just isn't a word the English-speaking world is familiar with,' Joan had said, and the temptation to reply, 'Well, call it something that rhymes and stick it there too,' was powerful, though resisted, of course. Joan already thought her half cracked. She had an idea not to make matters worse.

Sometimes I think of him with such a force of hatred that it shakes me. His square head. His posture. That sloping, selfish, swanking way he strides in, as if everything he touches, everything in his range, is his by right.

What has he ever done to deserve her? Just be him, that's all. A loafing, stupid man who leaves tiny hairs like ants crawling over the sink whenever he's shaved and hasn't got the sense to see when he's being duped, when the woman he's lying next to at night flinches at his touch, doesn't even love him; not one jot. And the thought that follows is always: how I'd like to shove him. While he sleeps. Launch myself at him. Push him. Thump him.

Bury his face in his pillow. Or, better still, smother him, force cotton and feathers into his face, crush it into his nose, feel his legs thrash under me, press and press, use all my strength, every last squeeze of it. Get rid of him. Have her all to myself, back how things were. He's skinny, he's limp, he's disgusting. What right has he to exist? He shouldn't put a paw on her; he's sickening.

As early as she dared, Pat went out to telephone Sam. Inside the booth it was chilly. Some kind of ivy plant crept through one broken windowpane and tickled her face. Her feet crunched on cubes of broken glass. Somewhere in the village she could hear the ugly shriek of a pheasant caw-cawing and when she closed the door to the booth, a cabbage-white butterfly stole in with her. A servant answered – Pat reckoned she must be the au pair. A girl with a pleasant voice, who called Sam 'Mrs Gosforth'.

When Sam got on the phone she immediately scuttled the idea of Pat coming to her.

'Don't be silly. I'll come next weekend. Gerald has rearranged his golf trip for then.'

Sam was whispering, her voice warm and familiar, but then it altered suddenly and she laughed and sounded breezy and somehow different, neutral. Gerald had come into the room.

There was nothing for it but to agree.

At nine on Monday, Smythson-Balby came by (thankfully, without her little friend) to drop off some paperwork about the ownership of the vehicle and pick up the article she'd left with Pat. She lingered, eyeing the black coffee in Pat's cup. Pat had not yet been to bed, but she felt light and refreshed, tap-tapping in her heart in time with the keys; she felt better than she had for weeks.

'Oh!' the girl said, hawk-like in her nosiness, whirling round. 'Where's your television set? You didn't manage to order it?'

'Coming later this week,' Pat replied, with a shrug. She was still smarting over that telephone conversation. So Gerald had rearranged things. So that was the reason their plans were all cock-eyed and slapdash: because of *his* plans to play golf. Holy crap. Why did Sam keep funking telling Gerald about them? So much time wasted! She'd promised Pat she would not duck out on it.

And then the damn Smythson-Balby accepted Pat's reluctant and not at all genuinely meant offer of a coffee. She plonked herself down on a chair at the kitchen table, crossing and re-crossing her legs, encased today in some bell-bottomed blue jeans with little flowers embroidering the hem. She asked in a cheery way about the article she'd given Pat to read. Pat had an idea the cheeriness was not at all how she felt. She handed the pages back. She watched as Smythson-Balby read her comments, neat and careful in their black ink.

Smythson-Balby looked up with a sunny smile.

'Thank you. I'll make those amendments straight away.'

Her voice was pleasant, controlled.

'I thought it a – a fine piece,' Pat said, suddenly aware that the girl was rather hurt. 'I was glad that you repeated that line – where is it? This one: "Calling her a mystery writer or crime writer is a bit like calling Picasso a draughtsman."'

'Oh, but it's true! I'm a huge fan of your work. Surely you realised that.'

Pat pulled out another chair at the kitchen table and sat down, to avoid towering above the girl.

'I guess I don't happen to care for . . . compliments. Matter of fact, I'd rather talk about something else. Other things.'

The girl sipped her black coffee. Pat had finally got the espresso machine she'd bought in Italy out of its box and, despite her initial reluctance to have the girl stay, was grateful to be shown how to use it. Smythson-Balby was practical, she could see that. And the coffee was good. Much better than that stinking Nescafé.

'I brought you a map of Suffolk. For driving. Izzie thought you might need one,' Smythson-Balby was saying.

'Have we met before?' Pat suddenly said.

Smythson-Balby swallowed loudly.

'No. I don't think so.'

'I keep having that feeling. New York . . . Paris? A club. Have I met you at one of those places . . . perhaps with someone else?'

She watched Smythson-Balby closely. The girl showed no reaction. One leg remained crossed over the other. The kitchen table was between them and Smythson-Balby rested one manicured hand lightly on the wood. The hand didn't shake and she didn't pause as she replied.

'Well, Paris, I've been, of course. And New York. And—'

'Greenwich Village?'

'I don't think so,' the girl carefully said.

'Huh?' Pat replied, puzzled. This wasn't quite fitting with the memory she was searching for, which definitely had a European feel to it. Mardi Gras ball somewhere, she felt sure. Her eyes covered with sparkly cardboard. Or the heat, the light, white light, sun-bleached legs. Positano?

'I have travelled in Europe, of course. And, yes, I was in the States for a while. I had a friend – Marijane – who studied at Barnard College . . .'

Pat did not care to mention that Barnard was her own old college or that she knew a young woman called Marijane and ask if it was the same one. She thought the girl was deflecting. She waited for more, but nothing was forthcoming, so she prompted again:

'Did you ever go to a restaurant in the Village called Potpourri? Do you happen to know a writer called Lorraine Hansberry?'

Not a flicker of recognition and the effort to continue the conversation was exhausting her.

Pat drank her own coffee and muttered, 'Lorraine waited tables there. Then she quit after her first play hit Broadway and was a terrific success. First Negro woman to have that honour. Thought you might know her.'

And we all knew her girlfriend, Pat thought of adding, but saw there was no point. Smythson-Balby said she did not know Lorraine Hansberry and the subject was dropped. Coffee-cup drained, she stood up to go, unwrapping the shoulder strap of her satchel from around the kitchen chair.

'Well, enjoy the car. London's about an hour and a half away, Aldeburgh about thirty minutes. It's lovely driving round here. Not too many cars on the road.'

As she spoke, Pat suddenly knew. It wasn't Greenwich Village. It was Paris. She knew it with absolute certainty. Pat had been there with an old girlfriend – Lynn, was it? – and there had been three women in the banquette in one corner, younger women. They'd joshed each other about them. They knew they were rookies, watching Lynn and herself avidly for tips. One had been a striking redhead with a green velvet cap and smoky black eyes. This young woman. A journalist – if she really was. Who, for whatever reason, didn't want Pat to know she frequented the lesbian bars of Paris.

Moments later Pat felt exactly the same certainty that she was wrong: it wasn't Paris at all but somewhere else, somewhere longer ago, and the girl had looked different, not a redhead then. It was infuriating and she decided stubbornly that she could match Smythson-Balby's opaqueness with her own and simply wouldn't ask. Let the damned girl be the first to volunteer it; she didn't care a hang if that didn't happen.

Smythson-Balby picked up her article and pushed it into the leather bag she now wore strapped across her chest, mailman-style. And she produced a folded road map, which she offered.

'I don't know how well you know it round here. I think you said you'd only been in Suffolk a few weeks.'

Pat felt sure she hadn't said anything about how long she'd been there. Another fact the girl had gleaned herself, from observation of the boxes that were still packed, presumably. She fought the temptation to unfold the map to the part she wanted, the part that would show her the route to London, to Sam. But she knew better than to do that in front of this girl.

As she was trying to usher Smythson-Balby out, she realised that she was being asked something possibly quite important. At any rate, she should have been listening.

'Her name is Frances. She's awfully nice. It will be terribly prestigious, you know. The BBC, if you agree to the interview. It will help. You know. In Britain. The same way you're known elsewhere in Europe, I mean.'

'Were you ever in a bar in Paris, near Notre Dame? I can't remember the name – red banquette seats? Small, you had to go down some treacherous steps to get to it.'

Damn. Pat had broken her resolve already.

'It doesn't ring any bells, I'm afraid. So shall I tell Frances yes? And she can write to you about it?'

'Yes, yes, I guess so . . .'

The girl smiled, and turned her head slightly to the kitchen door as they both heard a light tap. Ronnie. What a saviour. He was smiling. He tapped a thermos at the back window, and held up a small backpack. A picnic. She suddenly remembered they'd made this arrangement a few days ago. Ronnie was always dreaming up places he wanted to take her. Last week it was the Dolphin, a bar at Thorpeness. 'I'm the only light drinker in there,' he said. 'You'd feel at home, Pats.'

There was an awkwardness to the moment as she tried to introduce them – using Smythson-Balby's Christian name for the first time: *Virginia*. She was surprised to find she'd remembered it, as she continued with her hasty ushering out. Eventually that was done, and Ronnie – beaming his handsome smile at the girl – turned away from Smythson-Balby back to her and gave her a reassuring pat on the arm, stepping into the kitchen, removing his shoes and socks, then making his characteristic little hopping movements, like a robin, springing from spot to spot on the cold bricks of the kitchen floor.

'What d'ya take offa your socks for if we're going out?'

Her Texan accent sometimes reasserted itself around Ronnie, a sort of American swaggering that she felt he rather admired.

'I thought you'd need to rant at me for a good ten minutes first. I'm assuming some kind of animus towards our Smythson-Balby? One must always be ready as a courageous listener.'

This brought a grudging smile.

'Darling, if you need any laundry done I've found a smashing lady who will do mine for five shillings,' Ronnie said. Trying to be helpful, as always. Pat said nothing, only tipped some cold coffee from her cup into a pan on the stove and lit the gas to reheat it, planning to relate all. But first she took Ronnie upstairs to show him the snails – she'd added two others she'd found. Next to the snail she feared was dead, she'd uncovered a pile of powdery earth, which she'd explored with her fingernail. Poking around in it, she found a small pile of little beads.

She showed Ronnie. 'Must be their eggs!' he said. 'Splendid!'.

She would have to get proper tanks soon, glass tanks. The saucer was a temporary measure.

'Oh, and something else!' Now she was shy. They were standing by the window in her bedroom. There was a faint earthy, fishy smell from the snail saucers on the window ledge mingling with the smell of wood and sawdust. Pat did not like the intimacy that bedrooms always suggested and preferred to transform her own into a toolshed. Next to her made bed – with her coat laid out on it – were her wood-working tools, a Black & Decker, and a small bookshelf she'd been making for Ronnie. She now presented him with it, smiling with embarrassment.

'It's a bit wobbly, I guess. It's my first attempt. I won't be offended if you don't want it . . .'

'Splendid!' She could see Ronnie was genuinely pleased, as she'd known he would be. Ronnie had a great talent for both solitude and friendship, was capable of an unspectacular joy and endless wonder. That was why she felt easy around him; he was the perfect companion for a person of her character. Ronnie did not judge. There was only one characteristic of Ronnie that Pat might wish to alter, might *once* have wished to alter. That had been long ago and never acknowledged and would have involved a matching alteration of her own. In fact, these days she felt that had probably been a narrow escape because if the thought had been allowed to form then the friendship, the very real friendship she had with Ronnie, would perhaps have been over. If secrets existed between them it was because they didn't know how to tell them.

Now the bookshelf was admired, and Ronnie put the book on Gastropoda on the uppermost shelf and they both laughed when it slid to the edge and fell off.

'Splendid! Thank you, darling – how clever you are,' Ronnie repeated, with a sandpapery kiss on her forehead.

There followed a short discussion about the wood she'd used, and Ronnie's offer to fetch her some more from a chap he knew in Fram, because she had an idea to make something similar, or perhaps carve some bookends, for Sam. They returned to the kitchen, picked up the tartan thermos and the canvas backpack, now warm to the touch from the low October sunlight streaming in through the window, and suddenly a glorious fall picnic beckoned, with its promise of leafy-damp ground and horse-chestnuts to gather; there would be a church in Long Melford for Ronnie to sketch, good coffee in the thermos and boiled eggs on napkins, a piece of lemon sponge cake, remnants of gifts from Mrs Ingham. Ronnie would talk to her about the book he was writing, the interviews with local people, the young farmer who had said, 'I read quite a lot of novels but most of my reading is connected to pigs,' and that the dances he went to in Framlingham to find a girlfriend were mostly full of Mods. Framlingham was once called Frannegan, Ronnie would say, and a few of the old folk still used the name. He would be reciting poems (as he always was): 'Hours before dawn we were woken by the quake ... My house was on a cliff. The thing could take ... Bookloads off shelves. Break bottles in a row ...'

Thank Christ that, for now, the little hell, which was Smythson-Balby, Sam and the Problem, the proofing required for her last novel (which Ronnie described as 'nice drudgery' but on that she could never agree) and the terrifying interview she had accidentally just got herself into with this crank Frances, all could be, for a few sweet hours, forgotten.

And at last she's here, she's here: I'm meeting her at Ipswich station. I park outside, keep the engine running. It's a sputtering, inconsistent engine, given to roaring surges, like a heart surrendering to bursts of sudden joy ...

She's wearing a cream trench coat, neatly belted, her blonde hair, so gracefully piled up against her head, and perfectly made up, as ever, but in such a subtle and skilful way that only a good friend – or a lover – would know it. And a scarf, vivid colours of poppy-red and cornflower-blue, and that smell she always has when she kisses me: marzipan, sweetness, something earthy and feminine. We hug in a manner we hope is befitting of two good friends, and I carry her case to the car.

'You're a dab hand with that Black & Decker,' Ronnie told Pat. Another day, another picnic. An October picnic, close to Bridge Cottage, where they lay on the grass under the deep violet shade of a copper beech, eating boiled eggs from Mrs Ingham's chickens, and talked mostly of the books they were reading and writing.

He was so glad of the new bookshelf she'd made him, he said. He'd been rearranging his study – a bookshelf cull – and had inevitably become bogged down in the procedure. Of course he needed four different editions of *Emma*; of course it was distracting to gather the once read, the never read, the four times read and hug them in his arms, going up and down a dusty ladder to the very highest shelf.

The little floury cheese and pickle buns eaten and the thermos emptied, they were lying on the red tartan rug, she chewing the sweet stalks of the clover flowers that Ronnie assured her were edible. The fall sunshine tilted the English countryside and she stretched her legs and rubbed a cramp in her calf. Ronnie had been talking of a painter friend of his and how this woman had never changed the bedside offering on the bookshelves in the guest room: always the same books.

'Ancient gardening catalogues, *The Murder of My Aunt* by Richard Hull. That kind of thing,' he murmured.

'And why not? Why would you change the sequence? It's best to have books just where you want them, isn't it, so you can lay a hand on them immediately?'

She was thinking of *Crime and Punishment*; she'd been reading it again. She had been memorising passages. The lines 'an extraordinary man has the right, that is, not an official right, but an inner right, to decide in his own conscience to overstep . . .' and thinking of the terrible dream where the little donkey is flogged over and over, the whip flaying it in the eyes. She was thinking, too, of a story of her own, an early story – and had it been a memory, too? – about the ill-treatment of a terrapin. In books about murder, so much easier to raise sympathy for an *animal*, she mused.

They smiled up at the sky, heads now resting on their folded arms. It wasn't quite warm enough to be outside but they were both pretending otherwise. A bird, hunting, flickered in the sheet of airmail blue above them.

'Kestrel,' Ronnie pointed out. She thought he probably knew that a kestrel was the one bird in England she *could* recognise, with its unmistakable hovering stance that always made her feel like she wanted to spread her fingers and mimic the movements with her splayed hand, but Ronnie was a natural teacher, a pointer-out of things. 'I saw – I saw, the artist says, a tree against a sky or a blank wall at sunlight, and it was so thrilling, so arresting, so particularly itself, that – well, really, I must show you . . . There!'

This, Ronnie said, was a quote from Rupert Brooke, his statement of the impulse behind all art.

'Yes. "The thingness of things". As a better poet than Brooke said,' Pat murmured. She had finished two bottles of beer and was now feeling her drinks. She couldn't remember which poet it was. Was it the young American, the woman, who had committed suicide last year when her husband left her? For one instant, as the word 'suicide' formed, she felt she knew exactly what it was. To be on the receiving end of a suicide, to feel that dark stab under the ribs – Allela had done it, her girlfriend Ellen and Mother had threatened – the knife wound that would never heal. Sam says she's thought of it. She could do that to Pat: twink out her life with her fingers. And then the word, and its meaning, slipped back into shadows.

'So . . . your chap, your Stanley – what did the police call him, your fan? They haven't found out anything more about him?' Ronnie asked, as they folded the blanket and screwed the lid on the thermos and began packing things into Ronnie's backpack.

'No. I've had a couple of official letters forwarded from the French police since I moved, saying the case is closed – that's it. And, of course, they're sure that moving here would be the end of it. But . . .'

She felt for her cigarettes in the pockets of her jeans. Ronnie disapproved, but she needed one now. He lit it for her anyway, gentlemanly as ever, using her own lighter, cupping one palm around it against the wind and picking up a tiny piece of silver foil that fell onto the leaves at their feet.

'When I first moved in,' Pat said, exhaling the smoke, 'a fox killed Mrs Ingham's rabbit and there were some noises. At night, I mean. I had an idea that— At any rate, I guess I'm being ridiculous.'

'Yes, darling, you probably are.' Ronnie kissed her forehead.

He knew she didn't care to be touched, she involuntarily recoiled a little every time, but what Pat loved about Ronnie was that he understood other people's foibles but persisted diligently in being himself. He wasn't going to modify his own warmth one whit just because he'd met a chilly response. And at any rate, he was right: she didn't mean anything by it, she couldn't help herself. She'd never much enjoyed being hugged, unless it was sexual and *she* was open to it, like a switch being flipped. Other than that she didn't care to be caressed either. That was just how it was.

'But, after all, they were never quite – threatening, the letters, were they? Just the amount of them, and the mystery? Or the silly tone?'

She didn't know how to answer this without sounding foolish; she smoked her cigarette and didn't reply. No, they were not threatening in tone, but there were a great many of them and they frequently talked of death. One of them began: 'I've no idea why I'm writing this. You'll probably be dead for twenty years by the time you read it.' What could that mean? How could a dead person read a letter? And what the French police had failed to understand too (in the end she quit showing them the letters because standing there while an officer translated stupidly – who is this Frère Death, a monk? – felt like a further violation) was how intrusive they were, how much simply receiving them, anonymous letters, rattled her. The first one had been lying inside her apartment mailbox when she unlocked it; a flat white tongue in a slick black mouth. White envelope, one sheet of plain white paper. Typed, no sender's address and the signature typed too, one name. Afterwards she wished she'd studied the envelope – was it franked in Paris? Or did someone sneak in past the concierge and manage to drop it into the box while the mailman was delivering? Was that possible?

After reading it with its breezy 'I've found you at last! I'm like you: I love to hide behind masks and disguises so I'm not going to tell you my full name. I don't think you could call me an admirer. I find much of your writing strangely distasteful to be perfectly frank, but compulsive and I can't stop reading you . . .' These words (she had instinctively crumpled it into the wastepaper basket) told her that it wasn't written by the Stanley she knew in Fort Worth. He would not have had 'compulsive' in his workbag of usable words. And 'perfectly frank' sounded rather English, too, or at any rate, it sounded like a person with a better education than Stanley. She tried now to remember when the last letter had come. The day she left Paris. She'd ripped it open, but she hadn't kept it. That was the moment she had decided not to show them the letters – there were by now about a hundred of them: she'd suffered enough mockery from the Gendarmerie. Why did M'selle Highsmith think thees Stanley was following her? Why did such seemple phrases, like 'I love your new trench coat', cause her to feel *afraid*?

And, yes, they had suggested she see a doctor, and that experience, too, she remembered with shame. The word 'paranoia' was at any rate used, at least once. She didn't care to read her notes but felt sure – ha! Was this a further example of it? – that that was the diagnosis.

'What can this letter-writer *do* to you? I wonder why you feel so convinced this person – this Stanley, or someone else out there – means you harm?' the smooth young doctor had asked.

Birds twittered like maniacs in the window outside the consulting room as she had hunkered down in her chair and pondered that very question. *You are half cracked, Patsy, that's why I love you so much!* She had an idea that someone 'out there' did indeed mean her harm. She couldn't remember ever not feeling that way.

'So did you manage to see Sam at the weekend?' Ronnie asked, breaking into her thoughts. He placed his backpack in the trunk of the car and she sat in the front, turning the key in the ignition. They were going on a little trip to another church; evensong at Wormingford. Ronnie did not require her to express belief of any kind, but they both loved the singing.

There was a judder and a jolt as the engine cut. She had to pull out the choke to warm it up; she tried again. Eventually the engine was running smoothly.

'Ah,' Pat said. 'Slight change of plan.' She felt her voice sounded a little tight. Ronnie wisely said nothing, and the car bore them towards the cleansing dusk of Wormingford.

Once in the car, Sam bursts into tears.

She folds up, covers her face with her hands, and I'm shocked, as if it's me who is crumbling. The way I've heard men say they feel, seeing their father cry for the first time: frightened. Appalled. And then, perhaps, a little humiliated.

It's Gerald, it seems. The most ghastly, filthy fight. Minty didn't witness it, thank God, poor little mite, but it was frightful, really terrifying, bloody. He shoved her, he kicked her, he screamed into her face. At one point he hauled her by her hair towards the stairs and she felt as if the top of her head might pull away, like a teapot lid. She straightens, passes her fingers under her glittering blue eyes, widening them as she tries to wipe away the mascara without stinging. Her scalp still hurts, she says. She feels sure her hair might start dropping out. She runs her hands along her hairline, catches a tear at her chin with her hand and wipes at it.

'Oh, Pats . . .' she says.

I've never seen Sam like this. I've never seen her anything less than immaculately composed. I have not uttered a word. I felt blow after blow, one after another, a kick beneath the ribs, my scalp burning, as she told it. I stare at my hands on the steering-wheel: five white knuckles spark up, ready, and I hate Gerald like death, like poison. Mother always said I had such big hands for a woman; I could be a man in drag, she used to say. Ronnie is kinder, but he, too, has remarked on them, the long fingers, the spades of the palms.

The things I would like to do to Gerald loom up, white-hot evil things to teach him a lesson, things to silence him and remove him from our lives, blot out those black-blue eyes, throttle him for ever . . . but Sam is talking now, in a calmer tone, sniffing and pressing one hand to her lips, fetching a handkerchief from her purse, trying to pull herself together.

'Drive, would you, Patsy darling? I wanted to tell you, but now I want to talk of something else.'

'Not Patsy. Not here. Pat. Or Patricia. Ronnie has no trouble with it. You'll be able to manage it, won't you?'

'Oh, of course. Have you – you haven't had any further – you know – bother? Or letters or suchlike from him, have you?'

A pause, then I turn the ignition key and the engine splutters into life.

'Stanley? Nothing. No letters, no. No signs. No, no. I think I've shaken him off. There was a moment when I wondered – but it turns out a local girl is hipped on me. That's all.'

Sam attempts a smile. 'Should I be jealous?'

'God, no. The girl's . . . half cracked. The cute sort, you know? Nice figure, though, I'll give her that much. A bit leggy . . . Christine Keeler type.'

Sam bats me lightly with her blue scarf, the scent of her cologne whisking around my face. I pull away and, not knowing Ipswich, am soon lost in some back-streets by the docks. The rage of moments ago drained me: a feeling spreading through my veins as if I'd just been for a long run, a stitch under my ribs, breathless, and now I'm spent and hopelessly lost, and realise I have not been thinking of anything at all except Gerald and my loathing of him. I pull the map down from the nylon net above our heads and try to concentrate. We're next to a bar called the Sea Horse. Sam suggests asking someone but I shake my head at that. I trace a finger along the names of roads: Grimwade Street. Well named, we think. I'll get us home.

And at last we're here at Bridge Cottage and, as predicted, she finds it 'dinky' (a sudden picture then of Sam's elegant Highgate apartment, saturated with light, tall stems of orchids in a glass vase on a table in the hallway). There's a fire in the grate and I've made her an Italian vermouth with soda and wrapped her in an extra blanket and she's sitting on the sofa, trying to find something to watch on the television set. The image is fuzzy, like trying to see the picture through one of those snow-shaker globes, and it's boring anyway, more electioneering and politics. We switch it off. She wants to show me pictures of Minty: here's Minty in her school uniform, Minty with her blonde fringe, Minty watching *Bleep and Booster* in her nightgown, Minty holding a ladybird on her palm and grinning.

She's relieved Minty is back at school; sobs afresh a little when she thinks of her, and Gerald, and how *degrading* it is for Minty to hear Gerald bellow at her in that way, call her those ghastly names, let alone witness Gerald actually strike her. Yes, I'm thinking. At last, an acknowledgement that a child might know a thing or two. That children are not idiotic creatures to be endlessly duped and lied to. A pain twists inside me.

'*Did* Minty see?' I ask. 'You said she wasn't there.'

'Oh, not this time. But others, yes.'

And Minty. I look again at her. A blonde girl, sulky. A sudden flash of myself, dressed like a boy, in a cap and jodhpurs, six years old, just before we left Fort Worth. And Mother saying: 'Do you know, Patsy, you're a little bit cuckoo? Ready for the booby hatch, you know? Psychologically sick in your little boy's clothes. Come here . . .' and she would hold out her arms, sighing and scolding until I took a step towards her and she could snatch at me, hold me in an embrace so tight I could barely breathe.

'You have to leave Gerald,' I say. 'You've told me you hate him, sometimes. Matter of fact, many times. It's not good for a child to see – things like that. What's keeping you there?'

Sam sighs then, pressing one hand to her hair, feeling for the silver pin that pierces a skein of it at the nape. She's poised again. Whatever she let me see, moments ago, is smoothed over, like a magazine cover neatly closed.

'As if it were easy! The person you've been with since you were seventeen, the only life you know, the daddy your daughter adores! Your life, your home, your future, give it all up, just like that?'

'*Cuckoo you are, my Patsy, in your boy's hat and pants . . .*' Mother again and her cock-eyed pronouncements. At six years old I remember the taste of velvet in our Fort Worth boarding-house home: I'd developed a habit of putting my face into a cushion, opening my mouth and pretending to scream. Silent screaming: the stretch of your jaw, the velvet texture of the cushion in your mouth. I became an expert at it. I still do it some-times. Perhaps Minty does it too. I take the last photograph of her and stare at it.

She's younger than eight in this one, hair curlier and blonder, cuddly in a gingham school dress and genuinely tickled by the little creature she's admiring on one outstretched hand. But in later photographs the wary look has descended and the smile is false.

The person you've been with since you were seventeen, the only life you know, the daddy your daughter adores . . .

'One day – one day he might, you know, really *do* something,' I say.

'Oh, darling, he's such a silly man. He really won't.'

She kisses me then. Her face is hot from the fire and the taste of vermouth burns in my mouth.

Then she laughs and glances at the window in the front room to make sure the curtain is closed (it is). She gets up to try the television once more. We watch for five minutes, some teenagers with hair cut like black pudding basins, then switch it off again. She wanders around the house, roams upstairs, announces herself thrilled with my art room, managing to step in some blue paint in her bare feet – she's taken off her stockings, leaving them folded neatly on the sofa downstairs – treading it into the hall carpet so that I know I will never be able to see the nubs of cobalt there on the beige wool without thinking of her. The barely begun portrait she only smiles at – lifts once, puts it back – unaware that it's going to be of her.

She picks up a photo album of mine, flicks through it gleefully. Is that Stanley? I show her the photograph of my mother and stepfather on their honeymoon; him dazzling and proper in a blazing white suit and boater, she his perfect shadow – I always thought they planned the photograph that way – entirely in black, with a brim so wide it obscures her face.

'What did you say your mother did?' Sam asks, and I tell her about the illustration board that dominated any house we ever lived in, the portfolio Mother dragged from publisher to publisher, and the times she would say to visitors, 'Patsy is my best judge. Patsy is a little artist herself and she *loves* my work,' and the way the visitors would look at her and I would read their minds: *Huh! You think so?*

'Ha! That's just you. I'm sure everyone thought you were a charming little girl', Sam says.

There's only the one of me and Mother, from that time, me with my big bonnet mostly hiding my face, eyes downcast, wearing a dress for once, and long socks, legs outstretched on the grass. I guess I was four or five – I don't really remember it: it's just something I've looked at, as if it was another little girl, someone else's family. Mother has the haircut of the era – a modish bob, pressed to a perfect flick at her cheek – a dress of showy stylishness, her gaze, as ever, fixed firmly over my head.

Sam puts the album back on the art-room windowsill and follows me downstairs, where I need to add another log to the fire and check on the steaks under the grill. I remember my little pang of hurt when Sam mentioned how often a simple supper of steak and salad featured in my books. Of course, steaks back home, the fatter and juicier ones, were the height of luxury. I struggled not to feel wounded. Sam was surprised, too, that I looked hurt when she said we both knew that cooking was not my forte. I didn't know that, I'd said. And that day when Sam brought snails from Fortnum & Mason and I refused to eat them. I wondered if she would know what creamed chipped beef on toast was. Our first days in New York, alone in the apartment, that's what I'd fixed myself. A lifetime away from Fortnum & Mason snails.

The vermouth is finished but whisky spins in two tumblers and I hand one to Sam. I guess she would love to know more about my family and I feel like a heel for not wanting to tell her.

'You know I hate that Freudian voodoo,' I say.

'Your friend Betty said she'd heard from her. Your mother. And that she'll probably come and visit you in Suffolk while you're here. I'd love to meet her.'

'Betty said that? First I've heard. And, trust me, you wouldn't want to meet Mother!'

'She looks young – what is she now? Sixty? More like a sister in that photograph, than a mother. She's awfully glamorous . . .'

I remember something then. The grey blob, and the mouse.

'I had a . . . I don't know what it was. A sort of . . . well, I guess some kind of child's make-believe or, I don't know, a hallucination . . .'

'An imaginary friend! Delightful!'

'It wasn't. It was . . . a grey spot. Just at the outskirts of my sight, like a mouse skittering across the floorboards out of the corner of your eye – and I'd go look and it was never there.'

I can't bring myself to say more. Not the mouse but the other creature is what comes into my mind then, but I shoo it away. As I'm speaking I'm searching for the oven-gloves to lift the grill pan. I'm distracted and not really listening to myself, but Sam is listening hard. She's leaning against the kitchen wall and watching me intently.

'What did people make of it? The – grey spot?'

'I was ashamed to tell other people – I soon figured they didn't see it. But they all looked so shocked. At me jumping. I mean, whenever I saw it, or shrieking. It used to happen a lot when I was reading. Lost in thought. I saw it all the time.'

'Did it stop? How strange.'

'Ha. Granny gave me a cat for my birthday. It quit then. Let me fix you a refresher for that drink.'

I pour more whisky into our glasses and hand one back to Sam. She moves forward, goes to scoop my hair away from my neck to kiss it. I tremble and disintegrate: I've turned into sherbet. 'Don't feel sorry for me. I hate that,' I say, and it's true. I've noticed Sam always responds this way when I talk about Stanley and Mother.

Mrs Ingham's light is not on over at Bridge House. The curtains are closed, but who knows?

'So sad, darling,' Sam says, 'thinking of you as a little girl. Only Granny to ever care about you . . .'

'And Dan. My cousin. He was older – twenty, when I came along. He was an orphan like me.'

'You weren't an orphan.' She laughs, but we both know what I mean.

'We were like brothers more than cousins.'

'Brother and sister, you mean.' Again, she's teasing me.

Another memory, this time of trying to fall asleep at night and every time wondering: Am I going to die? Is this what death feels like? How will I know? It was because they always told me dead things were 'sleeping': my little cat; people in the graveyards at Fort Worth . . . No wonder sleeping filled me with horror. I used to sip water – keep a glass by the bed and try to sniff it up my nose; I thought that would keep me awake. It was painful: my nose burned and my eyes smarted. I'd read comics, *Ranch Romances*, the *Girl of the Golden West*, the *Girl of No Man's Land* and think about them trick roping, to keep my eyes from closing. I don't tell Sam this but she suddenly says: 'Did you ever think why not just give up, give it all up, it's too painful?'

'Please don't say that,' I murmur quickly. A feeling like a scalpel turning in my heart.

I am afraid to discover what she means. Is she talking about death, about suicide, or giving this up, giving *us* up? She *has* talked about suicide before – it was when I told her about my old

64

girlfriend Allela killing herself in '46 and how guilty I felt then, even though we weren't any longer together, and Sam's response: 'I can imagine killing myself, though. Can't you, sometimes?' I immediately felt my ears ring and the room spiral into a tunnel; I had to put my head between my knees to keep from keeling over. Now I let her rest her cheek against mine for the barest second. I pull away, a little stiffly, and begin laying forks and knives and folded red-checked napkins and the little jug of salad dressing on the table, next to the posy of flowers I'd put there earlier.

'What did you and Gerald fight about?' I ask her, pretending to be casual, spooning dressing onto curls of lettuce, after rescuing a leaf first and putting it aside for the snails upstairs. I pour us a glass of water each. I've been thinking of Gerald since she told me. Under everything else simmers Gerald. How soft and low his voice is. Everything about him is soft: disgustingly, toxically so. His belly, his smile, his handshake. It's as if he's purring or vibrating with the effort to contain his own hateful feelings, his loathing.

Sam doesn't answer. She is sitting at the table now, forks a piece of cucumber into her mouth.

'Was it us? Did you tell him about us?' I persist.

'No. But he said he knew there was someone. He assumed a man. He said: *Off to see your little friend to tell her all about it.* He was – you can imagine.'

Another occasion comes to me then. A publishing party. This time in a bookstore in London – Hatchard's, was it? – after we had begun to see one another. Gerald's brother was a writer and he liked to mix with authors. Little knots of people standing around and I, feeling awkward, was on my own, pretending to read the back of a book I'd pulled from a shelf. I glanced up when I heard raised voices. I was close to Gerald and a couple of other men. Somehow I gathered that someone had snubbed him, something trivial; someone at the party was talking about shares at the bank Gerald worked at, something dodgy, and Gerald took offence. Gerald: such a small man, slim except for that belly, like a snake that has swallowed an egg. Nothing altered in Gerald's demeanour as he stood there, grey shirt neatly tucked in over the paunch, holding a glass of wine, that sinister softness still hovering around him. But I knew. His smoothness had a silky, poisonous quality, like something foul and gaseous. A poison. Some have it in them, some don't, and that's all there is to it, and I saw at once that Gerald was like me. One of those who did.

The steaks are good. Colman's English mustard and a powerfully vinegary dressing make my cheeks pink and Sam's neck flush. We giggle over my descriptions of Mrs Ingham and the frilly nightgown, like something Honor Blackman might wear in *The Avengers* . . . We drain the bottle of whisky and the night burns warm and inviting and the chill horrors of earlier in the day start to thaw out. I will not let her touch me in the kitchen: that dark slit of night between the curtains always unnerves me. I venture upstairs first and put both bedroom lamps on, mine and the one in the cold green and beige guest room, as if to say: Here we are, safely tucked up in two separate rooms, dear world, in case you're watching.

'Low-flying spy planes?' Sam jokes, following me up the stairs. You never know.

Once in my room she falls on me, kissing my neck, my face, my throat. The sherbet feeling again, the desire to melt, to dissolve into a thousand grains. This is what she does to me. Such a naughty practised gesture, the way she pulls down my underpants. She, of course, knows exactly how everything she does feels to me. That is the trick of her and the skill: she's cocky, she likes to play the *femme fatale*. No gesture is clumsy, no movement without beauty. 'Lie down there,' she says, in a gravelly voice, clogged with desire, lifting off my sweater, unbuttoning my white shirt. She knows I never wear a brassière on the days when she is coming. She knows that my longing for her, which began much, much earlier in the day, will now be soaking me through and my nipples will be up and waiting for her touch, as she squeezes my breasts together to admire them, my body alert, prickling in a way that only she can produce. She cups my pubic bone; her fingers curl beneath, drawing deep. 'You first,' she says. Here, and only here, she is utterly the boss. The game is not to move. Trying not to buck, or thrust, or sigh, as the waves of pleasure dissolve me; her skilful fingers in a combination of vibrating taps and then deep, pulling strokes. My spine makes snapping sounds and I'm a fish on a hook, twisting and twitching, then finally throwing myself on the deck with a last great spasm as she plunges fingers inside me, her tongue in my mouth: giving myself up.

Later, I show her the snails. Another snail has dug a pit in the earth; another pair is mating. 'Yuk.' Sam shudders. I try not to be disappointed that she doesn't share my fascination. Ronnie will, I know. I'll show Ronnie again in the morning.

In the night, I'm woken by noises. A car driving up. An engine running, then a door opening and slamming, and thumping, thumping on the front door of Bridge Cottage. Sam is deeply asleep, blonde hair undone and all over her face, one arm flung across me. I shake her awake, try to lift the great heat of her from across me. 'Go in the other bedroom,' I whisper. She obeys at once. A glimpse of her white thighs, as she wriggles into a peach-coloured nightgown; the glittering sheet of her hair.

Gerald. Gerald drunk and possibly angry, although when I open the door to him, leaning there against it as if it's the most reasonable hour in the world, he appears infinitely controlled.

'We've met, haven't we?' he says. 'Edna O'Brien party.'

'It's two in the morning, Mr—'

'My wife here? The old girl? Just thought I'd join the party, you know.'

He's so slight, I notice again. The build of a girl or a teenage boy. He waves a bottle of Scotch at me and – not knowing what else to do – I close the door behind him and he steps over the mat at the threshold and into the front room. I go to the kitchen to fetch glasses. The smell of pipe smoke and tweed and Imperial Leather soap enters the room with him. He's already taking off his jacket and draping it over the arm of the sofa. My head is heavy, foggy, but I'm sober as a trout.

Gerald sits on my sofa, legs wide apart, spreading both arms along the back in the way that only men do. He is obviously taking in the unfurnished aspects of the room: the hard floor only partly covered by the Turkish rug and the welcome mat, my desk with its litter of papers and books haloed by the lamp. He picks a green hardback up from the sofa beside him: Karl Menninger, *The Human Mind*. He turns it over, as if its real title might be concealed elsewhere. He drains the glass I give him and shakes his head, a quick shake, as if to knock it down faster.

Sam appears at the top of the stairs in her peach silk night-gown but with the brown fisherman's sweater thrown over the top, smoothing down her hair.

'Good Lord, Gerald, what hour is this? Poor Pat was sleeping, and she has work to do tomorrow, you know, I told you didn't I? Is there something wrong? Is Minty—'

'Minty's fine. She's staying at the Dixons'. No crime to come and see my wife at the weekend, is it?'

'No, of course not. But all is fine here, as you see.'

'I could use some coffee,' I say, not wanting to be in the room with them, not wanting to see her like this, appeasing, *keeping him sweet*. I don't want to despise her. The door between kitchen and living room is always left open. I can hear them perfectly well.

'And as you see, I'm not with any fancy man, if that's what you expected,' Sam is saying.

'Ha! Well, what da y'know?' Gerald seems to be relaxing. When I come back in he is making himself comfortable, leans forward, undoes his brogues and eases his feet out of them. Socks in a disgusting mustard colour caught in a pool of light from my table-lamp. Thin, small feet. I have to look away.

'I left you the address didn't I? Why would I do that if I was hiding something?' Sam says.

'Well, that's what I thought. A double bluff, I thought. She's left me the address of this friend, and won't she be surprised if I just turn up there and find out there's no such *Pat* at all?'

'Well, now you see there is.' Sam sighs, accepting the coffee cup I place in her hand.

'Do you all mind if I go back to my bed now? You can sleep on the sofa if you like. There's a couple of plainly inadequate blankets in that cupboard just under the stairs, but you're welcome to them,' I suggest.

It's not that I want to leave them alone together. I don't happen to relish the thought of that pipe-smoking lunk sleeping in my house. But, I keep asking myself, what would I do, if I *was* just a friend of Sam's, a publishing friend or an author, someone neutral from an Edna O'Brien party, and her husband turned up? Isn't this what I'd do – offer him a bed, and pack them both off in the morning with tea and toast and marmalade?

And so I take my own coffee up the stairs to bed, clunking my head on the low beam across the ceiling on the landing at the top of the stairs, as I always do, and climbing back under now cooled sheets that still have that almond scent of her. Of course I'm prised open, wide awake. There's no way sleep will come to me, and I'm cocked like a shell, tuning in to hear whatever it is that's being said. I smoke two cigarettes one after the other, listening, stubbing them out in a saucer on the bedside table, switching off the bedroom lamp, listening again . . .

But perhaps I did sleep, perhaps I tumbled into a sort of half-dream because now, suddenly, there are raised voices, and something dark skittering across the floor and something trembling all around the house, and furniture tumbling and such a familiar terror in my throat and ears and heart and chest, sweat, sweat everywhere and thumping, something thumping in the bed with me, something huge and wild that I know is my heart-beat, and I think I'm back in my own little bed in Granny's

69

boarding-house and listening to Mother's voice, shouting, 'Did you hear me, did you *hear* me?' and then the sound of a stifled scream, and something heavy plummeting to the floor. The same familiar sensations: the salty smell of my own sweat springing out all over my body, the sense of falling, of my bowels peeling away, spiralling down a well into darkness. There's the Black & Decker drill next to my bed and I reach for it. The drill bit slips out and clatters loudly to the floor. I hold it at the drilling end, feeling the weight of the heavy metal centre with satisfaction, the electric cord and plug dangling beside me, creeping to the landing, crouching low so as not to knock myself out again on the beam and, yes, there she is, in the living room lit by the one little lamp, there they are now on the sofa, with him lying on top of her and she underneath him, her head hanging off the edge, head dangling to one side, in the strangest way, like he's already killed her; that's what I think at first, he's smothered her, God, no, he's killed her, and so I run downstairs but then I realise that under the thin blanket he's moving, the snaky bastard is muttering things, he's unaware that I'm here that I'm standing over them but she's not, her eyes widen, they meet mine; her mouth opens and she's crying, and she shakes her head a little, whispers, '*Don't*', and she's trying to twist away from him and he's like the most disgusting slithering eel under the blanket and he's saying in a low growl, 'You're still my fucking wife,' and Sam is twisting her head to escape his mouth, I see the little coil of gold chain at her throat, and it's that, the sight of that heart locket, I gave it to her in Paris . . .

'Get off her,' I say. I'm standing at the bottom of the stairs. One foot on the rug, the other on cold floor, next to the vile little puddle of his pants and shorts. The Black & Decker is raised and my teeth gritted so hard my jaw is throbbing.

'I said, get off her,' I repeat.

I'm close, I'm standing over them, close enough to tug at his arm and try to pull him off. He is drunk, I know that, meltingly, slitheringly drunk, and I don't know if he knows I'm here. I gather every ounce of strength, every part of me pounding with it, with loathing. In my hand – high up – is the lumbering solid metal drill and it's heavy, granite-heavy, and irresistible and the cord dangles and the plug grazes the floor as with the best swing I can manage I bring the full force of it down on the back of Gerald's head. It makes a surprising sound: a sort of crack, like a stone rattling across ice. His head is very close to the floor. I lift my arm and hit again, and this time he slides away from the sofa – like a seal slipping from a boat to the sea – and onto the floor, leaving Sam partially beneath him, her hands covering her face. I can't see how she can breathe beneath him.

I wonder for a moment what happened. I hit him again, harder. He groans – he, too, makes a strange sound, puffing, air slammed out of him – and collapses, like a blanket crumpling to the ground when a breeze subsides.

A spread of blood begins to form beneath him, fanning out in a deep red puddle. His forehead must have hit something. The brick floor beneath the rug. I'm tempted to lift my hand again and again, bring the drill down on his head again and again and again, mashing all the disgusting blood and hair and skull until it's pulverised – the joy, the joy, the joy of that – but I don't, I don't, good Christ, of course I *don't do that*.

I help Sam up. I drag her. It doesn't feel like a nice thing to be doing; she flops around, she's like a doll. Then she curls at once into a foetal position and lies on the sofa shaking. I don't believe she's crying. I stroke the hair away from her face. 'Honey, are you OK?'

She doesn't nod. She doesn't seem to be able to hear me, so I fetch brandy from the kitchen and then, lifting her head, try to pour some into her mouth. She splutters, and most of it dribbles out, but her eyes are open now. The shaking steps up a pace. I feel I can almost hear her teeth chattering. I pull her silk nightgown down for her; cover her knees.

Gerald lies in a great slump, like a skinny tree that's been felled by one blow. I guess I should get him some brandy too, or a cloth for that head, but let the son of a bitch sleep it off. He's going to be pretty sore for a week, and he'll have some trouble explaining the lump on his head, which I can see is forming under his hair beneath the clots of dark red wetness. There is blood on the rug, and on the Black & Decker. I take it to the kitchen and clean it with Fairy Liquid, a scrubbing brush and a rag. I find the black box it came in and fit it neatly back in there, shove it away in the cupboard under the sink.

Then back to the living room. I hesitate before touching Gerald's head. His pants, with the belt undone, and his under-shorts thrown on top are on the rug beside him and, after first covering his ghastly white buttocks with the blanket, I think better of that solution and – wanting to shield Sam somehow from the further indignity of seeing him like this – I pull up the white undershorts and pants, and do up the belt. He doesn't make a sound, or respond at all. As I feel underneath him for the buckle (not doing up the flies, I draw the line at that), his warm hairy stomach rests briefly on my hands for a moment and a dry retch heaves in my throat. I want to pull his shirt down and tuck it in but that would involve further touching. I sit on my heels on the floor beside him, wondering. There is a strange smell, ghastly and unfamiliar – something metallic and inhuman only partially masked by the pipe-smoke smell that always hangs about Gerald – and I don't know where it is coming from.

I flatten my cheek against his back, listening. There is no rise and fall. His body is warm, but – is he cooling? His cheek is crushed against the floor, eyes shut, the magenta-coloured blood pooling on the hard brick floor under one eye. The feet in the stupid mustard socks look stiff, heels angling upwards, toes jabbing the rug.

Sam is still curled at a distance from us, but she is watching me. If I pick up his wrist, she will guess. I move away, sip the brandy in her tumbler, lift the bottle in an offer of more. I put my arm around her and feel the trembling in her body vibrating through my own. My mind is racing, racing, racing. So many times I thought of this. The ultimate transgression, just as I said. Wondered, what would it feel like? And now I know. Except that I don't: I want to go back and replay it. It was quick: I was cheated, I didn't seem to be present – just a white hot blaze in place of myself. I want to go back; to savour.

I force myself to look at Gerald and imagine that even the hairs on his head are stiffening, are turning rigid; light as feathers. His temple was here, against the brick floor. If only the blow had been softened by the rug but that's all on the skew, over to his left.

'We should get him to a doctor,' I tell Sam, watching her face for signs that she believes me. Another wave of trembling in her.

'He's dead, isn't he?' she says, in a voice that seems to come from the back of the room.

'Yes, I think so.'

And the room itself seems to shake a little, rattle on its moorings. Now what? The hour is still early, but we can't sit here all night. My mind starts shuffling possibilities, weighing up. I reach for Sam's brown sweater and offer it to her. When she makes no sign I move over and put it on her, pulling it over her head, pushing arms through arm-holes as if she were a child. At one point she links her fingers in mine and I think: Not a child, but a monkey. A strange little animal.

'You always had that ability,' she says.

'What do you mean?' I think she's talking about my strength: is she saying I have the ability to kill someone?

I'm about to protest but she says:

'The worse things get, the calmer you become. It's – unnatural.'

And then she's sobbing, pressing her face to her knees, and letting her whole body succumb to it.

I watch her, and count up to 360. That's six minutes. That's all I can allow. It's still early, and still dark, and presumably no one knew

Gerald came here, no one has yet seen his car out the front. I glance at the clock on the fireplace: 3.10 a.m. That's fine, there's time, dawn is still a way off, but – we have to make some decisions.

'We must call someone,' Sam says. 'The police. The police. Shall we call the police? Or – a doctor or something. Who do people call at times like this? Oh – poor little Minty!' and then she's abandoned herself to crying again, returning her face to her knees.

'Do you think you could help me to lift him?' I ask.

'Lift him? What – shouldn't we— Oh, is he really?' She puts her face in her hands. She can't look at the shape of Gerald but it looms in the room, like a dark rolled thing that blocks the sides of our vision.

'Sam – I don't think we can call the police.'

I wait for this statement to sink in. For her to lift her face from her hands. I want to say: I don't care to see you crying. Where is your supreme poise? A week ago I had never seen you like this; I had not known you were capable of tears. I happen to prefer it when you are composed.

'What would it look like?' I say. 'He was – what he was doing to you. Won't they ask all about that? And then us, you being here. And then – I mean . . .'

I feel as if my face is burning as I say this. Scalding the room. Hot skin, then cold skin and then a sick feeling. I'm going to faint and it's the thought of it again, of what I did. The exhilaration. The pleasure, the release. Now it's the sickening sight of his skull that keeps making me think of one of my beloved snails, crushed, and the jelly-life seeping from it.

I gather myself. I'm aware of an accelerated heartbeat, a dry throat, and tension in every muscle, but a delicious slowing of my thoughts. Like the moments when plots form: my fingers on keys flying through something fast, something they do of their own will; but somewhere else, just at the corner of my eye, beside me or close to me, something shaping by itself, with the energy and volition of a livid dream.

'We can't both fall apart, honey. I need to think. They might say the blow was harder than required. We could call someone. But what – what will we say about the Black & Decker? Pretty grim . . .'

Her eyes widen. The shock is clear on her face; she does not look like herself.

'Oh, my God,' Sam says. I'm not sure how much is dawning on her. But at least her eyes are dry and, instead of tears, there is some solidifying, like wax cooling: she is returning to her own shape. She's right about my extreme coldness in a crisis, the adrenalin clarity that fills my head like a cleansing gas. I start tugging at Gerald's legs.

'It's a good job he's a skinny son of a bitch,' I mutter. 'Can't weigh more than a hundred and forty pounds. We could – outside, by the pond? Or, well, they would come to the house, then. And Mrs Ingham might see him. We need to get him away from here. No link to the house. Best of all would be to get him back in his car. I could use some help. Think you could help me lift him, honey?'

'Get him away from here? Are you mad? We need to phone someone. Tell someone what happened. Are you sure he's—'

And, for the first time, she crawls on her hands and knees towards Gerald and peers closely at his face. She extends a finger towards his cheek as if she was poking it towards a flame. She puts her face close to his mouth. She pats his back, lifts his wrist, lets it drop.

'Strange. It's cool. He was always such a hot person.'

Her voice curls. It's not like a voice of Sam's I've ever heard before. She kneels beside Gerald and seems to have no idea where she is.

'Honey – drink this!' I say.

I open the bottle and pour her another good measure of brandy. I cradle the back of her head while she sips. But now she's not crying; she's not really looking at me, at anything at all.

75

'Oh, why didn't you have a telephone in the house?' she says softly. 'Isn't there one outside?'

I hold her in my arms, stroking her hair. I hope that my heartbeat so close to hers doesn't give me away but I know I sound divinely calm and reasonable. The fisherman's sweater has that sour smell of wool that didn't dry properly, or air out.

'We need to move him, sweetie. It might be possible to put him in the car. I'll drive his; you drive mine. You think you can drive mine? We'll drive to – to Aldeburgh. Think you can do that? Follow the taillights of my car . . . and then, honey, then it will soon be over.'

How simple it sounds! I couldn't have planned it better. I didn't plan it, it was an aberration: it formed of its own accord, shaping and patterning off stage, or above and behind me, while I went about the business of living, but now it's done, and the shape of it can be seen, emerging from the vagueness with a dark clarity, its inevitability beautifully clear.

I search the room for Gerald's car keys, then steel myself to feel for them in the pockets of his pants. Then I remember he had a jacket, draped over the arm of the sofa. I find the keys: a door key and a car key attached to a mustard-leather fob, in the breast pocket. How he liked that detestable colour! My eyes rest on a stain, a snail trail of slime on my good Turkish rug, beside his groin.

I give Sam another slug of brandy before returning to Gerald and trying to lift him by placing my hands under his shoulders. 'You hold the legs,' I say. Sam glances at her husband's legs and collapses on the rug, weeping.

'Sam. Do you want me to go to prison? Is that what you want? The newspapers, the scandal, for ever more?' I try to sound gentle rather than hectoring but my voice comes out sharp.

'It's a scandal already! It will always be a scandal – Gerald . . .'

I'm finding his shoes and shoving them on his revolting feet. Doing up the laces. Holding him by each cold bony ankle to do this; 3.30 a.m., still time, still time. He seems paper thin suddenly but, of course, once we try again to lift him, he's heavy, truly heavy.

I grasp the shoulders; his arms droop beside him, hands dragging on the floor, like a monkey's; his head hangs against me, blood smearing my shirt. Sam grips his legs at the ankles, presses the dirty soles of his shoes against her thick wool sweater. We buffet him towards the door, like a battering ram; we pause while I manage to open it a little, glancing both ways along the road, sniffing the air, like a dog. (Ha! You'd think I'd done this a thousand times: a pro, I tell myself.) We lay him back down on the floor – his face horribly rested against the prickly WELCOME of the front-door mat – while I run to the kitchen for my shoes, for all the things he left: his pipe, his tin of Golden Virginia tobacco, his jacket, his leather billfold. Then we try again. A flashlight seems risky – someone might spot the beam as it flits around – so we do it with only the light from the standard lamp in the living room behind us and that seems too much, too shockingly bright, so I close the door to almost a crack.

We rest him against the car; Sam holds him there with one hand on his chest while I open the door with his keys, then run back to the passenger side before he slides to the ground. Sam wedges the passenger door open with her knee, while I try to haul his stupid trousered thighs into place. At any moment I fear she might throw up her hands and wail that she can't go through with it, so I'm saying over and over, 'OK, honey, sure, nearly done . . .' There is a moment when his head wobbles over and I think he might open his eyes and grin at me; the yellow interior light flashes over his cheeks as we are bending him at the waist and shoving him into the seat. The interior of his car smells of Gerald, of course: pipe smoke and tweed and grass cuttings and mustard-coloured socks. The human body is awfully heavy, unwieldy. We are both sweating with the effort.

Sam flings his jacket into the back and closes the car door, too gently, and has to reopen it and give a slightly louder slam. Gerald

77

is inside. I look up and down the street: what on earth to say if anyone sees us? He's drunk, we're driving him home? And then later, when he's found, how to explain that? I run inside to fetch a dishcloth from the kitchen (sad that it's a new one, pure white and soft) and wedge it behind his head so that no blood reaches the seat-back. There are no lights on in any of the windows of the cottages in Earl Soham. I run back one last time to get my own car key for Sam to drive *my* car, and I close the front door to Bridge Cottage as soundlessly as I can.

'They'll never believe you,' he says.

He forms a dark profile beside me, stares at the road ahead; are his eyes open? I slide my eyes a little to the side to look but can't tell. The country lanes are mostly unlit, the car a warm fug and my heartbeat louder than any radio. 'I was a pretty lad, married at eighteen,' says a male voice. Something Ronnie said once. Something Ronnie is working on; listening to. Voices, always voices, with Ronnie. That's all he does all day. Talk to farmers, John Grout, eighty-eight: I was a pretty lad. Samuel Gissing, eighty years: 'It all goes so fast. But a school morning was a whole lifetime.'

True enough. A school morning. Who can remember them now? Tadpoles in a jar, a caterpillar with a face like a little train, black dots for eyes, mouldering in a matchbox.

A low, inelegant shape darts across the road. Muntjac deer. I remember Ronnie telling me they were released long ago from a zoo or park or something and now they're everywhere. Aldeburgh is only half an hour away and a quick glance in the rear-view mirror tells me Sam is still following. The eyes of her car, white and bright, tailing Gerald's.

'There is nobody can say that you have killed a man.' Another line from Ronnie's notes. 'You got very frightened of the murdering and you did sometimes think, What is this about? What is this for? But the more the killing, the more you thought about living.'

That was the war he was talking about, at any rate. And I need to pull myself together; I need to think. It's so smotheringly dark in this car. There is no radio; that was another car, long ago. Gerald is smoking his pipe; I can hear his little sucks, smell the powerful choking tobacco. On his knee a map, an AA map of the local roads. And now he is chuckling: Think you'd killed me, huh? Think it could be that easy? And what now, how will you cover your tracks? Should have shoved me in the pond, like you meant to. Won't that old bitch Ingham have seen me, seen my arrival, heard the car? Won't there be finger-prints? Blood on the rug, blood on this car seat. And then there's Sam. How's she going to keep mum about it? You're an amateur here, for all your thinking, all your planning, all those years. You know nothing about it; you could never achieve it, no matter how many times you've imagined it, written it. Where are all your musings now? It's beyond you.

The car cruises along the loamy flats and Gerald's head lolls in my direction, emanating his dark, threatening smell. He is not hammering at me, no, no, it's fine, he's wordless again. He's deader than a shoe, deader than a pencil stub, deader than a cold Black & Decker drill neatly packed in its box. In a moment he might stretch out his hand and take the wheel but just now he is dead. He will say, as Mother did, 'Are you crazy? Are you ready for the booby hatch? Don't look at me like that! You're nuts, you know that, Patsy!' And that slap she always gave me, maybe Gerald would do it now, quick and hard across the face.

'Well, you old bastard, you finally got what was coming,' I say, out loud.

I'm driving, and I'm thinking not of Gerald, not of Mother, but of *him*, of long ago. Stanley. A sense of relief, of pleasure, is starting to steal through my blood and I want to laugh. I long to lean over and tap him on the shoulder and say: 'You know, you should have been nicer to me. You could have protected me from Mom, not taken her side all the time.'

Stanley, crouching to be the same height as me, his severe, Serious Father face, after I'd accused him of cruelty, after listening to the lobster screaming in its pot: 'You know, Pats, little girls don't know too much. They should never get their heads swelled, or think they know more than the grown-ups.' And I'd stood, hands on hips, roaring, 'I'm not a little girl!' and that made him smirk and bat my mother with his hat, saying, 'Ain't she just the funniest thing?' That other time, he snatched away my favourite words, telling me I was pronouncing them wrong. *Open Sesame!* The magic of it for ever spoiled, destroyed because of his crushing need to 'put you to rights about a few things'. Humiliate me, is what he meant. And that day, hopping between him and my mother at the park, they sharing an ice-cream cone over my head – *Give me some! What about me!*, one white blob splatting the sidewalk – and Stanley so tall, so way out of reach, laughing when I stretched for it, swinging the cone above my head and laughing again, but then saying, 'Aw, honey, you need a sense of humour,' when he finally quit, reached down to offer it, and I refused.

The sound of my childhood: jerky, angry voices coming from the hall while I tried to sleep. I would leap up and kick my door closed, but it never shut them out. 'I didn't *say* that!' Mother's voice. And then Stanley: 'You calling me a liar?' Doors slamming.

Car journeys: no wonder I think of him now. The metal and the plastic and the chrome, no way to escape *that* little hell, trapped with the beasts *inside* the walls. The explosive rows when Mother couldn't map-read – she couldn't ever – and Stanley took a wrong turn. The time he pulled over, dragged her out and punched her once on the side of her head, then shoved her back into her side of the car.

I held my breath on the back seat; I opened my mouth to scream but didn't. I wondered if I was even alive, put my hand to my heart to see if it was beating and, sure, there it was, skittering like a mouse. The engine growling and the sound of Mother softly sobbing, her face pressed against the window. I leaned forward to touch her shoulder, but she shrugged me off. I stared at the back of Stanley's neck as he drove, at the red and the white of his skin, at the tiny new black hairs growing. My whole body was trembling; I realised my teeth were chattering. If only she would leave him like she threatened, like she promised! If only, if only . . . One day he might *really do something terrible to her*.

One time, one night like no other, it had a different flavour and colour and taste from every other night, had fixed in my memory like a horrible work of art; that time the noises got too frightening, after I heard her hectoring voice and then her screaming, *Stanley, don't, don't, please*, and I'd run from my bedroom with such a torrent of terror in my heart and bellowed at him that I was going to tell Granny Mae, that I was going to tell my cousin Dan what a bad man Stanley was, and he put his face close to mine and my six-year-old pride and power exploded as he said: 'OK, I'm a bum, so what? You're just a little girl. They'll never believe you.'

And so in the back of the car, as a *little girl*, I nursed it. And when the little mouse of my heart calmed down, I thought: Not only am I alive but I'm more alive than before: this is what being alive is. That's how it began, the monster. The heat in the car, sullen and cruel. For six whole hours, my bladder full to bursting, I simmered and swelled behind Stanley's long, dark head with my big idea: how to murder Stanley.

Some little things must be the cause of me, bad seed that I am; a multitude of tiny things, like sand grains to a dune. But those years, those years with Mother and Stanley, those millions of minutes of a child's life, car journeys and vacations and that low, grim hum of constant quarrelling, that's when the piling up of grains began.

Aldeburgh at night reveals not a single cottage with a light on. It's just after 4 a.m. We might be in luck. I park down Crabbe

Street, a narrow unlit road, a gull greeting me with a long cry as the car door is opened. There is only one van parked here: *Ray Felton Chimney Sweep*. The sea-wall is just about in view next to some Tudor building that Ronnie pointed out to me – Moot Hall. I can't see the sea but I smell the tang and hear it: a regular great shudder, like an elephant harrumphing. In the night air the sailboats' masts tinkle, like someone jingling change in a pocket.

Sam pulls up just behind me in the Anglia and hurries round to my side of the car, tapping on the window, her face pale as the moon or a white balloon with blackened eyes. She's wearing only the long sweater over the silky nightdress and her black suede pumps without stockings, her legs white as uncooked spaghetti. She hasn't seemed to notice the cold. I can see that she's still in shock; that I have perhaps an hour before reality defrosts her, and after that, I will not be able to rely on her.

'Help me get him out. Make it look like we're helping a drunk,' I whisper, opening the car door.

There is no one: no lights, no late-night dog-walkers.

I glance up and down over the frosted pastel lozenges – the sleepy cottages – in the moonlight, then to the sea-wall that edges the beach. Again, no one, and coming around to his side and reaching into the car, I put my arms under the slumped Gerald and haul him out, his feet catching a little and having to be lifted one at a time. Then I lean him against the side and hold him there with the flat of one casual hand. If anyone were to look, they need to think we're two women friends helping a filthy drunk to stand up. But there is no one, only the briny scent of the sea, the waves rolling as if someone is exhaling loudly beside me.

So between us we begin walking him to the beach, draping one of his disgusting arms around each of our necks. We climb easily over the low sea-wall and the sea arrives in grey frills atop the black. Gerald's head sags against my shoulder. The crunch of pebbles is a sudden, shockingly loud sound – I have a horrifying sensation, as if I'm stepping onto the shells of snails.

We drag him across the shingle, past Moot Hall – one fat gull with its rump stuck inside a chimney, as if jammed there – and the black lumps of the fishermen's empty huts, *Fresh fish, crab for sale*. Fishy smells waft our way. Gulls squeak occasionally, like creaking doors suddenly opening. One of us on each side of Gerald, his flaccid weight lugged between us like an effigy, like the penny-for-the-guy that Sam once told me about, her English childhood of burnings and bonfires. It's harder than I imagined, our toes sometimes finding an indentation, kicking up a pebble or slipping, the skinny, feeble Gerald an awkward weight, and sweat is starting to pool in the narrow of my back with the effort. The desire to glance over my shoulder and make sure no one is following is strong. Up to the pearly edge of the water we go. And now the sound of sea grows closer, very close and intimate, like a dog lapping at a bowl.

I whisper to Sam: 'Go back to his car now. Wipe all the handles and the gear stick and everything you can find in the car with that dishcloth I brought. Check for a bloodstain on the passenger seat. Get rid of the dishcloth – bring it to me. Then lock the car and wipe the key fob too.'

But, hey, fingerprints. How likely is it that the police would be looking for fingerprints, or anyone else, in what is patently a suicide? Fingerprints have to be anticipated, dusted, there have to be suspicions. A long glance up and down the beach: what if someone has a notion to take an early-hours stroll, an insomniac, or just the usual crackpot? And should I have brought a liquor bottle, make it look like he needed one last drink? Too late. Nobody.

Gerald lies at my feet now, like a stupid doll, pointed-toe brogues sticking up to the sky. The sea rolls in and away, like a restless sculptor, over the stones, and I think of Ronnie briefly, Ronnie's stories of herring days in Lowestoft and his way of describing his friend Britten as 'oceanic from the start'. Waves, he says, make land seem like a very trivial business. The sea inside us, tidal pulls. Yes, yes. I'm doing you a favour, Gerald: returning you to the sea.

I watch Sam's dark figure stumbling a little as her foot kicks an abandoned lobster pot, going back to the car. Better she doesn't watch me undress him. Hear the clanking buckle of his belt hit shingle. Better not to see the pitiful white body; the foolish, floppy, ghastly white appendage wilting over to one side like a dead fish.

I pile clothes, shoes, billfold on top of the jacket on the pebbles near to the water's edge. It needs to look deliberate, but not too controlled. I try to think how a man would do this. Would he place pants folded under shorts? Would he hide the billfold inside a shoe? Would he coil his belt neatly? That's too neat. I kick it to make the snake-shape spring open. How calm is a suicide? Calm enough to go through with it. Not so calm or considered that it actually looks as if someone else did it, as an afterthought. A noise makes me turn my head sharply, but it's only the scrape of stones scuffing together by my walking on them.

Then I think: If I get rid of the billfold it will take them longer to identify him accurately. It will give us a few hours. So I pick it out from inside the shoe and hurl it as far out to the black sea as I can. I'm too far away to hear the splash when it lands.

I glance up and down the beach. Darkness. A few pricked lights of cottages far away; they might even be stars. Occasional white frills on the black waves. And the water is icy, bracingly cold, as I go in with my shoes on and drag this naked white man with me. My arms around his chest, the wet curls of his chest hair flattening in streaks, like bits of seaweed, his body limp, like a rubber doll, his flesh yellow where the water shades it. No signs of rigor mortis yet. Perhaps it's too early? Don't corpses get gas in them and bob around? All that research on the progress of a corpse, where is that knowledge now when I need it?

The sea bites at my ankles in their jeans and slops around in my shoes. How far will I need to go out? The tide is coming in, I feel the water deepening by the second; my plan is to wade deep enough to ensure that he's carried away – I need him to sink

84

under the waves, rather than float – and I don't want the bastard washing up on the shingle immediately, for all to see. Let him wash up, but later.

I'm already exhausted and hoping I won't have to go out too deep, stumbling against the force of the waves and with the slippery stones jabbing through the soles of my shoes. The salty taste is in my mouth, the spray on my face. My pants wrap around my legs, stickily, bitterly cold. The mumbo-jumbo sound of the sea around us. Further in, up to my knees now, and wrapping the cold wet nastiness of Gerald with my arms, as if holding a lover.

Surely the tide will lug him away from me (then offer him back; endlessly returning, endlessly offered back). Too late I remember about the blow to his head and hope that the cut will seem like one produced by a fall, knocked about on a rock, perhaps, or be washed spotless by the briny sea. Maybe by the time they recover the body his skull will be too bloated and waterlogged for the cut to be visible, or pecked at by gulls (though even in my hopefulness I suspect that, in fact, the cut will be opened up, yellowed and bleached and gaping . . .). His eyes are black. I can barely see him in the milky light but I see them open suddenly, staring at me, like the gaze of the eeriest white monster from the deep, some serpent-like shape, evil and ever-present: I'm close enough to kiss him. Didn't you always know there was evil in the world, didn't your childhood show you it in the purest, whitest form? And here it is again: like a gull sweeping to pluck at your eyes, a white slice of fierce bone, hasn't it travelled beside you night and day from the beginning? What made you think you would ever escape? And here Gerald is laughing and laughing and suddenly liberating himself from my clasp, flinging himself head first into the waves, then bobbing like a ghostly white seal on the surface, and I'm thinking of those times when I submerged my head, all those occasions when Stanley taught me to swim, the yellow garter snakes I was afraid of, the shadowy depths. Now it's just a mouthful of salt, and icy water up to my waist, and a noseful of sea-flavoured mucus and it's done – if I go an inch further the tide will claim me too; I've already stumbled once and am icily cold up to my shoulders. With a last spurt of energy I throw him away from me, away at last, and for ever! I watch the white form plunge under a wave and spin away, bob atop a dark crest and vanish again.

Yes, I see the little man there, the Thing, I know he is there, atop a wave. But I don't turn to look.

I stride back to the beach. My jeans slip and slop against me and my feet slurp inside the wet shoes and my ribs give a stabbing pain as I try to catch my breath. I pause for a moment to check: no one has appeared. No lights have appeared. I glance back at the black sea and hear it rush in my ears, like distant gunshot, like a prowling beast, but I do not see the white of him, though it must be bobbing somewhere. No sounds of a car engine starting up, not even in the distance.

I walk past the little pile of his clothes on the pebbles, everything grey in the darkness; even the nasty mustard-coloured socks have been soaked up by a deep, absolving grey. Extraordinarily easy. I feel delirious. Denim slapping wet at my calves, water slopping in my shoes, striding towards the two neat cars. How modern and dry and alive and civilised those cars look. The epitome of ordinariness, I suddenly feel. And not a single witness! All these years. Whoever would believe it could be that simple? His life snuffed out in one big swat, the way you would crush a mosquito. Almost unbelievably lucky, as if the world was on our side and agreed with us that it was a better place without Gerald in it.

Two parked cars, and the dark figure of a lovely woman, smoking a cigarette and waiting for me. She hands me Gerald's car keys and the cloth with the blackened stains on it and I make one last dash towards the white spume of the waves, to wrap the keys in the cloth and throw them away from me, out towards the curling rush.

*   *   *

Inside, my car is dark and innocent, with its familiar smell of warm orange peel and traces of Smythson-Balby's powerful perfume. I daren't risk a glance at Sam, but the interior is filled with the soft sound of her sniffing and sobs. Easing myself into the driver's seat makes obscene sucking sounds as my wet clothes grip the leather, and I stifle a giggle. The car starts obediently. Seawater pools at my feet and my body is suddenly convulsed with violent shivers, my teeth chattering. I'd like to ask, 'Say, could you pass me that blanket on the back seat to dry myself?' but I don't.

And now the journey to Hades and a watery underworld is to be replaced with a journey back up to the light – perhaps, perhaps, but only if Sam will allow it. I wait for the car to warm me a little and my teeth to quit chattering. Then I try, in a tone I hope is intelligent and firm, the tone of a reasonable person, a friend (not the tone of a murderer trying to cover her tracks, no: not that!):

'Of course, you have to say to the police – or whoever – that when you left yesterday morning, Gerald was home. They'll hammer at you. Say that nothing was wrong and, no, as far as you know, he had no idea, no plans, you know, to – do anything foolish. You could add that maybe he had gotten himself a little depressed. He was sometimes a little hysterical. Jealous of a lover he imagined you had. No, don't mention the lover. Everyone knew Gerald liked the liquor. But, then, what if Minty mentions you had a fight? OK, say you had a fight. You have to report him missing. This evening, I guess, when you get home. Make out you feel some, you know . . . some *worry*. The amount of worry of a worried wife whose husband is not home when she expects him to be. But not too *much*. Can you do that?'

Sam makes no reply; her unreadable blonde head is turned towards the window.

A hot blade of fear slices through me. I try again:

'Of course it's going to be tough. The questions. But after that. They'll quit. They'll find him. Once they've found him, and the car and the clothes, they'll quit. There'll be the funeral to get through, of course – didn't you say his parents are still alive? But then most wives barely function at funerals. No one will find that suspicious. Then after that. Much easier, OK, honey? The relief – not having him in your life. Not being afraid. And after a time, after whatever we think is a decent time . . .'

But I can't finish this sentence. What on earth is Sam thinking? I suspect she is thinking about Minty, and here I am lost, I have nothing to say, nothing at all to offer to the world of mother-hood, the dark reaches of mothers, a murderous species if ever there was one, a space I've always been excluded from. I shift on my seat, shivering violently again. The wet clothes clinging to me are deeply unpleasant. I will have to try and dry the car out tomorrow with a hairdryer (but, then, maybe Mrs Ingham will see this and it will look queer?). A grey blob – a weird vision of Gerald, bobbing away from me – floats into the corner of my eye. I shake my head briskly. Sam has quit her crying and from the position of her shoulders I see now that she is stiffening. Stiffening her resolve, perhaps? I hope that this is a good sign.

'Goddamn it,' I try. 'He did some god-awful things to you, Sam. I know that wasn't the first occasion.'

I want to say: Do you really think a man like Gerald, a wife-beating, sinister, slimy, deceitful man – a violent rapist – should be allowed to live and be happy, and that happiness should be denied to you and me? Silence. Trees loom mustard-yellow and sinister in the headlights, like a forest that wants to clamber into the car with us.

'There will be questions, Sam . . .'

I can hear her breathing. My lungs tighten; the interior of the car is full of an oppressive lack, an absence of something, of air or oxygen, something that threatens to end us, to choke us both.

'You know, don't you still have the death penalty here? That John Christie case. It's being debated. Or, even if it's abolished, I'd go to prison for a very long time. They'd never believe me, Sam,' I say.

They'll never believe you. Stanley's long, dark head and his insolent smile leap into the car, and I have to grab the wheel tight to prevent us swerving off the road.

'Once . . .' Sam says slowly. 'One night Gerald came to bed and I wouldn't, you know, I wasn't in the mood. And he started right on, and actually I had the curse, that was the reason I hadn't wanted to, and he didn't put the bedroom lamp on, and he didn't see at first. There was blood everywhere. The bed. The sheets – I had to get rid of them. When I put the bedside light on it looked like a blood bath. And afterwards Gerald said: "You're filthy. You make me feel sick."'

Sam turns a soft face to me and puts her hand on the wet denim of my knee. A surge of happiness flies up. Everything will be OK. And after that a feeling of deep exhaustion and relief descends. Like waking, and a nightmare that kept stopping and starting is finally over.

'And then other times. He was so charming, wasn't he?' she continues. 'So smooth and soft and clever. All charm at work. So sorry and so loving. That day when the whole house was filled with flowers, roses, every colour, every kind of smell. Do you remember? Something happened at work, some shares went up or something, and he was thrilled and he wanted everyone to know it. And always he was hanging on, going to those events, so jealous of his brother's world. The arty-farty world, as he called it. It was confusing. The worst time. The worst thing I remember. He trapped me in a doorway. Can you imagine that? I was coming through and he started pushing me and closing the door, trapping my shoulder and my arm – in our kitchen, a heavy wooden door, he was calling me a bitch. I can't remember what I'd done to infuriate him but I saw that look and I was screaming at him to release the door because my arm hurt so much and then I saw Minty appear and run away again. Minty didn't come to help me – she didn't know what to do.'

Her voice has become hushed: she's talking to herself.

'I hated Gerald then. I was screaming, I was in pain, but I was furious too and degraded and that's when you have degrading thoughts, isn't it? My poor little girl, growing up like this. Poor Minty, seeing this.'

I glance at her and notice only that a forgotten hair-grip dangles from a long strand of fair hair, like a tiny ballet dancer, clinging to her by one outstretched leg. Then my eyes return to the road: empty, desolate. I have to concentrate hard, hold on tight.

She continues softly talking and now her voice is warmer, dreamy.

'I think that's what attracted me to you. I could tell you were – you *knew*. You weren't one of those people who read the paper and say: "I can't imagine it – what on earth makes people *do* such things?" You remember that dinner party? I'd just read the first scene of *The Blunderer*. God, that scene is vicious. And I remember thinking: This woman knows. The feeling of hatred, of wanting to do something sordid. It's – *pungent*, almost. She's like me, I thought.'

Cool, poised, profoundly competent and graceful Sam, like me? I don't want her to say that. She's not like me: she's everything I'm not! Good and clean and . . . I'm concentrating, my eyes on the road; my usual replies form but I don't utter them – *Of course an author must be able to write of things that he or she has not experienced, imagine them*. I'm aware that I'm gripping the steering-wheel with way too much pressure but it's because any minute I might take my hands off, throw them up into the air in front of my face, let the car swerve and buck and shimmy and do whatever the hell it likes with us, offer us up into the Suffolk blanketing dark, like a little cup of stars; my hands feel thick with blood throbbing with something strange and ghastly that tiptoes towards me getting close, closer . . .

'People who have never felt in fear of their lives can't know what a horrible feeling it is, sordid and corrosive,' Sam says, staring at the windshield and not glancing at me. 'I've sometimes looked into prams – you know the nannies on Hampstead Heath

– and thought: Well, how do you make a child into a murderer? If a child has never had its dear sweet trusting little face bellowed into, then does it ever learn the depths of terror? I know Gerald was brought up in that way – in *fear* – and somehow I always knew that you must have been too, dear Patsy. Before living with Gerald I had no idea I could feel – *imagine* – such violent, ghastly things to do to another human being. It was either kill him or kill myself, I often thought. There were many times when I wanted to do to Gerald exactly what you did.'

Don't ever talk of killing yourself, I want to say.

The road blurs and undulates, rears up like a snake. I rub at my eyes to try to refocus, wondering at the tears that slide from my chin. I must not take us off the road. I must not drive into a tree. I must stay calm. I must think only of the sweetness of Sam beside me, the dark wild sweetness in my bedroom earlier. I must think of that, and how best to capture it, which words will net it (though none will, none will); only thinking of that, only work, the austere servitude of words, the thoughtful peck of fingers on keys, only that will save me.

Back at Bridge Cottage, I roll up the rug and prop it by the front door, exposing the red-brick tiles beneath. I scrub them with a rag, which I burn on the fire. Sam goes upstairs as if to bed, then reappears, running her hands through her hair and saying: 'I left my seconal at home – do you have a sleeping pill?' When I say no, she hovers by me in the kitchen, murmuring: 'There's just no chance whatsoever that I'll sleep.'

I heat up some milk in the pan on the stove and catch it just as it swells to boil. Carrying the mugs into the front room, I hesitate: somehow it doesn't feel OK to sit in there. It sizzles with too much – *atmosphere*. So I carry the mugs – white china with bluebells on them – back into the kitchen and set them on the table. If Mrs Ingham is looking out from her window across the garden, out in the direction that Bunnikins used to have his hutch, or scanning for a fox, this is what she'll see: two old friends at five in the morning, drinking hot milk from bluebell mugs and smoking, at a table with a posy of flowers on it and folded napkins piled at one end.

'I remember when I couldn't bear the taste of milk,' I say. 'A bit too *real*, isn't it? Makes you think of cows.' Sam says nothing.

When the sun comes up, Sam gets her bag from upstairs and I drive her to Ipswich station. In the car we barely talk. I want to say, 'Is everything OK between us?' but I hardly know how to. I can't think what possible reply Sam can give to the woman who just killed her husband.

As we part, she now wrapped in the tightly belted trench coat and clipping along the station platform in her black suede pumps, I try once more to plead with her. 'You remember Ellen Hill? I told you about her, didn't I?' I ask nervously. Sam nods. 'And you remember she was always talking of . . . doing away with herself, and after I'd been through that once with Allela, it made me mad as hell. Matter of fact, I felt she was torturing me, making me responsible for her life, for whether she lived or died. And in the end—'

'Pats, my train. I've got to go,' she breaks in, as the noise thunders overs us and the carriages roll to a halt beside us. She steps inside with only the curtest of kisses, barely looking back.

She'd said she'd call the police station tonight at about 10 p.m. She will say casually that it's Sunday now and she was expecting her husband home and that he has not returned, and he hasn't phoned, and she's a little worried. Then she will call the telephone outside Bridge Cottage and I will be there, waiting.

October. It was liquid and insecure. October was falling, slipping; things losing shape. Solid things – leaves, ground, love affairs – turning to mush. If she had been six years old and in Fort Worth just now, she would have been burrowing inside the straggly orange flesh of a pumpkin with her knife, carving two dangerous, dark, unseeing eyes. Here, October slid towards the end of the year: low sunlight, soggy leaves, equal parts sunny and cold, runny and solid, good and bad, like the curate's egg. The children in the English village seemed not to celebrate Hallowe'en; not to know that October was the crack in the year when the ghosts came out to play.

She was in the car with Ronnie, hands resting lightly on the steering-wheel, the handbrake still pulled on, engine cut. And then Ronnie said: 'I heard about her husband going missing. Chap I know knows his brother, a writer. Says Gerald was erratic, volatile.'

'Yes,' Pat said, staring at her hands, at her big splayed fingers. She did not tap them, but she counted in her head. Five long seconds passed.

'Have they heard anything more? Less than a week . . .' Ronnie said. 'That's not very long. He could just be . . . were there problems at the bank? Did he have a mistress?'

'There were rumours of mistresses, yes. He was hard to get along with.' She wondered whether to add more. Conversations with Ronnie were not like those with others: he was not much of a gossip and sentences could end with a clear thud and silence reign and Ronnie, she knew, wouldn't notice.

'Still. For Sam, it's rotten . . .' Pat added. Her voice wobbled a little on Sam's name. She started the engine and swung the car into the road without a glance in the mirror. It was rare to meet another car round here, only tractors and bicycles. Was Ronnie going to say more about Gerald? The inside of the car was fraught with held breath. She felt her cheek prickle and was sure that he was staring at the side of her face, although she didn't dare glance at him to check. She felt his gaze beside her, and somehow she felt, too, his fear of her suddenly. His gaze, his eyes, seeking hers. She stared at the road. She would remember this minute all her life. Something strange seemed to pass between them. Some idea, some awful hint, something hideous, some slip understood on both sides. Was Ronnie looking at her the way Razumikhin looked at Raskolnikov in *Crime and Punishment*? Did he *know*?

The moment she'd had this thought she felt its foolishness, its falsity. He can't know anything: his eyes aren't piercing straight to your darkest thoughts, he's not a mind-reader, what can he possibly know? *You're making things up – matter of fact, you might be half cracked at this moment, if you want the truth.*

'I heard about your Dagger, too.' Ronnie's voice came from nowhere. But it sounded gentle and kind, not accusing. She breathed out in the fug of the car. 'The award party is in a month, I think. We could go together? That is, if you felt like driving us?'

Was it only this? Ronnie was always shy about asking for rides? But he was more social than she, too, and convinced that writers gained immeasurably from being around other artistic people, having had that initial input himself as a boy from the composer he described only as 'a thin, crinkly-haired figure'. Pat had felt a little high, and then a confusion of shame, in being told she was shortlisted for the Silver Dagger award. Best foreign crime novel. It would be published in England now at any rate. But a prize was nothing great.

Pat's distaste for parties amounted to a phobia. Her talent for aloneness was powerful, and although Ronnie shared her skill in solitude, their intermission requirements were different. Her solitude was punctuated by a need for intense sexual and passionate experiences that left her drained and hungry for aloneness again. Ronnie needed something else. Something intellectual, green, healthy. Not the degrading immersion that she went in for. A shudder passed through her as she remembered.

An October stillness hung in the air; bells were already ringing and dusk liquescing the countryside. On the dashboard lay Ronnie's attempt to make a corn dolly. 'Looks more like a voodoo doll,' Pat muttered, holding the curious stick figure up to examine it, while Ronnie gave her directions to the church and remarked on the loveliness of the sunset; like a pink ice-lolly slowly melting.

Ronnie's corn dolly was the goddess Ceres, imprisoned for a year in a cage of corn, to promise fertility. He said that, traditionally, it was always the men who made them and she was not to josh him for his efforts, made in the proper way from the last sheaf of the harvest. As she studied it, hunched and stiff, the arms sloping by its sides, it was the stick-thin Gerald she saw. And maybe something pretty shady. Out of the corner of her eye, something else.

I'm closing the door of the telephone booth at our agreed time on a milky blue night under a full moon, trapping brambles and leaves in with me. From the crunch underfoot I notice that another of the panes of oblong glass has been smashed into little cubes. The phone is ringing already – almost leaping off its cradle like a black snake – and I snatch it up. 'Sam?' Yes. 'What did the police say?'

'Nothing much. Name, a description. When did I last see him, that sort of thing.'

'And how did they sound? You know? What kind of person did you speak to?'

'Oh I don't know. Just as you'd expect. A British bobby. Not that intelligent. Not that – oh.'

And then a little kerfuffle at her end, and I realise that her daughter Minty must be in the room she's calling from and there is talk of 'cocoa' and 'toothbrush' and 'Don't worry, darling, you'll see him tomorrow,' and murmuring, and then she's back on the line.

'I didn't realise she was awake! She might have been listening outside the door for all I knew.'

I'm not too concerned. If the child picks up on her secrecy she'll just assume it's the usual adult thing, the whispering and hiding of painful truths that parents do routinely to children: Daddy hasn't come home and no one knows where he is. I long to say something useful and soothing, something to tilt the mood and make Sam friendly again, not wary, like this, not tired-sounding and quietly hostile, but there's nothing I can think of.

'Well, call me again tomorrow,' I say. 'I'll be in the phone booth at ten in the morning. Will Minty have left by then? Will you be able to talk?'

Yes, Minty will be in a car with her little friend Hermione Dixon and the Dixons' nanny will drive her to school. That is, until the news, of course, when she knows Minty will be fetched back again and she has to face her, her tears and dramas or, worse, her dry, too-mature-for-words stoicism. Her voice is dulled, quiet. I guess that some of the reality is seeping in; it's only natural, I suppose, that she might feel a little sad about Gerald, but that will pass, surely, when she realises what it means for *us*, what freedoms it affords us . . .

'I never feel sadder than seeing little Minty all dressed up with that blazer and beret and with her little case on her way to school,' Sam says.

'Well, now that – now, perhaps, you can make your own decisions about which school she goes to. Won't that be nice?'

I have to say this quietly, of course. Everything in a whisper because naturally, at this point, we can only know that a husband is missing, that he didn't leave word of where he was going, that his wife returned from a weekend visiting friends and found that he wasn't there and that she is worried enough to call the police.

I close the stiff booth door and dash over the road to Bridge Cottage; rain falls in fat wet blobs on my head. I decide a large glass of whisky topped with water from the faucet will help me sleep but in fact it jolts me awake, and lying there stiff and alert for an hour or so, breathing in the scent of Sam's hair on my pillow, I give up and wrench myself from the warmth of my bed to take up my writing.

My bathrobe is hooked on the back of the door. I don't wear it when Sam is around: I know it's unsexy; I feel like an old man in it. But it's comforting now: the deep plum-coloured wool, the Harrods label, the familiar cream and lilac stripes on its cuffs, the striped woollen belt. It smells of me, I suppose, this thick, draping garment, whatever that smell is – how can a person know their own smell? It was Sam who told me I have a talent for aloneness. I had never heard it expressed that way. 'Hey – I get lonely sometimes!' I'd protested. And I feel it now. Like a child alone in a plane, appraising the world. How far this tiny, silly, pointless village is from everything and everyone. What on earth am I doing here? Why am I always . . . why have I always been cut off like this, rattling around somewhere like a nut in a sealed-up doll's house? There's Texas, Paris, Europe, New York. The world, with Ronnie and books and people in it. And here I am. None of them knows where I am just now and *what I did*.

Except Sam, of course.

My fingers curl around the shell of a snail in the pocket of the bathrobe, grazing its sticky horns before it draws them in. I move to add it to the ones on the window ledge. A hobney-dod, Ronnie had called it. There are lots of them now: various pairs of differing sizes, some found in the garden. The garden ones are in a washing-up bowl on the window ledge so that I can observe them and figure out if they're pairs of the opposite sex. The original snails in their saucer contain the eggs, and I check these every time I pass and replace the snails who have crawled over the rim and sometimes ended up on the window-pane. The eggs have turned a pale grey colour. I keep a magnifying-glass close by to observe them but even in the lamplight these are now clearly visible. One pair in the washing-up bowl is now digging a pit; happily, there will surely be more eggs soon.

I've crossed a line that very few people cross. It is – as I always knew it would be – an extraordinary feeling. Nothing else matters. No rules, no silly behaviour, like putting out milk bottles on the step, filling up the car with gas, opening a bill from Eastern Electricity Board – none of these things seem real any longer, or necessary. Surely I now live by different rules, like the delirious pleasure I felt as a child if I bunked off school, the secret feeling that no one could find me, the delirium of terror in case they should.

I pour myself another glass of whisky and take a big, burning gulp. I only feel up to the *Plotting* book, not the novel, not the immersion required for that. I'm too prickly and alert. Aroused. Provoked. Not exhausted, not yet, but I can feel it waiting to engulf me.

I write then take another glug of the whisky (this one is good, a smoky single malt, golden in colour, delicious), turning at last to the novel, lifting my fingers to begin.

And then he turns up again, making me jump out of my skin, appearing at the bottom of the stairs, simply sitting there, fully dressed, small and bent like a coat-hanger, tapping at the heel of his pipe and looking over his shoulder at me with that soft glow and those small dark piggy eyes.

'You should have weighted the ankles,' he says. 'Weight the body down so it won't pop up again and betray you. Why didn't you think of that?'

He gets up. He stretches in the low-ceilinged cottage. Jerks one finger at the rolled-up rug, leaning against the stairs.

'You'll have to get rid of that. Blood and semen and who knows what else? They do tests, you know. Won't there be a post-mortem, too? You're so much more of a rookie than you think . . .'

Tests! What tests? They only do tests if they suspect something. The whole point is – you're a suicide. That's why it's fine for you to bob back. That's why it *wouldn't* be fine for you to have weights around your ankles. And they don't always do a post-mortem. I've looked it up, a giant legal tome at the library. Post-mortems are expensive, and distressing for the family, prolonging the grieving process. They don't do one after every death as a matter of course.

'You took an awful risk with that blow to my head,' he says. 'The skull does have its weak points. One is the pterion, known as the temple. Just beneath this thin bit of skull is the middle meningeal artery. If you get clonked in the temple, this artery can rupture. That must be how you did it. Not the back of the head but the temple.'

99

How did he get to be so knowledgeable? I don't remember him having any kind of Irish accent, either, but there is the faintest trace now. He's right about that blow to the head. I have been worried about that. But then, apparently, the thing to be aware of when determining death by drowning is that other injuries – head injuries – might be caused by the fall into the water, or by contact with a boat, or even in the moment when the body is hauled from the water, which sometimes involves hooks and ropes and further insult to the head . . . And then there is a knock on the door – late as it is – and the Thing, it, *him*, whatever his name is, disappears and dear kind Ronnie is there, in darkness, knocking at the back door.

I switch on the kitchen light at the same moment as he opens the unlocked back door, bringing in a blast of rain-soaked air, shaking his head with that ever so slightly too-long mane – it makes him seem like a vain man, which he isn't. 'You were writing,' Ronnie says, with the greatest civility. 'I'm so sorry.'

I assure him it's fine. It's late for Ronnie, gone midnight now, and Ronnie is more of a morning person, but he's been at the church, evensong, then stayed to interview someone for his book, and when he went to cycle home, he discovered he had a flat. He tries to wheel the great muddy thing into my kitchen but I draw the line at that.

'Leave it out there. Mrs Ingham won't make off with it.'

As I open the back door there is a low ghostly sweeping movement in the huge elms. The return of my grey blob?

'Barn owl,' Ronnie says. 'She's hunting. Aren't they beautiful with their little heart-shaped faces?'

We close the kitchen door against the rain and chill. My kitchen is not much warmer.

'You talk to yourself when you write,' Ronnie says, glancing at the tumbler of whisky I'm holding. I offer the bottle, standing on the kitchen table, to him; it seems to make a rather servile ducking gesture, like doffing its cap.

Ronnie accepts a small one to warm up. 'Doesn't everyone?' I ask.

'Why no fire?' Ronnie asks, wandering into the front room, and immediately sets about making one, kneeling in front of the hearth to sweep the cold ash with the little dustpan and brush. Then his eyes land on my bathrobe: 'Or were you on your way to bed?'

I tug the plum-coloured robe tighter and redo the belt, following him into the front room, shaking my head, reaching for my cigarettes and the gold lighter in the fluff of the pocket. I let Ronnie light the fire – tearing up the copies of the *Ipswich Star* and using the last of the kindling and, yes, though I didn't think of it before, the room is cosier with that crackling sound and smell in it.

But there is the rug I've rolled up and stood on its end, meaning to be rid of it. And beside that the recently cleaned bit of red-brick tile; bare and scrubbed and dramatic. Flustered, I go to fix us some buttered crackers, the only food I have in the house, wanting Ronnie to follow me into the kitchen until I can somehow shove the sofa over the bare spot. Ronnie produces a brown-paper bag he's brought of Blenheim Orange apples, his favourite. I chop one of the miserable-looking apples into pieces, place them on the tray with the whisky bottle and a glass of water to dilute. 'It's only midnight,' I say. 'Plenty of hours left to write.'

'Ah, but . . .' Here Ronnie is shy, apologetic. His mouth tucks under a little as he asks: 'I wondered if you'd mind terribly, darling, if I stayed over? I can't quite face fixing that puncture tonight in the rain, if you won't let me bring the bike into the kitchen. I do have a puncture kit so I promise I'll be off first thing in the morning.'

I nod, trying to seem as if I don't mind the disruption. Ronnie knows me too well for that.

'How many words today?' he says.

'It's been a strange day, I guess. I couldn't settle.'

He nods. No need to explain to Ronnie how it is.

'The only useful thing I did was rethink the title. *A Lark at Dawn* is goddamn-awful. *The Schizophrenic We* – what d'you think of that?'

In fact, I've only just thought of it. And I'm not sure it's any good either, and Ronnie agrees.

He purses his mouth and shakes his head.

'Sorry, darling. I don't like it.'

We both sip our whisky.

'Well, Pat, you've made it very homely in here.'

This is a joke. He strides again from kitchen to living room – to be nearer the fire. I see Bridge Cottage through his eyes. Plain beige lining of the green velvet curtains, drawn closed. The lamp craned over my typewriter. Books in a slow, overflowing ooze from opened boxes to floor. My desk a litter of ashtray, half-empty glass, the core of an apple, another saucer of snails. The television set, looking awfully dead when it's not switched on.

The orange flames of the fire snap merrily and I seize on this:

'It's cosy enough now you're here.'

This seems suddenly to be a flirtatious remark, though I didn't mean it to be. Ronnie's blue eyes glow at the compliment. He crosses his knee in the leather chair; I perch on the sofa. A loud plop from a drop of water falls into a glass bowl I've placed on the floor in one corner of the room. Ronnie looks at it questioningly.

'How on earth is rain getting in *there*?' he asks.

'Not rain. The upstairs bathroom. Plumber's coming tomorrow to fix it.'

'Let me,' Ronnie says, and goes upstairs.

I follow him up at once. 'No need. Man from Framlingham is coming first thing.'

Ronnie is in the bathroom, doing something with the ball-cock. He stands on the lid to reach the black cistern above his head, rolls up his sleeves and comes back downstairs to rummage in my toolbox – horribly close to the Black & Decker in its own black box – and then goes back up again. I follow him at one step every time, saying: 'Leave it, it's late, why bother?' but then he pulls the long chain and flushes the lavatory and the gushing sounds cease. He dries his arms on the guest towel.

'There.' He smiles. 'Why pay good money for that?'

I'm not smiling. He sees my expression and stretches out a hand to touch my cheek. 'Pats, sorry. What is it?'

His touch makes me want to bite his fingers, like a cat. Instead I grab them and kiss them.

Ronnie allows it, smiles, and strokes my hair with his free hand.

'Such a funny mood you're in this evening,' he remarks. His face is close and our eyes meet. Suddenly he looks startled, frightened even, and I have to step back, wondering what he saw there. We're now on the landing and in sight of my bedroom, the door open, the bed with its crumpled silky counterpane on the floor in a pool of emerald green. I somehow don't want to get back in there on my own so I say to Ronnie: 'Come with me. Let me see you undress.'

This is not the first time. But it was long, long ago, and surprise now rolls over Ronnie's face. It was the time of his essay on George Crabbe, his obsession with where Crabbe's leech pond might have been. The era of his experiment with the siren voices of fiction.

'So sad, tonight, aren't we?' he says, and kisses my forehead. But he obliges, following me into the room, undoing the belt of his khaki pants, and unbuttoning his shirt, then stepping out of the white shorts, his suntanned ease in his body that of a man who spends hours swimming naked in rivers, who works shirtless chopping wood in his garden. But my room is cold and he leaps, shivering, under the covers, tossing the pants from his foot and almost tripping in his haste to get warm. I take off my bathrobe and watch him lie there smiling as I take off the pyjamas and climb slowly in beside him.

'So beautiful you are,' he says. Again, not for the first time. The bedside lamp is switched on, the bedside table at Ronnie's side of the bed (Sam's side is how I think of it), and Ronnie moves to switch it off, but I put my hand over his.

'Let me look at you,' I say. He sits up; the covers rest at his waist. My hand traces the light fur of his chest, then I murmur: 'Ronnie, what's the worst thing you've ever done?'

I put my head down to kiss him on his sternum, his tiny pink nipples. Ronnie's body is smooth, carved, like a fine boat, like a canoe that has been sanded and sanded, then further scribed by the sea. All wood and sunshine and heat – how hot men always are, compared to women – honest edges and muscle. He smells like the oil from his bike, and the smoke from the fire, and the tart green apples he's been eating, and the fine healthy sweat of the cyclist, of one who sleeps deeply and well. As I kiss him, planting one after another soft, small kiss on his chest down to his belly button, he strokes my hair. I know from the way he does this that he is trying to soothe me, dissuade, not charge up. I can't see his face just now so I try again:

'Have you ever been so low you thought of suicide? You remember I told you that two of my girlfriends took it up, and one was rather successful.'

Ronnie says nothing, but he follows my eyes to the portrait of me that Allela did and says: 'Your friend who painted you back in the forties? She had – prescience. You look about the age you are now. And you certainly look cross with her.'

I stare back at us from the wall, fierce in my red jacket, a frown line between my eyes. *Yes, I will live a long life, and I will always be angry with you, Allela, for abandoning yours. Abandoning me.*

'Twenty years. The irony . . . In the end, after downing the acid, Allela recovered in hospital and was sorry! Her girlfriend told me that. I never went to see her. She'd slipped into a coma and died by the time I heard.' And it wasn't my fault, everyone kept saying. Our relationship was long over by then. But I re-read her letters to me, and she came back to me with such vividness. Sweet little Allela, with her bug eyes in her glasses, like some kind of insect. I should have tried harder; I should have understood.

'I read your novel,' I tell Ronnie. 'I love the way you talk of the boys in the school, that line about being neither shy nor respectful of death, only disgusted.'

'Well, if you did read my manuscript,' Ronnie sounds rather pleased, 'you'll remember the line where the old girl says these days she wishes we still traded in nuances rather than amateur psychology.'

Ah. I smile, opening my mouth a little against the warm skin of his stomach. *Touché*. So clever, Ronnie. So enclosed. So private.

'Did you ever *steal* anything? Ever really want to *hurt* somebody?' I persist.

'Of course I've wanted to,' Ronnie says. 'It's not a bit the same as *doing* it, is it?'

I sit up, feeling danger swell close beside me, hover at my face. 'I went into the garden today to try to – kill some snails. I wanted to see if I could do it. See what it felt like to snuff out the life of something, a living thing . . .'

Tears hammer at my eyes as I feel it again, the horrible crunching, the jelly-life oozing out and the strange sadness, the inevitability of how I felt about myself as I looked at the little crushed shell my hand. I'm just as Mother always said. Sick. And evil.

I lift my face to his and our eyes meet. It seems to me that Ronnie sees all, sniffs out my soul, my darkest little-girl past, but – what? What does he do with the information, the knowledge? He draws in his antennae and retreats.

'I worked on my book today,' he says. 'I was at the church, talking to Tender.'

I picture the church, perhaps the same one he took me to, with the huge blowy churchyard, the lichen on the church tower, and on the drowned sailors' tombs. 'Of course, Tender's not his name. The gravedigger. He inherited it from his father, but it's not his real name.'

I press myself against Ronnie, crush my breasts against his chest. He's unmoved. He smiles – he laughs at me, actually, with a kind of sunny beauty, but he's unmoved. I shift slightly away. And now he's laughed at me, should I give up? Because Ronnie either has no ugliness inside him (I think this is true) or he has no access to it. Both states bore me.

'Tender's been digging graves since he was twelve years old. Before his voice broke! The work never upset him, he took it in his stride. Graves are my vocation, he says.'

Now Ronnie laughs again, a gusty, genuine chuckle, and switches off the light. He shuffles himself further down in the bed, and I rest my head on his chest and continue to stroke him, compulsively, my hand straying deep into the rougher hair beneath his stomach, but not quite that far.

'He says that he's buried one woman three times. She keeps cheating death and giving them all a shock. His point is: using a mirror is no good. You should put a piece of cotton where the lips part and if there's the least bit of wind it will flutter. And he says he can always tell from the eyes. When seeing has ended.'

When seeing has ended. I think of my snails again. And a terrapin that Mother once cooked in a pot of boiling water for a stew. Watching the agonised creature frantically scrabbling to escape – Mother humming happily, reaching for a spoon, the same way she would have twinked out my life, given half a chance: washing me away, drowning me in turpentine.

And now Ronnie is talking softly, and consolingly, of death. I listen to his heart beating and the vibrations in his ribcage.

'Dust to dust, they say. More like mud to mud. Half the graves round here are waterlogged. Foxton is a terrible wet place.'

I keep my hand compulsively moving on Ronnie's warm skin. I plunge, daringly, with my naughty, wilful, transgressive hand. But there's no desire for me there: just softness, Ronnie's sweet kindness, his tender pity for me. I think of the phone booth suddenly, with its brambles and bushes, the heated conversations trapped inside the closed glass door. Ronnie sleepily comments that the gravedigger didn't read, didn't like to think too hard, had seen death so often, every day of his life, that his own wish was simply to be cremated – ashes thrown straight into the air. Then Ronnie's breathing grows deeper, with a nasal vibration at the end, and I know he is asleep. Dear, sweet Ronnie. The war has washed over him, over all of them in this little place, left its residue. He believes in art, as I do. And now he wants only to sleep.

Sam rings at 10 a.m. as arranged; she sounds cold; wary. The booth smells of wet grass, cats and blackberry leaves. The glass panes are faintly furred with green; a beer bottle knocks against the toe of my shoe. I can barely hear her words, between gulps and sniffing and great long inhalations of breath.

'Is Minty there?' I ask. A sound that seems to be 'no'. Have the police been? Yes. In person? Yes, two of them. A man and a woman. Young. Horrible. What did they say?

'They found the – the clothes, you know. And the car. Early this morning. And they wanted to know if he was – if I thought he was – depressed.'

'What did you say?'

'I said no. I said I don't know!' she wails.

I guess this crying is good. The hysterics will make it all look authentic; if her husband had just gone missing, she would certainly be upset. I try some soothing words, but my mind is elsewhere, on the problem of the stained rug, which Ronnie has now seen rolled up and leaning against the stairs, and which I need to get out of the house by some means, just in case. In case of any visit.

'Did they ask you anything else? Where you'd been for the weekend? Did you mention me?'

'I said I left Saturday lunchtime and he was fine then. That he drove me to the station to get the train to Ipswich and his golf clubs were in the car and I'd thought he was going – golfing. They didn't ask me your address; they didn't seem concerned about that. That when I got back Sunday and he wasn't there I reported him missing.'

'Maybe you should have hinted. Not so fine. A girl at work. The argument you had, you know . . .'

'What?'

'Told them about the fight between you. So that – they have a reason.'

She simply sobs. She tells me she has to go, she has to ring the school and let them know, and then she cries: 'What to tell Minty, oh, what do I say to Minty?'

'Well, at this stage he's only missing, it's only the clothes they've found, so keep it from her for now. Yes, keep it from her,' I say. 'At this stage Gerald might turn up.'

'*What?*'

'I mean, for all we know he might. That's what we would be thinking if . . .'

Through the broken pane of the telephone booth I glance over at Bridge Cottage. A cobweb strokes my face; a pheasant is call- ing somewhere, repeatedly; a bus appears at the top of the road, on its cosy, normal way to Framlingham. Tra-la. How life in a village goes on! Then I see Mrs Ingham appear at the front door of Bridge House, which, being higher up than mine, situated on a small raised incline, can be seen easily from the booth. She puts two empty milk bottles on her step, bending stiffly to place them in a wire crate with *No Milk Today Thank you* and *Silver Top Please* all pre-written on little cards that simply need turning. She picks up a package the mailman has left for her. She's fully dressed and she returns in a moment wearing a navy coat, clutch- ing a red purse, a pillbox hat pinned to her head, and her little dog, Reggie, yapping away and tugging on the lead beside her. Promising. Maybe I can put the rolled rug in the car while she's out.

'I have to go. I'll call tomorrow. Same time. Honey, try to . . . It'll be OK.'

Sam is still crying when I replace the black telephone in its cradle. I should have been kinder, but I'm distracted, heart pumping a little. This may be my only chance. I nip back into the house and carry the rolled-up rug out to the car, pressing my face against its ghastly roughness and smell. Opening the trunk, I flop it down and shove it across the back, but there is a prominent spare wheel in there and very little room: the trunk won't close. I have to find the mechanism that allows me to push down one of the back seats and dump the rug across it. I glance up and down the street: only the mailman still making his rounds, up ahead, his back to me. Bits of carpet underlay, like black moths, flutter all over the road and cling to my clothes as I'm manoeuvring it. I see the departing figure of Mrs Ingham and her dumb little dog trotting up the street; she doesn't look back.

Next problem, where the hell to take it? What do the English do with their old carpets and rugs? I certainly know where I can *buy* a rug – Abbott's, the large, barn-like second-hand furniture place in Debenham, if I want to replace it – but getting rid of it is much trickier. I jump in the car, aware that the rug is visible to anyone glancing in through the window. Well, that's fine, isn't it, at this stage? I'm just a householder getting rid of an unwanted rug.

Virginia Smythson-Balby is suddenly tapping on the window at the driver's side. Holy crap! What's the idea of turning up like that every five minutes?

'Hello! Miss Highsmith! Going out for the day? I wonder if you have time for a word? It's about the interview – Miss Highsmith. I've spoken to Frances. Would this Friday be a possibility? I'm sorry it's such awfully short notice.'

'Friday's fine.' I jump in the car, making it clear I'm in a hurry. This seems to make her smile. Or something in my behaviour does.

'At two p.m. I'll drive you down there, if you like, as she's a friend of mine,' she says. 'That is, unless—'

'Huh? Oh, sure. See you Friday.'

I begin winding the window up. She gives me a startled expression through the spotted glass and then another big smile. Her perfume gusts in through the window. I turn the key in the ignition and pull away from her. In the side mirror I see that she is waving happily, a coat with some sort of silver fox fur collar up to her neck, as if she just secured a coup of some sort. I'm right about her being hipped on me. Damn her: what did I just agree to?

The fields round here, deserted though they are, seem somehow filled with patrolling farmers. I have an idea to drive to the dockland area in Ipswich. For some cock-eyed reason the docks appeal to me. The old gasworks and the Cobbold Brewery, this area glimpsed only once, the time when I was lost with Sam after picking her up from the train station, has the dirtiness and industry that I need: people moving things around, shifting things, dumping things. I seem to remember seeing giant vats and skips for garbage. I'll just plonk the rug in one of those. Easier to look innocent in an industrial setting than a deserted rural one.

The sumptuous colours of the trees and fields start to lift my mood as I drive. There is a whiff of rot in the air: leaves, apples. I sing a Doris Day number . . . and picture Gerald for a moment, the great lunk whistling as he put his golf clubs into the car, fooling around and reckoning on a jolly weekend with his buddies. This thought produces a pang of something but I can't tell what. Then I think: He wasn't in golf slacks when he arrived at Bridge Cottage. Does that matter? Does it have any bearing? Would he have been? Should I have thought of that? Also, why didn't the police ask Sam for the address she was visiting at the weekend? Wouldn't they at some point ask her about that? Then again, no reason to get nettled, the story is this: Gerald didn't care a hang about golf, he's been having trouble with a mistress, or several (or work, something dodgy there, wasn't there a hint of some bad dealings, some investigation, who knows what?) and, worse, he has long suspected his wife is in love with some arty-farty guy, so he drives to the coast in a half cracked state and does away with himself – why Aldeburgh? Is it near the golf course, perhaps, and a last-minute change of plan? I pass the green-painted water pump. Crows squawk overhead like village busybodies. I drive towards the sky of graded blue as if into a screen of dip-dyed cloth. It reminds me of a scarf Sam has. And now I'm thinking: Some day soon I'd like to wrap her in that scarf, in nothing but that vivid, violet-blue gauzy material, blazing the colour of a Texan bluebonnet in spring and then slowly unwind her, twirl her until she is fully undone.

They found the body. It was in the *Ipswich Star. Man, missing for over a week, found washed up near Martello tower. His car was found at Aldeburgh; his clothes and belongings recovered on the beach. Believed to be Gerald Gosforth, senior partner at a London bank* . . .

Sam doesn't think I should come to the funeral and we have a fight on the telephone, which I win.

'You hardly knew him. It will look odd,' she says.

I know she's right but my motives are complicated. I feel tightly wound, like a ball of cotton. I can't risk not being there. I have to keep some kind of vigil over Sam. Maybe she'll betray us with a look, some comment, a gesture. I *have* to be there. A voice inside me screams, *I wouldn't have dreamed of doing this if there were any other way* . . .

A rooster crows somewhere as I leave the phone booth. I'm nervy, strung out, and I'm going to be this way for a good twenty-four hours. I find a black leather vest – what do the French call it? A *gilet* – to wear with a skirt and white shirt and plain flat shoes, and I know that I look . . . well, not exactly the toast of the fleet. Lumpen, more like a ranch-hand in drag, but there's nothing I can do about that.

Ronnie needs a ride and I'm glad of the company. He knew Gerald a little, and he knows Sam. He will notice my sweating hands on the wheel, my lip permanently folded under my tooth (Ronnie notices everything) but, being him, he will assume it's just my shyness, my dread of social occasions, my fear of my love affair with Sam being detected, and put no further spin on it. I am Sam's friend, after all (well, Ronnie knows it's more than that but that's OK), the friend she was staying with during the weekend when her husband went missing.

A surprising number of people are here. A couple of other writers. People from the bank. Parents of Minty's friends. The Dixons. The Polk-Faradays. Neighbours, friends from the bridge club. Golf buddies. Gerald's much-envied younger brother, Hugh, the one who worked in the publishing world: a skinnier, more ridiculous version of him in a shiny suit and glasses that perch on the edge of his nose, giving him the look of a parson. We're at Sam's place, back from the crematorium. Damned good luck that cremation was what Gerald plumped for in his will. Once he is ashes no one can examine the head; no further clues can ever be uncovered. And because of the shame, the whisper of suicide, the coroner's questions have been hasty and respectful, Sam said. His opinion was that the law should be as Christian as allowed, under the circumstances, Ronnie repeated to me. No post-mortem was suggested by the coroner: there has been a certain haste.

My heart is drumming its tattoo and I pull the leather *gilet* around it, as if others in the room might see. I'm watching Sam, while trying to look as if I'm not. My hands tremble around a tiny glass of sherry, which threatens to slip from them. And Sam? Where is she? She's wearing a simple black silk number, elegant as ever, and lizard-skin high heels. I'm conscious of her even when not watching, as if she's the only lit thing in the room, and always in my peripheral sight. Is she acting naturally? Is she saying the right things? The answer is no, she's acting like an automaton, like a zombie; she's stiff and slightly crazed, her nose too powdered, her blonde hair too rigidly pinned in its bun. But that's fine, that's fine, no one will expect otherwise. *Who is she talking to now? What is she saying? Did that woman just glance over at me? Was my name mentioned?*

The smoke from my cigarette drifts upwards, slow and unbroken. Sam goes to talk to another little group – an older couple, perhaps relatives. My heart jumps. *Who are they? What is she saying now?*

No one will be surprised either that I'm sitting here alone, sipping at this tiny tot of sherry, blowing out smoke. That is what's known about me. Reclusive. Unfriendly. What does it matter how they describe it to themselves, if they think of me at all, which I've learned to persuade myself is unlikely. 'Nobody is thinking about *you*,' Mother used to say, when I used shyness as an alibi.

Minty is passing round little plates of cakes with disgusting coconut shreds on top. She shook everyone's hand as we arrived, including mine, and said solemnly: 'Thank you for coming.' She didn't meet my eye and I was glad, because the hand she held was slippery with sweat, and my eyes, I felt, were frightened. At any rate, she has the same handshake as her father: snatching only your fingers and letting go as soon as she picks up your hand, as if it's hot to the touch.

At the crematorium I relaxed for a moment. I thought: That ridiculous curtain, the music blaring, the rigmarole. What are people protecting themselves from seeing? And I thought of Ronnie's gravedigger, Tender, who buries nearly two hundred people a year. Brother Death. Does he have some secret knowledge the rest of us don't? A more precious take on life because he's closer to death every day and sees how it is? You could say the same about writers who write about death. Trying to face it down, but failing every time. Words aren't death – typing them doesn't move you closer. If anything, it makes it more fanciful, takes the teeth and claws out because you've captured it and survived, pinned it to the page. That late-night tremor, the quake you feel when you get a *real* glimpse. That just edged further away.

And then the thought flies suddenly at me: Where *is* Gerald? His face flashes up for me with details I'd forgotten I knew, a small pock-sized scar under one eye, pale lashes, a rather fat mouth, a little obscene. Are you really gone, then, *really* and for ever? It makes me shudder, thinking that Gerald feels more vivid, horribly nearer than ever.

And if anyone cared to question me, ask, am I different now? Sure, I'm special, because it puts you in a very small minority, a small percentage of the human population who've done what you've done. I can just imagine what others – weaker types – would like to ask me, and it's all about regrets. Well, naturally, I regret the loss of a human life. But you have to understand. The man was despicable. It was the heat of the moment. He was raping his wife and not for the first time either. You think a man can't rape his own wife? Well, I'm here to tell you he can.

They'd *so* like to ask me, Miss Highsmith, could you ever see yourself, you know, committing another murder?

Well, I'd hope not to, of course. But under certain circumstances . . .

And at any rate. Murder is a tricky thing. Sometimes we dress people up in certain clothes and outfits, soldiers, executioners, abortionists, and say: It's OK for you to take a life. But not for others. Not for others to exercise their own judgement. Only those we decree. How does a judge, a man who has sent dozens of people to Old Sparky, how does he square his conscience at night? And maybe, just maybe, those ideas are conventions, ideas that change with the era and the situation. One time or place illegal, unthinkable; another time, another place, not.

Sam moves around the room as if she's on castors or sliding on ice. She's wearing the lapis-lazuli pendant I bought her, the heavy point of blue on a gold chain slipping just inside the neckline of her black dress. Now some woman – who is it? Perhaps someone from the bank, someone from Gerald's work – is kissing her and they are putting their cheeks together for a moment while the woman hugs her. I sit a little more upright. *The more you thought about killing, the more you thought about living. There were six Turkish boys and we butchered them right quick*. Ronnie's book. His interviews with people from his village. They're all obsessed with the war, as if it was yesterday. Not even the Second World

War: some of the old men in the village are still talking about Gallipoli, the Somme. 'My mate went off like a firework,' one says. 'All the cartridges strapped to his chest were exploding.' *The more you thought about killing, the more you thought about living.* Ronnie lets me read the drafts. I don't know what to say. Ronnie's book is so far from what I'm writing. I would never let him read my drafts but he doesn't mind. I just tell him the word count.

Fear trickles through me as I realise someone just asked me something. It's Charles Latimer. He apparently knows I'm living in Suffolk and is saying something like did I see the Beatles at the Gaumont Theatre in Ipswich last year? 'Do I look like someone who would care for the Beatles?' I ask, not bothering to explain that I have only been in Suffolk for a few months. Charles laughs. 'Ah, darling, how I've missed you!' he says. I pretend not to know what he means. Then, to provoke me further, he leans in close and says: 'I believe the Beatles are back in Ipswich this very month. Young women are already queuing for tickets . . .' He turns away, chuckling, to greet a young publicist with buck teeth and cheeks dusted with the desiccated coconut. I stay seated, rigid, my cigarette done, nothing to do with my hands. But he turns back to me and continues in a quieter voice: 'Dear Gerry was depressed, wasn't he? I could see it. He mentioned a few times, something about her "spending a lot of time away". What do you think?'

'I can't talk just now!' I say, and leap up, leaving him staring after me. Is it my imagination, or does Sam shoot me a frightened glance from somewhere in the room?

Such a strange, strange child aren't you, my Patsy? I'm cursed to know you!

Mother. Why is Mother's voice never far away?

In Sam's elegant bathroom I lock the door. I splash my face with cold water, sit on the closed seat of the John, my head in my hands. I splash more cold water on my face and then notice it's making dark wet spots on my blouse and am reminded suddenly of the wetness of the bottom of my blue jeans, of the sea sloshing into my car. Maybe Sam has a pill in that medicine cabinet I can take. I fan my face with one hand. I stare at myself in the mirrored cabinet: I look terrified. I see myself talking to some solemn grey bewigged judge, an English judge, and saying: *Sam had nothing to do with it. Leave her out of it. She took a lot from him and, matter of fact, it was me who snapped . . . m' lord.*

The room swims a little and I wish I'd brought the sherry in here with me for a top-up. It's all black and white hexagonal floor tiles, oversized white bathtub with feet, and blue glass bottles, high windows pouring in light. The contrivance of it, the schematic colours in here surprise me. Blue towels, blue china soap dish. I'm stung suddenly: what must Sam think when she comes to mine, where she's lucky if there's a clean towel and a new bar of Wrights Coal Tar soap? Oh, Sam, oh, Sam. How will she cope? Sure she's cool, she's a holder of secrets, ordinarily, but is she up to the task? My heart beats wildly. I find I'm staring at the bottles in Sam's cabinet. I don't know if I'm thinking of anything at all except that.

A bottle of Fenjal Creme Bath – my heart is going like sixty. Plix by L'Oréal, 'for a double-life set' – the phrase from the ad comes back to me, and the stiffness of Sam's hair today. A tin of Cuticura. I really must catch a breath, drink some water. A box of Lil-Lets. A wrapped bar of Imperial Leather soap. A jar of Endocil beauty treatment cream – I open this and sniff it and, yes, this smells like Sam, like her cheek when I kiss it. Senocal sleeping pills. (Her doctor's name, written on the side, is Dr Death I think at first, incredulously, then squint again and see that the writing says Dr Deacon.) Morny Lily of the Valley talcum powder and the packaging for some bath tablets, empty. Elizabeth Arden lipstick, colour Sheik: a sort of tasteful pink that Sam leaves in mouth-shaped blots everywhere, on wine glasses or white china cups. Something makes me gasp, blurs my eyes with tears. In a box, some contraceptive jelly and a plastic scallop-shaped container with her diaphragm in it.

I close the cabinet, put my hands over my eyes. *Of course, of course*. She said they rarely made love but – well, what married lover admits otherwise? (A horrible flash here, Gerald's white ass, his pants puddling around his ankles.) There are voices outside the bathroom door, perhaps raised voices. A tremor of alarm streaks through me. My hand is shaking as I go to flush the John, aware that I've been in here awhile. Just outside the bathroom door is the woman who was hugging Sam earlier. She gives me a condescending smile (she's wearing a grisly shade of peach lipstick) as I pass her on the landing.

'Are you all right?' the woman says, and I force myself to nod and say, 'Sure, fine, thank you.'

The son of a bitch is dead now, I tell myself. The Problem, such as it was, is over. There Sam is, downstairs – I peek over the banister (this upstairs landing is all muted colours, lilac and grey) – talking to a friend from the bridge club; her fine ankles in her lizard heels, her simple, elegant, understated silk dress, her necklace dripping down the front of it, disappearing between her breasts. We're free to carry on now, everything is fine, we can begin at last, begin again, start afresh. I stare at my hands – my big hands, how Mother always laughed at them – and they're gripping the banister like they intend to break it. Notes from a piano plonk up to me: Minty, no doubt, playing for the guests. Good God! Is there no end to the torture that child must endure? Why can't you leave the poor girl alone, get off her back for one goddamn minute?

I take a deep breath. Several. I release my hands from the banister and the wood has made red marks on my palms. I smooth down the shirt beneath my leather *gilet*. I put one hand into the pocket of my skirt, reaching for the snail, take it out to check on it. Some nacreous silvery patches gleam among the workaday brown. It's an ordinary garden snail, a moist body the colour of milky coffee. It pulls in its horns – its little eyes on telescopes – and I slip it back into my pocket.

No one is looking up here. Sam has gone to have a lie-down, I hear someone say. I have to believe in her, that's all. There will be months, maybe years, of this. It's just as I once said: I'm alone forever. I could scream over the banister at the top of my voice: I did it, I killed the bastard, and all the faces below would tilt up to me . . . like petals turning to the sun.

But I won't. I'm smoothing down my shirt. I'm walking back downstairs and I'm about to say to Ronnie that I have a headache, that I don't care to stay. I'd like to go home now.

And so Friday afternoon arrives and the damned girl turns up perky as ever to drive me to London. Why I didn't insist on driving myself I can't now remember, but too late, I have to endure a couple of hours of her blatting at me. She puts my bag in the car with a quizzical look: a weekend bag – am I planning to stay over? I shake my head – so nosy! – and she slams the trunk with a flourish. And today she's wearing a caramel-coloured leather jacket, a suede skirt, cream satin blouse and achingly bright yellow scarf tied round her ponytail. Also jingling necklace and huge hoop earrings. She passes me her cigarettes and asks if I'd like the roof closed. It's windy: of course I'd like the fucking roof closed.

As she's driving I'm thinking about Ronnie's warning. Where did he get the idea she was a biographer? And how can I find out if he's right and head her off at the pass?

'Is it going well, then, your novel?' she says, after a noisy suck on her cigarette and a ridiculously exaggerated exhalation of smoke. The painted nails, frosty pink, tap on the steering-wheel and she keeps admiring them.

The most banal question ever. I guess it will get me in practice for the goddamn interview ahead.

'I've changed the title twice already. But I do know it will be a suspense novel without a murder in it.'

'Is it set in America? Or here in Suffolk?'

'An American man is married to an English woman, living in a house very like Bridge Cottage. And he fantasises all the time about killing her, and the reader isn't sure whether he really does, or whether he simply imagines it and she goes missing or perhaps commits suicide. That's what I'm writing at the moment, at any rate. There might be a murder by the end.'

'Not the prowler one?' she asks. I'm surprised she remembered. I'm tempted to say: Didn't you realise it was a lie? I was deflecting you, but I let it go.

I try to indicate then, with a sort of hunkering down deeper into my seat, that I don't want to talk more, but the damn girl is inured to subtlety and blithely carries on.

'I'm glad you're setting it in Suffolk! I thought I saw you in Aldeburgh last weekend. Very late – Friday, or was it Saturday night? Were you there? I think it was you. You were with a friend, a woman, though I only saw you from the back, just getting into your car . . .'

I dive forward suddenly, head on my knees, then put my hand on the car door handle. Smythson-Balby glances worriedly across at me and rapidly changes down a couple of gears.

'I'm sorry – I feel a little car sick,' I mutter.

'Oh dear. You do look – pale . . .'

She pulls into a lay-by and wrenches up the handbrake. I jump out of my side and am sick, loudly and ingloriously, into some brambles. Thorns snag at my shirt as I climb back into the car and a purple blot appears on the sleeve where a late, leftover berry squished itself against me.

'Damn!' I say, twisting the material round a little, to study it.

'Oh dear.' Smythson-Balby rummages in her purse and flourishes an embroidered handkerchief at me. I think I notice a family crest of some sort.

'Go ahead – spit on it,' she says. More tempting than she could possibly know.

I dab dubiously at the vivid mark on my sleeve and am not surprised when there is no impact whatsoever. She starts up the engine again.

'Terribly sorry! I really am. I'll drive slowly. I used to get terribly car-sick as a girl. Daddy said I had to sit in the front and stare straight ahead. Maybe that will help.'

I'm still pressing the dampened handkerchief to the stain on my sleeve, pretending to be more concerned than I really am about it; hoping to distract her. A cold prickling creeps around my hairline, as if someone was enclosing it in an icy brace. If she feels guilty for her damned awful driving, or worried that she's made me fret, which will make the interview difficult, perhaps it will take her mind off what she just said about Aldeburgh. Though I have a contrary desire to probe her about it – what did she see, exactly? What time was it? (It must have been when we were returning to my car, about to drive home together. What on earth was she doing in Aldeburgh in the early hours of the morning? Did she see us from a house window, or another car, or was she actually out and about somewhere near the beach? Surely she would have mentioned Gerald, at any rate, if she'd seen that a man, a drunk, was propped up – dragged like an effigy – between us and left behind! Or if she'd seen me stride out into the sea with him, fully dressed.)

This is my one moment to ask further questions about her comment, and for it to seem natural, to discover whether the remark was innocent or not, what she saw and what she would say if ever asked about it (by the police, for example). If I raise it later it will surely look contrived and betray anxiety. But the moment passes. She moves on to other baloney – chit-chat about where we're heading for in Soho to do the interview, and then a lot of garbage about a pirate station called Radio Caroline, which is broadcast from a ship off the coast of Suffolk, pretty close to us, in fact: have I a radio and have I listened to it? And how she can't admit to this woman – some distant relative – who is going to interview me, Frances, that she listens to it, when it's, you know, illegal, and stuff, and Frances works for the BBC . . .

And so the journey goes, with the harvested fields looking

disgustingly bleached and shaved; exposed. Naked. Smythson-Balby's nose could use some powder. My dread of the grilling ahead intensifies with every mile.

We arrive at the bar in Frith Street at ten minutes to two, after a ridiculous amount of time spent finding a parking space. We emerge onto the street, press a buzzer, beside a black, unprepossessing door. Smythson-Balby announces herself in an insufferably silly voice into a button, then we trudge up some stairs to a small landing and a room behind it with dark wood, and smoke, and visible whisky bottles at the bar, and a masculine air: the first good sign of the day. Smythson-Balby shuffles her backside into a red leather chair beside me and – it's too much, I mean, I really have been a paragon of restraint – I burst out: 'You're not staying for the interview?'

Smythson-Balby's eyes widen innocently as she plays for time, retying the yellow scarf around her ponytail. 'No, of course not. I thought I'd just do the – the introductions, you know. And then I'll – I can come back here and drive you to the BBC for the next part. How does that sound?'

'At any rate, I can get a cab on my own.'

'Oh, it's no trouble!'

I bet. She takes out her cigarettes and offers me one. And then, just as she's fumbling to light mine for me, a small woman with dark clothes, a skirt suit in a strange style of inexplicable randomness, a hat with black feathers and a kind of tippet that seems to be feathers too – so many flounces and flutters – strides over to us. A crow or a raven, I picture at once, hopping around a lump of road kill. Me.

'Frances!' Smythson-Balby leaps up.

'Who else?' the tiny woman growls.

I stand up and hands are offered, drinks ordered and chairs shuffled. The feathered hat and tippet are removed and Frances reduces significantly in size but not volume, revealing rather shorn, reddish-brown hair capping her head. And then Smythson-Balby wriggles her arms back into her caramel-coloured leather jacket and says she'll see me downstairs in front of the black door in around an hour. She looks as if she wants to say more, wants – I'd guess – to offer some half-assed reassurance of some kind, maybe even an apology, but thankfully thinks better of it. Her bouncy derrière disappears down the stairs.

Two Scotch and sodas are brought. Frances accepts a cigarette. On the table in front of her is a copy of the new newspaper the Brits keep going on about: the *Sun*. She taps it with her fingertips and says, 'Ghastly rag, have you seen it?' before stretching over to slap it onto another table. She speaks in a smoker's dry voice, one of those crispy voices that suggest an old, used-up throat. I guess she does a lot more talking than listening.

'So what has our little Ginny told you about me?' she asks.

I shake my head.

'Isn't she a cutie?' the woman continues. I refuse to rise to her bait, even to give her the benefit of letting on that I know what she's talking about. A pause; the woman inhales, blows a smoke-ring. I expect her beady green eyes to be on me – glance at her to see if she's appraising me – but find her instead fiddling in her pocket book for a mirror, flipping it open, rubbing at one eye with a finger, removing a smudge of flicked-up black eye-liner. She snaps the compact away.

'I'm a biographer,' she says, then goes on to name her books: a couple of writers I've never heard of and one woman novelist I *have* read. 'I know more about that woman than any person alive,' she adds.

'Did you meet her?' I ask, as I met her once, too, at a party, and remembered her as shy, a woman who wanted to melt into the cloakroom and vanish into the boots and cast-off furs.

'Didn't need to. She's a phoney. I can't stand phoneys,' Frances says. She tosses back her Scotch, bangs the empty glass down on the table. 'I've read all your novels, of course. It wasn't my idea – the interview. I've done a few for the Beeb before. It was Ginny.

She discovered where you were living. Little thing was so excited. Near popped, she did.'

The English vowels are the same sounds Sam makes. But here the grating is intense.

'I'm from Sussex,' she says, reading my mind. 'But I certainly know Texas and New York, the places you grew up. Daddy was an ambassador. We travelled. Rome, Venice, Paris. I know all the places you know awfully well.'

I know more about that woman than any person alive. And yet not bothering to meet her. In a few years she's going to be saying the same thing about me. I remember dimly that the woman novelist we're talking about had an affair with a friend of mine, back in the late forties, guy named Don. 'Did you speak to Don Parkin about her?' I ask.

'Ah, him – he knew nothing,' is the barked reply.

'But how can anyone know everything?' I venture, stuttering. 'I happen to have— A friend of mine is in analysis. Every week, talks her heart out. Every week for five years. I'm sure that shrink – she happens to be a woman – *thinks* she knows everything about my friend. And, boy, is she wrong. Here's one thing she doesn't know: my friend's husband is a terrifying son of a bitch and she's feared for her life more than once, but *that* she doesn't talk about—'

'Maybe he doesn't beat her up and your friend is lying to you,' she interrupts, clearly unable to listen to another person for more than one minute.

I am a little startled by the interruption but I carry on.

'My point is, does that shrink – who thinks she knows everything, and certainly knows some secrets – but does that analyst *know* her?'

'Well, but see, that's shrinks for you. I'm a biographer. Better than a shrink. More like a *detective*. Looking for clues . . .'

'Is the life itself a crime, then? Your metaphor rather implies it.'

'Ha! *Touché!*' She clinks her empty glass with mine and her eyes glitter; she's enjoying this.

I give it one more stuttering go at explaining.

'You might – you might read the diaries, say, know all the facts of their lives, birthdates, where they went to school, all the details and dates. And still if you have no – no imagination, maybe if you haven't plumbed your own depths, you know nothing. Then another person with insight, intuition – or the gift of *imagining* . . . *that* person might get closer. Knowing someone is not about knowing *everything*, every little detail, anyways a crazy impossibility, it's about intuiting the things that matter, the secrets and—'

'Baloney,' she says.

And I'm thinking in fury: Me, for instance. That's my gift. I'm like Mark Twain: I know that folks are like the moon – all of them have a dark side and it only takes me five minutes to winkle it out. What's Frances's dark side, then? Not much hidden, that's too easy. She's a parasite, a vampire: she only feels alive when she drinks the blood of others. And mine? Mine is so bottomless one book couldn't contain it. (Which is why I'm writing others.)

I take my own drink in tiny burning sips, trying to hide the shaking in my hands and shoulders. I'm thinking that those who *don't* have the skill of being able to make people come alive using only words and paper never appreciate how unique, how supernatural a gift it is. I'm pretending this is a playful discussion rather than a matter of life and death to me. Luckily, Frances is, as I suspected, so tuned out from the best clues a person gives that she is hammering away regardless.

'Never like to be in once place long, hmm?' Frances is saying. Her hair is like a stiff wire brush and rather fascinating in its severity.

Back on safer ground. I swallow hard and attempt a light tone: 'A few years. Suck all the juice out of a place and move on.'

'How are you finding Suffolk, then?' She guffaws, a great screeching laugh that opens its wings and flits all around the room. I try not to retreat too visibly, but I'm sure I somehow do, edging back further in my chair. She's loud. And she doesn't care.

She's noticed her empty glass at last and is now jerking it in the rudest way towards the young barmaid for another, making a cursory nod towards my glass too. I accept and, in a spirit of overcompensation, thank the girl profusely. She's pretty, with a wide mouth and a low neckline, and she beams back at me. The second Scotch goes down in a ribbon of fire and I find myself wanting to laugh.

'You may as well know I'm writing a book about you,' Frances says, after a further huge glug of Scotch. 'An unauthorised one, of course. And Ginny is doing an itty-bitty piece of research for me. I didn't feel the need to tell you – I didn't feel the need to meet you – because I know there's not a cat in hell's chance you'll give me your blessing.'

Ah. Does being right about Smythson-Balby in my suspicions, or at least finding an explanation for why she keeps materialising, change my feelings about her, make me less or more anxious? I check myself but find no answer.

'I guess I'm right? And you're flattered that I'm writing it,' the woman says.

'Why would I be flattered?'

'It will give you the status you need. Cement your reputation. As a subject of Frances Balby – no one will call you a blasted crime writer after that. You'll have your place, you know, where you'd like to be. In the canon or whatever you people call it.'

Now here I do feel something. A fizz. And I'm ashamed of myself, because it's pathetic and unworthy and because I've spent a lifetime saying I don't care. I deliberately conjure up Ronnie – so many conversations with him about *writing*, never about *being a writer*. Ronnie is my talisman, a sunny golden shield against what she offers: the devil's bargain, held out. It's not even possible, it's hopeless to desire it, yet she wants me here slavering because, after all, every writer craves it. This scrap: the *place in the canon*.

She finishes the second Scotch as quickly as the first and produces a notebook and fountain pen from the purse beside her, leaning under the table to do so, and spying mine.

'That's rather an extraordinary handbag. What do you keep in there?'

I consider telling her, and decide against it.

She waits for my answer then, seeing none is forthcoming, asks: 'So now that I have my cards on the table, are you planning to skedaddle? Skip the interview, the BBC?'

'No . . .' I say.

'Splendid. That I didn't expect. You're a push-over, then?' She cackles.

I tap my cigarette into the ashtray. No, not a pushover. Not at all.

'Good,' she says, folding the notebook open at the first clean page. 'I'll just do a few prelims. Then off with our saucy Ginny to La La Land it is. Two more Scotch and sodas, please.' And the mad black crow is once again there on the table, screeching, dancing and jubilantly shaking her wings.

There is a commissionaire at the entrance to the BBC building who greets us. Smythson-Balby is beside me, Frances a couple of steps behind, so I think this is probably a safe moment to peek at the snails in my purse. But, damn it – the clasp opens wide as I try to do this surreptitiously and the commissionaire catches sight of what's in there. Our eyes meet.

A head of lettuce, and six of my favourite snails, along with many of the babies – which look at the moment just like pieces of grit.

The commissionaire takes his cap off and readjusts it on his bald head. Wrinkles his nose at the fishy smell emanating from the opened purse, the pieces of dark slimed lettuce inside the damp brown paper. I close the purse quickly. I'm conscious of my pulse quickening.

'Well, I suppose you can take a lettuce into the studio,' he mumbles, in some sort of London accent.

Smythson-Balby gives him – and me – a bemused look; Frances Balby is a little distance from us, preoccupied with lighting a cigarette – trying to hide the fact that it's her last, not wanting to feel obliged to offer it to either of us – and I'm pretty sure she doesn't see. What do I care if she sees, at any rate? Only that it will end up in the interview somehow, be turned into something eccentric rather than a perfectly practical solution to taking care of them when away from home. No doubt it will enter the mythology about me. The Famous Grouse, with the snail obsession, that kind of thing.

I remember little about the interview. It feels like a series of ducks, left hooks and parries. At one point Frances says: 'Is your prose *deliberately*, wilfully unlovely? There is rather a relentless quality –' to which I mumble my reply: 'A novel isn't a series of brilliant one-liners.'

She punches back at me: 'What would you say it is, then?'

I don't have any idea, I want to say. Why are you asking me? If I knew, do you think I wouldn't quit, find a better way to spend my time? It's an unrequited love affair. A letter to a lover who sometimes loves you back. It's a compulsion; it's something I have to do; it's not for you, actually, or anyone at all; I can't quit; I couldn't tell you who it's for or why. Leave me alone, can't you? *They'll never believe you.*

'I think perhaps writing successful fiction has a supernatural quality,' I venture, 'making people think – *believe* – something that may or may not be true.'

'A dark art? Or one big con-trick, in fact?' Frances replies.

The research I've been doing for the *Plotting* book suddenly comes to my rescue and I remember a quote from Ford Madox Ford. I clear my throat and murmur: 'No. I believe it's nothing less than "a medium of profoundly serious investigation into the human case".'

This is more of a poke under Frances's ribs than a proper hit.

A vivid dream, I should have said. A vivid, sustained, illogical dream. A grey blob. A candle flame. A tiny whorl of snail, the pattern its grey belly makes when you turn it over, the words that fail you when you try to describe the tenderness you feel for its vulnerable horns, flailing wildly; when you really *look*.

She laughs then, and presumably a thousand radio listeners laugh with her. 'Ha! With plenty of murders and fist fights thrown in for good measure. Well, that's all we have time for, I'm afraid. Splendid, thank you Miss Highsmith.'

And afterwards the usual clamour sets up: I'm such a damn fool, why can't I filter what I say, why is it that others (Ford Madox Ford for one) are so sure about what it is they're doing; how can it be that as recently as a week ago I heard a writer of crime fiction state, once again, 'I think we are all equally capable of committing murder, given the right circumstances'? And I wanted to scream: Oh, yeah? You think *you* could do one, even if you needed to? You think it easy, do you, to pick up that great heavy thing and bring it down on the head of whoever is driving you nuts? If it's so easy – go ahead, do it, why not? Have a go, why don't you, instead of just talking about it. Or what? You believe your great-aunt Lucy, who never hurt a fly, is as likely as young George, the ruffian at the local dance-hall, to have exactly the same amount of hate juice inside, solidifying into the same violent lava? All those plots where characters have *motives* – ha! How laughable I find these *motives*. How rational, how thought-ful. For Christ's sake, is this what most murders are about? Victims are just the people who are in the way, the girlfriend or wife or guy at the receiving end: there's no design. Murders are about one thing: they come out of murderous *feelings*. The grey blob at the corner of the eye, the fears, the feeling of deep, chok-ing, agonising fear, the simmering cauldron bubbling in the centre of the heart and stoked up daily. *I take an axe to Mick's head.* An old line of mine. Plot, storyline, cause and effect. Look around you: is that what's going on? Does that man plan to begin a lifetime's addiction to strangling his lovers? Does that man *plot* to lose every girlfriend he's ever had by an epidemic of violent rages? It's not controlled, plotted, planned and deliberate: it's all just an explosion of *mess*, of *feeling*. Feelings directing everything.

And what it comes back to is this: I always suspected myself one of the rare individuals (even rarer among my sex) with more of this lava than others. I knew I was that uncommon being, capable of murder. And Gerald has allowed me to prove myself right.

The journey back is silent. Dark, yellow-lit hedges and fields, picket fences sepia in headlights. The red eyes of a fox sliding in front of us. I'm relieved when we're back on the bit of straight, the A1120, leaving London and Frances Balby behind.

'Are you offended then? I suppose I should have told you,' Smythson-Balby finally says. It's clear she's been trying to think of a way to broach the subject for the last fifty miles.

'You have a fine nerve but, hey, I don't happen to give a snap,' I say. Sure, she damn well should have told me, but it's done now. So Ronnie was right, and she's pretty shady and a vampire. Biographers. Leeches every one of them. Isn't it a kind of murder, a half-baked idea to steal a life, and make it your own, live off the reflected glory? But what good would it do to say so?

'I – it was your novel. *The Cry of the Owl*. I love that novel – it's brilliant! So spooky and sinister. And his ex-wife is so – monstrous. She's really crazy, frightening, but she makes him feel that he might be going mad. I was telling Frances how much I loved it and she said she was writing about you and then, well, when I found out from Izzie that you were moving to Earl Soham, it just seemed so extraordinary.'

'It's fine. I guess you could have mentioned it, that's all.'

We pass the butcher: John Hutton. A milk churn by the road-side lit up in car-lights. I don't know why but I find the solid cream shape of it troubling: an odd combination of cosy and sinister. 'Ambrosia Ltd', the dairies round here all say. And they make me think of Texas, of Grandfather's wagon delivering the Fort Worth *Star-Telegram*, or the milk-delivery wagon with the orange wheels and the pretty white horse. Or the taste of steel-cut oatmeal. Of grits: yellow as scrambled egg, homely as porridge.

'I hate to part on this note,' she says. 'I really do feel – well, terrible, Miss Highsmith. I do agree, I should have mentioned the biography and the fact that I was doing some research for Frances. And, of course, I would quite understand if you didn't – you know – want to talk to me again.'

Her voice sounds a little choked. She's not about to cry, for Christ's sake? The girl is young, I suddenly remember. Ambitious young journalist – what was that crap she was telling me about winning some prize?

'That wife. In that novel. Nickie,' I offer, throwing her a line. 'A girl I knew who acted just like that. Jealous, crazy. She had a dislodged mind. Fire Island. You said you knew it there.'

Smythson-Balby neatly changes the subject, as she does whenever I mention my old haunts.

'So I heard a little of your interview with Frances,' she says. 'They had the radio on in the green room. I laughed when you said you were sick of writing about psychopaths. That they were too easy to nail. Went really well, I thought.'

I don't agree.

'Your friend has a hell of a nerve. She thinks if she flatters me with all that bull about not being a crime writer or suspense writer but just a writer I'll fall in line. I can see through her. Ronnie never categorises me like that. I write to Paul Bowles, Gore Vidal. Did you know that?'

She says she didn't.

'And they write back.'

I could use a drink. I tell Smythson-Balby this, meaning for her to call by a country bar, but to my surprise she jabs her hand towards the glove compartment.

'There's a bottle of Dewar's in there. And a glass. It's not clean but . . .'

I pour myself a wobbly glass and down it in one.

'I've been fending off would-be biographers for a while. Why can't they wait until I'm dead?'

She laughs at this. One of her intemperate girlish guffaws.

'Pour me a shot,' she says. The yellow scarf is releasing the moorings on her ponytail and her black eye-liner is smudged into shadows at the sides of her eyes. She's infinitely prettier when not so well composed. I consider telling her this, but think better of it, and pour her the whisky instead. I'm wondering how to ask her again about Aldeburgh, without making her suspicious. I need to know what she saw.

She keeps one hand on the wheel while she knocks back the drink. Her driving is no steadier than it was; I guess I should be more concerned.

'Well, as I told you before, Miss Highsmith – Pat – I really am a fan. I'd hate to – blot my copybook, as it were, with you over this.'

'Forget it. But what about a trade: tell me where we've met before.'

Now her gaze, straight ahead, seems to glaze in some way. A shield. There's definitely plenty she's still not telling. I persist: 'I get the feeling you've lived in many different places, like me. But, strangely, they're the same places. At the same times. Would you say?'

She laughs. 'We've never shared dates. I've been in New York, Greenwich Village, yes, and Berne, Switzerland – and Paris in 'sixty-two, I think. Is that the same as you? Yes, odd, if it's true.'

She's cool, very cool. But then she delivers a blow.

'And I think we have a friend in common. Samantha Gosforth? Her husband was in the papers recently, a sudden death. Very sad. I knew them both. Actually, I was briefly an au-pair for them. I knew Hugh Gosforth too, Gerald's brother. Their daughter, Araminta, was just a baby then.'

This time, I'm not going to throw up. I'm controlled. Is she doing this deliberately? Releasing her scraps of information in drips? First she saw me in Aldeburgh; second, she knows Gerald and Sam. And third, surely, some deep but resonating hint that she knows stuff. Plenty of stuff. How much, I'm not sure but it goes back a while, too. But if she really knows Sam, why didn't she put together that Sam was the woman she saw with me that night at the coast? And – I struggle to remember – when I mentioned to Sam that a young journalist was sniffing round, did I give 'Virginia Smythson-Balby' as the name? And what had Sam replied?

A violent stab suddenly as I wonder: Were they ever lovers? Is that what she's hinting at?

I put the whisky back in the glove compartment. I need to feel sharp.

'Sure, I know Sam Gosforth, a little,' I say casually. 'Terrible about the husband. I believe the daughter is eight or nine?'

'Minty. Poor little mite. I was invited to the funeral, it was last week, but I woke that morning with the most filthy migraine – did you go?'

'Yes.' Here I'm struggling to find words relaxed enough in their delivery to convey, yes, I knew them a little, sure, I went to the funeral and, yes, there's nothing more to it than that. I'm scared that my voice will betray something, that my laboured breathing is visible. In fact, my chest is so tight I'm not able to take a breath, and I feel as if all of me is clenched.

Smythson-Balby recognises me, I know that. And Sam is a sexy, attractive woman, and if Smythson-Balby knows her well, she *knows*, meaning she can know about us. Migraine. The very mention of it brings on one of my own, sweeping down on me like a hood. We're nearly at Earl Soham. Now her yellow scarf, the ponytail, has come undone entirely. A great launch of chestnut hair rolls over her shoulders; she's well aware of this, I think. Aware of her charms; all the tricks. Aware from the start.

'Come in. I could use a coffee,' I say. 'I'll let you fix it. I'll give you the odd snippet for your friend Frances and then maybe she'll leave me alone.'

'Oh, Frances is a bloodhound. She'll never let go, now she has the scent.'

We're drawing up to the outside of Bridge Cottage and she's parking on the opposite side, next to the telephone booth. Could I take her to bed? If I have to. If it's the only way to sucker her in; get her off the track. Or find out what she saw that night and who she might mention it to.

I notice she leaves her jacket heaped over her purse on the back seat of her car. Does that mean she'll only come in for a short while – she's not counting her chickens? Or perhaps it only means it's Suffolk, the safest little place on earth. She doesn't trouble to lock it.

She places the little percolator on the stove, moving round my kitchen with a confident air, a girl who is used to fixing coffee in the kitchens of older women. I fetch the liquor bottle to add to it. I notice Mrs Ingham's light is on in the house opposite the kitchen window and wonder, Didn't I just see a figure there in a high-necked gown? Matter of fact, what I really long to do is to telephone Sam, to hear Sam's voice, but I don't care to think about that now. There's work here to do.

I run my fingers through my hair, tuck my shirt a little tighter into my jeans, undo the second button, run my tongue along my top teeth to make them feel cleaner. I glance at my bangs in the mirror in the downstairs bathroom, pulling down my lower eyelids to see how red the insides look. Hmm. I wonder if I can even remember how. Smythson-Balby is sitting at the kitchen table. She flashes me a wide – too wide – smile. She too has tucked her satin blouse in tighter at the waist but this crummy effort is hardly necessary with every button straining like that, those breasts like performing monkeys, out to catch the eye.

133

'I feel as if you're still cross with me,' she says. 'About the biography. The notes. I feel rather awful, actually. I mean – I could say to Frances, I can't do any more. Stop now.'

'I happen to think there's no point. I guess you've already told her plenty.' I pour a good slug into each cup and offer her milk from the bottle, which she shakes her head at.

She crosses her legs, untangles the yellow scarf from the last strand of hair and lays it on the table. It's flat and long. For some cock-eyed reason the idea of a nylon stocking, without a leg in it, pops into my head. Snap out of it, I want to tell myself.

'Just the things we talked about. The interview. The things in the paper. There's nothing more, really. Of course I've figured out who your gentleman caller is and done a précis of each of your novels for her, breaking them into themes, looking at the message of the work . . .'

'Message? Holy crap, not really?'

Her bottom lip comes out then, a little stubbornly.

'There clearly *are* messages in your work. You know, the ordinariness of evil lurking in domestic settings, the doppelganger theme – the bad guy and the good guy who change places, who are the same person. And there's the murderer celebrated as ultimate rebel, an amoral or subversive hero, the forces of law and order as toothless against evil, the victim as repulsive or contemptible or silly in some way and deserving of death . . .'

And here, suddenly, I forget the business I invited her in for and feel my blood start to pound in my brain.

'I wonder why reviewers and critics always put it like that? As if I'm writing in another language they need to translate? Why should I go to the trouble to make up characters, plots and settings and all that? You talk as if a story is just a bottle to hide a message in. Ornamental words to hide a rational thought, which no doubt you think is the *true* thought.'

'I'm so tempted to write this down.'

'Well, don't! Can't this conversation be private? I happen to think that it's the only way to contain the truth. *Art* is understood not just by the mind, is it, but by the emotions and by the body itself? Fiction is my first language. Reducing it to another one – *messages*, for Christ's sake – is radically, destructively incomplete.'

'You do think of your writing as art, then, despite what you said to Frances before?'

'Oh, fuck off. What are you selling your soul to that damned bitch for anyway? Are you in love with her?'

Well, so now it's out there. Not with my usual skill but it hits the mark. Her eyes blaze at me and a deep red colour slides, like a bloody cloud, from her throat to her face.

'I most certainly am not! She's a distant cousin, for God's sake.'

'They're all in love with their cousins round here. Why should you be different?'

So, it's a stand-off, then, and a fight, after all. Sordid and unsubtle. All plans to make it otherwise have gone to hell. Smythson-Balby scrapes her chair back and stands, snatching up her yellow scarf, earrings wobbling, flouncing like a girl of fifteen.

'I should go.'

'Where is it you live, anyways? You seem damn close – you pop up often enough.'

'I'm staying with Izzie in Aldeburgh.'

This time the way she says *Izzie* has a flavour to it. She is at least conceding that. Her next tight little speech is in response, I know, to my throwing up earlier in the day. But, thankfully, she put another spin on it.

'Look,' she says, bold now, the drink loosening her up, 'Izzie and I, we'd been for a midnight dip. Toes only: it was jolly cold. We saw you and your friend. You were going back to your car from the beach, your friend wasn't wearing a coat. I recognised the car first. But you needn't worry. I never intended to add that – you and your friend – to the notes I'm giving to Frances. I don't see – well, I don't see that it's anything she needs to know.'

And if she'd recognised this friend as Sam Gosforth, now would be the moment to say so, yes? I wait for a second before nodding. She manages to look both prim and coquettish at the same time, scooping the hair up from her neck and winding it securely in the yellow scarf. It's not just vanity: I really don't think I'm wrong about her feelings for me. They seep from her like that powerful, unsettling perfume – the smell of a girls' locker-room – whenever I'm around her. And will these be useful in the end, or will they lead her to a greater and greater interest in me, to an endless pursuit? In fact, is it my imagination or has she in fact been pursuing me with a crazy, spectacular kind of compulsion already?

'You know, it's an open secret,' I say. 'Sure, people keep asking me about *The Price of Salt*, whether I might republish now under my own name. But there's still Mother and Granny Mae. And Fort Worth. I don't know why that should matter, but it does.'

'It's an absolute smash at the L. The same status as *The Well of Loneliness*. But I don't think it's known here, or the name Claire Morgan either.'

She's let her guard down now, and what that last remark tells me is that she knows the L in Greenwich Village. And probably the Grapevine and a deal of others too. So I wasn't far off in those early musings about where we'd met. But the flavour of the night has altered. I want to talk to Sam so badly that agitation has snuck into my movements. I'm practically rapping my fingers on the table, willing Smythson-Balby to leave. She, at any rate, has sensed this and is putting on her jacket.

'They can write what they like – tinker with me all they want – after I'm dead,' I mutter. It's not much of a reply to all that has been said and unsaid between us but it's all I can think of and for now it will have to do.

In the night-time phone booth with its silly little royal crown above the door and its now so familiar smell of nettles and warmed-up paper, the over-baked telephone directory, the line rings and rings, but Sam doesn't answer. I picture her in that fancy London apartment, with her long hair in blonde plaits, Heidi-style, the way I've sometimes seen her fix it before bed, and drinking neat gin in a priceless glass, and . . . what else? I feel certain she's there, ignoring the telephone's scream. Punishing me somehow. And I have an uneasy feeling that I'm being watched, that despite hearing the red car roll away, Smythson-Balby is still here somehow, waiting to pounce.

What part of our conversation will she relay to her little friend Frances? And how could I have imagined that seducing her would achieve anything, secure her silence, when it would surely only stoke her interest, give her added excuses to visit more and more often?

I click the receiver dead and then, an afterthought, one last dial. And this time, on the first ring, a breathless voice: 'Hello?'

'Honey. You're still up!' I say.

'I just came in. Gerald's parents wanted to talk about the urn. They're still cross with me that it wasn't a proper burial and want to order an engraved plaque to put on the urn. Should it say "Devoted husband and beloved father and son" or "Beloved husband and devoted father and son"?'

She sounds drunk. She sounds bitter or angry or something unreachable, and a great panic wells in me as I try to reel her in, soften her up.

'Honey . . . if only I could hold you now, and stroke your hair . . .'

The snuffling at the end of the line tells me that she's crying, and I press for an advantage.

'Come visit soon so that I can do that, just as soon as you're able.'

But her reply comes back sharply, with a wail: 'How can I? What about Minty? It's impossible – she needs me. She's so shocked, Pats, it's horrible. She hasn't said a word about it. But I know she's thinking: Daddy left me. He didn't care a hoot about me, he *wanted* to leave. And that's the worst part because, of course, no child likes to feel that a parent *chose* to end their life. If only I could say to her it was a ghastly accident . . .'

My ribcage contracts, as if someone is squeezing all the life out of me.

'You wouldn't say that?'

'You have no idea – it's so easy for you. You don't have to walk around the house, see his things, see Minty's stunned little face . . .'

Such a trite, traditional sentiment, I think, and crush the thought. Her voice is childish, sulky.

And now more sobbing and there's nothing I can do but cradle the receiver (actually I'm not cradling it at all, I'm slapping it in my hand, not listening to her deep inhalations and choking sniffs, giving myself time to compose myself so I don't say anything rash). But the sobbing just continues, and after a while, the coins run out and I tell her in a desperate voice that I have to go, that I'll call again tomorrow, that she's got to be strong, that I love her. She'll calm down, I tell myself. It's early days, it's understandable: Gerald has only been dead for a matter of weeks! When Minty is back at school and life is back to normal, she'll see sense, we can resume, she'll realise how easy it's become now to see one another, without the Great Impediment (as I always thought of him) getting in the way.

A dash across the road, and back at the cottage, I turn on the faucets for a soothing bath.

Pats. I think we should cool things for a while. I'm not going to be able to come to see you any more. She didn't say that. It sounds much too composed: she wasn't in a state to say anything so rational. But still, in my head, I hear that phrase as if she already said it: my worst fear. I know it's coming.

I pace around the bathroom naked. I check on my snails. I think: I did it for you, for *you*, Sam. I risked everything. Can't you be a little bit grateful?

I try to undo that thought. It's beneath me.

And then something Sam said about Minty resurfaces: *Daddy left me. He didn't care a hoot about me, he* wanted *to leave.* And I think of Mother – that year she left me in Fort Worth with Granny, and that same breath-stealing feeling creeps back into my chest, hands twisting my heart, and I have to sit on the bed and put my head in my hands.

When I raise my head, I see something. A mouse. A small grey shape, racing along the skirting-board, under the window. Fear trickles along my spine.

'Leave me alone, why don't you,' I say, quietly.

There's a sound of breathing in the room. And then unmistakably from somewhere: a burst of laughter.

That year: 1933–4. The saddest, the longest of my life. After Mother had betrayed me, told me she'd divorce him, then gone back to New York and Stanley, leaving me in Fort Worth. My little bedroom at the back of the boarding-house, above all those rooms. The boarders, mostly salesmen, those great lunks in their square-toed boots and overalls, eating Granny Mae's steel-cut oats and sorghum. Their masculine smells of tobacco, of cattle-dung. They'd ruffle my bangs – *How you doin', Toots?* – and I'd fly up to my room and comb it back again. My first taste of pure, sweeping longing: *Come back, why don't you come for me?* Whispering into the pillow.

I'd hear a train moaning. Was it on its way from Texas to New York, to Mother? Or was it bringing her to me? When would she come? When would I see her again? I'd kiss her creased photograph, under my pillow. *Just me and you and Granny Mae, that's what you said. Come back now, Mama! Your Patsy needs you.* The moan of the train again. A wild sound, pure sorrow.

Sometimes I think that year was preparing me for something. Teaching me who I am. This is going to be your lot. You are going to spend your life longing for something to arrive, someone, something who never shows up. Here it is: the feeling that's yours alone, the special one. Are you ready?

Will you come back? Will you ever come?

I picture Granny Mae, creaking down beside me on the counterpane – crochet squares of every colour, moth-holed and
unravelling – stroking my hair. 'What is it you see, honey-pie,
that's so darn frightening?' she'd ask. And then she'd give a little
frightened jump when I'd scream again, and she'd look at where
I was pointing. Scolding me fiercely then: 'Darn fool girl, you're
scaring your old granny now. I'll fix you some hot milk and you
get yourself on back to bed.'

So I told her. It's a mouse, a little grey mouse. And she bought
me Sparkie, who slept purring in a black coil beside me on my
pillow. But, after all, the mouse was just the beginning. The
mouse was – I realise now – the warning sign.

That first time. That glimpse. Just a movement at the corner
of my eye as I'm snuggling under the covers. I forgot about it.
The second time, I'm restless and sleepless on top of the covers,
the heat of the day barely seeping away, light streaming in
beneath curtains that I'd parted to open the window. My
bedroom door ajar to make a cool through-draught, but none
has materialised. I'm sweaty, limbs flung angrily in a star shape,
staring at nothing. And there it is, standing in the light where
the bedroom door is ajar: a little stumpy figure – a child? a doll?
– some kind of monstrously disabled man, a dwarf, a mongoloid? It has an outsized head, it's wearing boots.

I leap from my bed, rigid, run to the doorway. It's looking at
me. My body quivers from my toes to my teeth. A great swilling
heat pours through me, as if I'm about to faint. I run back, climb
onto my bed, whispering: there's nothing there, there's nobody!
And for a while, it was true . . .

*Oh, God, don't think of it, don't think of it now. It can't come
if you don't think of it.* Think only of Sam. Sam will come back
soon. This is about Sam, about fear, isn't it? Sam is not like
Mother, like all the rest. Sam loves me.

I have a strange, ridiculous desire to shout for Granny. That
first time after the shock, I thought, no, not a dwarf, one of the

boarders, one of the salesmen, must be playing some kind of trick on me. And then it slid towards me, as if on ice, backing me into my bedroom. Now it's saying something to me, something indecipherable. That whispery voice, not a human voice at all. It's all in your head, I say, but I can still hear it.

So I check under the bed, open the wardrobe where wooden hangers knock emptily; shut it again; open and draw closed the curtains. All in apple-pie order. There's nothing, he's not here. I didn't hear anything. Heat starts ebbing away from me and my breathing slows to normal. Am I half cracked? Snap out of it. It's just – emotion. Missing Sam, that's all. The aftermath of what we did.

A shocking thought about Sam, about the power she has over me: one word from Sam now will detonate me – police, scandal, prison, shame, end of career, end of my life, everything. And then something comes to me with violent clarity: *I already felt like this*. Before killing Gerald. That's what loving Sam is: I felt it the minute I fell for her. I've never been in love like this before. I gave her the power to demolish me. I never gave myself fully to another woman after Mother. It was a mistake to do so this time, but it's done now.

After a while, my pacing soothes me. There's no sign of him, the little man, the little figure, I need my head examined. I go to the window, pulling back the curtain to stare out over the dark garden, a sky spotted with only a few dull stars. I put my hand to my heart until it slows to an even beat. I lick my dry lips, tasting salt. No sign of Mrs Ingham, but who knows if the Mad Bat is lurking somewhere along with some invisible fox, bent on tearing the throats of the chickens, snapping rabbits' heads from their bodies? I remember Betty and Nell, two friends in Islington, London, saying how they kept a timer in their guest bedroom. Every night light went out sharply at eleven thirty. Should anyone care to spy on us – and for us, ever vigilant, we had to assume they were – they must have wondered who was the tyrant for time-keeping, Betty or Nell.

I chuckle a bit, then breathe out. Drop the curtain again and turn my attention to the snails on the window ledge. Watching my snails always relieves tension. There are a few more plastic bowls and saucers of snails now. I crouch to observe the glass tank, my latest addition, which is too big for the window ledge and is on the floor near the bed.

Further dirt heaps have appeared, spilling their little beads of eggs, which I transfer to the saucers until they grow big enough to escape. I fetch my purse from downstairs and replace the bigger mating pair in another bowl, and watch them for a while. A mating can last for a whole day. It's supremely consoling and mesmerising, so unhurried, so without any other consideration – if snails can be said to have *considerations*. I ponder this for a while.

By the time I step into the bath I feel better. My pale body is longer and skinnier than I remember, like a great long yellow fish, the water giving it a sepia tint from the rust in the plumbing. I scrub myself with a thin sliver of white soap, veined with black, remembering with a twinge Sam's glamorous bathroom. I must get some decent soap. I was being foolish and paranoid about Sam, about the return of *it*, of the Thing. There's no one here. She's not going to break off with me. Being in love with a beauty like Sam makes you skinless, is all. She's a grieving widow and needs to play the part. It's been one hell of a shock for her and she's risen to the occasion magnificently. At any rate I should support her in her efforts and give her time; time is all she needs.

'Nobody else sees me,' the Thing used to say. 'Maybe I only belong to you. Why should the others see me?'

A quiver of pride, laced with fear. *Special.* I miss him, I realise. Maybe I wanted him to reappear. So familiar, so inexplicable. Mine alone, he was. Maybe I loved him.

In the morning writing absorbs me. For some reason I wake refreshed, despite a night of dreams of Gerald, Sam and

Smythson-Balby in a passionate threesome, and other things I can't remember but know were pretty shady. Losing myself in the new novel for hours means that it's noon before I wash, brush my teeth or fix myself breakfast. The delicious chaos of a successful writing morning. There's nothing much in but a paper bag of button mushrooms I bought for the snails, but they rejected, so I fry them up with a clove of garlic and masses of butter and pile them on toast. There is a loud rapping on the front door at twelve thirty. I lift the curtain a little to see a cop car, and two policemen standing there.

The room starts a curious drumming and shifting, as if I'm in a sandstorm. I unlock the front door.

'Miss Highsmith? Miss Patricia Highsmith?'

'Yes.'

'May we come in? Some routine enquiries.'

'Of course. Nothing's happened? There's nothing—'

'Nothing to be alarmed at, ma'am. Like I say, just some enquiries.'

They step in. Great clod-hopping black shoes. An older one and his little stooge: a young, pudgy one. Taking off their caps, holding them by the chin straps and standing awkwardly, taking in the fact that I'm wearing the robe over pyjamas and the floor is a welter of manuscripts and books; the smell of the recently fried garlic and the sound of my stomach rumbling. I put my hand on it. I scurry to push some papers away, to make space on the sofa for them to sit down.

'May we come in?' he asks again.

They are in, but I nod distractedly.

'Of course, I'm sorry. Do sit down. Care for a coffee or something?'

'No, thank you, ma'am. Just a few questions, you know.'

The older policeman puts his hat on the sofa so that he can produce something from his large pocket, in a plastic sealed bag.

'We found a wallet. In fact, a fisherman handed it in. The most curious thing.'

Gerald's billfold. The nasty-coloured leather, darkened by seawater but otherwise, well, it doesn't look much the worse for wear. Something so mundane, as masculine and ordinary as golf clubs, as pipes and tobacco pouches, as tweed jackets and leather buttons, now transforms itself into something sinister. Dead, chilling, waterlogged.

I find I can't say anything.

'Fisherman found it on his boat,' the officer continues, 'tangled in some nets. Like it had been flung there. He thinks perhaps the owner did just that. Pretty amazing when you think of it, if he was trying to throw it away but accidentally landed it on a moored boat.'

I swallow and my voice comes out a little high. 'Yes! Extraordinary.'

'Unbelievable,' the tubby one interjects.

'And how does this . . .'

So he opens the billfold with painstaking slowness and the tubby one smiles inanely at me, as if we're on a television game show together, waiting to hear the question read out. Nervous thoughts jab at me. What is in the billfold? What are they doing here? What is it that links Gerald to me? I almost expect – crazily – some kind of note in there, some full account of what happened, written up by Gerald to damn me for ever. I run my tongue over my teeth, wishing I'd brushed them this morning; wishing the acid, frightened taste in my mouth would go away.

'The wallet belongs to a gentleman called Gerald Gosforth, who passed away a few weeks ago at Aldeburgh. Money still there. So we know he wasn't robbed.'

They know he wasn't robbed? What does this mean? Where is it leading? I feel my face becoming hot, and I flatten my cool palm against it, trying hard to keep my eyes on his.

'We've assumed he committed suicide, actually, from some clear indication we've had from others, you know. Let's just say he wasn't the most faithful of husbands and might have got himself into a tight spot with money at the bank where he was a senior director, too.'

He looks directly at me to be sure I follow. He must have noticed how red my face is, and what meaning will he put on it? I drop my eyes, and can only hope he thinks I'm embarrassed by the implication, by the mention of Gerald's unfaithfulness. I swallow again, trying to moisten the dryness in my throat.

'So, just one small thing. Inside the wallet, we find this.'

He unfolds a small square of paper, and hands it to me. In Gerald's writing, *Pat Highsmith, Bridge Cottage, High Street, Earl Soham, Suffolk.*

The effect is like a mule-kick, a blackout, a falling off an edge. I hear myself murmuring something incoherent while my mind is going like sixty. *Holy crap.* Gerald's writing: how ugly it is, like the writing of a big, sloppy twelve-year-old boy. And the great lunk wrote my address down. What to say? I glance at the window, the opened curtains, and a figure – the milkman – passing. At the dead ashes of the fire in the grate. At my typewriter: perky, waiting, a clean sheet of paper rolled. All paused, waiting, my life seemingly clicking past me on a strip of film while I stare at the piece of paper in my hand, and Gerald's dumb, dreadful, condemning writing.

Why didn't I look inside the billfold? Destroy it? Fear surges like a bubble bursting in my heart.

'I – sorry, I have go to the bathroom.' I shove the paper back at him.

The room shakes again, contracts. My papers and my novel – the sheets bolt upright, sharply alert at the typewriter – swerve into view as I rush past them to the stairs, thunder up to the bathroom. What light can they possibly put on my strange behaviour, on my burning face, my obvious upset? Think, *think.* What to say, what to *say?*

The two officers look embarrassed when I come back down. There's the loud rush of the cistern flushing above our heads.

In the bathroom I'd splashed cold water on my face, buried

it in a towel. Tried to think, to calm down and prepare something. I could say that Sam was here, sure, we're friends, that's known. (Hadn't she said the police *didn't* trouble to ask the address of where she stayed that night in Suffolk? What an extraordinary blunder! How casual they are, these cops, how foolishly British around well-spoken beautiful ladies.) I could say she was hiding here from him, hiding a (male) lover from him, Gerald was chasing her, she'd taken refuge with me; they had a row, he drove off to the coast in anger, must have waded out to sea?

Now I'm rubbing slightly damp hands on my bathrobe, pulling it tighter at the waist, redoing the tie, and they're watching me closely.

'Of course, Miss Highsmith, we don't need all the details,' the cop says. He's been scratching at one slightly out-of-control curly eyebrow with a fingernail.

I'm wondering what my face is doing, what my heart is doing, beneath my ribcage.

'It's not a criminal investigation. Family affair. Routine enquiry.'

The other man, the younger one, makes a sound, a nervous sound, not quite a cough. They seem to think I'm following. I shake my head a little, but my thoughts still won't clear. I'm thinking of Sam, Sam, lovely Sam, fiddling with her necklace, that habit she has of bringing the lapis-lazuli pendant up to her mouth to touch it with her tongue, unaware that she's doing it . . .

'A man has died and his wallet has been found. It would help to know the – ahem – circumstances. We don't necessarily need to pass them on to his – ahem – bereaved wife, upset her with details about things she probably has a strong suspicion of already, you understand?'

Sam's tongue, edging towards vivid blue. Pauses. I try to take in what he's saying. They don't need to pass the details on to his wife. Because they think it's simply this. Gerald was having an

146

affair. They are asking me this. *I'm sorry to have to ask you, ma'am. Were you the mistress of Gerald Gosforth? And he visited you at this address? And the date was? And you last saw him at . . .?* The older policeman makes notes. I hardly hear my answers. He asks me something more – was Mr Gosforth begging me to go away with him, perhaps? No, I manage. He was asking me to rekindle an old affair. I refused.

The only crime a British cop can imagine from a woman like me: having intercourse outside marriage. He replaces the cap on his fountain pen.

And now the cop is staring again at Gerald's note. 'We will convey the property to his wife – we have to do that, of course. But I don't see any need to include this, do you?'

The square of lined paper, torn from a notebook, Gerald's writing. The cop is – astonishingly – folding and tearing it, striding over to my cold fire and scattering the pieces there, on top of the soft grey ash. Gerald's handwriting, the one piece of evidence that links Gerald to this house, to me, in tiny pieces.

I run a hand through my bangs. I feel that my face has cooled, during his questions, the blood draining. Perhaps I'm very pale, now. And the room, with all the trauma and shapeshifting that's been going on, stills.

I try to look like the secret mistress of a man like Gerald, and a tragic, guilty one at that.

The two cops stand up. Tweedledum and Tweedledee. One reaches for his cap on the sofa arm; the other swings his by its strap. The body has been cremated, the billfold found and explained, what other possible evidence can there be? I'd like to dance around them, rubbing my hands. Instead I rub at my eyes, as if holding back tears.

I recover my voice. 'Thank you,' I say. 'Matter of fact, it's been . . . you know.'

'Of course. We'll see ourselves out. Good afternoon to you, ma'am.'

The older officer takes the sealed plastic bag and the billfold and drops it back into his deep pocket. The younger policeman smooths down his jacket over his portly stomach and replaces the hat on his head. The back of his neck blazes with reddening shaving burns and a crop of spots. Rookie. *Just failed to sniff out your very first real-life murderer, you foolish, foolish child*, I can't help thinking as I close the door behind him.

After that first time, my first sighting of Sam at that publishing party, her perfect heart-shaped face imprinted itself indelibly. The Grace Kelly elegance of her neck, her stylish hair, her elongated lines, and eyes the colour of a blaze of Texan bluebonnets in spring. That little fizz between us at the table after Gerald's outburst. I knew she had registered me, as I had her. I tried to remember where I'd heard the gossip about her having an affair with a woman, and if it was reliable. Was it Peggy who'd told me? Peggy was the host of that first dinner party. Or maybe Rosalind – who was more to be trusted: Rosalind was in a long, open relationship with a woman, had lived in Britain, knew the London scene. Because one didn't want to make a stupid move with someone like Sam. Nothing crummy or ugly; not with someone so . . . poised.

After a while, Sam was all I thought about. I found out from Peggy her address and next time I was in London I took a bus to Highgate and walked down her street. Sparrows twittered madly at me as if I was stepping into a birdcage and I walked with my heart jabbering louder than they were, rendered almost breathless by the terror of being discovered. Was that a blonde head at a window? A slender hand? Would she have vermilion geraniums in her window box or were those hers – the blue hyacinths (I preferred to think of hers being the blue)?

I wrote her a letter and tore it up. In the letter I told her she reminded me of my very first love, Rachel Barber, a little flame-haired six-year-old I'd played dolls with in Barber's bookstore in Fort Worth. And I began to get sick with thinking of her and it never occurred to me that she thought about me too. And then one day a miracle happened, it really was a miracle, and she appeared in the vestibule outside my apartment in Paris, where the concierge had let her in, flopping white gloves onto her pocketbook – *thwack* – and saying in that English voice: 'I hope you don't mind? Peggy gave me your address. I'm in Paris for the weekend. I thought you might come to the theatre with me because I don't speak a word of French . . .'

I shut the door on her. I can't believe I did it, but I did. And then I heard her tinkling laugh and got my first gust of her perfume, a light smell like pale jasmine tea, as I reopened it a crack. She was smiling, and so was I.

Later, she said: 'That's when I knew you felt the same about me! You were so shocked at seeing me there. That door closing was pure reflex.' It was. I closed the door because a dream had just become real. I wasn't ready. I hadn't even brushed my teeth. And there she was, shimmering in a shantung silk shirt dress of cobalt blue – fragrant, graceful, and impossibly lovely. And such confusion drummed in me. What could I make of it? Was I reading too much into it? Was she even there alone? She surely hadn't travelled all that way *just to see me*.

I thought back to that other moment, the first glance between us across the dinner table. The fizz. What had our eyes registered? Perhaps simply this: that we already knew one another from somewhere. That we would be friends. No, that wasn't it, that wasn't the feeling at all.

So then she swept into the apartment – my usual litter of ashtrays, half-drunk whisky glasses, papers, books, coffee cups – and I mumbled my apology for the state it was in and she smiled and her big naughty eyes widened. She waited while I put on a clean white shirt, some black slacks I hoped might be smart enough for the theatre. She sat primly on the sofa in my study – the only room I had besides my bedroom – and I peeped at her through the open door; noticed her earrings, big cream buttons, the jacket that had been hung over her arm now folded on the sofa. How neat she was! Like a fashion plate! And then a feeling like a snake, electric, speeding through my body, as I pictured something else. Tumbling. Her tumbling on my bed, her dress askew, her legs bare. What on earth was under that blue silk, all that tautly held perfection? What level of need, desire, could drive a woman that *contained* to come to Paris to see me?

In the theatre – a bad Molière as it turned out, *Le Misanthrope* – she leaned in close and whispered: 'I read a novel. A marvellous novel, called *The Price of Salt*. Nothing had ever moved me as that novel did. I thought: *Ah . . .*'

I was grateful for the dark: I knew my face would be flaming. Mention of *that* novel, even now, years later, always brought that welter of feelings. Not quite shame, no. More, a simple horror of exposure. I literally squirmed in my red plush seat.

A couple of theatre-goers beside us tutted in annoyance as Sam leaned in again to whisper:

'And then Peggy told me. Claire Morgan – she's here! She's in London, in fact her real name is—'

'*Pardonnez moi, Madame, mais*—'

'So sorry! *Je m'excuse, Monsieur!*'

She giggled lightly at her poor French accent, turning her charming smile to the behatted creep behind us, who had just leaned forward and tapped her shoulder. 'Shall we go?' she said suddenly, and stood up.

Outside was a blue evening, soft with rain, the sound of it sizzling, like fat bubbling in a pan. The trees showed the tiny buds of spring, sharp as arrows. The smell of her wafted towards me, imprinting itself. Something earthed, something sweet: pastry. I thought of a cake store I knew in Paris, in the rue des Feuillantines near my favourite library, a place that we would one day soon sit in together, and the fragrant things that would be between us then: tea, cinnamon, Hawthorne. Matter of fact, why didn't I ask her straight away? 'When can we see one another? Will you have lunch with me?' It wouldn't have been the first time: in New York I was known for my bluntness knocking up against my shyness. Something about Sam silenced me.

'Do you happen to have a cigarette?' I managed to ask, and she fetched one from a silver case inside her pocket book.

'Do you suppose there's a place to get a coffee round here?' Sam asked. We were in the Latin Quarter, standing in the street, while I searched for my lighter. I felt in both pockets, then realised I'd left it at home and had to hand the cigarette back. A child with chocolate-button eyes had been watching us standing there, me frisking my pockets, and he was immediately in front of us, presenting his dirty palm for a coin. Sam fumbled in her pocket book again and handed him some francs, looking at me, and my heart made an answering leap as the boy ran away.

'Are you always so quiet?' she asked me, across two white cups of burning black coffee, two dried-up sweet pastries between us. Her pocket book and gloves were carefully arranged on the chair beside her, her jacket draped elegantly behind her. The smell of tobacco, coffee, the smell of Sam came at me in gusts: I was feeling delirious.

'I guess.' I didn't know how to say: only with you. Usually my shyness made me garrulous.

'And you gave the women a happy ending. In your novel, I mean. That was marvellous. That was bravest of all – I felt.'

'Why not?' I ask, unable to think of any other answer.

'Well – because most people consider women like Therese and Carol as unnatural at best and wicked at worst. The Church says we're evil and there's no support from families either. We can only experience rejection.'

'We', she said. She said 'us'. The most extraordinarily bold admission; she must have thought it had been said already. She wanted me to know.

'I don't care. I'm inured to rejection,' I said, leaned across the table and kissed her on the mouth.

She pulled away from me as if I'd struck her.

At that, I had to laugh. 'Look around you,' I said. 'There's a peer group here.' The bar was quiet, and she had failed to notice that the half-dozen patrons, all those sitting at little tables with tasselled lamps, hugging their *pastis*, leaning towards each other, holding hands or perched at the bar, were women. Matter of fact, now I looked, a couple of them were dressed like men, and that might – on first glance – have confused her.

'You have a surprising voice,' she said, widening her eyes and nodding, trying to recover her composure. Her mouth had felt warm, her lips soft – faint flavour of lipstick and coffee. I could still taste it. My heart was racing like a locomotive up a hill but I knew now that, outwardly, I had the greater control. She picked up a little pack of matches from the bar, began tearing one off. Her hands shook.

'It's a posh voice, isn't it, not particularly American? I suppose you've lived in Europe for so long you don't sound at all Texan. Cultured. You speak slowly . . .' She was determined to smooth things over.

Here I had to smile. '*Posh?* That's rather a statement.'

'And you say "rather" a lot.'

When I looked quizzical at this, wondering how on earth she could deduce that from such a short conversation, she added: 'I heard you on the radio, talking about Hitchcock making a film of *Strangers on a Train*, and there was some silly chap who kept trying to trip you up. I had to pull over, actually, to listen on the car radio, because your voice was so pretty, so calm and so soft. And you're not a bit calm!'

She'd read my novel, she'd listened to me on the radio. All those months she had been as hipped on me as I had on her.

'And what of all the lies we have to tell everyone, our colleagues, our family?' she said plaintively, returning to her former subject.

You're speaking for yourself, I thought. You have to live that way with a child and a husband, but not me. 'Some of us don't.'

'You aren't deceiving your mother and father?'

'My mother and stepfather. They both assume I'm queer. They wish it were otherwise but they're not in any doubt.'

She pulled out another cigarette for herself but instead of smoking it she laid it on the table and lit a match. 'Blow,' she said, holding the match in front of my mouth. I did, and I caught her wrist, and held her hand there, in front of my lips, her elbow resting on the table. A slender wrist, circled by a fine gold bracelet, nails carefully shaped, white and girlish. She tugged a little and laughed. I held tighter, and she shook the dead match free onto the table between us.

The bartender's eyes flicked over us. I looked into her huge cornflower blue eyes. A confident, flirtatious gaze. A gaze of naked feeling came back at me. I thought: No one will ever make me feel this way, and now I'm in a spot. The smell of sulphur lingered, as she finally dropped her eyes, picked up the cigarette and struck another match.

All the things I loved about Sam were there from the start. Her strange mixture of boldness – she had come all that way, she had spoken so openly – mixed with something profoundly conventional, cautious. Her tremendous grace and poise, like the calm surface of a dangerous lake, with the promise that trembled within it of something utterly unruly. Her maturity, the kindness, her thoughtful, logical self, the loveliness. And fire. Whenever Sam was in the room flames were somewhere close.

Later, much later, at the end of that first, long, weekend, I remember us standing outside Notre Dame and Sam saying, 'You think I'm so good' (I had used this very word) 'but I'm not. When Minty was a toddler, in the early days of my marriage, I fell for a girl. And I tried to – finish myself off, with pills. Gerald never knew the reason, but he said suicide was a very, very wicked thing. He said I should see someone, you know, a psychiatrist. And it's only down to him that I'm still here.'

We were staring up at the roof of the cathedral, those ghastly gargoyles – one great beast biting off the head of another, one open-mouthed with claws and outstretched talons, one a sort of foul-tempered Pan, head in hands, sulky. Of course, the most terrible fear ran through me as she said that. Rain was still falling, the spray visible in streetlamps. I kissed her so hard, I felt suddenly frightened, and we laughed, and held each other close, letting rain trickle down the necks of our jackets.

And then the bells of Notre Dame started chiming, I don't know why, a clanging, wild-in-God's-glory sort of sound. Such enormous bells, such deafening vibrations. A chime and then a smash, again and again. We put our hands over our ears and laughed.

'What on earth?' she asked, as the clanging went on and on, tumultuous, crazy, on and on. Perhaps it was midnight. Perhaps it was some French celebration we didn't know about. And just when we thought it was over, it started again, on a different note, like a new set of smaller bells, or like a small heart clanging in a chamber.

Sam pulled a face and said, 'Let's go', as if Notre Dame was admonishing us with its centuries of rebuke, its dominating sounds. But I heard something else. I heard joy and glory. I heard celebration. Ancient, tribal blood-pumping.

I love her I love her I love her

The bells rang out, as if our lives together would be charmed, as if they would never cease.

Then, after the cops have gone, I think: What am I afraid of? The world isn't interested in seeing justice done. I telephone to make an arrangement to see Sam, and she sounds – what does she sound? – she sounds willing to see me, at least. She suggests next weekend and that we bring Minty with us, take her to the zoo. Given that a while back I was mentally chiding her for forgetting Minty, I'm surprised to find myself terribly disappointed by this suggestion. An image of Minty with her dark eyes and penetrating stare imprints itself on the windowpane in the phone booth, against the dark November green. I can hardly say no. I've been reading an early draft of a novel Ronnie is writing and lines come to me from it. He's writing about boys – about a particular old spinster's dislike of boys, as 'embryo men' – and then writes: 'Their pain was an unpleasant snivelling. Their joy was a guffaw ... Like green plums their skins might glow, but remained essentially nasty.'

Boys: essentially nasty. I almost laugh, thinking of this, and what a surprise that Ronnie can write so well about the mean-spiritedness of others, of bitter old ladies. I might be wrong about his understanding of me, after all. The memory of the white, clean pages of his manuscript – piled so neatly on the floor beside my bed: I always take special care of anything belonging to Ronnie – comforts me, and allows me to murmur the right things to Sam down the line about bringing poor little Minty along. I long to rush back to my bedroom, snuggle into my robe and pyjamas and abandon myself to reading. Perhaps I can find a hot-water bottle somewhere. Didn't I perhaps unpack one and leave it lying on one of the shelves in the airing cupboard? Or was it the cupboard under the sink? (No, that was where I put the Black & Decker, its cord tightly wound, its drill bit replaced and lying with the others.)

And it's when I'm looking in the airing cupboard, just after my hand has taken out the cold rubber bottle, that I come across it, with a short vicious shock. A letter from Stanley. In a sealed envelope, stamped, franked, postmark unreadable. Holy crap! But unopened. My stomach plunges, a feeling as if my bowels were falling away from me. How the hell did a letter from Stanley find its way into the airing cupboard?

So when my mind has gone wildly through who has been in the house, who could have left a letter there – Mrs Ingham, Sam, Ronnie, Smythson-Balby, Gerald, all possible, inexplicable, crazy – it dawns on me. Didn't I put some rain-soaked letters and the damp local newspaper into the airing cupboard to dry only a few days ago? Was it possible that this letter was among them and I didn't see it? Is it possible that this sealed envelope has been lying there on that wooden slat, face down, drying itself toastily under the *Ipswich Star* for several days now, and that when I finally picked up the paper to read the other day, I didn't see it?

I force myself to pick it up and look at it again. The deeply familiar feeling of dread begins washing over me on staring at the typeface. The slightly raised letter *e*. The address set out badly, sloping too far to the left . . . It's just like all the others. The same cheap white envelope. The stamp that's always a little on the skew, as if hastily stuck. No postmark visible. I have a horrible sensation, as if icy water is trickling down my back. Perhaps it is. Perhaps I'm a tipped-up egg-timer and my sand is draining out.

He's found me.

I fetch the whisky bottle and take it to the sofa with me, and the hot-water bottle, and the moment I take a deep, deep sip I know what's coming.

The moment my eyes close the tiny grey blob is there, crouching, and when I open them it skitters fast across the cushion and down beneath the sofa. I search for the hot-water bottle, wrapped in a flannel, and place it on my stomach, and screw my eyes closed again.

This time the dream is of the desert between Fort Worth and Albuquerque, the view seen from a train. Beautiful colours, tan and green. And blood red.

Again, I will myself to wake up. Because here he is and, sure, this time it's a dream, but in every other respect, he's real, and he's the same. The little man. His stumpy, squat body.

And then the dream ends and a train somewhere sounds – mournful, low – passing its long lonely journey from then to now along the tracks of the night, tearing me awake. Me aged twelve, at the door of the boarding-house in Fort Worth, Red Alley behind us, Granny Mae hovering inside and Mother on the doorstep with her lizard-skin cases, a glowering Stanley in his white suit beside her. And I'm crying, and clinging to Mother's legs. The Justin boot factory looms behind her, the sky horribly blue, like a vast blue dish, pressing down on her. The bricks of the factory building horribly red, the men pouring out for lunch like a stream of booted black ants.

Mother's legs are the only thing that's real. The taste of my own tears, and her nylon stockings, scented with the Buffalo Trace bourbon that she favours, that she might have spilled some time. 'You said you were going to divorce him!' I mumble into her legs. But what child can get away with accusing her mother of lying, of inconsistency, of being spineless?

Instead I have to straighten up and step forward for her kiss (and his), listen to all the platitudes about how an independent year in Texas with Granny Mae will be so 'good' for me, listen to the impatient snap of Stanley's heels on the step of our wooden-framed house, while she tells me how much she loves me, and suffer her stupid presents for me: a jumping frog and a new sketchbook and a set of watercolours.

'Funny how you love the smell of turpentine, Patsy,' she once said, 'when, after all, I did once try to get rid of you by drinking it.' And at my horrified expression she laughed and added: 'It was your father's suggestion! Don't look so shocked. And it didn't work, did it? You're still *here*.'

And I think of that, and the lightness with which she told me. That she tried to 'get rid of' me. Abort me. Murder me. That, really, she didn't want me at all, never had, and it was only my strange persistence and stubbornness that had brought me here and was keeping me here. *You beastly child, I wish you had miscarried, you beastly husband, I wish I had never married* ... Lines from a poem come to me whenever I think of her. And the final lines are my reply, wondering often why it is that I'm still here, alive, after all: *You hear the north wind riding fast past the window? He calls me. Do you suppose I shall stay when I can go so easily?*

I must have been a horrible, dreadful, monstrous, evil child to be so violently unloved.

I said this once to Sam, and her reply astonished me: 'Why do you say that, darling? Mightn't it be that Mother was the monstrous person, unable to love her child? Some women are like that. And to divorce your father nine days before you were born, that's quite the thing in 1921, isn't it? There must have been something seriously wrong between them for a woman back then to think of divorcing a husband when so heavily pregnant and going it alone. She must have had her reasons?'

The curious thing is, I don't know those reasons. Was he violent? Did he beat her, have affairs? Did she?

One time when Sam asked me where I got my almond eyes, my Oriental beauty from, I wondered with a start was my father – Jay Bernard Plangman – inside me, looking out at her. I told Sam, 'I like to think I have Cheyenne blood.' Anything but what I really thought: I have no idea. I met my father for the first time that same year, that sad Fort Worth year, and also once when I was a young woman and, sure, the resemblance was alarming but I didn't want to talk about it.

There was something I did want to talk about, a question that had long troubled me. Sam was a mother, and I had often wondered, was it normal for a woman to leave a baby, as Mother did, when the infant was only three weeks old? Would Mother have been fully recovered from the birth, would she still have been bleeding, her breasts full of milk? She left me with Granny Mae. She did come back, of course, but I had always puzzled over it. Was it perhaps unusual behaviour for a young mother?

Sam's eyes swam with tears when I asked her. 'Oh, darling,' she said. She bit her lip, but then couldn't resist adding: 'Most mothers can't leave a baby next door for an hour's nap when it's just three weeks old.'

That confirmed it. I was the most unlovable child who ever drew breath.

I'm hotly awake by now. And there's only one cure for this level of insomnia: writing. I creep downstairs to put some of these thoughts directly into type. The letter from Stanley simmers beside the typewriter; I still haven't opened it. I throw it towards the grate, where it lands with a soft pat; I'm unable to prevent myself noting from its weight that there's probably only one sheet of paper in it. Then I rescue it. It's somehow impossible that I should burn it so I put it instead in the leather hod where the kindling goes, beneath the neatly chopped sticks.

'How does this letter-writer, how does he – or she – know the name of your most hateful stepfather?' was the only question the doctor in Paris was interested in, pushing his stupid glasses further up his nose (he should have shoved them up his ass). My answer – 'Yes, that's it! How does he know so *many* things about me?' – did not interest him at all.

The consensus was that a letter-writer who knew some facts about me and wrote nothing much that was threatening except to say that he was not an admirer of my work particularly but found it addictive was not something to be concerned about. Matter of fact, it was my concern that troubled everyone most. 'If you write the books, people will read them,' the doctor said. 'And these readers, they will have their opinions about you. And this you cannot prevent. You should, in fact, be pleased, no, that you have these – how do you call them? – these fanatics who follow you.'

The police had been even more dismissive. My feeling that someone was following me was ridiculed. Sometimes I had noticed in the street outside my apartment that someone had moved trivial things to show me that they had been there – once a glove placed on a low wall, once a stone positioned near the entrance to the building. 'Why should these things distress you?' the police said; it was not a crime to pick up a lost glove. Other times, a car would move away as I came out of my front door and I'd think the same thing: someone was waiting there, and watching. And more and more, the people I told (what kind of letters? Matter of fact, it's fan mail. Oh, well, thees is OK, isn't it?) made me feel that my own neurosis was the question, that my responses, my anxiety and fear of the letters were the problem and nothing more.

One gendarme told me, in barely suppressed exasperation, that being a writer of 'the crimes' I should surely know that the person who wrote letters with phrases like 'I am obsessed with you and your work and I don't know why' was probably not the same kind of person who would leap out and stab you or break into your house and wait behind the wardrobe for you, and therefore there was nothing to be done. Crazies existed, and since letter-writing was not a crime, we had to put up with them. But how could the authorities be so sure? Didn't even 'types', straightforward creeps, turn into psychos and buck a trend occasionally?

'When did they start, the letters?' Sam had asked. Sam and Ronnie, the only friends who showed any kindness, any concern.

I honestly couldn't remember. Paris, 1960? A year or two before I met Sam. The first was innocuous; it didn't frighten me. Beyond the observation that the name Stanley was the same as my stepfather's (which anyone might know) and noticing that it was franked in Paris, with no address or signature or anything further; beyond that, I made no observation. I think the first one simply said something friendly, like 'Hello, did you think I'd forgotten you?' as if the person knew me, and there was nothing threatening in the tone. It was when they stepped up that I became alarmed. Almost one a day during the writing of . . . Which book was it? *The Two Faces of January*, perhaps.

'Could it have *been* Stanley? I mean the actual one?' Sam asked. And, strangely, on that I was certain. After all, I had letters from Stanley. I had his handwriting (his letters were never typed like these), his phrasing, his syntax, his style, to compare. Even his choice of stationery. No. The one person I could rule out was Stanley, my stepfather.

I turn back to my writing, the ghost story I'd started yesterday: 'The Yuma Baby'.

And then here's Mrs Ingham. 'Minna,' she says. Can you believe it? Her first name is Minna, and she insists I call her that.

'Yoo-hoo! Miss Highsmith! I saw the bobbies – for heaven's sake. What did they say?'

She's knocking on the back door, having shuffled down the steps on the path from her house to mine in a curious pant suit in dark green and some yellow fluffy slippers, which are now stained and darkened by the wet grass. She looks down at them, following my eyes, and we stand in the kitchen together. I have hastily hidden the liquor bottle in the cupboard. I'm brewing coffee, matter of fact, the gas is sizzling and the kitchen steamy, so there's no chance of not offering her a cup. I go to the cold-store to fetch the milk and hide my expression.

'I'm sorry, I hope I'm not interrupting your work,' Mrs Ingham says, settling herself into my kitchen chair. I wince at the ghastly noise as she scrapes it across the brick floor. The door is open between kitchen and living room and my typewriter looks bereft, to me, slightly nettled at being abandoned.

'No.' I pour milk into two cups and the bottle shakes in my hand, splashing a little onto the wooden kitchen table. I make to fetch the dishcloth to mop the milky pools, then remember that it's gone. Gerald. The back of his head.

'Did the police say anything useful? Find anything? It wasn't about Bunnikins and the fox, was it? Has there been – you know – any other nuisance?'

'They . . .'

I offer her the coffee and, after a pause, sit down opposite her. I don't want the old snooper in the living room, possibly noticing that the rug has gone and the floor looks strangely bare where I haven't yet replaced it.

'Or was it about Saturday night? A couple of weekends ago. Thought it might be the fox again. I didn't want to say anything – you know, make a fuss, knock on your door. But I heard strange noises again. Thumping sounds. I even thought I heard a man's voice,' Mrs Ingham is saying.

'No, no, they weren't here about that.'

This is one of those occasions when too much talking looks suspicious. Let her come up with the answers herself. I sip my coffee. I'd rather drink it black; the milk is a concession to Sam telling me I'm fading away and wanting to feed me up. This thought is saddening, because just lately Sam has had no such interest in my thinness or much else.

Mrs Ingham glances up at my calendar, as if needing confirmation of what day it is. Three little kittens in tartan collars, supplied by the Framlingham dairy, gaze down at her.

'My Reggie is going deaf. I could definitely have relied on him, once upon a time,' she says.

And thank God for that, I think, taking a large slug of coffee. Another dash of whisky would be good. Thinking fast, I've decided that the best lies are ones that contain the truth.

'I'm awful sorry about this. Matter of fact, I probably should have mentioned it. I did have a prowler, a sort of crazed fan, when I was living in Paris, used to send me letters. It went on for a few years. He might have followed me places, too. I never had proof, just the feeling sometimes . . . the kinds of things he knew. How'd he know I'd been wearing a new coat that day? Lucky guess? Or did some seedy young bum see me leave the house in it? That sort of thing. I guess a kind of paranoia developed. In the end, doctors put me on medication. And I moved here, and the letters stopped.'

'But now you think he's found you?' Mrs Ingham glances at the mailbox as if he might materialise in front of our eyes. Her mouth is a small perfect O. Have I gone too far? She will want to see the letter, and I don't care to show her it.

'No – that is, I *have* had a letter, that's all.'

'Oh, my goodness. What did it say?'

'Nothing much. I gave it to the police. He doesn't *do* anything, you understand. Just letters. He signs himself Brother Death or sometimes "Stanley". Stanley is the name of my stepfather. Of course I asked my stepfather, first, but it's not his writing and – the letters from Paris were locally franked. Stanley is in New York, these days, or Texas with my mother.'

'How jolly awful for you. Death threats, that sort of thing?'

'No, no. He sends fan mail and cut-out pieces from reviews. He's not unpleasant – or not always. And sometimes little snippets of information that tell me he knows where I am, where I'm staying.'

'You've never seen him?'

She hasn't touched her coffee, I notice. The milk is forming a scum on top. She gives a little shiver, though whether from fear or excitement, it's hard to tell.

'No. The cops said it's a hazard of the profession. Crime-writing, you know. Draws the crazies out of the woodwork.'

A huge concession there, though she didn't notice it. I called myself a crime writer. But it does make a better explanation and I know she'd see that, too. Writing about crazy guys lures them to you. I glance up at the kitchen window where a huge spider is bouncing in its web, like a badly wound ball of black cotton.

'Couldn't you, you know, have the handwriting analysed? I've heard—'

'They're typed letters. That sort of thing only happens in pocket-book novels. Ordinary folks don't get that much police time or attention. You know. Writing letters, even a lot of them, without signatures, is not a crime.'

'Well. Really. I do hope he hasn't found you here.' Now she's tugging at the lapels on the green jacket of her pants suit, as if she needs to cover up, as if she herself might be under attack next. I see that the story has enthralled her, that it will do the trick. (So useful that my narrative skills are never fully otiose.) This story fits beautifully with her idea of a writer and the strange trouble they carry around them, like a bad smell.

We drink our coffee, and she makes small-talk about her chickens; would I like some eggs, she'll drop me off a half-dozen, did I know the mobile fishmonger calls every other Friday, very good haddock it is, too.

I manage by a sort of twitchiness and a glance into the living room to indicate that I need to get on with some writing, and finally she leaves. I wave to her from the window as I wash up in the sink, in tepid water, moving my fingers inside the cups in the absence of a cloth. She wobbles up her steps to her own front door in the silly yellow slippers, while I think: If only she could slip on the concrete and crack her head open, like one of her eggs. And then: Do other people have these thoughts, or am I, as Mother often said, wicked through and through?

Before that, I'd been in the garden. Pretending, in case Mrs Ingham, the damn fool *Minna,* is watching, to be checking the place for footprints, for signs of the prowler. In fact, I'm merely striding in my brogues among soggy wet leaves, and hard, persistent fungi, staring down at the little brown stream moving as slow as gravy, and thinking about Sam. Is she seriously going to continue with that weekly analysis – paid for by Gerald? From what she's said the woman shrink talks of *inverts* with such revulsion and excitement – why can't Sam see this? – that any sane person would assume her to be struggling with the same persuasion. And the shrink had not had the wit to tell her to leave Gerald, only that when Sam gave up her 'tastes', the marriage might stand a chance. And what if Sam now felt the desire to confess? Were shrinks like priests? Were they allowed to keep schtum?

Something is unravelling between us and I have to knit it back. It's not just about Gerald: it was there before. It's Sam, it's her . . . conflict, her desire to live the life of a conventional wife and mother, be acceptable, accepted.

That time, that first weekend together in Paris, the happiest ever. After making love, she said to me:

'Your novel. The thing that pleased me most was that on my copy the cover says, "a million copies sold". All those women . . .'

Sam was one of those strange women who'd partly believed she was the devil itself, and entirely alone in her secrets.

Not me. About the age of twelve, I had this picture-postcard, 'Mabel Strickland: The Lovely Lady of Rodeo'. Dan, my cousin, the only one sorry for me, the only one noticing my loneliness, that terrible year said: 'Mabel Strickland's in town. You want to go to the fat-stock show and the rodeo with me and see her?'

'Were you always so sure, Patsy, or are you retelling it how you wish it were?'

So I told her about the flame-haired little girl, Rachel Barber, maybe six or seven, and the rubber Felix-the-cat toy we used to bat around between us, over in Barber's bookstore, among all the pocketbook novels and the dusty mysteries and the love notes I stuck inside books – risky! – for Rachel to find. And that was innocent enough but, yes, it did feel right, because in my secret heart I imagined Rachel felt it too. Rachel opened my letters and giggled; she ran away, but she came back, she read the notes, she didn't turn me over to the adults.

Mabel Strickland, *the lovely lady of Rodeo*, was a less inno-cent feeling and I wondered if Dan knew it. 1933: I was twelve by then. I'd read endlessly about Mabel and others like her – Tad Lucas, another favourite – in comics like *Ranch Romances*. Later I saw her in a movie with Bing Crosby, *Rhythm of the Range*, but not that year: that year I hadn't seen her in the flesh, only dreamed of her. I dressed like a boy, like Jackie Coogan in *The Kid*, with a huge cap pulled to one side and a pudding-bowl haircut, and neither Dan nor Granny Mae ever said a thing about it, although I knew Mother would make a stink when she saw.

That day Dan bought me corn-dogs and sweet lemonade and a box of crackerjack, and we sat hollering at the trick roping and the calf wrestling, the air filled with tobacco and the smell of cattle urine, while Dan necked Buffalo Trace bourbon from a bottle and asked me not to tell Granny Mae. By then Dan was already a rodeo rider and radio announcer but that day he kept me company in the stalls, and we watched, mesmerised, hearts hammering, as the little clods of red earth flew up under the horse's heels, waiting for the star of the show. Dan loved Mabel, too, and gave a great holler as she tore out there, black hair shining, her famous white boots with the playing-card shapes cut into the leather, the white tassels on her leather waistcoat streaming out behind her.

My eyes welled with tears. My heart seemed to be trying to climb out of my body. The crowd was roaring and Mabel with the violet eyes was performing at breakneck speed – hippodrome stands, vaults, and then, heart-stoppingly, even slipping under the belly of her horse. Sweat had begun to spring everywhere on me: what on earth was happening to my body? And as the horse – a dark bay with a blaze on its face – thundered past, the tiny white girl with the knockout smile clinging to it, so did a train out on the prairie and that long, powerful, gathering sound moaning and picking up speed as it raced away made me flush through with heat, and I realised *I* was shaking, thundering too, that something had hold of me and was tossing my body in its grip, and it was Mabel Strickland. I knew then. Dan looked at me strangely. I could have used some air, but I didn't care to say so. No one had to tell me what I was experiencing. This was love, mature love, which men spoke of everywhere, which the poets wrote about, which all my reading had prepared me for. Love for a girl: so what? They were all in love with a girl.

When I told Sam this, she giggled. 'A cowgirl? Well, I guess you did live in Texas. She was the only cheesecake available to you, poor darling.'

'Ah, Mabel, you couldn't call her cheesecake! She threw a steer to the ground in a perfect *bust*, breaking the world record – twenty-four seconds!'

I was still loyal to Mabel after thirty years.

For Sam, it was so much more complicated and delayed. She'd met a young woman when she was at a bar, alone, after she'd married Gerald, a kind of prostitute, as it happened, from a different class than her own, and this naughty girl had kissed her briefly on the mouth and gazed up at her with big brown eyes, letting her know at once such a world existed and that she, Sam, belonged in it.

Later, Sam said this occasion was a mistake, a confusion. She had gone back with Steffie, but they had only sat together and talked; Sam was scared to do more. The girl had been troubled, and desperate, and 'not really my dish', Sam said. The feelings, Sam said, were probably only pity for the girl or an awakening of a maternal instinct. 'Bullshit,' was my reply. After that there were others, too, mentioned by Sam, never fully fleshed out, never fully admitted to. Most of our conversations were about Gerald. Once I knew of his violence, her fear of him, most of her energy went into figuring how to survive, how to keep him sweet.

And now I need to talk to Sam, and see her, and make a new assessment of The Problem and where we are with it all. Everything has changed, and instead of being relieved, or thrilled, I feel some other miserable thing, a weight, an impossibility, an overwhelming bleakness about the future, about the point of anything. Didn't I always say – didn't I say to Smythson-Balby, in fact? – how extraordinary this feeling would be? Of exclusion, of fear, of aloneness – not guilt, not that exactly, only *terror* that, having done this thing, you can never, all your life, again feel free. Because you never know when – or how – you will be undone. How many guys are walking around with that secret in their hearts?

The only person I can share this with is Sam, of course. And yet. We've hardly spoken. She mentioned last time that her dreams were vile: snakes and strange green textures that had no proper form but drove her screaming from her bed. Minty is back at school, and despite her claiming that it was only ever Gerald who sent the girl away, I notice she's made no effort to change her boarding status, to have her at home with her.

I feel impatient with her. Why do people fool themselves, say one thing, so often, and do another? I hate it when Sam behaves as Mother did, pretending an affection that her actions belie. I immediately want to suppress this criticism as unworthy. It's surely the first time I've had such a *disloyal* thought about Sam; I don't like the way my thinking is going. We're in this together! I must telephone her and assure her of this at once!

A chilly wind suddenly snatches up a few strands of my bangs and ruffles my thin shirt. It's been weeks since the funeral and surely enough time has passed for a friend to visit a grieving recently widowed woman friend? I turn back towards the house, and as I do, I hear a ghastly crunching underfoot. Lifting my foot in its wet and shiny brogue as if it's mired in glue, I hardly dare turn the sole over to look.

Another snail shell, hideously crushed. A scattering of pieces of brown shell and jelly: the poor little thing quite dead; quite without any hope of rescue. Tears slide down my nose as I pick the darling object from my shoe, despair once again rushing up at me, for all the pointless, senseless deaths of all the most tiny, beautiful and deserving of creatures. Crushed underfoot or eaten by birds! Doing no harm! The little face of that terrapin, turning to look at me one last beseeching time. I crouch at the stream to place the snail there, watch it sink beneath the brown-grey soup with a soft little plop and bob back up again, the shell filled with air.

No point wishing for the death of Minna Ingham, or obsessing about Smythson-Balby and what she may or may not know, or what's in the letter, the possible or imagined reappearance of Stanley. They're not going to be the ones, are they? There's only Sam can really do it; there's only Sam to fear and, as ever, as always, how could I have been so stupid? Sam is the only danger. Of course, of course.

After Mabel Strickland my next big crush was Veronica Gedeon. New York, 1937. I was sixteen. I had a crazy true-crime addiction and was unable to walk past a newsstand without spending ten cents on one. *Daring Detective, True Detective, Master Detective, American Detective, Official Detective Stories, Startling Detective*, I loved them all with their gorgeous smell of wood pulp and their vivid covers, and sexy pictures of naked girls always cringing and shame-stricken but naked, at least, and that was what mattered and the only way you could get a hold of them. Inside, the stories were entrancing, lurid and stimulating: 'Ghost of Killer – Widow sighted at Fayette County Gaol'; 'Crimson Trail of San Francisco's Gas Pipe Killers'; 'I Am a White Slave'; 'Pretty but Cheap' . . .

That day I picked up a copy of *Inside Detective* and, if you want the truth, it's exactly like the French describe it – a *coup de foudre*. I'm thunderstruck, struck dumb, love struck immediately. There she is: Veronica Gedeon – Vonny – a delicious blonde with dark, frightened eyes, a desperate, pouting mouth, one arm thrown up protectively, shrinking in a position of shame and degradation, her flimsy dress pulled down over one breast . . . Oh, my, that girl was so peppy, that picture gave me palpitations. And the story inside was even better: the model on the front who had starred in other magazines, such as *Front Page Detective* and *Detective Foto*, had – get this – in real-life been raped and murdered! And with her mother lying under the bed, unknown to Vonny, having been dispatched an hour earlier by the same brutal killer! It couldn't get any better. Matter of fact, it did – when photographs of Vonny, taken by amateur photographers, began appearing in all the newspapers, nearly all of them draped in a bit of voile, but easy to see all of Vonny's charms on display: her tiny waist, her well-proportioned, well-spaced breasts, her lovely stomach – she was obviously sucking it in for the photograph, which made you love her even more. I kept them all. I cut them out and put them in a photograph album, bound with antelope skin. I couldn't let Mother see them, of course, and this was the year before I went to Barnard so I was still living at home with her and Stanley, but I could swoon over the photographs – that was definitely the word, *swoon* – alone.

The passion went on for months. And not just mine but the whole of New York, no, the whole country, when her slayer was found and began his own confession in the *New York Times*. Oh, we were in for a treat then. Oh, my. Details we'd never have conjured on our own, some too obscene to print, we were told. That did it. That sealed me, sealed my fate. It took Vonny two hours to die, and over and over I'd imagine her during that time and swoon and swoon again.

That was probably when it began. I read so many of those magazines, they began to seep into my dreams and colour my sweat. I guess they shaped and formed me; alongside Dostoevsky and Edgar Allan Poe and Karl Menninger, sure, they can be said to be an influence. And when I met up with my father, Jay Bernard Plangman, that's a whole story in itself. Maybe I'll tell it, maybe not. Guess what he shows me? The latest semi-clad newspaper photograph of Vonny. That's all he can think to talk to me about. 'That's what I call a girl' – his exact phrase. His not-so-subtle way to let me know that he found me, his boyish daughter, far short of the ideal.

It doesn't take a genius to point out that every girl I've ever loved does end up in the same delicious state: cringing, shame-stricken and brutally murdered in the end. But only in my fiction, of course.

In real life they simply leave.

Later that day – late afternoon, 5 p.m. – Ronnie arrives to take me to the party. The Crime Writers' Association of Great Britain Dagger Awards. He waits while I choose a clean white shirt and fresh white socks, while I insist on re-ironing my best black slacks, and polishing again my smartest black brogues. He waits while I fasten my snakeskin belt, comb and smooth down my hair, helps me fasten the silver catch to my locket at the back of my neck and then watches as, trembling, I strap to my wrist the watch I saved up for all those summers ago. He pours me a large Scotch when he sees that I'm shaking and can barely buckle the watch strap, knowing it's the thought of the party and of having to walk up to the podium if I win that is making me tremble. He takes my arm and says gallantly: 'You should be proud – it's something to be pleased about you know, winning an award.' And he waits patiently, too, when I run back upstairs with my big purse, to get the essential award-party guests: a large head of lettuce from the fridge and most of my snails.

The party is the usual god-awful affair. Filthy wine in little plastic cups that nearly fold in your hands. Matrons in floaty numbers over slacks; peppy little blondes in dresses so short they look like négligées. That mournful feeling, whenever there is a break in the conversation, or someone moves away from me, of gazing round helplessly for Ronnie, like a child in an empty stand searching for its mother, and seeing that I'm alone, utterly alone. Once or twice I put my hand in my purse and close my fingers around a cool smooth shell, feeling the stickiness at once retreating shyly. Pull in your horns and hide: if only it were possible.

Charles Latimer bounds up and I'm glad of him, at least. 'Darling! Congratulations! And, you know, it's a real dagger – made of silver and everything. Have you seen it yet?' He seems a little high.

I have to go up there and collect it, it seems. More torture. And here is the dreadful Frances woman (a peck, and she hops off) and a bunch of English writers, whose names I should know but don't, and once again, I'm on my own. I draw on a cigarette. I try to make my face into an expression of worldly sophistication, as if standing alone like this in a cloud of competing perfumes, in the midst of chattering, madly socialising people screaming with laughter, is something I want to do. Holy crap. *Where, oh, where is Ronnie?* And why should I care if I happen to seem a little odd? For some cock-eyed reason, most people in the world are concerned simply to be exactly like everybody else.

Virginia Smythson-Balby is in front of me, drink in hand, smiling rather hopefully.

'I – hope we're – on speaking terms? I wanted to say, you know, congratulations and all that.'

'Of course we're on speaking terms, why wouldn't we be? I'm having a hard time finding a drink – where did you get yours?'

I'm feeling swimmy already – but I don't tell her that. Her cup is full and she happily grabs one from the tray of a passing waiter and hands it to me, neatly depositing my empty cup on the same tray. White wine, but it could be the vinegar that pickles are drowned in. I down it in two glugs and reach for another.

'Would you like a lift back to Bridge Cottage later?' the persistent girl says. Her shiny chestnut hair bounces on her shoulders, and she's wearing an emerald green dress in some gaudy fabric with swirls on it; a dress so flighty it's barely skimming her thighs.

'I drove here. I brought Ronnie.'

'Oh, but I just spoke to him. He told me he had met a friend here and intends to stay in London.'

Sure, Ronnie told me that earlier, too. But she has a fine nerve.

'That's fine. I'm happy to drive alone.'

She looks a little shifty then, embarrassed. Nods towards the cup of wine in my hand.

'Well you can relax then, can't you? Have another drink and not worry.'

'It's only seventeen shillings on the train to Ipswich,' I say sharply. 'I could get a cab from there.'

'Oh, but do let me! We could leave your car here and I'm *awfully* horribly sober, and we can have a nice chat on the way home.'

Sure. A chat. A powerful urge then to ask her about the letter from Stanley, or is it 'BD' or Brother Death? Did she know anything about it? Did she ever write letters, strange, meaningless letters, the kind of letters a fan might write, letters that simply say: 'I know where you're living', or 'Hello, I'm still here', letters that say nothing very much but are written for the purpose of making me shudder? She looks like the letter-writing sort. Intense. A bit cracked, perhaps. Did she send letters to me, now or in the past, or even drop one in my house, perhaps sneak one into the airing cupboard on pretence of going to the bathroom one time?

The latest letter from Stanley is still unopened, so I've no idea what it says. Maybe this one is worse than the rest. Maybe the writer confesses at last. Maybe he – *she* – knows something about Gerald.

Another tiny cup of wine is downed, then the room is called to attention and the voices lapse to a hum and some crazy with a microphone is making a speech about the Crime Writers' Association of Great Britain . . . and I'm picturing not writers but criminals, wishing, longing, dreaming up their deeds in smoke-filled studies across Britain; and then not criminals but strutting pheasants – seen so many of those in Suffolk lately: how stupid they are, and how many of them I see at this time of year, scooping up their tails like women lifting their skirts, scurrying across the road, with their white collars and their swanky colours, and how they dart out just as the car approaches, and then it's my turn, my turn to step up there and say something, some thanks or jokes (well, yes, people are laughing and smiling, I guess I'm making some jokes), then accepting the narrow cardboard box and flipping it open to see the dagger lying there, silver, thin, pretty deadly, weighty – I really do think it could probably stab someone in the throat (perhaps the head of the Crime Writers' Association?) – and then I make another joke about the dagger and there's polite applause, and now I have to make a speech, it seems; I bite back my usual argument about how I'm writing 'suspense fiction' and mumble something instead about how happy I am that there is such affection for crime fiction in this country, wondering if the charming pleasure English readers take in vicarious acts of violence, in reading about wicked things that others do, makes a healthy outlet for society (some argue that pornography serves the same function, easing pressure that might otherwise turn fine men into rapists).

Then in the middle of speaking I'm trout-sober and thinking again of the pheasants now crossing the road, thinking that they look like a stream of little vicars, lifting up their robes, the white collar at their throat, trotting, that funny mix of pomposity and timidity, as if they really do have some kind of ludicrous death wish – didn't one bat itself bloodily against the car the other day, a startling thud that made me jump, as if someone just threw a hard snowball? *Vicars, vicars*: how they tell Ronnie that the world is full of taboos and people used to live like animals. Children were welcomed, each one was 'the little dear' – oh, sure, everything as natural and healthy in the country as little yellow chicks, unless it was born out of wedlock and then it was shunned and hated. What of a child whose mother had tried to get rid of it with turpentine? How would they feel towards her? I want to ask. Could they turn the healthy yellow into a dank and skewered green? But Ronnie has no answer for that.

And then I mention (oh, sure I'm still making a speech) – lightly, very lightly – an alternative view, that rather than the ever-growing love for crime fiction *releasing* society from some of its evils, letting off a little steam, as it were, perhaps such fiction is stoking a fire, making violent behaviour, violent acts ever more *desirable* and appealing, exhilarating, keeping us ever entertained, ever aroused to their potential excitements, always happening to and being done by other people; protecting us from the hurtful, sordid glimpse of how such things really are ... I trail off here and there's some uncertain applause and then I'm allowed to step down, melt back into the crowd, the faces ballooning up – Ronnie, smiling, the sun behind him as always, Ronnie telling me something important that actually matters, like *a scythe cost seven shillings and sixpence in Wickham Market and we did the reaping by hand*; how I long for something clean and true like that, instead of this god-awful stupidity and clapping and the spotlight and the podium and the sickness, the dirty wicked sickness, sweeping through my body.

*   *   *

174

Smythson-Balby drives me home. Of course she does. She had an idea of that all evening. I can't remember where I've left my car but she *says* Ronnie knows and we can go back for it 'on the weekend'; she'll drive me. So, not just one occasion to drive me but two. She's taking advantage. It was she who planted more and more tiny cups of wine in my hand, and now she has her reward. I'm slumped in the passenger seat beside her and she's singing, I swear she's actually singing along to the radio, Brook Benton . . . *Hotel Happiness (tra la la la)*.

She's chattering, too. All sorts of things. Did I see Muriel Spark at the party? Had I read the latest Edna O'Brien? Could she take another peek at the little silver dagger lying in its box, and when I pass it over, 'Oh, how pretty! One could use it for a letter opener!'

I'm struggling to sober up. I'm slumped against the cold of the car window and I've taken off my shoes and am curling as close to the foetal position as I can manage, in the cramped seat of her Triumph. I must stay alert. She might mention Gerald, Sam, Aldeburgh, and something might slip. Her lurid green dress with its swirly pattern is rucked up, and I can see the top of her panty-hose, and I have to deduce: she's got a fine nerve. She doesn't care if I see it or not.

Now her chatter is about her family: Daddy who is – good Christ – a high-court judge; one younger brother, a sort of mongoloid it seems, in an institution somewhere, I can't remember the word she uses; an older sister, nicknamed Bonnie, very fat, 'poor darling'; an older brother who runs the family home, the estate, with his own giant brood. They're practically in the car with us. Another sister, who does something with horses, or is that the same fat one? On and on it goes until I sit up a little straighter, and ask: has she ever written weirdo letters to anyone? Fan letters?'

A light laugh. She doesn't blink or give anything away. Impossible to tell what she's really thinking of my question but the answer comes easily and pleasantly, pink-painted nails on the steering-wheel, a little tug at the hem of her dress: 'No, I don't think so. Is this about . . . is it because I said I loved your work? Do people write to you? And you find that – unsettling?'

I shake my head. The Suffolk roads are dark, flanked either side by trees that always make me think of a film set, a false front. I know what's behind them: hills and further darkness, a waiting blankness. At Cretingham (I think of the brother she mentioned – perhaps 'cretin' was the word she used), a ghostly owl sweeps in front of us and the headlights suddenly pick out an old-timer in a flat cap, sitting in the back garden of his lone cottage with a pipe – at past midnight – like a gnome.

She laughs. 'What's the story there, do you think? Old chap had a row with the missus and come outside to smoke?'

'Probably just buried her. Surveying his handiwork.'

'Never off duty, are you? It must be exhausting dreaming up all the horrible things people are always thinking and doing.'

When I say nothing to this, she starts up again: 'And yet they're not, are they? I mean, most people are law-abiding. It's just a little fantasy. You said it yourself, when we first met. How many murders was it in England last year?

'Three hundred,' I say.

'Yet if you read – sorry, I don't mean to cause offence – but if you read novels like yours, you'd think they were happening willy-nilly, to everyone!'

'Most of my novels aren't set in England. In fact, this one is the first.'

The feeling then: this is the point of her conversation, to find out more accurately what I'm writing and report back to dear Cousin Frances. I bite my lip.

'And murder is happening sometimes, even here, isn't it?' I say. 'Look at Christie. Not Agatha! I meant John Christie. Eight women, wasn't it, most of them hidden in his back yard?'

She nods. This has been in the news again lately, a new investigation ten years later, because one of the victims was blamed on Timothy Evans. Radio, television, newspapers: it would be hard not to know the details. Strangling them with their own stockings; raping them once they were unconscious.

'And that thing they say, crummy guys who didn't know him at all. He "kept himself to himself" – how often do you hear that when newspaper men interview the neighbours? Meaning: I didn't know him but I want my five minutes of fame so I'm going to say *something* about him. Everyone loves it, the frisson, the glamour of being associated with a murderer.'

'Well, Daddy says they took a vote this week in the House of Commons. And the death penalty really is going to be abolished . . . dragging up the cases again and poor Timothy Evans, well, it has achieved something. Ghastly though it all was. If you believe that the death penalty is barbaric. But perhaps you don't. I suppose a lot of Americans, Texans, wouldn't agree with me.'

'I do happen to agree with you,' I mumble. I'm not your average Texan.

I file this information away: no death penalty, then. I somehow knew that would happen, a reprieve of sorts, punishment withdrawn for a crime no one has yet uncovered, and doesn't it take some of the sting away, making it less of the ultimate risk? But Smythson-Balby is pleased, and rattles on about civilised behaviour or something. Now she just seems young. Young, idealistic and sweet. I put my cheek against the cold car window, suddenly feeling icily sober.

'And another thing,' I say. 'You're getting yourself confused. Between fiction and fact, I mean. An author makes things up. Their skill is to lie, to deflect and head-off, not to give you a shining pathway to their innermost self.'

I read the sign saying 'Saxtead 2, Debenham 5', which always makes me think of Ronnie, and she changes down a gear as we reach the road that runs alongside Bridge Cottage. There are no lights on in Mrs Ingham's house – Bridge House – but I have the strong feeling that Minna's standing there anyway, watching. There's a hesitation after Smythson-Balby has wrenched on the handbrake and is wondering whether to cut the engine, and then she does, and the interior light flashes on. An unexpected feeling wells up in me. Her cheek is rather pink; her bottom lip pouting a little. Her big eyes blazing. Another dangerous thought as the light and silence fill the car, then fade away: *I'm lonely. I miss Sam.* And, God, that girl has good strong legs.

I reach for my purse, which has travelled carefully on the back seat, with the clasped frame slightly open for oxygen. My hand is shaking a little on the inside handle of the car. 'You fancy a nightcap?' I ask.

She says she does.

This must be the most dangerous situation I've ever found myself in. This girl wants to know about me, and I want to tell her things. My love affairs often begin this way: the tease and charge of sharing, revealing, confessing, then making full about-turns, snatching it all back. I'm swimmy with whisky too. *Dangerous.* I'm rarely interested in getting to know the other person. I'm excited by what they want to know about me and how many secrets I can hold tight.

I take her from room to room upstairs, handing her one of the spare toothbrushes I keep in packets in the medicine cabinet; unsurprised, she takes one dutifully and brushes her teeth, spitting noisily into the basin.

Then I show her the snails, returning the ones who have been journeying with me back to their rightful bowls (there are many more of them now: I've bought proper tanks for several of them). Although she wrinkles her nose at the smell and seems surprised at first, she stands for a while watching as they make love. Abelard reaches down to kiss Héloise.

'How can you tell he's the male?' she says.

'You can't. There's no difference between them.'

Héloise had reared on the end of her tail, swaying a little under Abelard's caress. We watch for a while, and I'm thinking of absolutely nothing. Then the swellings begin to appear on each side of the snails' heads. The sticky lumps grow larger and touch. 'How they adore each other,' I murmur, and drag myself away with reluctance, feeling her interest slacken.

'Ginny', as she insists I call her, now wants to see the study (she assumes it's where I write, and is surprised to see only the wood-working tools, the bench, the easel, the half-squeezed tubes and little glass jar of paint brushes in muddy, stream-coloured water). There is the portrait I'm doing of Sam as a great long white orchid, stretching and arching, gazing down at me, but at least it's safely hidden behind other propped-up sketches, and I don't allow her to flick through them. I kiss her in the door-way, figuring that will be the best distraction. She groans and practically melts to my feet but I manage to steer her towards the bedroom. Her mouth is lovely, warm, tasting of wine and tooth-paste and a hot smoky flavour that is all her own.

There she strips off entirely – under the swirly green dress is a black slip with lace, whipped off in a second and pants and pantyhose briskly abandoned – and leaps into bed, like a child, pulling the sheets up to her chin, coquettish and giggly. I have a flash of white skin, the youthful flanks of a lacrosse player, slim waist, fine, developed arms. I hope she's not expecting me to undress in the same reckless way. I leave her there while I pad downstairs for whisky and glasses, the tremble inside me that wars with the sensible voice saying, *What are you doing have you lost your mind completely do you want to be undone?* and the other self, the deeper one, the one I've always listened to, that goes steadily on, pouring drinks.

So I hand hers to her in bed and she sits forward and kisses me and puts her glass down with a clunk on the coaster – a picture of a little church in Lavenham – on the table beside her. I step out of the brogues and leave them neatly by the bed, toes pointing outwards. I take my shirt off, and unclip my brassière, then my jeans and underpants. I fold them and leave them on the rug beside the bed. I climb in beside her. Her big eyes seem to swim

179

up at me, dazzled, and she smiles a big, crazy kind of smile, and I'm almost, for one second, mesmerised, made dizzy and sick by the delicious extravagance of her; of her youth, her gorgeous excess, the ridiculous loveliness of those girlish breasts, that tumbling hair, that mouth, that smile, those big, big, Bambi eyes . . .

But where to next? How experienced is she? Our naked skin is chilly to the touch. I'm afraid to be crude, too knowing, too rough: I don't know here what she's used to, though it's clear from all she said, from every hint about 'Izzie' and various clubs, that we both know she's no novice. She begins at once to feel for me under the sheets and probe and stroke and knead with rude confidence; well, I guess people are the same in bed as they are elsewhere, and that's her style – boisterous (she strokes my back as if rubbing dry a dog), gauche, devil-may-care and sure. In the end she's skilled enough, and her strength (one arm at my waist, pulling me closer), her kisses (on my neck, my breasts) and her fingers are producing a flow and a heat and a rhythmic certainty that I'm craving, yes, that's *it,* I'm thinking, surrendering at last, opening my eyes to smile at her as her fingers melt a little deeper, letting her know that the ball of her hand is pressure on exactly the place. I want to be here and there and also dangerously far away; how would it feel to be peeled, found out, to give it all up? I put my mouth to her breasts. How would it feel to cease to exist?

In the early hours I am bolt awake and something cold is washing over me. Sweat. Shame. Oh, God. Sam. My darling Sam, all alone in her grief, in that big draughty home in Highgate. Sam. What on earth will I say to Sam? I'll have to tell her because – because Sam is the only one who knows me, who knows everything about me, the worst of me; if I have secrets from Sam I'll lose everything. I'll never feel close to her again.

The whisky bottle is empty and I can't remember finishing it but the feeling in my head, as if four sharp fingers clamp my scalp in a spiteful grip, tells me that I did. *Oh, Sam, Sam, darling, I'm sorry!* I feel for my pyjamas, under my pillow. I must put them on under the coat and slip my feet into the cold brogues and go out; telephone Sam. A hot solid lump – of Ginny, as I now think of her – is beside me, rumbling lightly with snores; the low threat of a volcano.

And then, under my gaze in the semi-dark, the volcano erupts. She opens her eyes and mutters: 'I love you.'

Holy crap. *No.*

Rain is spattering the window – a sliver of splashed glass appearing between the curtains with the pinky-gold glow of dawn – and I lie on my back staring up at it. A cold, ugly, familiar feeling tiptoes up my body. How I despise those who fall for stupid, ridiculous, wicked and murderous me. How sensible lovely Sam is in never declaring herself, so that I can respect her.

How to answer this silly slip of a girl? How not to hurt her but to make it clear, absolutely clear? I slip my arm out from under her head. I roll over and immediately cover myself in the unsexy bathrobe, tying the waist tight. 'I'll go fix us some coffee,' I say. Her smiling face instantly freezes. That was not the answer she expected. She pulls the sheets up to her chin and a frown line appears between her brows, but she says nothing.

When I come back up with two cups of coffee on a small tray and milk in a separate jug, she's all bounce again, and sitting up with her black slip on, and asking for cigarettes. I light one for her and she nods her thanks.

'Daddy says I'll grow out of it. It's just a phase but he says he should never have sent me to an all girls' school.'

'Your father knows? The high-court judge *talks* to you about it?'

'He said Izzie had dyke's thighs. That was the giveaway. Daddy had lots of experiences – he went to Eton. One grows up and gets married and tries not to succumb. That's what he says will happen to me.'

Ha. I roll my cigarette in the ashtray absently, thinking about Sam. Desire flickers again as I notice that Ginny is letting the strap of her black lace slip fall a little as she stretches her white neck, lifts her hair. (Maybe if I'm going to give her up for ever – go cold turkey – I could have one last binge.) She's a hot, heaving sort of presence. I realise that from the first occasion I met her she always gave me this vividness, this availability, possibility. The opposite of Sam, with her grace, her restraint, her infuriating coolness. Ginny wants to present it, offer it, that audacious body! And then leave it to you to make the first move so that the responsibility is never hers. Despicable female behaviour. Yes, exactly like a child.

'Avoid it all you want,' I say. 'I know girls like that. It won't make you happy.'

'But you're the most unhappy person I've ever met! And you're open, as open as it's possible to be.'

Sudden fury at this jibe gives me the energy to rid myself of her.

'What makes you think I'm open? What a damn stupid thing to say. Who can be open? In a place like this? You're not going around saying that about me, are you?'

'No, no – of course not. I wouldn't say a word. I shan't say a word. I understand the rules.'

'I wrote a novel about it. But wouldn't you think that if someone published a novel under another name they didn't care to have the whole world know?'

She nods, trying to appease me, I can see. So I say: 'This – it can't happen again. Biographers don't make love to their subjects, do they? Or only in their writing.'

She even smiles at this and settles herself into the covers as if not deterred at all, planning to stay awhile. 'But I'm only the research assistant! It's perfectly legitimate, surely, being a biographer. Perfectly human – nosy, sure, I'll grant you that, but not wrong to be fascinated by someone. To want to tell the story of another's life. To study their work.'

'Let the work speak for itself. It's all there, if you're any good. Then it can mean something different, more or less, to whoever cares to read it.' I finish the cigarette and roll over onto my side to stare at her. She certainly is a beauty and I see that she knows it; she watches me and the direction of my glance, all the time trying to catch a light there to ignite. The devil with Ginny Smythson-Balby. I'm determined not to give so much as a glimmer.

'One minute you claim you don't care if people know you're queer, you don't care for the opinion of others . . .' she says.

'When did I say that? I never said that—'

'But biographies are so fascinating,' she interrupts. 'Haven't you ever read one? What about Dostoevsky and the fact that he was almost executed and reprieved at the last minute? Isn't that relevant when reading him and his thoughts on life, on how we want to cling to life, no matter what?'

'There you go again. Confusing his characters with his own position. As if a writer wasn't capable of putting things in a character's mouth that he didn't happen to feel. Or spread them between two characters. I happen to think the white space is where the meaning is held.'

When Ginny opens her mouth to disagree I've suddenly had enough and cut her off: 'At any rate, what I've mostly learned from biographies is that someone has some pretty bad habits in bed or is a lousy tightwad about tipping in restaurants. So what?'

'Oh, I'm sure that, one day, you'll be glad people remain interested in you. Don't you keep diaries, after all?'

'Some people just like writing to themselves. That's what a diary is, if you want the truth. Leave the novels alone – the unconscious bits should remain unconscious.'

Her wide, finely carved shoulders and creamy skin were starting to work on me, like alcohol. I should get up. I should go downstairs and fix breakfast, at least squeeze us some orange juice. I could even slip outside and telephone Sam, because I'll need to go to London today and suddenly I can't go another minute without speaking to her.

'I need to make a call,' I tell her. 'I have plans to confirm. I have to go to London now on the train from Ipswich and pick up my car. You were kind to bring me home.'

I see the misery in her eyes but there's no avoiding it. My eyes stray to my window ledge, the snails, inert at this time of day, in hiding. The most curious thought pops into my head, one I haven't had since I lived in Pennsylvania with Marijane. 'Did you ever think you were going to have the most unusual experience, one that you are marked out for in life, and you always knew, even as a child, and then, finally, you did?'

Ginny beams at me. I guess she thinks I mean her. This is enough to calm her; she reaches for her clothes and swings her legs from the bed to come downstairs. Matter of fact, I'm thinking of something else entirely that I felt fated to do and a feeling I'd forgotten I'd had. But it was the right thing to say. A last romp would be ill-judged, if enjoyable. I see that now. Ginny meant it when she declared herself in love with me. I need a drink, and yet the whisky bottle is empty and I can hardly go and buy another at this hour in the morning. Another dreadful mess. And, as ever, of my own making. Making a mess, upsetting people, that's what I do best.

At the age of three I remember making a mud pie for Mother. I spent hours in the garden at our house in Fort Worth. I dug up the rich smelly black soil until it was deeply under my fingernails and smeared over my clothes and I imagined that it was the black gold – the oil that everyone spoke of – and patted it down into one of Granny's flowered plates. I added little flowers and decorated the edges with blades of grass. It looked so pretty; I thought Mother would love it. So I ran in from the garden and held out the plate to Mother and said: 'I made you Chocolate Mud Pie. Eat it.'

'No, Patsy, sweetie, it's just earth and flowers. It looks disgusting. I don't want to eat it.'

'*Pretend* to eat it!'

'Why would I do that? You'd know I was pretending – and look at you! Look at your overalls – they're disgusting!'

'It's a lovely pie. I've made it for you.'

'Patsy. It's soil. It's dirt. Goddamn it – it's make-believe. I'm about to go out. You be a good girl now and take a bath and—'

'EAT IT!'

Then I got a slap, a hard one, across my face or the top of my head or wherever she could reach as I scampered away from her, balancing my plate on one hand, like a head waiter. *That* was something. I knew where she was going that evening and I knew who with. The hateful Stanley. And I might have annoyed her, but she had hit me: that was something at any rate. It meant she knew I was still there: I'd gotten under her skin. That pleased me.

'I could give you a lift to the station in Ipswich,' Ginny says, pulling her green dress over her head. I guess there's no avoiding her. Just as I reckoned: for those hopelessly, unrequitedly in love, even hurtful attention is worth it. A slap or coldness, it's all the same to us.

The trip to the zoo is not a success. The day pings with tension, things unsaid. What is Sam thinking? Does anyone suspect us? Have the police made more enquiries, or are we safe now? We're like two birds on a high wire, with a strong wind blowing, clinging on by our toes.

I keep glancing at Sam for signs. Her face, the way she is drawing her fur stole up to her throat, the gestures of her hands in pale blue gloves. What kind of gestures are these – and in what light would others see them? Does she appear nervous, guilty, ready to pop like a bubble and confess at the merest provocation? And when to make *my* confession, when to mention Smythson-Balby and get that out of the way? I walk beside her quick firm steps on the slick wet sidewalk with Minty on her other side, and none of the answers are clear.

The Christmas lights are on in London; it's dark by 4 p.m.; car tyres swish sadly as they roll through puddles. Minty's eyes do not light up at the dangling white and red Santa Claus outside a department store, and she says nothing when Sam remarks softly: 'If only this rain would turn to snow like last year . . .' Minty is a watchful, shrewd girl in a raincoat over a pinafore dress, with big dark eyes and a sullen expression. She misses nothing; so much like myself at her age. She has her mother's fair beauty but Gerald's sneaky, sinewy quality, and gives one the horrible feeling that she is only biding her time, enduring her childhood for as long as she has to; waiting for the moment when she can rise to her full height and take up her place as the judgemental country matron she was always destined to be, presiding over husband, children, hens, whatever.

Only the fat sea lions being drizzled on in their concrete bunker produce a spark of interest.

'There's blood on that one,' Minty says, pointing to a long, slug-like shape and a sly eye, and, sure, there is: a wet patch, gleaming under the rain, of dark blood.

'Oh, poor thing. They must have been fighting,' Sam explains, although my first thought is not fighting but mating. There's another sea lion enduring his cell with him, smaller, clearly female, and there's blood on her rump, too. But I don't say that, of course. Sam is fiddling with an obsidian pendant, oval-shaped, nestling in the dip in her throat, lifting it, dropping it again. I long to put my hand over hers and still her.

Minty doesn't laugh, as the other children do, when the keeper puts a hat from a Christmas cracker on a chimp, and tries to get a little one and its mother to pull the cracker apart; they simply hit each other over the head with it and begin chewing on it. Sam looks worriedly at her, and then at me, and says, in her warmest tones: 'Oh, darling, aren't they funny?' but no one is responding.

And I know I am brooding, and Sam will accuse me of this later, of not trying harder to be talkative, or fun, for Minty's sake, of shaking off the rain in Liberty's café, and drinking my cocoa in silence, but the possibility of *not* thinking of Gerald is not there. It looms between us: a great cloud of extraordinary proportions, a noxious gas, something we're breathing in but not breathing out. I long to tell her about the visit from the police, of Mrs Ingham and her suspicions, of Smythson-Balby, of all the small tribulations and terrors I've borne – for her sake, for her sake, of course – and I long to have her reassure me, tell me that nothing has happened in the weeks since the funeral, no further conversations with policemen or anyone else. That all is fine between us . . . But she's said nothing, she's . . .

'Children can't grieve openly. It's so cruel,' is all Sam says, *finally*, when we're back at hers, our legs aching, our hair and coats soaked through, the smell of miserable, cooped-up animals still clinging to us, our umbrellas making puddles in the large ceramic pot in the hall. Minty is in the bathroom, drying her hair with a towel. I don't care for the discovery that it's Minty she's been thinking about all day, rather than the anxieties I've been suffering over *our* predicament (and what to do now that Gerald is out of the way) but I say nothing.

Minty's footsteps thud dully overhead and Sam stands at the bottom of the stairs and calls up to her that she's to go to bed; she'll bring her a hot-water bottle and some warm milk in a little while. Another twinge of irritation pangs through my body. When will Sam turn her attention to *me*, quit worrying about all that apple-pie order here? When will we get to *our vitally important* conversation?

While Minty was on the stairs on her way up to bed, I had put my coat back on and stood at the front door as if to reopen my umbrella. I called goodnight to her over my shoulder and then, once she was safely away, I stepped back into the living room, removed my coat, and sat down in front of the hearth.

A fire crackles there and the room is full of the smell of burning; Sam has barely noticed my charade about leaving. She is trotting up and down the stairs with things for Minty and I hear murmurs of the maternal conversations I presume to be about tooth-brushing and when bedside lamps must be switched off and then at last – *at last!* – she appears in the living room beside me, a bottle of wine and two glasses in her hands, the corkscrew awkwardly under one arm.

How to move us along to the main subject, the subject of us, the future? How long must we wait? What should we do now? Would she move to Suffolk? She opens the wine and pours some into my chilled glass, a delicious Pouilly-Fuissé, so light and refreshing, from a case in Gerald's cellar. Perhaps we should go to France, I'm about to say, sipping it. I'm feeling restless again, and rather done with Suffolk. Or could I move in here with her, or nearby perhaps? Once the child is back in school, of course, and . . .

And then she's telling me, I think she's telling me, that our love affair is over. That what happened between us can't just be *absorbed* – I picture blotting paper, black ink, stains dispersing – that her feelings for me since Gerald's death have *changed for ever*; that she doesn't feel she will recover from her grief, her 'blackness'; she's finding her old depression – not felt since the early years after Minty's birth, the time she started seeing the analyst – has descended again, it's unbearable and she's very afraid she's *going under*. She refers only to Gerald's 'suicide' and her 'guilt' – she doesn't say what this is about – and waves a hand as I try to interrupt.

I'm staring at the wine in her glass, its delicate pale green colour. There's still a fire in the hearth, although it's low, glowing, and needs more wood. There's a leather hod next to the fireplace and in an idle way I wonder: Should I put another log on the fire? And then I'm staring at the stem of her wine glass, which will surely break if she rubs it between finger and thumb like that for much longer; and I suppose I hear her but I don't hear her and when I open my eyes again the world has altered and I'm alone in it.

All this I did for you. So that we could be together. I was willing to risk everything, anything, for you, and in the end, you are conventional and what you want above all is a life like everyone else's. This is nothing to do with Gerald. You are a coward and that is all. You are not – worthy.

Sam is softly crying. More tears, which shame me. I stare at her with a combination of loathing and devotion. She struggles to find a handkerchief in her pocket book and I hand her mine – a big, clean, ironed one – and she sniffs and blows her nose, which could use some powder. Samantha. The woman I want above all others, the only one I have ever wanted like this. As spineless as everyone else. I sip my wine again; and now it tastes only of greyness, of salt. Somewhere a window has been left open and I think I hear rain swishing down a drain or a gutter. A car horn sounds and some drunken voice gives a brief burst of 'O Little Town of Bethlehem'. The brakes of a double-decker bus cut it short with a hiss.

I pour myself another glass of wine and inch ever so slightly away from Sam along the sofa. Only half consciously, I place a dove-grey velvet cushion between us. I do not want to touch her, or comfort her. I have a temptation to stand up, move away from her and sit nearer the fire, but I don't. I'm thinking, composing. What to say, what is the one thing that will change her mind?

Some Christmas cards on the fireplace catch my eye. A couple are not Christmassy at all but clearly say: *With Greatest Sympathy*. A small tree bedecked with only a couple of silver balls and one hand-made pomander, a shrivelled orange with cloves stuck in it, a cheap red ribbon around it, and dangling from it on a white, snowman-shaped note, in a child's handwriting, *To Mummy, love Minty*.

And a torrent of pity washes through me, staring at it. Minty. Alone, in bed, face buried in her pillow, dry-eyed. Her father gone, and her mother down here crying for herself, disappointing, treacherous, like every other mother in the world. The sound of a train far, far away rattles through my brain with its familiar melancholy wail: here it is again, here it comes – my life, years – to torture me. I think of box-cars, and my longing to jump one, a fantasy I had when I was Minty's age, how I would just run along the track and fling myself on, let the train carry me far away, a long tunnel in Hell, who cared? To anywhere. I remember the smell of my mother's hair on the pillow; that one time she suddenly decided to sleep in my bed. Painfully awake, fitful, afraid to disturb her, afraid that even if I twitched my shoulder it would be enough to make her leave. Listening to the vibration of her soft snoring. And in the morning she was gone, the pillow flat, as if she was never there. And what I said to myself then is the same now: *This is how it is for me. They are all heartless bitches. That's just how it is.*

Sam sniffs loudly, dabs at her nose and hands the handkerchief back to me. Swallows. Smooths her dress over her knees. Straightens her shoulders – I have a glimpse of the strength in her slender body, her power – and glances at me over the top of her glass.

'Are you going to sit here brooding all night? It's too late now to call a taxi. At least we should go to bed . . .' she says. And, curiously, it's not Sam I see then but a girl in summer camp, a young woman called Rose – wasn't she the tennis coach? She was so strong, and muscular, too. More vibrant than Sam. More real.

Sam stands up, her back to me. She's wearing a cream dress, discreet, chic. Cream wool, with wool-covered buttons all the way down the front, a neat belt at her neat waist. She will always look chic, I think. She's like a long-stemmed orchid. And then, angrily: *She's all about style over content.*

Rose, Miss Rose, the tennis coach, wore a pleated white skirt and had a peculiar way of doing her hair up, using a long, thin sock to bind it. That summer we were playing, all the girls were playing, dress-up. I had an idea to change into Miss Rose's clothes – the white tennis underpants, the pleated skirt, the little blouse with the small embroidered motif, and, of course, it all smelt of her, of sweat and cut grass and tennis-shoe-whitener, and the smell made me tremble and fizz. The other girls were striding round the camp, it was camp counsellors' day where the high jinks were to dress like this, to swap and be each other; that was the whole idea of the game. And so I found Miss Rose's sock and wound it round my hair and her little hair clip and put that in too. And then there was that moment: I was in the dorm and she burst in, she must have seen me at the window with my hair fixed up like hers, mimicking her tennis serve in front of my bedroom mirror – swinging her racket twice before hitting the ball.

'Girl. What the hell—?' Miss Rose said.

I lowered the racket.

'Oh – we're all doing it, dressing up as the counsellors,' I said, in a shaky voice. 'I'm – I – it was a game, Miss Rose.'

She was staring at me; I could not meet her eyes.

'Miss, everyone was doing it . . .' I petered out.

This was the shared room, the girls' dorm, and I was afraid another girl would step in, step into the fuzz of the atmosphere that was sudden and sizzling between us.

She looked at my hair. 'Take that out,' she said and grabbed at the sock, snatched at the hair grip, so that it pinged onto the floor. I longed to pick it up but found I could not move.

'Miss, the other girls—'

Miss Rose stepped closer to me then bent quickly to pocket her hair grip. It was strange that we had to call the counsellors 'Miss'. The girl was probably eighteen, a calm girl, icily deliberate in every last stride and comment.

'You . . .' she said, '. . . need to understand something.'

And then she said more, words too cruel, too plain, words I would never be able to unhear.

No. Not me. She doesn't feel that way about *me*. And throughout this confrontation with Miss Rose I'd been miserably removing each item until I was wearing only the underpants and a long white tank. Shame now stuffing the room with a choking, poisonous gas. Miss Rose looked wordlessly at the white underpants, as if deliberating whether to ask me to take those off too. Then she turned on her heel and stalked out.

Oh, that phoney, that little round-heels, that bitch . . .

Mother, Rose, Sam, all of them. The smell of the chalky whitener on her tennis shoes. The whisk of air as she stalked past me, scooping my humiliation up in one hand and tossing it, like pebbles, behind her imperious ass. *What are you so fucking afraid of?*

'I meant to tell you,' I say to Sam now. 'I went to bed with someone else. The young journalist, remember her? Ginny Smythson-Balby. Gorgeous little thing, she is.'

An expression crosses Sam's face that gives me a deep, ugly pleasure and I glance down into my glass to hide it.

'Oh. Well. I suppose I deserved that,' she says softly, hesitating, then making a step towards me, holding out her hand, her eyes glittering. Then: 'Come to bed, Patsy. Can't we stop warring and just be good to each other?'

Girl, you're heavenly . . .

A fragment of a song I loved, once. And it – and the gesture, the hand outstretched – makes something leap in me, flick its tail. My heart still on the hook. But.

Every part of me aches with the sadness of knowing that this is not a reconciliation, that she means it; that cool, decisive Sam will never go back on her word. 'Come to bed' does not mean to reconcile but only to sleep. And an impulse to push her and hurt her keeps surging in me just as it did with Miss Rose all those years ago.

Watching her, the room oscillating slightly, I imagine my hands around her throat, just tightening there, exactly where the shiny black obsidian pendant hangs, my fingertips pressing a little, digging it into her throat – how much pressure would it take? Not much, perhaps, because she is so, so delicate, these days, and that elegant Modigliani neck is like the stalk of a tulip, ready to snap. But it would end things, put an end to it, and I have to do that.

'Or . . . well, shall I open another bottle?' Sam asks. She's swaying, feeling her drinks but halfway to the door to fetch it. I nod.

'I happen to think,' I say, finding my voice at last. 'We could get past these troubles.'

'I'm so sorry, darling,' Sam says, in a rush, agonised. 'I'm sorry, but this is how it has to be.'

I fall silent. You lack courage, I want to say. You're like all the others. And this: I never saw you cry in all the time together and just lately you're all tears, like a weeping saint. A line from Karl Menninger's *The Human Mind* – how I loved that book! – floats to me out of context but vivid and jarring: *The adjuration to be normal seems shockingly repellent to me.* My face, I'm sure, is a little red, with the wine and the fire, but otherwise betrays nothing.

She fetches a bottle of Frascati this time from the kitchen, and solemnly pours us both a fresh glass. Icy cold slips down my throat.

And then later, much later – matter of fact, dawn is bleeding under the curtain in a trickle of red – I tiptoe from the guestroom to Sam's bedroom, opening the door creakily, leaning over her and shaking her.

'Sam . . . you awake?'

'Hmm?' she says, sitting up, blonde hair mussed, skin shiny.

'I feel . . . logy,' I say, and lie beside her on top of the sheet. She's always strict about this. Minty mustn't see us. I was meant to have left earlier, and now we'll have to explain my staying over, which is bad enough.

'Logy? I don't know what you mean, you feel ill?' Sam asks, her cool hand on my forehead. The scent of her, almonds, frangipani, is sickening.

'Something's wrong. *I'm* wrong. I'm sick.'

It's my hands. My hands feel wrong, like they don't belong to me. And my tongue, too, is sticking to the roof of my mouth. 'I'm logy, I'm logy . . .' My words come out fat and stupid.

Sam springs up. She brings me a big glass of water, from the bathroom, holds her hands over mine to raise it to my mouth. In her eyes is something new.

'Oh, Pats,' is all she says.

I refuse the water, spilling some on the bed as I pluck at her but she wriggles free. She's in her nightgown, now reaches for the robe hanging on a hook on the back of her bedroom door and runs out to the hall where the telephone is. I follow her. I feel like a big lumbering Frankenstein, my hands fatter and fatter and stranger and stranger.

'My head! My guts! I feel terrible. Don't leave me Sam,' I say. A last beseeching effort. 'Don't let Mother take me away!'

'Sssh sssh, you'll wake Minty – you're shouting, Pats! It's early, let's not wake her!'

I think the room is shaking or someone is shaking me – is Sam shaking me? – or is it just me, a trembling and a heat that surges through me? I'm sick, I'm sick. I'm not shouting, she's gone crazy.

'Sam, not water – fix me a proper drink.'

'Oh, my goodness, is it, is it – should you stop *drinking*? You're shaking . . .'

'No, no, don't be – dumb. I could use a drink. That's what the problem is. Bring me – have you got Scotch? I could use a whisky, Sam, or bourbon, I could—'

I hear her on the telephone, and she's saying: 'Yes, I'm terribly sorry it's so early, Dr Deacon . . .'

And then I stagger from her bedroom to the landing and the pale lilac walls are rushing towards me and the grey carpet comes roaring and charging – a huge grey horse shaking its mane – hurtling into my face.

January. She'd always loathed the month she was born in. It was a month of ugliness, desiccating like the roses around the cottage door. Nothingness, whiteness, days slipping; nothing solid. January made her think of sand trickling away, of flipping an egg over and over, shaking the year to its end, its horrible new beginning.

She woke in her own bed at Bridge Cottage, and saw a film of snow outside on the window ledge. Where were her snails? Beside her on the bedside table was a bowl of cold pea and ham soup – a lurid green – and a glass of water. She looked for Scotch. She leaned out of the bed, the silky counterpane sliding to the floor, to root for her bottle of J&B – there should be one just under the bed – but her hand touched only fluff and dust and wooden floorboards; she couldn't find it. She went to open the curtains and was a little surprised to see that January had also brought a soft lace-work of snow to the windowpane; snow sat on her car and the oak tree outside in daubs of white, like ice-cream dollops.

There was a noise downstairs, a small grating sound – a drawer being opened. She jumped, and felt her heartbeat quicken. Involuntarily she glanced around her bedroom for the flicker of the mouse, for *it*, the Thing, but saw neither. Burglars? Someone was downstairs, in the house. Her mouth was a little dry as she glanced around for a weapon. Where was the knife she used to groom the plants? Snoopers? Smythson-Balby again? She looked for the plum-coloured bathrobe to cover herself, and wished she had the Black & Decker.

As she stepped out on the landing, ducking to avoid the low beam – at least she'd remembered that – she saw Ronnie coming

195

from the kitchen, carrying a tray with a glass of orange juice and a plate with two of the Limmits cookies she'd bought months ago. Ronnie. She stared at the tray: No doubt he thinks they're *real* cookies, then wondered why such a mundane thought popped into her head then. Ronnie's hair was longer and fairer than ever; it grazed his shoulders. His knees creaked as he started on the bottom stair, and then he looked up at her and beamed. She imagined him hanging up his duffel coat and yards of knitted scarf on the downstairs peg.

'Feeling better?' he asked.

'I don't appreciate people moving my snails,' she said, as her heartbeat returned to normal and she advanced wincingly – the light was shockingly white here – down the stairs.

Ronnie took the tray into the kitchen to show her the snails through the kitchen window. They were out in the garden, near the shed, all the bowls and tanks under an ugly iron canopy, buckling under its weight of snow.

'They were filling up the house, my dear. The smell was atrocious. Your mother insisted. I built it myself. And they do so prefer the outdoor life.'

Mother. Mother was here at Bridge Cottage. Had she – had Pat locked up her novel? Yes, she had. And, yes, she remembered Mother's visit – Mother in Suffolk, as bizarre and exotic a species as a big white leopard – but she'd rather she didn't.

The alcoholic blackouts – this wasn't her first – meant that things were piecemeal and came back in shreds. What she remembered most was a dream she'd had, a terribly sad dream, in which little snails crawled towards her across her bedroom floor over the body of a girl she recognised as Veronica, the pin-up Veronica, the girl who had been strangled in New York. She simply stared at Veronica and the snails with the deepest of sadness.

'I could use a cigarette,' she said now, to Ronnie.

Together they searched Bridge Cottage for cigarettes, finding a half-empty packet eventually in an old jacket pocket, the leather *gilet* hanging in her study, which she hadn't worn since the funeral. At the first drag, the first deep hit of nicotine, she felt a surge of gratitude and affection towards Ronnie. It must have been him who had brought her the soup upstairs.

The room smelt powerfully of turps and old coffee; there were several dirty cups and ashtrays on the desk in the corner. They were surrounded by her sketches, several charcoal snails, various cats about to strike, dead rats and dead birds, a pencil-and-paper drawing of the kitchen at Bridge Cottage, cosy with its sprigged curtains and posies in vases on the kitchen table, its hanging knives. Ronnie, she knew, found it easier to admire her sketching than her novels and he picked one up now – a line drawing of Sam, sleeping – and told her how fine it was.

'Sam took me to *her* doctor?' She remembered that. She remembered most of it, actually, the ride home in a taxi, paid for by Sam, but thought it wise to pretend she didn't. She remembered the return to fetch her car, too, and Mother's visit: the sudden image of a wire coat-hanger, brandished at her, narrowly missing her eye with its round hook. But there were gaps, and she had the strange, unvoiced sensation that she'd perhaps been ill for longer than she realised. She didn't want to ask Ronnie, to find out, so she fell silent, and nodded her permission for him to look through her sketchbook, and smoked.

'I did it, you know,' Pat murmured, at last. And the relief of confession was just as sweet as she'd long imagined. Huge and sweeping and unique. Like an orgasm. Long, colossal, drawn-out and salty. 'I killed someone. I killed Gerald.'

'Hush, darling, of course you didn't,' Ronnie replied infuriatingly. She was shocked to discover she'd said it to Ronnie, out loud. 'Why don't I heat the soup for you?' he persisted, moving as if to get up to go next door to her bedroom and fetch the tray.

'No.' She tugged at his arm. 'I did. I mean it. I murdered him. And—'

'Suicide is a ghastly business. People always blame themselves – perhaps that's the intention. I've always thought that if someone is determined to end their life, no one could stop them. The wonder is that Gerald did not consider the child in all of this.'

'Suicide,' Pat repeated. 'Sure.' Then, suddenly uncertain again, plucking at Ronnie's sleeve: 'But they didn't find a note, did they? They found a body, but no suicide note?'

'I believe they *did* find a note. I'm sure someone – Charles, perhaps – mentioned it to me at the funeral. *Yes*. Gerald had a lot of problems, darling, at the bank. An investigation. Other women, you know.'

'Suicide,' Pat repeated again, like a child. Then suddenly remembering: 'But what about the head injury? Wasn't there a head injury?' She felt muddled, faintly dizzy.

Ronnie stared at her with a puzzled expression. He gave her a look so sympathetic that neither of them could bear it; he quickly turned back to the drawings. He murmured quietly: 'I don't know anything about a head injury. There was no injury to the head. He drowned himself, that's all.'

Silence for a few seconds. Pat breathed heavily.

'I've been writing,' she said, from nowhere, as if in answer to a question Ronnie had asked.

'Not *drinking* too much. Writing too much.'

Ronnie smiled. 'And drinking too, darling.'

He had been kneeling on the floor to look at her drawings and now gently replaced the sketchbook with the others, tipped against the wall. He leaned back on his heels for a moment to watch a new flurry of snow fret the windowpane, murmuring to himself: 'Britten once told me how he would leave a shiny black piano downstairs and find a matt white one when he woke up. Old, old flour would drift down on it from the seamy beams all night.'

Pat struggled to think harder about Gerald, to take in what Ronnie had said. Of course. No head injury. A suicide note – did she know about that? The body washed up at the Martello tower. Something came back to Pat then. Some painful hastening feeling, like gathering fear: was it really over with Sam? But surely there was something she could say, some line, some way to convince Sam of how much she loved her. And then a slap of shame as she remembered Sam's calm, firm words, and muddlingly, maddeningly, another thought: lines from Ronnie's novel, a novel she'd read when she first came to Suffolk, a novel about a young man, Dick Brand, that she took to be a version of Ronnie, because Dick Brand lived in Suffolk and was destined for the Church but wanted to be a writer. It had amused her, this novel, because she recognised so much of Ronnie in it, as one always did in reading novels written by friends. It also reassured her that she and Ronnie, as she'd always believed, were opposites in personality, and in their writing style they were centuries apart. His syntax, his sub-clauses and his vocabulary, not to mention characters with names like Quenny and Old Yockers, his positively Forsterian tone, made her feel exhilaratingly modern, almost hard-boiled; made her feel positively *swinging* in comparison.

The line that flew through her mind then was when Dick Brand complained of having a kind of 'literary mattress' wedged between him and life; a poetic, intellectualising sensibility that got in the way. She felt it now. Ronnie had an advanced intellectual capacity; she envied him that. He was cleverer, kinder, more cultured, better read and better educated than she, better in every way but one. She had the ability to feel – to name – the blast of things. In that alone she was his superior.

'I don't see why you think it impossible that I might—' she began, meaning to prolong her confession, to enjoy again the delicious relief of saying the phrase to Ronnie, but he cut her off.

'I love these charcoal snails,' he said, picking up two sketches that had been abandoned, pages torn from a pad and thrown across the room in the direction of the wastepaper basket, remaining where they fell. He studied them for a moment. 'That one looks as if somebody tipped it out, almost as if the body is made of liquid,' he said, and then: 'They're in nice new aquaria outside. You mustn't worry, darling. I bought them myself from the pet shop. I rigged up the canopy too. They had become rather a lot, hadn't they? They kept on laying eggs, I presume, and multiplying . . .'

Ronnie's tenderness, his quiet solicitude and acceptance, touched her. But the need to unburden herself was strong and she made one more attempt:

'Sam, she doesn't care to see me again. She thinks we will never get past our troubles. And it's over because – well, she knows that Gerald's death was my fault . . .'

Ronnie stood up, knees creaking, and replaced the sketches neatly on her desk. He looked closely at her, his eyes meeting hers, then resting somehow on the jam-jar containing paint-brushes dipped in an inch of grey water on her desk. He said: 'I saw that you were out of Quink. I bought you a little bottle. I'll get it. When you're feeling better we can go to the church I wanted to show you at Fram,' and he began to make his way downstairs.

She followed him, first going to her bedroom and wrapping the bathrobe round her pyjamas. She was thinking of the night she'd watched Héloise and Abelard making love, had stood there with Ginny . . . How long ago was that, and why does it feel more real suddenly than a long love affair with Sam? She remembered a detail she'd read somewhere – of snails mating for life, of a snail crossing a long, high garden wall with great difficulty in order to find its mate. That was her definition of true love: it should last for ever and involve suffering; perhaps it should cost you your life.

Mother, in her crude way, all those lifetimes ago: 'Are you a les?' she'd thrown at Pat when Pat was twelve. 'Because you're starting to make sounds like one.'

'Have I been ill?' Pat asked Ronnie now, pausing halfway down the stairs.

He turned over his shoulder: 'The doctor came,' he answered. 'You were sedated.'

'Oh.'

'And Gerald committed suicide.'

She wondered again: how late in January was it? How long had she been ill? Other memories loomed up, billowy, ill-formed. The grey blob, the little shape, skittering at one side of her vision. The blankness, familiar to her from previous alcoholic phases, snatching pictures away.

'I think you had . . .' Ronnie was saying now as they reached the front room. He picked up a cushion distractedly, plumped it and threw it back. 'Well, it was down to Mary that you weren't locked up. A breakdown, she called it, and simply insisted the doctor treat you here. She nursed you. We should go for a walk now you're brightening. The Martello tower . . .'

'Mother nursed me?'

This didn't fit at all with anything that Pat could remember; anything from childhood. Nursing? Did Mother even have it in her? With the name Mary, or Mother, there came always only the stretched, snaking feeling that something about her was profoundly wrong, foul and unlovable, because what girl in the world had a mother who didn't want her – worse, didn't even like her?

'I think we fought, if you want the truth,' Pat murmured. 'I think I fainted when Mother arrived.'

Ronnie laughed, an easy laugh, as if he already knew this.

'I think she might have – attacked me, at one point,' Pat said, one finger rubbing at a place in her eyebrow where she can feel a small cut healing. 'Can that be true? With a coat-hanger? Was the doctor here then? And did we have to be separated?'

Ronnie glanced down now at the desk in the living room, at the little bottle of Quink he had placed there in a brown-paper bag; embarrassed or amused, she couldn't tell.

'Hush, Pats. You weren't well. Mary is – well, she's extreme, isn't she? I suppose she's had – her own privations, to make her that way.'

'She made a stink, you mean,' Pat said, and Ronnie laughed again, glad, he said, that she sounded more like her old self.

The cloud was clearing, and a few memories peeked through the shreds.

There was Ginny Smythson-Balby in her silky black slip. There were her manuscripts, her diaries and her *cahiers* and the novel she was writing: she saw it as if in a dream, pages and pages covered with typed script that seemed to mass on the page, like murmurations of black starlings in a white sky. There was Sam's apartment, the shiny harlequin tiles in the bathroom, and then this, suddenly: imagining herself standing next to the medicine cabinet, with a container of pills; holding Sam's reading-glasses close to her nose, reading the warnings on the seconal pills and thinking: How easy it would be to give those to Sam and make it look as if Sam had done it to herself. The capsules split with nail-scissors, the powder, almost invisible, scattered along the cold white porcelain of the bath. And how she could drop them so easily into the wine glass, Sam's glass with the Elizabeth Arden Sheik crescent on the rim.

The sordid way her mind worked, this she was ashamed of. Did others do it? She had always done it, and now the habit had crossed over to addiction. She indulged herself, imagining leaving the apartment, glancing back at the scene behind her: Sam's blonde hair spidery, Sam lying face down on the sofa. Someone reaching inside her chest, and twisting her heart with their fist. She pictured herself washing her own wine glass in Sam's kitchen, squirting inside it with washing-up liquid, the water trickling hot over her wrist, her palms stinging red as she wiped the glass with the dish towel and put it away. When she left there would be only the one glass, next to Sam; she imagined it tipped up on the floor beside her, empty except for the traces of wine and perhaps tablets. Innocent or sinister; whatever one wanted it to be.

Other thoughts now, equally murky, snatches of a dream, or . . . pages of her writing. *If there were secrets between us it's because we didn't know how to tell them*. She would have to think of everything for this scene to be convincing, imagine it all in the fullest of details. She would need to convince herself, first.

So, perhaps it could be like this: the child, Minty. OK, she'd say to the police that her mother's friend, the writer Patricia

Highsmith, had been visiting earlier that day; they'd been to the zoo together; they'd bought some iced cookies in the shape of Christmas trees in waxed paper in a delicatessen near Regent's Park; they'd had supper at home, but then Miss Highsmith had left; she'd seen her put on her coat, then say goodnight to Minty and her mother; that would have been around 10 p.m. And the time of her mother's death would be – let's say – 3 a.m. Yes, that would be the right time to choose. Then she'd have the police come. The cops would conclude that this lonely hour was the one that had got the better of Mrs Gerald Gosforth and made her down those sleeping pills, the pink bottle of seconal, the capsules of pills all snipped up in the bathroom, the powder carefully dissolved into her wine. The loss of her husband too much to bear, poor woman. They'd believe it was suicide, not murder. Perhaps – if the police knew Pat was there, if she had Minty let slip this part, just to add a little pep – well, they might assume Miss Highsmith had been there confessing to an affair with the deceased husband and exonerate her entirely. That would be the piece of information, the final ironic piece, that made Sam's death – her imagined death – seem like a convincing suicide. Genius! That one little detail about her own address in Gerald's billfold – she'd often wondered where that had floated in from – would now add up perfectly. This satisfied her. She almost purred with relief. This she could make believable, she felt.

Suddenly, Pat said to Ronnie: 'I'm writing a novel. About – you know, all of this: Suffolk, Sam. As well as the *Plotting* book. As well as the other novel, now called *The Story-teller*. First person singular, and rather confessional in style, you know. It has one murder – of the husband – and now perhaps another. I may abandon it.'

Ronnie was in the kitchen, pulling on boots and suggesting she grab her coat. She looked down at the shine of his luxuriant shoulder-length hair. He turned his face to her. He seemed to be biting his lip, stifling a smile or tucking some words away, but that was just Ronnie's expression, the way he always looked: impish, she thought, with his small mouth, his slightly rounded cheeks. Mischievous, like a small boy struggling to keep quiet about a prank he just played on you.

'A difficult form – the first person singular. I thought you mostly wrote in third?'

'I do,' she said. 'I've gotten rather bogged down in it . . . It sounds like more of a confession. I'm not even sure it's a novel.' (Was that true? Matter of fact, she felt certain for the first time that it *was* a novel, just then.) Deflated, as she had once put it, like a soufflé lifted from the oven too soon.

Was it over? she wondered. Could she still finish it, that novel? If she knew everything that happened, it was never such fun to write it. She liked to surprise herself first. She felt emptied. A thought swam to her, as she dressed and found a cigarette in the pocket of her coat and put it to her mouth, that her plotting was all wrong, all those details she'd thought of a moment ago, the Sam-suicide part – all of that would have to go.

Ronnie was pulling on his duffel coat and leaned forward with it half on, one sleeve dangling, to light the cigarette for her. At the first inhalation a sensuous abandonment trickled through her. *Such bliss to feel this blank. How would it be not to care about anything very much at all?* And then Ronnie's voice waylaid her: as they stepped out of the back door onto the crisp bite of snow she realised he had been saying something.

'So I told her, no, but give it a week. I'm sure she'll be up to it in a week.'

'Who – Mother? I thought you said she'd gone back to the States,' Pat asked, blowing out a smoke-ring.

'No, the little Smythson-Balby girl. She's been calling most days. She's pretty intense, isn't she? I'd call it a major crush, darling. I've fended her off because I didn't want – all of this finding its way into her notes. But she's awfully persistent.'

The toes of their boots, their heels crunched on the step outside the kitchen door, leaving satisfying marks on the virgin white – like marks from a typewriter key biting into a page. Blankness lifted from Pat; she felt the last remnants of her illness dissolve in the snap of the white, bracing air. So. Vigilance required, as ever, she thought. A lifetime's awareness of the loathsome nature of things, of the direction they were likely to travel in, of course, of course. The journey was always from bad to worse. And the solution? Work, above all else. Work, discipline, vigilance.

She had almost, for a second there, forgotten. Hadn't she always been pushing, fighting? Hadn't her own mother tried to poison her in the embryonic stage, wipe her out? Ha. This discovery, once she'd recovered from it, had powered her. She was like the devil himself, like desire, like a searing bleach or the plague. There was no checking or combating her. There was only this: secrecy. Nosy little bitches, biographers, vultures, all of them, trying to worm their way into your secret heart, winkle out the darkness and deceit, take your life – a kind of disgusting symbolic murder – and make it their own. Sure, she might throw you a line, here and there. Night fishing, who knows what you might drag up to the surface? But Patricia Highsmith was no fool. It was a joy to be hidden, she knew. But the greatest joy was if she was never to be found.

Smythson-Balby arrived a few days later and found Pat sitting at the kitchen table, writing a cheque for the milkman. A milk bill had come from Framlingham Dairy for the last quarter, for one pound three shillings. Pat signed her name and folded the cheque, shook the snow from the bottom of the milk bottle onto the dish towel and poked the folded cheque inside.

'Yoo-hoo,' Smythson-Balby said, just inside the door, singsong style. She had already let herself in, and was now slapping her gloved hands together, dripping wet slush onto the kitchen floor. Pat stared at the girl's outfit: wellies, pink, bell-bottomed slacks, rabbit-fur hat and coat with white fur cuffs. The tip of

Ginny's nose was pink and her eyes bright, her breath steaming up the windows.

'Still snowing out there, then,' Pat said, getting up to rattle the slatted lid closed on the breadbin. But she was thinking: The girl looks really pretty; it's a shame she's such a jerk.

Ginny took off the rabbit-fur hat and shook out her hair. 'Whoo-eeee,' she said childishly. Pat made a grunt.

'So glad you're up and about,' Ginny said. 'And looks like you've been writing, too.' Her eyes fell on a diary, next to the bottle of Quink and Pat's fountain pen. Pat quickly closed it. 'Shall I make us some coffee?' Ginny said, as if she hadn't noticed.

Presumptuous. Proprietorial now, Pat realised, and shuddered. *I love you.* Whatever else, she hadn't forgotten the – the audacity of *that*.

'Matter of fact, I wondered how long was I ill for.' Pat wanted to know.

Ginny glanced up at the kitchen calendar and flipped the page over from December to January. A robin gazed out with beady eyes. 'Today's the eighteenth, I think.'

'My birthday tomorrow.'

'Ooh, lovely – we should celebrate!' Ginny's back was to her, as she stood at the window, shaking the old coffee grounds into the kitchen garbage can.

Danger, danger. Every inch of Pat was alert, although she appeared to be merely watching Ginny as the girl spooned ground coffee from a screw-top jar on the shelf in the pantry, then came back and lit the gas under the little pot on the stove. Ginny was at home here, finding cups easily and now – it took only a minute or two for the coffee to brew – handing over Pat's drink just as she liked it, strong, with no milk. Pat sipped it while it was tongue-burningly hot, holding the cup in hands that trembled only a little and could be explained by her recent illness or even – let's face it, Ginny knew it well enough – her alcoholism.

In Pat's head, Ginny had died fifty times already. A crack to the head, a tumble down the stairs, a fall in the garden, face mushed down in the stream, something lethal slipped in her tea. But all of them improbable and provoking suspicion, Pat felt, because they would centre on Pat, on Bridge Cottage, and bring the law here and further investigation. So many things could look like accidents. That was in her favour. Cars sliding off the road in the snow and the slush, for instance. Drivers a little the worse for wear. Police in English villages don't automatically suspect foul play, and why should they?

'Not on the wagon, are we?' Pat asked. 'There's a brand new bottle of J&B in that sink unit. Shall we pep up our coffee?'

Ginny obliged. Now the hat sat on the table between them, like a big furry barrier, and Ginny's coat shouldered the chair. Underneath she wore a baby pink turtle-neck and three strings of pearls that rattled wildly as she bounced around the kitchen, pouring things, putting bottles away. Pat sensed the mood Ginny was in – it came off her like steam. No doubt the irritating girl would like her to take her to bed. Again.

'I suddenly wondered,' Ginny began shyly. 'That woman you were with that night in Aldeburgh when I was with Izzie. It was dark, of course. But she was tall, I saw that. Slim, and with blonde hair. I thought it at the time, actually. Was it Sam Gosforth?'

The kitchen was so quiet Pat could hear snow falling outside. Sliding past the salmon pink walls of Bridge Cottage, coating the trees, freezing the stream, weighting branches, icing the whole of Suffolk in Christmas-cake white. She was thankful she'd defied Ronnie and Mother and brought her snails back in from outside; they were safely snuggled in her art room. The phone booth would be frosted over, the door packed and stuck. The oak tree weighted, and poised. And what of the silly statue, the totem, as Pat thought of it, in the village? Eric Gill weird, now blobbed with snow like an ice-cream cone.

Pat poured a giant slug of whisky into her coffee cup and shook her head.

'No. It wasn't. Peppy little numbers like yourself – not married women – are more my dish.'

Ginny simpered, then suddenly looked as if she ought to be offended, trying to suppress her smile. It was impossible for Pat to know whether Ginny believed her. She suspected she didn't, but would let it go. For now.

'So,' Ginny said, with insane cheerfulness, 'is the writing going well?'

Pat made a sound that could mean anything, but she got up, and they moved into the living room, where the fire was dying in the grate. Pat prodded it with the long poker – Might the poker do? she wondered, twirling the end, almost wanting to lick it, to see it sizzle – and added another log. Ginny sat down, cross-legged, on the floor in front of the fire, and giggled for no reason. She seemed a little high already.

Pat's pages were piled next to her naked typewriter (that is, the cover was off) on a new work table, one that Ronnie had found for her in Abbott's, the second-hand store in Debenham. Pat had protested that it was foolish to buy new stuff when – she could feel this now, somehow – she wouldn't be staying in Suffolk for much longer, but Ronnie had replied that he'd like to keep it after she'd left so it wouldn't be a wasted purchase.

'You know,' Ginny was saying, off on one of her schoolgirl-debate-society subjects; 'why do men like Gerald beat their wives?'

'How do you know he did?' Pat asked, startled.

'Oh, you remember I worked there? As an au-pair. Even then I knew Samantha was afraid of him. He had a filthy temper.'

A pang of jealousy throbbed through Pat at the thought of Ginny, a young Ginny, in Sam's home.

'I've been thinking about this. About the sort of cases that Daddy sees. I've often wondered why it is just men. Women have as much reason – if not more – to be violent, to erupt.'

'And what pearl of wisdom have you come up with?' Pat said. She had brought the whisky bottle into the living room. Of course she was meant to quit drinking. Ronnie was too polite to mention it but she knew the doctor would not have been constrained. She poured a generous slosh into each cup. The coffee had gone now and it was more of a whisky slush with a coffee aftertaste.

'Well,' Ginny persisted, 'men might be . . . trying to attack their own desire. The women they love represent *vulnerability*, the one thing that can hurt them. They want to crush it. And since women are more *comfortable* with their feelings, feelings of weakness – that's our lot, most of the time – we don't need to attack it. Kill it in others where we foolishly imagine it lives. If you see what I mean.'

Ginny's last words came out rather slurred: she was showing her drinks already. Pat glanced out of the living-room window and glimpsed Ginny's little red car, all spattered with white, like something covered with a lace doily, parked there at the front of the cottage. Again she imagined it veering off the road, tyres sliding on black ice, Ginny's hands on the steering-wheel, a tree looming up. Too much to hope for? Many drunks drive home safely, in conditions worse than these. Maybe a further helping hand is required.

'I don't happen to agree. Wives, girlfriends, prostitutes, the women in their lives – they're just in the wrong place. They're just who men can get at. Murderous rage. And women are spineless. Nothing more sophisticated than that. Women are pushed by circumstances instead of pushing. Your explanation is so much Freudian voodoo, if you want the truth,' Pat murmured.

Killing your desires – what hooey. Killing, crushing, despising what you desire, whatever makes you vulnerable; your own feelings of desire, in fact, being repugnant to you. Pat was thinking: Maybe the library in Ipswich has a book on car maintenance. Tampering with brakes. Is that possible, or is it just a movie cliché? I mean, why wouldn't a driver just tug on the handbrake? Ginny was not much intellectually and a damn fool driver. Woolly ideas about men and feminism. Pat's eyes strayed to Ginny's sweater. At the voluptuous strings of – probably first class – pearls. The girl caught her look and smiled, stretching out the legs in pink slacks. She glanced at Pat over the rim of her cup, trying, Pat knew, to be flirtatious. Pat edged closer to her. Put one hand on Ginny's thigh. That was all it took for the girl to drop her head against Pat's shoulder, and sigh.

And then Pat reached for the little zip at the front of the pink slacks, flipping the button free from the button hole and pulling the zip with a ripping noise so loud that they both laughed. Pat's hand there on the metal felt extraordinarily hot. She paused to pour them both more whisky. The burning taste of that, too, melted the room to one tightening, brown-toned embrace. Ginny Smythson-Balby stretched out in front of the hearth like a cat and allowed Pat to tug the slacks from her body, wriggling and lifting her backside (her lovely fat derrière, Pat couldn't keep from thinking, though she wished she were less entranced) to help her. She wore small pink cotton underpants, with a daisy embroidered on one hip. Pat kissed this, then peeled the cotton, kissing the dark pubic hair, rubbing her face in the warm salty heat at the centre of Ginny, until the room itself trembled and groaned around them, and the fire blazed at Pat's cheek and once again, for a while, all other thoughts were soothed.

Mother. On the doorstep at Bridge Cottage, a suitcase beside her. Mother, glittery and smart, snappy in her silver fox fur with her newly dyed black bob and leather gloves, saying: 'Well. I found you through some friends of yours in Islington. You're still the same stingy little shit. You might have telephoned or arranged a cab for me from Ipswich. I've been on that butt-freezing station best part of an hour. You didn't get my letter?'

A letter that apparently told Pat that Mother was arriving, and dates. A letter Pat hadn't opened. And Mother always acting as if her own behaviour – bent on chasing Pat halfway around the world – was perfectly normal, as if no one would accuse her of being anything less than sane. Pat was in some kind of smog of despair and not really functioning and it was a shock to open the door to her.

'I didn't get any letter.'

Pat wanted to ask: how the hell did you find me? But that would let Mary know how much she'd rattled her. Her mother stepped in without wiping her boots on the welcome mat. She sighed and lifted her lizard-skin case over the threshold herself. A tiny case not much bigger than a weekend case: the only reassuring sign.

'No Stanley?' Pat asked, kissing her on both of her icy cheeks, because Mary turning up in Suffolk from Texas was extraordinary enough. Who was to say who else might come?

'Why in God's name would Stanley come?' was all her mother said. She puffed herself onto the sofa without taking off the fur coat and looked around the front room of Bridge Cottage with undisguised repulsion.

'Jeez, Pats. These places get worse! No telephone. Don't you even have *heating* here?'

'I was working! I can fix a fire. You didn't just come from— Where did you fly from?'

'I've been staying in Islington. With friends of yours. AS I TOLD YOU IN MY LETTER.'

And then, with a chilling, creeping feeling stealing from her toes to the hairs on the back of her neck, Pat thought: It can't be. The letter she'd thought was – the letter that was like all the others. She had never opened it. That letter? It was from Mother.

She fetched it from under the newspapers in the kindling. It was covered with flecks of wood. Pat's hand was trembling; she tore it open. It contained one page in Mother's round hand. Signed: Mother. Not Stanley. Not Brother Death, or BD. Not typed, nothing threatening. Actually, not like the other letters at all. No '*I know where you are*' or '*No one will ever believe you*', just a limber, chatty, folksy letter saying she was coming to visit, with flight numbers and times and . . .

'I can't believe you didn't read it!' Mary flounced, watching Pat with small dark eyes. Currants, black buttons. The dead eyes of a snowman, or a gingerbread boy. She was shrugging her arms out of the coat, wafting the scent of Chanel No 5, making the front room of Bridge Cottage smell like the beauty parlour in Fort Worth. Saturday afternoons. Hairspray and red-polished nails.

'I thought . . .' Pat said, and flipped the envelope to the front again, to study the typed address. But that part *did* look the same. Surely the same typewriter.

'Did you type the envelope?' Pat asked her.

Mary leaped up then. 'Let me take a look at that! What's so goddamn interesting about an envelope?' She snatched the envelope from Pat and examined it, and Pat wondered again: did her flustered shoving back of the envelope at her mean that realisation had dawned and she understood she'd made a revealing mistake? Usually the envelopes on letters from Mother were handwritten. The letters from Brother Death or Stanley – the letters that had pursued her and alarmed her and blighted her life for the last few years in Paris, the letters from, well, she knew now who it was – *they* were always typed, both inside and out, with that wonkily pasted-on stamp, and the address not quite aligned properly.

Mary's mood changed at once and she gave a sharp laugh, like a bark, and a sly smile.

'Can't a mother let her daughter know she's thinking of her? If that same goddamn daughter travels all over the world and never writes her, and tries to cut her mother out of her life . . .'

'Is that a confession, then? You're owning up to them?'

'I don't know what you're talking about!'

She sank back into the rickety sofa, which made an odd assortment of clicks and creaks, as there was a pile of metal coat-hangers beside her, which Pat had been meaning to take upstairs.

'Wine, Pats? You gonna offer me some wine? Or a highball?'

Pat went to the kitchen to fix her a drink and give herself time to think, time for her heart to quit its crazy ticking. She was like an overwound clock. Snap out of it, Pats. She can't stay long. What can she want? At least she had found out about the letters. Although what was truly frightening (and confusing) was that, as the police in Paris pointed out, the frank on the envelope, if you could read it at all, was usually local. Which meant . . . what? Mother had got someone to mail them for her in Paris? How the hell had she managed to go to so much trouble? Still, she did know a lot of people, friends of Pat's, and it did make sense of how he – 'Stanley' or 'Brother Death' (that name from one of Pat's own novels too) – always knew where she was.

'Shall I fix up the fire?' Mary called, never able to quit her habit of interfering, and of continuing a conversation with Pat regardless of which room she was in.

Pat ignored the singsong voice and bit her lip, putting two glasses of Frascati on a flower-patterned tray. She glanced at the clock in the kitchen: 10 a.m. It was going to be a long day.

Mary was shaking out her hair, arranging her skirts and preening, gently pushing the coat-hangers away from her, when Pat came back into the room. She was nowhere near the fire and had no intention of fixing it. She had simply meant: you go fix us a fire. So Pat did, glad that the leather hod next to the fire was filled with kindling that someone – presumably Ronnie – had left there for her, and folded copies of the *Ipswich Star*, which she began wadding into balls.

'You've lost weight,' Mother said.

'I've been ill.' In fact, as Pat suddenly realised, she'd been mostly in bed since leaving Sam. There was something large and balloon-like that pressed at her chest, a physical illness or an emotional one, she didn't know. She glanced down and was surprised to find she was dressed in Levi's, her lizard-skin belt and a clean shirt, though her feet were bare. Had she been intending to do something when she'd been interrupted by that brutal, startling rap at the door? Sure. She had been coming downstairs to start work on the novel again. Out of the corner of her eye a mouse ran along the skirting-board. Mother watched her glance at it, watched her face, and laughed.

'You could use losing a few *more* pounds.'

Pat looked at the Levi's, which were bagging around the thighs and hips and didn't say anything, hoping Mary would go no further.

'Sitting on your ass all day, drinking. No wonder you're fat!' She sipped her wine and glanced at Pat over the top of the glass, before breaking into another little peal of laughter, which she no doubt thought was girlish and becoming.

'Last time I weighed myself I was one hundred and ten, tops. I don't happen to think that's fat.'

'Ha! I'm just telling it like it is, Pats. Your best friends sure wouldn't tell you. It's a mother's unwelcome task.'

Pat struck the match and the newspaper caught, blossoming to a blue smoky flame and a crackle. She sipped her wine. 'We could go for a walk later. Ronnie's been showing me some pretty churches in Suffolk . . .'

'Ronnie! Schmonny, what kind of name is that?'

'Matter of fact—'

'And, anyways, don't you find these English country places so *little?* I brought my paints. I thought I'd paint for a day or two. But the scale is already boring me. The pretty-pretty Suffolk. No colour like fall on the east coast. It's all so *subtle*.'

Ha. Subtle. Not her forte.

'Well, ain't this nice?' she said, when her glass was drained, holding it out for a top-up. Pat had anticipated this and brought the wine bottle in on the tray, so she obliged.

'Catching up,' Mary continued, 'mother and daughter. And you've been getting some nice reviews. And your friends in Islington – Betty – said you'd won a prize or something? Oh, and an old friend of yours, Lil. Did I tell you about her? Exposed herself to Stanley. That's right. He was downstairs mixing drinks and she followed him down and sat on the top stair. He turned around and she was letting him have it. Can you believe that? Bent on making my husband. That's what your little friends are like.'

'Those letters. Paris. Signing them "From Stanley" . . .'

'Letters from me and Stanley? What's your problem? I don't get it.'

'Do you know I went to the police about them in Paris?'

She laughed gaily.

'Oh, Pats. Have you been to a doctor lately? Had any black-outs? How much are you drinking?'

'I thought it was some creep, you know. A prowler or something. It got so that—'

'You always were paranoid. Tip you over the edge, did they? Well, I always said you were a crackpot.'

More laughter. Pat was standing, kind of towering over her mother, aware that she was clenching her fists. Mary swatted at her knee – the only part she could reach – with her hand.

'You know I spoke to Dr Carstairs about you. He has some very interesting theories.'

Ignore her. Pat asked tightly if Mother wanted some olives, or crackers and cheese to go with that wine. Took the tray into the kitchen, trying to gather herself, knit herself back together, fend off the buzzing in her ears. A sound, she realised, that being around Mother often produced. She took a long while to arrange crackers on a plate. Added a knife. Unwrapped a wedge of English Cheddar from waxed paper. And then went back in.

'Oh, and you know,' Mary was saying, 'I'll tell you. I'm done with that schmuck! That son of a bitch! I've left him, Pats. I can't stand another day of it.'

There was no need to say anything. This was familiar enough and this was how it would go. Pat hadn't thought Mary would come all this way, travel halfway across the world at sixty-two years old, just to pummel her with it, like – like someone throwing snowballs at a fence, but she'd clearly underestimated her mother.

'I've been telling your little chum Betty and – what was her name? That other one. The bull-dyke. Nell. They were awful nice. They sure were understanding. I hope you will be too, Pats.'

And out they came. Stanley's latest crimes, oiled with the rest of the bottle of wine. They were no worse than they had been on any other occasion. Pat at first felt resigned: so Mary's need to regale her had not abated, her conviction that Pat's job since early childhood was to be a listening post, an absorbing handker-chief. As Mary shifted excitedly on the sofa the coat-hangers rattled and chattered; she seemed not to notice and kept blatting at her. What it amounted to was this: there was some task, a faucet that could use fixing in the yard, always some task like this, something that Stanley hadn't tackled. And she'd tried not to nag him, folks would tell you she'd held her tongue, she'd been a saint, other women would have cracked sooner, but, no, that man had gone *weeks* before he'd even got off his ass . . .

Holy crap. Halfway across the world to tell Pat this?

And if Pat had replied, if she'd said what she longed to – Why don't you leave him? You know you hate him. Nearly forty years you've been telling me this crap, how much more do I have to take? – what would happen? But she didn't. Mary sucked all the words out of her. Look, there they were now: fleeing from the typewriter, flitting up to the ceiling, like black flecks from a fire.

The expectation of – what? Her mother's response. A stinging humiliation, shame, a slap, the buzzing in her ears, the arrival of flickering pains, flickering little movements, the little man. The ache of that time when Pat had thought her mother had left Stanley, for good, when she had believed it would just be them, allowing herself a little surge of hope. Maybe it would be calm between them. Maybe they would have some good times together, as she'd promised. And then her sudden about-turn, the day Mary had dumped Pat at Granny Mae's in Fort Worth and turned on her heel with a smacking kiss and gone on back to him. Since then, her talk of Stanley felled Pat with a misery and dumbness like no other. Impossible to untangle who was right or wrong, which one of them had committed the greater sin against the other. Childhood constantly reshaped itself and Pat was unable to decide. Sure, he had a violent temper, though he was on a long fuse. But Mary cursed him daily, loved to sneer and turn her face away from anyone who loved her; there was something cruel in her, too. She'd never leave him.

Having her at Bridge Cottage felt contaminating. Pat glanced helplessly at her desk, anguished by the nakedness of her work, the ghastly vulnerability of her words there. Would her mother pick up the pages, glance at them, do that thing she did, reading out a line and mocking it? 'Such a *cruel* imagination you have, Patsy . . .'

One time, that night after she'd thrown Stanley's dinner in the sink when he'd come home later – perhaps as little as ten minutes later – than they'd agreed. And in her fury Mary had scooped up everything else around to throw in the garbage – his tobacco, his letters, his magazines – and her haul had included two notebooks of Pat's. The inclusion was undiscovered until it was too late: the notebooks were soggy with coffee grounds, beyond rescue. Mary had screamed at her when Pat mentioned the notebooks; all very well for Patsy to *express herself* all over the goddamn place, didn't she care about *her*?

If it had been affairs, other women, drink, other men even . . . But no. For Mother it revolved around how *bone idle* Stanley was: the shelf that needed fixing; the back door that still squeaked after she'd told him a hundred times, a million minor misdemeanours, like the kind she despised in her daughter too. She just seemed to enjoy having something to beef about. She thrived on it. She absolutely shone, twitched with a feral excitement once she started about 'that damn fool husband of mine'. Everything about Stanley was despicable to her. She was never happier than when she was baiting him and then enjoying the full battle that ensued.

'That man is a goddamn *pig*!' she'd say, showing Patsy the hairs he'd left in the basin after a shave, how he hadn't rinsed them down.

And while she spoke of him Pat would think of all the things she would like to do to him. How they would get rid of him, she and Mother together, be left alone, in peace, just the two of them. Then Mary would shift, a volte-face. It usually happened if Pat uttered a word, if she tried to appease her by agreeing with her. Mary would come over all coy and say, 'Of course, you can't help that you have no i-de-a what a woman feels for a husband. You know, I've always preferred men myself. You're so clearly going to be playing for the other side, Pats,' and somehow, then, rather pleased with this observation, Stanley would begin his transformation in her eyes, from shiftless ne'er-do-well to devoted stepfather and tireless champion of his delinquent stepdaughter . . .

'Well, I guess I'm luckier than some women because I have a husband I really *adore,* who took on this little one as if she was his own,' she'd say to anyone in the vicinity, as if the rest of her words had never been spoken.

And for the first time – was it the first time, really, perhaps the first time she remembered? – Pat snapped.

'Stanley! I happen to know you're never going to leave him – and what's the idea of boring me with this crap?'

And Mary was up, leaping from the sofa, knocking her wine glass over, instantly in tears.

'You're so cruel. I can't believe it! You always were mean, self-ish, wicked – that man gave you everything, he took you on as if you were his own.' She took a little kick at the glass, tried to move it away from her.

Pat unclenched her fists and took a step back. She was think-ing of nothing, nothing at all, trying to keep her mind as blank as a sheet of paper. But onto it floated a picture of Sam as she had been in Pat's imagination – face down, dark hair fanning out, the white upturned heels of her feet on the sofa. And a feel-ing, a seizing feeling, of such piercing, cork-screwing pain arrived that it left her reeling. A startling, clear thought: Sam is not dead. But I've killed her.

'Cuckoo, you are! Nuts! Oh, yes, your little friends have told me all about you. The things you've been saying. You shoulda been locked up years ago and I've a mind to organise it while I'm here. You've finally lost the plot. You have so many shameful little secrets – you're *seething* with them. Your own friends – quite frankly, they're afraid for your sanity. Betty says she heard you on some radio programme and, holy crap, you think you're Dostoesvky!' She was spitting out her words now, in her old style, and she'd stayed on her feet, her head lowered, the way an animal – a bull – drops its head before a charge.

'I haven't been well.'

And then Mary was launching herself at Pat, grimacing, baring her teeth like a dog, screwing up her nose – it would have been funny if it wasn't so familiar to Pat and blood-curdling – and she was reaching for the nearest thing to her on the sofa and snatching at one of the coat-hangers and she's poking it at Pat, trying to bat her head with it, or poke her eye out with it, and Pat screaming, '*Those letters made my life hell*' (or one of them is screaming, someone is screaming) because neither woman hears the bike arrive or the kitchen door open but here is Ronnie – suddenly Ronnie – and he's wedging himself between them and he's saying, 'Calm down, calm down,' and all Pat feels is the stinging, piercing blows from Mary on her shoulder, her cheek, the metal jabbing, aiming for her eyes, and some blood above one eye where Mary hits her mark. Pat's hands fly up to her face and, despite the fear and the foolishness, there might be a place where she's enjoying it, where a voice inside her is saying: *Why don't you get rid of me like you always meant to and put us both out of our misery? Bring it on, Mother, I've nothing left. Why don't you go out and finish the job?*

So, it turns out it was Ronnie who called the doctor, and it was the sedation that Dr Lynn – a small, kindly man, with round glasses and strands of hair drifting from his bald patch – the injection he gave Pat and drugs that he prescribed that wiped out most of the days that followed, the rest of Mother's visit.

Amusing to Pat to think that *she* was the one who had to be sedated. Mother was assumed to be – by the time Dr Lynn arrived – in perfect control of herself; she was the one considered to be sane. Pat was ranting, Ronnie told her, later. Some very queer, troubled things about 'murdering' Gerald, and Sam too. Ronnie thought Gerald's suicide had affected Pat more than anyone had realised and he kept reassuring her: 'Sam's not dead, darling.' Dr Lynn said Pat had been hitting the whisky too hard for too long. He'd like to see her 'exercise some restraint'. The three of them put Pat to bed and, as Ronnie told her, Mary nursed her for the rest of that week before returning to Fort Worth. The only signs that she had been there are her letter, innocent, handwritten, not a letter from Brother Death after all, the bent coat-hanger and the snails relocated outside.

It seems I confessed, then, but was not believed, Pat thought.

Mary never knew that Pat had met up with her real father when she was seventeen, for dinner. Oh, she knew he'd come to the boarding-house at West Daggett Avenue, when Pat was twelve, a brief visit, organised by her cousin Dan, their first official meeting and nothing great. So, he came, she saw him, he drank some lemonade on the stoop, he went. This time, five years later, was different.

Pat organised it herself, looking him up in the *Yellow Pages*: Jay Bernard Plangman. The name Plangman was still on her birth certificate and made her shiver, reading it. Mother and Stanley and Pat lived in New York by then. She had left Fort Worth at six years old, but of course she visited. Matter of fact, she was just visiting Granny Mae in Fort Worth and happened to notice he lived just a block away.

Her father – Pat couldn't think of him as that and in her mind called him Jay B – was a little surprised to hear from her. *Yes, you schmuck, you've had years to fix up to see me.* She didn't say that, of course. He suggested they meet in the Stockyards as he had a little business there. What business he had Pat could only guess at, since he was an illustrator, like her mother and Stanley, and teaching art at the Fort Worth public school. But the Stockyards had the bars and the whorehouses; Pat wasn't naïve.

When he arrived she was sitting in the lobby of the Stockyards Hotel, pretending to read the *Fort Worth Star*, her thoughts coming in stabs – *Look, the great lunk didn't want to see you, why fool around with him?* – as she leafed through the comic section. The fan overhead flicked the smell of horse-dung, cattle urine and tobacco onto the steaming hot street outside towards Leddy's store, the White Elephant Saloon . . . Through an open door she heard the periodic crack of whips and soft whistles of the ranchers, the tinkling of bells as the longhorns were driven down the bar-lined streets towards the pens. To Pat's eyes this hotel – Jay B's suggestion – was a swanky one: six huge fans over-head, giant potted plants, candelabra, red velvet walls, huge Oriental-style lamps painted with birds and flowers, gilded mirrors.

She had a moment to observe him before he saw her. That black, oiled hair and the round glasses. The money-like features. Black moustache. She had always despised moustaches.

And his first remark to her, his opener, was a nod to the news-paper in her lap: 'Did you read that confession by the Mad Sculptor? That's some confession, huh?'

He meant the murder of Veronica Gedeon, Vonny. Even the *Fort Worth Star* had finally caught up with it: the slayer's confes-sion had mesmerised the nation, and the joy was, the naked photographs of Vonny just kept on coming. In this one, here she was, a nightgown just slipping over one shoulder to expose a breast. 'She always had a smile for the receptionist; she never "ritzed" the office boy,' Pat read.

Jay B snapped his fingers at the girl in the wooden reception booth. He asked Pat what she wanted to drink and she said, 'Lemonade,' then quickly changed it to 'Beer.' She didn't like beer but guessed it would be what Jay B drank. As he sank down heavily next to her on the leather sofa she could smell that he'd already had a skinful and was feeling his drink. This pleased her. That he had to get drunk to meet his daughter; yes, that felt good.

He leaned over and grabbed the paper off her, read some choice bits out loud. She was shy. This wasn't the conversation she'd expected to have. She had been hoping to practise her German phrases on Jay B, since his was the German side of the family. She knew he'd been to the Chicago Academy of Fine Arts and hoped they might discuss art, and perhaps – only if he asked – she might show him some of her drawings, tell him about her dilemma between becoming an artist or a writer. In fact, she had a sketchbook with her, inside a leather satchel, which suddenly felt pretty schoolgirlish. She tucked it a little further under her feet as the beers were brought and the two bottles placed on a round marble table in front of them with a clunk.

Jay B was saying: 'She's a honey, isn't she? A knockout! You read what he did? It took him two long hours to kill her. Imagine that. His hands at her throat for two hours – *wheeee*. What was the rest of him doing?'

He stared into her eyes. His were dark, goggled behind the round lenses, and – a horrible jolt this – unmistakably familiar. Like hers. Like Pat's. And she could see he was excited by Veronica, like her, too. She had often wondered about this. If the world is full of pictures of girls specifically arranged to arouse, how come the world expects only half of the population to respond? Wouldn't it get to the girls, too, in the end?

He was staring at her appraisingly. She put a hand to her bangs and brushed them away from her eyes a little.

'You got you a boyfriend yet?' he asked.

'No.'

Jay B stretched out his legs on the sofa, his eyes skirting the room, his boots the predictable Justins with the pointy toes. It was mainly full of other men – stockmen, railroad workers, ranchers in Stetsons – and the odd girl in a frill-bottomed dress. The fans whirred noisily. She suddenly felt self-conscious in her blue jeans and blouse. But one thing she knew already, she understood, with a sinking despair. Jay B was not looking at her the way a father looks at a daughter.

'I got better pictures than those,' he said suddenly. 'You want to see them?'

He glanced around the room and stood up. She stood up too. This was the moment to run, to give up the fantasy. Jay B was not cultured. He was not going to offer any respite from the little hell that was Mother and Stanley.

Curiosity, fear, devilment, what?

She went with him up the red-lined walls, the soft-carpeted stairs. He had a room in the hotel. That was why he'd suggested it for the meeting place. She went with him to his room. From somewhere came the smell of hickory smoke; food. The room was number twenty-six. She let him close the door. She sat on the bed – a slightly dirty pale blue counterpane – while he showed her some pictures, and he watched her face with a little sweat appearing on his brow. The pictures were lurid, strange and ugly, and there could be no doubt about their purpose, or his. He moved in to kiss her and she allowed it, curious again as to what she might feel. His tongue was very hot, and rather fat. He tasted of beer and sweat and strong tobacco. He put a hand on her breast inside her blouse, his fingers coarse at the ends, and she watched him for a moment, then edged away, as politely as she could, and he said, a little sadly: 'Doesn't do it for you, huh?'

She shook her head; didn't care to pretend. She couldn't tell him that it was Veronica who did. She couldn't tell him that she had already lost her virginity to a boy and it had been rather . . . scientific. They moved a little further apart on the bed, and Jay B suggested dinner.

'You look just like me, Patsy,' he said, over dinner in Riscky's steakhouse. 'Like I would look – if I was a girl.' They had *kapusta* soup – Polish – at a bar and then steaks, with the curved horns of an enormous longhorn steer guarding the doorway. She liked the stockyard smells and flavours and felt at home there. She drank

J&B Scotch for the first time until the room swam (it seemed to have his name on it: the red letters on the yellow background for ever spelled Jay B to her) and he leaned in and said, 'God's gifted you with some good looks – it's OK to appreciate that,' and she pretended to be flattered, placing a napkin under her glass of whisky so it wouldn't slide off the wooden table. She knew it was true, sordid and terrifying, that she was like him. An overwhelming sense of self-loathing settled in her. Growing-up was now complete, her character formed, she felt.

That would have been the end of it – she never made an effort to see him again, and never wrote about it, not even in her diaries – but the other thing, the troubling thing, was the arrival that day, in the hotel room, of the little man with the whispering voice and the heavy Justin boots. She saw him as Jay B kissed her, when she opened her eyes. He was standing by the door and laughing at them, of course, and she started a little. Jay B jumped too, breaking away from her and glancing guiltily at the door in case someone had knocked on it. Pat said nothing. She knew Jay B saw no one there. She knew the little man was not real, and yet he was. She had once asked the little man why others couldn't see him and he'd assured her that she was special, there were not many who could, and that thought gave her comfort.

Her birthday dawned, and as she was 'brighter', Ronnie proposed a walk to the Martello tower in Aldeburgh. She wondered whether he thought she was all right in the head. He was polite and would never have given any indication of doubting her, she knew. The day was chilly enough to make their noses pink and their fingertips tingle, and they walked at a lick to try to keep warm. They were discussing writing, as they always did, but Pat longed to return to the discussion of Gerald, to feel again that cleansing relief of trying it out, of saying, 'I killed him.'

Ronnie said: 'That's the funny thing about writing of any sort, the worst or the best. It can't ever say *exactly* . . .'

'What if the fantasy life is the real one? What if – well, what's that Virginia Woolf quote about us living two lives at any time and one of them being the life of the mind, the imagination? Who is to say that isn't the most valid, the most *real* . . . At any rate I can never find that Woolf quote when I look for it, but I know I read it somewhere.'

Pat was breathless and a little frightened, a feeling she had on the rare occasions when she expressed an opinion that she believed in, that mattered to her.

'In the end novelists are either about forgiveness or revenge. I do suspect your talents lie in the revenge department, darling,' Ronnie said.

She laughed; somehow remarks like that, when they came from Ronnie, never wounded her.

'I've been thinking of selling Bridge Cottage,' she told him. 'Switzerland again, perhaps. I mean, now that Sam . . . and my novel is nearly finished. I'm just wrestling with the ending. How would the murderer be found out, was there a witness or nosy snooper who finds out something . . .'

'Does it have to end like that? Couldn't the murderer simply get away with it?'

'Oh, no. The reading public is not pleased with criminals who go free at the end. You rather have to get them to prison.'

'But that's your particular talent, isn't it? To have us root for the criminal?'

Now Ronnie was asking about Virginia Smythson-Balby:

'So what is your beady-eyed spy up to? Have you found out anything further?'

'She promised she'd be cautious with stuff passed to that old witch. Small mercies. Haven't heard from her in a while. The crazy way she drives that car, in this filthy weather. I keep expecting to read of her driving off the road in some god-awful accident, and learn about it in her obit.'

Ronnie glanced at her in a puzzled way, but patted her shoulder and smiled, the wind making brief jabs at their faces and whipping some long strands of hair across his. Beside them the sea hissed over the shingle.

'Such intrusion of privacy, biography. Although I did help Forster write an index for his biography of his great-aunt, long, long ago.'

'You're full of surprises.' Pat laughed.

'Well, I know there are writers whose books are intensely autobiographical, about their bodies and sex and things like that. I think that's perfectly all right. But not for all of us, no. Writers must be allowed our privacy if we choose it.'

'Sure.'

'Mrs Dalloway said that love and religion would destroy the privacy of the soul. A lot of people in my stories say things like that,' Ronnie said.

She hadn't known Ronnie wrote stories. He was indeed surprising. Yesterday he had said, with great tenderness, out of nowhere: 'All loathing is a trick done with mirrors. Someone has annihilated you, you now despise yourself and you try to fling the darkness away from you.'

And now he produced a book shyly, from his duffel bag, and said: 'Happy birthday, darling. Administer at random. Whenever you are next in a bleak mood.'

John Clare. A slim volume. Pat turned it over, mumbled a quiet 'Thank you.' She was thinking of his own book, the manuscript Ronnie was working on. The voices of farm labourers, blacksmiths, teachers, the district nurse. How he described it as simply his 'listening to my own world talking'. And how restrained he was, because she thought the book read like an angry lament to a passing way of life, yet Ronnie's voice was never insistent or biased. He was, as Joyce said, the true artist, off to the side, paring his fingernails, letting the work speak.

They stood on the shingle and she thought of the colours of the longhorns being driven through the Stockyards in Fort Worth – every shade of rust, pinky-cream and biscuit – just like the pebbles on the beach. The wind was strong and plucked at the pages of the book as she tried to open it. Her nose and ears stung with cold; the sound of the masts tinkling reminded her of other times she'd heard it, always like someone nervously jingling change in the pocket of their pants. She picked a page, began reading:

Then off they start anew and hasty blow
Their numbed and clumpsing fingers till they glow . . .

'Clumpsing?' she asked.

'Numb with cold, like today. He's a Fen man. Not too far from here. And he – well, famously he had rather a spectacular breakdown.'

'Ah.' Ronnie's kindness again, his tact. Like an arrow to the heart: this will be his only reference to whether she was all right in the head. Guilt, shame, all the undeservedness, awareness of her own wickedness welled up again. Perhaps, she thought, she should avoid the naturally good because their condition brought on hers more powerfully.

'For those moments when you tell me life is meaningless,' Ronnie said. 'I know you don't believe that—'

'Matter of fact, I do. I wrote it only yesterday.'

'But, darling, acceptance of death when it arrives is one thing, but to allow it to upstage the joys of living is surely ingratitude.'

She slid the book inside her coat, and they linked arms to continue their walk along the shingle. After a while it became too tiring to keep picking their feet out of the stones, twanging their hamstrings painfully, so they continued by walking along the built path towards the tower. The tide was high, a tumbling, broiling grey broth with occasional spurts of white, like bursts of fireworks – like a great spray of white feathers – as it hit the jetty beside them. Ejaculations. Joy, or anger. The sea a prowling beast, its rumble persistent beneath their conversation, like distant, rolling gunshot, like a war going on always somewhere else in the world.

227

Thoughts of Gerald, of Gerald's pale limbs, flopping like pastry, drifted into Pat's mind. A seagull gave a long and haunting wail. *Did that really happen?* she wondered. And the answer rose up.

'Isn't meaning to be found in your work?' Ronnie was saying. 'I don't altogether mean the novels themselves but simply in the *doing* of it, day after day, the application of the seat of the pants to the seat of the chair, the belief, the absolute belief, in the sustained, vivid dream you're creating on the page.'

The dazzling winter sun bounced off the icy puddles and the windshields of the cars parked on the wide sea walk. There it was: the Martello tower. Squat and stumpy, like a building cut off at the waist, maimed. Ronnie said: 'Look, darling, there it is! Splendid!' But Pat did not agree.

Gerald again. How could he have stepped into that sea? Icy, chilling, a monstrous grey beast . . . The sound was agitating, exhilarating: as if inside the blood, like being a screaming child, picked up and flung out, out into the icy surf, over and over. And out of the corner of her eye Pat saw a familiar figure: a young woman who was always, *always* near to her. She refused to look in her direction.

To change the subject she said: 'Matter of fact, I'm thinking not Switzerland but France. Fontainebleau. I've looked at a place called Samois-sur-Seine, too. I wish I had your rootedness. But, as you see, I don't.'

They walked a little in silence, then Ronnie said:

'I won't pretend that it's some great romantic thing. It's simply the countryside. I take it very much for granted. I'm not infatuated with it or anything like that. It's a normal place to live. If you go for walks with a friend in the countryside, that is a lovely experience. But if you live as I live in the middle of nowhere by yourself, that's another experience. There's nothing mystical about it, but it makes me dream. Surrounded by fields every day, something happens to you. I don't know what it is.'

228

'Yes,' Pat said. She doubted they were thinking of the same thing. And now they were at the tower and staring at it.

'It's a quatrefoil, you know. For the four heavy guns. To protect us from Napoleon,' Ronnie told her.

'It's exactly the shape of a sandcastle,' Pat said. And then: 'You know, I've had creepy ideas since I was very young. I gather you haven't. The countryside doesn't cure me. It rather stokes them. And the one that interests me most is what goes on in the mind of someone who has . . . killed somebody.'

Ronnie nodded, matter of fact, as he always did when her thoughts took a turn like this. She was picturing the sandcastles she'd made as a girl, turning the buckets upside down, the fat shapes, close together. Then kicking them, making the whole thing crumble.

'You're quite wrong about your little friend, her wretched driving being the death of her. She's very much alive,' Ronnie murmured. He gestured to the figure approaching.

And the girl waved, a huge wave, pretending spontaneity; affecting surprise at seeing them there. She wore the rabbit fur hat and the pink bell bottoms. She was smiling, and waving, and Pat thought: She exists. There was nothing she could do about this.

On the way home, for a 'birthday treat' Ronnie wanted to show her the church of St Michael in Framlingham, a church he'd talked about often. 'If you're moving on soon, you must take a look. It has the most extraordinary tombs.'

It was cool and echoey in the church, after the tight coldness of the day on the beach; a relief to be out of the wind. She stared without interest at the marble tombs, dutifully read the little plaques explaining, 'To the right of the Glory is one of the finest pieces of sixteenth-century monumental sculpture . . .'

A middle-aged woman, hair tied up in a knotted scarf, swept a corner and called out: 'Don't mind me!'

Pat stood close to Ronnie, feeling a little shy. 'You should have been a priest. There's still time – don't you think?'

'No – nonsense,' he replied quickly.

Pat thought he looked alarmed, and so for devilment, she persisted.

'Why not?'

'I actually think the laity is enormously important. The laity means the people of God,' Ronnie said very quietly. They were almost whispering, self-conscious because of the sweeping char-woman at the other end of the church. Pat wished they were alone. She wanted to ask him again – she longed to; she could no longer bear not asking him.

'Have you ever done anything really wicked, Ronnie?' The powerful desire rose in her once more, the desire Ronnie alone elicited, the desire to confess – to what? – and be absolved.

Ronnie froze, one woolly gloved hand about to reach out to touch the pale-veined tomb of Mary Fitzalan. Sunlight latticed her marble deathbed in an exquisite leafy pattern. In the marble was carved the most charmingly serene face. Looking at it, Pat grudgingly concluded that, if anyone could be said to be at peace, it might be Mary Fitzalan.

'You know, darling, you alarm me when you start talking like this,' Ronnie murmured.

Yes, she thought. Books, liturgies, prayers. But not – ugliness. Not little men that no one can see. Not bloodied dish-cloths and semen-stained carpets. She trembled for a moment and didn't know if it was anger. To disguise it she made herself read a little leaflet about Mary Fitzalan: died at the age of seventeen, after a hasty marriage and a stillbirth. Ha! So. Matter of fact, the sculptor of the peaceful tomb was lying, like everybody else.

Ronnie was standing now in the chancel, batting his gloved hands together and admiring the great east window. Pat stared at his figure, his back in the navy blue wool duffel coat. She wanted to thank him then. She had never met anyone like Ronnie, and now she would be going away and probably never see him again. She would write him; that was all.

'It's a very beautiful thing to be holy,' Ronnie was saying, as she came to stand beside him. 'It's aesthetic as well as sacred. It means whole. Completion. It shouldn't be cut off from ordinary existence. Everybody should be holy, really.'

She knew he was speaking to her, no matter how delicate, how tactful he was. It reached, for a moment, and she was grateful. She knew, whatever his protestations, that he might just as well have been standing in the pulpit.

The novel is finishing itself, writing itself, teeming at me, creeping into my dreams and seeping into my sleep. I dream I'm a man, walking in jeans and brogues, then suddenly an old woman with a strange shape, like a fat ball. Then all at once I'm aware that I'm me and saying to myself I'm having a dream about being myself, how banal! The words of the novel keep steaming at me, like a racing train I can barely fling myself onto, scarcely catch as it thunders by. I need to run beside it and at the perfect moment jump, grab on – longed-for and hard-won, a mesmerised, drugged dream-state. Waiting and working, service. Until the time, the next time, I can feel this alive: the next time it happens.

Ginny Smythson-Balby. Here she is, frisking about the place, tossing her long hair and whinnying. Now she's making up a fire in the living room, next she's opening with a pop some very good red that she says she 'nicked from Daddy's cellar', and handing me a glass, saying, 'No, no, let me!' She's humming and trotting back and forth between living room and kitchen where she's cooking us a meal, something she calls a 'pasta dish'. Two words that make me shudder. 'No steak?'

'No, silly.' She bats me with the dish towel. Steak doesn't go with pasta.

She's wearing a fluffy pink angora sweater with turtle neck and short sleeves, and her creamy arms are covered with smuts from the fire, her ass wiggling as she bends in front of it. I sip the wine and watch her. She's absolutely charming, like a little pink show pony.

'Come on, Ginny. You can tell me now. We *have* met, haven't we? Long ago. Was it New York?'

She turns around. That perfume she wears, the smell of a girls' locker-room, fuggy and feminine. I'm not hating it as much as I did at first. She sits beside me on the sofa, and we both glance at the spot on the floor – the carpetless spot – where Gerald's head was caved in. She glances away first.

'Paris, 1952. I was sixteen. I think I told you I was older,' she says quietly.

I find I can't speak. I stare at her.

'Daddy had sent me to a finishing school in Paris. You know, hoping to sort me out after I'd fallen in love with a girl. And I read *The Price of Salt* and someone said you went to the club we called La Petite – you remember it?'

I can't move to nod, or reply.

'And I went to seek you out. Yes. The one novelist who had given us a happy ending. I had to meet you and tell you how much I loved the book. But then I lost my nerve and . . .'

'Did we go to bed?'

Now she pouts and pretends to be annoyed.

'Of course we did! You don't remember? You were my first and . . .'

Thirteen years ago. There were a lot of girls. And a lot of alcoholic fugue states. I would have been thirty-something and . . . The one I'm thinking of – could it have been her? – was the runaway child. Like something in an Ann Bannon novel. The Beebo Brinker type. La Petite bar. I had a certain fame there, which I briefly enjoyed. Hitchcock was making a film of my first novel. *The Price of Salt* had just been published and plenty of people knew that the pen name was mine. I do remember a crazy girl. Could that have been her? A creepy feeling even then. Too keen. A girl I was happy to romp recklessly with in the hours of darkness (she was noisy: her orgasm, I remember now, was one of the rather alarming sort, too loud, bucking and feral; why didn't I remember this when I took Smythson-Balby to bed? But, of course, the girl has matured by now, had other lovers and learned to be more temperate); in the morning her hot limbs around me felt like the snaking limbs of Medusa. Girls who were too keen on me always made me edgy. Dark eyes that didn't seem right with her hair. Which wasn't long and chestnut like this but a blonde crop.

'Did you have different hair?'

'I was a bottle blonde for about six months. Daddy was furious – made me wear a wig when he caught up with me. I went back to school in the end. But I felt better. You helped me. And my first time! With the author of *The Price of Salt*! I—'

'Did you follow me about? When we met here at Earl Soham—'

'Well, there's no need to take that tone! You must have followed women – you write about it often enough.'

She reaches out to stroke my hair but I pull away.

'Novels. You're confusing my writing with me again. I have no wish to be adored,' I say. My voice trembles with anger.

Sure, I once drove to the house of the – the woman I think of as Carol and watched her come out to her car and leave but I could never have let her *see* me, know me. What kind of person wants to be *seen*? Or watched? *Only a snail*. To be adored is to be eaten alive, sucked in. Being pulled, pricked out of its shell with a pin, stretched towards a waiting mouth. I put my glass on the floor and sit up straight.

'I think you should go,' I say.

'Oh, no, please. I'm sorry. Please, don't . . . The pasta is just about ready. Come into the kitchen and see how pretty I've made the table.'

I allow myself to be led to the kitchen. She has found a way to pull the sprigged curtains – which never quite met – completely closed, securing them with wooden pegs. A candle shoved into the wooden candlestick, sprigs of holly around the base and a silver-sprayed pine cone resting on white linen napkins. Like something a very young girl would do. But she must be . . . nearly thirty? And what kind of vortex have I stepped into? Keeping that candle burning – I glance at it as she lights it now – for thirteen years?

'After dinner you should go,' I say. I pause, then nod as she holds the spoonful of pasta over a bowl and gazes at me.

'And . . .' a new, sudden thought so piercing in its clarity '. . . did you, were the letters – they were you, too?'

'Please, sit down. Let's eat, shall we? I wish I'd never told you. You liked me yesterday – you liked me last week!'

Last week I was trying to figure out how to tamper with the brakes on your car, I think.

I pull out the chair and sink down. The letters float in front of me. *Brother Death*. Didn't Ginny admit to knowing all my novels? Doesn't she show a knowledge of my work, a kind of scrutiny and close-reading that Mother never did? And Brother Death is my own phrase, the way that Jenny Thierolf – the suicide – thinks of it in *The Cry of the Owl*. Mother would never remember that. Mother wouldn't care to read me that closely. Mother: in the end I thought Mother confessed during our fight but didn't she merely quit denying it? Is it possible she had no idea what I was accusing her of? 'Letters from me and Stanley? What's your problem? I don't get it,' she'd said. And maybe she didn't.

What kind of girl is Ginny? I'm in a spot now – I know that much – but how bad is it? What sort of creep keeps up a vigil for this long? She must be nuts. An oddball. A blackmailer? What's her plan?

'Ginny. You know that – we can't carry on like this. I'm much too old for you. And I already have plans to move on. It will – I don't want to hurt you. I can tell your feelings for me are—'

'Don't say it! Don't say it,' she squeals. 'Please let's eat. We can be friends, can't we? There's no reason for you to be – scared of me. I've given up all of that! Letter-writing! They weren't so bad, were they? Not threatening. I wish I'd never told you. I just want to, you know . . . Be your friend.'

* * *

But there is another, much more powerful, reason for me to be afraid of her: Ginny comes downstairs from the bathroom after dinner and makes me a gift of it.

'I couldn't resist a look in your art-room,' she's saying, as she clicks down the stairs in her kitten-heeled slippers, straightening out her little pink jumper over her little pink midriff.

She doesn't even say: I hope you don't mind. I do mind. I'm blazing, and she can see that. But she has her own sly power now, and she can't wait to use it.

'Beautiful. Such a lovely – you have quite a talent. It's even dedicated to her. There can't be any mistake, whatever you say. I know it's Sam Gosforth.'

'Yes, it's Sam,' I say coldly. The portrait was finished from memory and propped up, in front of others. There seems no other way to play it. 'And now you promised you would leave.'

'Oh, I'm not sure I want to leave now! I haven't had my port – and I brought such a splendid bottle with me. Let's open it, shall we?'

'Ginny, I'm tired – I—'

'Oh, just a little one, eh? A teensy-weensy little one? Because, after all, now we have so much to talk about! About how lovely Sam was and how it was *indeed* her that night when Izzie and I saw you in Aldeburgh, the night that Gerald so sadly chose to do away with himself . . .'

And so it sets up again and when it comes, the familiar clamour, I don't know if it's a welcome relief, a release, or just exhausting. Here it is: should I push her under a car? Might she run out in front of it so I can drive it straight at her, blood and guts and mashing, mashing, can I do that? Should I just use a cushion – here's one beside me on the sofa – and smother her now? But then there's the old problem, the perennial problem: how to get rid of the body. So it has to be suicide – but two of those already! Is that pushing my luck? Though Ginny is an obsessive, a prowler, by definition something of a crazy, maybe it *would* be plausible. OK, if not suicide then an accident – yes,

236

this time an accident: could she fall down the stairs in this house? Could she slip – she's drunk enough, one glass more of port would do it – in the garden outside and drown in the stream there? But if it's *here* it will bring attention to me, bring the police, the newspapers *here*, there would have to be an inquest. So what can it be that throws suspicion away from me? It has to be somewhere without witnesses. An accident that involves her alone, with no link to me.

Picturing it now: the Martello tower, that child's sandcastle tower as real as real can be, but just exactly like make-believe. The ejaculations of that angry white spray as it splashed up against the jetty. The long drop behind the wall. The signs: *Danger! Unguarded drop*. High tide. Icy cold. No one could climb out in darkness, hold onto those slippery wooden posts. Anyone who walked there alone, and had the misfortune to slip off the high walkway in high tide (a shove in the darkness, a scream that no one so far from those sugared-almond-coloured houses could possibly hear or know was human) – do seagulls scream in that haunting, disturbing, wailing way, piercing the low hypnotic howl of the sea, or are they silent, sleeping at night-time in that lonely spot? I feel almost sad and sorry, thinking like this. But I have begun and now I give my wicked self the rein.

How to lure someone to their death? Make them go to the place you want them to? Well, pretty easy if that person has a habit of following you. Perhaps has been following you for several years.

After she's left, after I've heard the little red Triumph tear away, I have the strongest instinct that she's waiting further up the road, that she hasn't gone far at all. She'll be somewhere, if possible, where she can watch the house, see if my bedroom light goes out. She probably picked up on my prickly mood; on the fact that I didn't seem to be getting ready to go to bed, despite my insistence that she left. Perhaps she thinks I've some unfinished business, something to tidy up in Aldeburgh or some-where else.

In any case. If it's to happen, it has to be tonight. I gather my coat, the flashlight and a leather thermos, into which I pour a good jigger of port. I leave lights on in the house downstairs, so that if the old hag Mrs Ingham is watching she will think I'm still at my desk, working. There is a huge fat moon, which is rather too bright, turning the pink walls of Bridge Cottage a lurid shade of blood-orange, but it can't be helped.

No one sees me leave the house. I slip into the car and it obedi-ently starts up. Take the route towards the cemetery, past the well, and the telephone booth and the strange sign – *Christ who died upon the rood, grant us grace our end be good* – which makes me think of the little church in Fort Worth and how as a child I thought, What is the 'rood'? A misprint of 'rod' or 'road'? Deliberately misspelt to rhyme with good?

I don't pass the Triumph. Such a noticeable, flashy car, it would be hard to miss. She must be skilled at this, has had enough practice. Knows how to wait somewhere discreet, perhaps parked behind another car. Could I be wrong about her? Has she given up, gone home? I'm reminded of that night I took a walk, early in my stay at Earl Soham, the intense feeling I had that night of being followed. I reach to the overhead nylon net in the roof of the car, feel for the map, then remember that I lent it to Ronnie and no longer have it. No matter. The names of the villages fly by on signs: Saxtead, Brandeston, Debenham. Each has an associa-tion with Ronnie somehow: a church; a crab-apple- or black-berry-picking occasion; the blue-violet sloes we picked for gin; the scent of the creamy white elderflowers that made sweet cordial . . .

Not Ronnie. No good thinking about Ronnie now. No good remembering that occasion when he asked what was my earliest memory and told me his and of course it was something green and healthy about oaks and the ancient boundaries of flat land Debach. Even before I told him mine I was thinking: Anyone who has lived three years as a baby and has never had their small face screamed into by a mother whose spittle they can feel on their skin – that comment Sam made about baby-carriages and how fear turns to evil – is probably going to be all right. Is going to grow into something nourishing. And I told him mine: Fort Worth and the boarding-house garage. Mother dumping me to go on her first date with Stanley. Those two men, for some reason I think they were travelling salesmen, who visited that day and carried me to the bench in Granny's garage, and lifted my dress and did something mysterious and ugly to me; and Ronnie suddenly had such a pained expression, such a bleak, sad look in his eyes, and murmured, *Oh, Pats, you always take such sides with the past, with others' damnation of you*, which surprised me, and I quit what I was saying and said, 'What? What do you mean?' and, of course, we were tongue-tied and could say no more and I had to change the subject just to make his sad expression shift. And then remembering another comment of Ronnie's. I was complaining about biographers – was it Frances or Ginny? I can't remember who – and he said in his ridiculous, random way: 'Well, darling, she's just a barnacle on the cruise ship that is Patricia Highsmith's life.' And *that* one I loved, and it makes me smile again now.

At last. Headlights in the rear-view mirror and the shape of the low sports car that could be hers, I can't be sure. I drive on regardless, faster than normal, taking the bends rather recklessly, hands a little slippery with sweat, heart knocking against my ribcage, like ice in a glass. What time is it? Must be past midnight. The main glitch will be witnesses. Anyone who sees my car, sees her following me or walking on the path to the tower. Anyone who sees me in Aldeburgh. But at this hour? The British licence laws seem like a blessing for the first time: the bars will have been cleared by now, the last drunks gone home. I pass the church of St Peter and St Paul, with its arch that, Ronnie showed me, frames the first lovely view of the sea at Aldeburgh. But that's daytime. Ronnie's concerns are daytime ones: who is buried there, which poet is commemorated here. Tonight the church is unlit and unlovely and cannot save a single soul.

I park on Crabbe Street out of habit, then think that too far to walk and drive further, up towards the yacht club. Slaughden Quay. Something Ronnie said about a whole village being lost to the sea, here, long ago. So. One little person should be a cake-walk. Where *she* parks is her own business. All I need concern myself with is witnesses. Making sure no one sees me walk to the tower. If they see her – if they believe she's taking a late-night walk alone – no problem.

The moment I cut the engine I hear the masts of the sailboats, from the yacht club to my right, jangling in the wind, demoni-cally. Sounding not so much like coins being jingled in a pocket now but the bells of jesters, jeering, rattling in the strong wind, gathering into a high-pitched inhuman sound, a soundless scream. And down a long tube of years I hear it again: the stock-yard back home in Texas with the great steaming hustle of long-horns powering down it; the jingling spurs on the men's boots, the cowboys' jangling whistles, the clinking bells around the necks of the dumb massing beasts. To my left the sea throws itself at the wall, smacks and retreats, over and over. Abject dark-ness. I think I heard another car engine being cut, wheels popping slowly through shingle and ice-puddles. I don't turn to look: I pretend I've no idea I'm being followed.

I grasp the flashlight in my pocket, feeling the switch with my thumb but keeping it unlit. I swig the port and wipe my mouth with the back of my hand, walk briskly along the stony high wall, once tripping slightly over an abandoned piece of rope, the sea snarling and growling alongside me, hair whipping into my face. There's no sign of her and I wonder for a moment if I'm wrong, if my whole plan is hopeless. Curious that every occasion when I *didn't* want to see her – the party in London, the Victoria, the BBC interview, the night of Gerald's death – she contrived to be there. What are the chances of her letting me down now? If she does, I'll simply take an invigorating walk – stimulating for the brain when writing and therefore never wasted – then go home. And yet I know I won't. I finish the port, sweet and hot, and I'm conscious of a fast, pattering heartbeat, stinging cold nose and ears and the wind dancing around me, snapping hair into my eyes, taunting. To my left, if I were to flash the light towards them, are the warnings. *Unguarded drop. Beach levels may vary. Danger! Keep clear of the edge*. A feeling of the icy sea creeping up at me, like the tongue of a huge dog. Fear. What am I afraid of? Being followed? This makes no sense. I wanted her to follow me here. Not another soul in sight.

I stride out, away from the shingle, along the parking lot and the path that leads to the tower. There is enough moonlight to see the edge of the walkway I'm on and the dark, glowering hump of the tower in front of me. The white edges of the sea's mouth, its fathomless interior yawning beside me. It makes me want to giggle. Silly Ginny! How she tried to get me to talk about my characters as if they were real people, based on real lovers or women in my life, whereas every writer knows that a character is both real and a secret ungodly form from somewhere else entirely.

Now I notice a light sweat on my palms despite the cold and a dripping feeling down my back: is that sweat, and fear, too? I stumble again on some goddamn bit of old fishing stuff, and kick a bucket, and it makes a startlingly loud sound. Did I hear steps behind me? Is she behind me? Did I smell for a minute that smothering perfume, that sickening *feminine* smell? Sure, that's her – I see her at last, a dark shadow with a ponytail clip-clopping towards me.

She's even calling, 'Wait! Sorry, I'm sorry, let's not fall out! I'm not going to say anything at all about Sam, I promise. I only want to be with you. I love you, Pats,' and I have such a powerful desire to scream, 'Shut up!' She's as bad as Ronnie, with her ridiculous belief in this four-letter word. Instead I duck behind a broken remnant of wall in front of the tower, shivering on the icy grass, coiled in the position of a child, the sea glowering beside me.

I hear her footsteps running up to me and one slip, one push as I leap out and surprise her and that's all it will take – I spring out and grab at her ankles, she's down like a skittle with a great thump and over so fast, slipping, and then – well, in the end it almost *is* an accident, I'm not sure I ever really meant to do it. I don't think I even push her. It's icy here, we're twenty feet up, it's naturally slippery, she slipped – the drop into black vastness, I barely even hear the splash, just a grey lump tumbling and then the sea swallowing her in silence. I look over and see nothing. Not even the Thing is there, though I half expect him to be and stare into the blackness searching for him. Very few people have seen him in their lifetime, but I have, I'm one who has, I tell myself. I think I hear her voice. The masts have quit their clinking, the wind has dropped, and the air is bracingly silent. And then it's not her voice I hear but another young girl's – is it Rachel Barber, the flame-haired girl, is it my first love? – saying, *Oh!* and the voice is not much like Ginny's or Rachel's either, but like mine. A *girl's* voice; a squeak of surprise. I've thought of this so often; this is what I've been thinking of virulently since the age of eight. I've tried it in every shape, visited it on others, every which way, over and over. Has it made it any easier? Am I any nearer to being able to imagine it? Brother Death: a sibling, a seed, a dark twin; something we each carry in us from the start and spend our lives desiring and refusing to know. Only a small shock now about the *when* or the *how* of it, and realising what I guess we all know but spend our time not knowing: we're all on our way there. Here we go. Perhaps it's only ordinary. Perhaps it's as Ronnie once said of our friendship: simply tender and true.

Acknowledgements

I've long been addicted to Patricia Highsmith's fiction and I hope that fellow fans will enjoy spotting the many references to her novels and short stories and echoes of her favourite themes and literary conceits in *The Crime Writer*, as well as some real events from her life, as documented by her biographers. For those not familiar with her work, the following information might be helpful.

While living in Bridge Cottage in Earl Soham in the 1960s, Highsmith was writing – among other things – the novel *A Suspension of Mercy* (published in the United States as *The Storyteller* (Doubleday, 1965) and she used the cottage and the house beside it and the Suffolk countryside as a setting, as I have. That novel tells of Sydney Bartleby, a scriptwriter who fantasises endlessly about killing his wife.

The non-fiction book Highsmith was also writing while at Bridge Cottage was published in 1966 as *Plotting and Writing Suspense Fiction* (The Writer, Inc, 1966).

Stalkers are a favourite theme of Highsmith's, most notably in *This Sweet Sickness* (Harper & Brothers, 1960). Poison-pen letters are a device in her novel *A Dog's Ransom* (Knopf, 1972).

Many will know that Highsmith had a deep love of snails and her biographers describe her taking them to parties in a handbag or smuggling them from France under her bra. The descriptions of the snails were suggested by Highsmith's novel *Deep Water* (Harper & Brothers, 1967) where Vic Van Allen watches his beloved snails mating and nicknames them Hortense and Edgar; and by the short story 'The Snail Watcher', which appears in the collection *The Snail Watcher and Other Stories* (Doubleday, 1970).

The character of Sam is in many ways an evocation of the eponymous Carol from Highsmith's famous novel of love between women, *Carol*, (first published as *The Price of Salt* under the pen-name Claire Morgan; Coward-McCann, 1952). Carol, too, is elegance personified, in a troubled marriage and the mother of a daughter, but unlike Sam she is braver about defying convention.

The scene where Highsmith imagines how it would feel to be interviewed about the murder she has committed is a pastiche of that idea in *Strangers on a Train* (Harper & Brothers, 1950). The scene where Highsmith suffers an alcoholic blackout was suggested by a scene in the same novel where Bruno starts to suffer from the DTs and finds he can't speak properly or use his hands.

Highsmith's memory of being caught dressing up by Miss Rose, the tennis coach, was inspired by the famous moment in *The Talented Mr Ripley* (Coward-McCann, 1954) when Dickie Greenleaf surprises Tom Ripley in the act of trying on his clothes and reacts furiously. The device of carrying the corpse of Gerald to the car and pretending he has committed suicide is of course the same ploy Ripley uses to rid himself of the odious Freddie in the same novel.

The concept of the little man who appears to her occurs in Highsmith's short story 'Not in this life, Maybe the Next' collected in *Mermaids on the Golf Course* (Otto Penzler Books, 1988). Her biographers also tell of a hallucination of a little mouse or 'grey blob' that she saw as a child.

The terrapin scene is an echo of Highsmith's story 'The Terrapin' in the same collection. The mother in that story (a commercial artist like Highsmith's mother) was the inspiration for the character of Mary Highsmith in my novel. The coat-hanger attack scene in Bridge Cottage is an actual one, which took place in 1965 and resulted in a local doctor, Dr Auld, having to sedate Highsmith, as recounted by both her biographers.

I'm grateful to those people who helped me with my research. In particular I owe a debt of gratitude to Highsmith's authorised biographer Joan Schenkar for meeting with me and for the generosity of her response to my requests. Andrew Wilson's biography of Highsmith, *Beautiful Shadow*, is a model of fairness and compassion and a fascinating read. If readers would like to know more about Highsmith's life and work I urge them to read her stories and novels along with the biographies and memoir mentioned below. I'm grateful to Liz Calder, to Ronald Blythe for his kindness and generosity, and to Lord Bragg for pertinent and helpful insights. I was lucky enough to meet the bookseller Brian Perkins (Senior) in Fort Worth, Texas, who knew Highsmith as a child. I'd like to thank him for clearing up the mystery of the little 'flame haired girl' – Highsmith's first love.

My thanks go as ever to my editor Carole Welch and my agent Caroline Dawnay and their assistants Jenny Campbell and Sophie Scard. Special thanks must go to Carole and to my husband Meredith Bowles for being my first intrepid readers and for their skilful interventions, invaluable comments and input. Fellow writers Sally Cline, Louise Doughty and Kathryn Heyman have, as ever, kept me going with their support and friendship. My friend Geraldine Harmsworth supplied me with a brilliant line – and I hope she enjoys seeing it here. I'm always grateful to my family Lewis, Felix and Poppy for their forbearance while I'm writing.

I'd like to acknowledge the following books and sources:

The Talented Miss Highsmith by Joan Schenkar, St Martin's Press, 2009

Beautiful Shadow: A Life of Patricia Highsmith by Andrew Wilson, Bloomsbury, 2003

Highsmith: A Romance of the 1950s by Marijane Meaker, Cleis Press, 2003

The Mad Sculptor by Harold Schecter, Houghton Mifflin Harcourt, 2014

'Love is a kind of madness' on page 1: These were Highsmith's words to Melvyn Bragg in a *South Bank Show* interview in 1982.

'The low, flat, compellingly psychotic murmur' on page 41: This brilliant description of Highsmith's voice in her fictions is the phrase of Joan Schenkar.

Extracts from Ronald Blythe's *Akenfield* appear on pages 51, 78, 106, 114 and 174. Published by Allen Lane, The Penguin Press, 1969. Copyright © Ronald Blythe, 1969. Reprinted by kind permission of the author.

Extracts from Ronald Blythe's *A Treasonable Growth* appear on pages 155, 224 and 226. Published by MacGibbon & Kee, 1960. Copyright © Ronald Blythe, 1960. Reprinted by kind permission of the author.

Extracts from Ronald Blythe's *The Time by the Sea: Aldeburgh 1955 – 58* appear on pages 83 and 198. Published by Faber and Faber Ltd, 2013. Copyright © Ronald Blythe, 2013. Reprinted by kind permission of the author.

Ronnie's comments on pages 52 and 53 about 'the bookshelf cull' and his reference to *The Murder of My Aunt* by Richard Hull are taken from an essay of that name in *The Bookman's Tale*. Published by Canterbury Press, 2009. Copyright © Ronald Blythe. Reprinted by kind permission of the author.

Extract on page 157 from *Lightly Bound* by Stevie Smith, from *The Collected Poems and Drawings of Stevie Smith*. Published by Faber and Faber Ltd, 2015. Copyright © Stevie Smith, 1944. Reprinted by kind permission of the publisher.

JILL DAWSON

The Tell-Tale Heart

When a teenager dies in an accident in rural Cambridgeshire, it affords Patrick, a fifty-year-old professor, drinker and womaniser, the chance of a life-saving heart transplant. But as Patrick recovers, he has the odd feeling that his old life 'won't have him'. He becomes bewitched by the story of his heart, ever more curious about the boy who donated it, his ancestors and the Fenland he grew up in. What exactly has Patrick been given?

'Immediately engrossing' Melissa Katsoulis, *The Times*

'A searching and gently philosophical novel . . . moving and intriguing' Suzi Feay, *Literary Review*

'This deft, intelligent novel explores the human anxiety that replacing a heart is the closest one can come to replacing a soul.' Alfred Hickling, *Guardian*

Lucky Bunny

Crime is a man's business, so they say, though not according to Queenie Dove – a self-proclaimed genius when it comes to thieving, who learned her skills in London's East End during the Depression. Daring, clever and sexy, she went on to thrive in the Soho of the Krays and the clubs of Mayfair, fell wildly in love, and got away with it all. Or did she?

'Gloriously enjoyable . . . Queenie bursts out of these pages, longing for life, as we are drawn into her world by Dawson's terse, electric prose.' Philip Hoare, *Sunday Telegraph*

'Dawson, as ever, delves deep into her subject matter, combining fast-paced narrative with astute, piercing reflection' Leyla Sanai, *Independent on Sunday*

SCEPTR!